Praise for *Sylvanus Now*

"Like the rock where it was born, Morrissey's voice is at once haunting and heartbreaking, lyrical and pure. Anyone still looking for identity in Canadian fiction can call off the search."
 —Brad Smith, author of *Big Man Coming Down the Road*

"Deft and deliriously romantic ... When [Morrissey] steps back and lets her characters do the talking, the results are electrifying ... acute and bleakly funny ... It is a novel to be taken to heart."
—*National Post*

"There are detailed descriptions in this novel which are dazzlingly unique. Both physical and emotional land-scapes are charted with care. A splendidly unique novel."
 —Alistair MacLeod, author of *No Great Mischief*

"An epic novel of love and loss ... It is an arresting tale, recounted in powerful, lyrical prose ... Morrissey's strong descriptive powers elevate the landscape of Newfound-land to the status of a living, breathing character in the novel."
—*The Gazette* (Montreal)

"Morrissey's strength is in the way she evokes the dialogue and lost culture of Newfoundland outports."
—*Ottawa Citizen*

"[Morrissey] vividly evokes the Newfoundland way of life with refreshing honesty. With its details about a fishery so stunningly destroyed, *Sylvanus Now* is infuriating and troubling. Yet what's hopeful is the [characters'] love, both heart-breaking and enduring."
—*The Daily News* (Halifax)

"A beautifully written story about the struggle to maintain a unique identity ... to remain true to ourselves as the world challenges our beliefs; and to continue to follow our dreams, despite things not always going as planned."
—*Downhomer Magazine* (St. John's)

"Absorbing human drama, in Morrissey's best yet."
—*Kirkus Reviews*

"Morrissey generates a remarkable intensity of emotion here, and if the novel often seems oppressively sad, it is buoyed by the crispness of detail and the author's ability to vivify the slow process through which an inner life is transformed."
—*Booklist*

"Brilliantly displays multiple conflicts: between the individual and the state, tradition and progress, alienation and acceptance, and love of the land and the love of another."
—*Literary Review of Canada*

Praise for Donna Morrissey

"There's a sense in Morrissey's writing that William Faulkner has met Annie Proulx ... Morrissey is almost certain to set new boundaries in fiction in Canada."

—*Atlantic Books Today*

"Morrissey's voice, innocent, wise, funny and boisterous, and so expertly tuned to the music of the Newfoundland dialect, is simply irresistible."

—*Books in Canada*

"A Newfoundland Thomas Hardy."

—*The Globe and Mail*

"If you haven't read any Donna Morrissey, there's a trio of wonder waiting ... as lively as Newfoundland and as sweet as the sea."

—*The Sun Times* (Owen Sound, Ontario)

"Morrissey knows of what she writes."

—*Toronto Star*

PENGUIN CANADA

SYLVANUS NOW

DONNA MORRISSEY is the award-winning author of four novels, *Kit's Law*, *Downhill Chance*, *Sylvanus Now*, and *What They Wanted*, all set in Newfoundland and all subsequently translated into several languages. *Kit's Law* won the CBA Libris Award, the Winifred Holtby Prize, and the American Library Association's Alex Award. Both *Downhill Chance* and *Sylvanus Now* won the Thomas Head Raddall Atlantic Fiction Prize, and *Sylvanus Now* was the winner of the Atlantic Independent Booksellers Choice Award. Her screenplay, *Clothesline Patch*, won a Gemini Award. Morrissey grew up in The Beaches, a small fishing outport in Newfoundland, and now lives in Halifax.

DONNA MORRISSEY

Sylvanus Now

PENGUIN
CANADA

PENGUIN CANADA

Published by the Penguin Group

Penguin Group (Canada), 90 Eglinton Avenue East, Suite 700,
Toronto, Ontario, Canada M4P 2Y3 (a division of Pearson Canada Inc.)

Penguin Group (USA) Inc., 375 Hudson Street, New York, New York 10014, U.S.A.
Penguin Books Ltd, 80 Strand, London WC2R 0RL, England
Penguin Ireland, 25 St Stephen's Green, Dublin 2, Ireland (a division of Penguin Books Ltd)
Penguin Group (Australia), 250 Camberwell Road, Camberwell, Victoria 3124, Australia
(a division of Pearson Australia Group Pty Ltd)
Penguin Books India Pvt Ltd, 11 Community Centre, Panchsheel Park,
New Delhi – 110 017, India
Penguin Group (NZ), 67 Apollo Drive, Rosedale, North Shore 0745, Auckland, New Zealand
(a division of Pearson New Zealand Ltd)
Penguin Books (South Africa) (Pty) Ltd, 24 Sturdee Avenue, Rosebank,
Johannesburg 2196, South Africa

Penguin Books Ltd, Registered Offices: 80 Strand, London WC2R 0RL, England

Published in Penguin Canada paperback by Penguin Group (Canada),
a division of Pearson Canada Inc., 2005
Published in this edition, 2009

1 2 3 4 5 6 7 8 9 10 (WEB)

Manufactured in Canada.

LIBRARY AND ARCHIVES CANADA CATALOGUING IN PUBLICATION

Morrissey, Donna, 1956-
Sylvanus Now / Donna Morrissey.

ISBN 978-0-14-317032-7

1. Newfoundland and Labrador—Fiction. I. Title.

PS8576.O74164S94 2009   C813'.54   C2009-903803-X

Visit the Penguin Group (Canada) website at **www.penguin.ca**

Special and corporate bulk purchase rates available; please see
www.penguin.ca/corporatesales or call 1-800-810-3104, ext. 477 or 474

To her babies,
Milton, Verna, and Paul

Come and see. and I beheld, and lo a black horse;
and he that sat on him had a pair of balances in his hand.

And I heard a voice ... say, A measure of wheat
for a penny, and three measures of barley for a penny;
and see thou hurt not the oil and the wine.

And I stood upon the sand of the sea, and saw a beast rise up
out of the sea, having seven heads and ten horns, and upon his
horns ten crowns, and upon his heads the name of blasphemy.

—Revelation 6:5, 6:6, and 13:1

PART ONE

Sylvanus

SPRING 1949 TO SUMMER 1953

CHAPTER ONE

A MAN'S WORTH

SYLVANUS NOW had just turned fourteen that morning when he burst through the school doors for summer, shoved his dory off from the calm shores of Cooney Arm, paddled through the narrow channel protecting the cove, and headed for the choppy waters of the open Atlantic. Tucked inside his pants pocket was a credit note for his confirmation suit, priced at thirty-two quintals of dried salt fish (on hold at the merchant's), and tucked around his feet were two coils of fishing twine, the end of each tightly knotted to a cod jigger.

Rowing half a mile along the rugged coastline, he anchored two stone's throws from where Pollock's Brook rushed out of a small estuary into the sea. Wrapping his fishing twine around each hand, he tossed the ends holding the jiggers overboard, their hooks more silvery than the underbelly of a herring as they sank into the sea. Rising, he planted both feet firmly on either side of his boat and began jigging: left forearm up, right forearm down; right forearm up, left forearm down. Thirty-two quintals of fish. A hundred and twelve pounds a quintal. He figured he could do it.

After scarcely five minutes of jigging, his left jigger hooked.

"Ah," he grunted with satisfaction and, sitting back down, pulled in the fish. Ten pounds it felt. Fair size for drying and marketing. He grunted again. It was this, the immediacy of it, that fulfilled him. That even as he was twisting the jigger out of the cod's mouth, he was already tallying his own worth—unlike the hours spent over school books, studying letters and figures that made no sense.

Pulling a skinning knife out of his rubber boot, he cut the cod's throat to bleed it, cursing the gulls swooping and screaming overhead, one flapping so close he swung his knife at the yellowed eyes menacing him. Laying the fish aside, he tossed his jigger back into the sea and rose—left forearm up, right forearm down; right forearm up, left forearm down; up, down; up down—a sturdy figure in his father's black rubber pants and coat, unyielding to the rocking of his dory, his sou'wester pulled low, darkening his eyes as he faced into the sun and the gannets swooping black before its blaze as they dove into the sea a dozen feet below his boat, beaking back the caplin that were luring the cod to his jiggers.

Fourteen pounds. A day's jigging ought to land him half a quintal or more. With splitting, salting, and drying the fish on shore, it would take all three of the summer months, he figured, before he was able to dodge up to the merchant's and barter the price of the suit—for *thirty*-two quintal was the price he was figuring on paying, not the forty-two the merchant was asking. Perhaps he was poor

at book learning, writing his numbers and letters backwards and trying the patience of his teachers and elders
alike as they tried breaking him from the foolishness of his
habit; but he could figure, sometimes for hours on end,
about such things as how many cords of split wood to fill
a twelve-by-twelve crawl space, or how long to leave a fish
curing in brine, or, no doubt, how many hours it took to
cut and sew a size-forty suit and how many quintals of fish
to make a fair trade.

Another hook—a hard one. Real hard. Excitedly, he
leaned over the side of his boat, pulled in his fishing twine,
hand over hand, seeing a fathom down into the sea and
the glazed eyes of a cod whose tail flicked confusedly as it
was hauled from its brackish bed, up, up, up, breaking into
the startling light of the sun.

"Whoa, now, who do we have here?" he asked in
astonishment as he pulled the forty pounder half out of
the water, the brown of its back glistening wet, its belly
creamy as milk and swollen with roe. A mother-fish.
Rarely would she feed off a jigger, busy as she was, bottom
feeding and readying herself for spawning. Reverently, he
unhooked the jigger from the mouth of the quietly struggling fish and watched the sun catch the last glimmer of
her gills as she dove back into the deep, the sack of roe in
her belly unscathed. He felt proud. The ocean's bounty,
she was, and woe to he who desecrated the mother's
womb. The gods smiled, and within the minute he was
pulling another fish up from the deep, a twenty pounder,
twice the normal size for a hand-jigged cod, and his heart
pounded as he flipped it into his boat.

Two hours later, the twine was chafing his hands and
his shoulders had begun to weaken. His father, before the

sea took him (along with his eldest brother, Elikum), would've held out jigging till the tide ebbed. Come evening, he would've returned again, filling his boat for the second time that day, getting home late, late evening, working long into the night, gutting and splitting and salting his catch. And perhaps I might, too, row back out for the second tide, he thought. If I gets the morning's catch gutted and split and sitting in brine, and a good scoff of Mother's cooking filling me gut, I just might. And perhaps, by summer's end, I, too, might spend the whole day standing and jigging with nary an ache nor wish, like Father done.

Perhaps so. For now 'twas the most he could do to bleed the last fish, pull his anchor, and will his leaden arms to lift his paddles out of the water. Shoulders groaning, he rowed against a growing squall, plying harder on his paddles as he swerved back through the choppy waters that always choked the channel's narrow neck. One last long haul on his oars and he hoisted them inside, gliding toward the shoreline of Cooney Arm. Then, as he'd seen his elders do after making it through the neck in worsening weather, he rose, raising his eyes as if in salute to the wood-coated hills that cuddled the scant few houses of the arm from the wind and sea.

But Sylvanus's wasn't the salute of his elders. This morning's lop was a duck pond alongside the squalls they had survived. His was the salute of pride, for despite his having drawn ashore dozens of times before, sometimes with fifteen, maybe twenty pounds of cod for his mother's pot, today he was straddling a hundred and twenty pounds or more—a few pounds more than a quintal—from just four hours' fishing. A fisherman's catch, for sure, and to be bartered at the merchant's. And this thought cast his eyes anew upon the hills. Yet, unlike his elders', his sought more the rock gorge to his right and the thousands of fathoms of white foaming water crashing down its cut and spewing across the meadow into the embodying arms of the mother sea as she buoyed him and his bounty to shore. Water. God's blood, the elders used to say. And in his moment of pride, Sylvanus Now would've traded his last drop of red in gratitude.

THREE MONTHS LATER, the thirty-two quintals of fish bartered and stored in the merchant's shed, he dodged home, a deep satisfaction filling his chest and the suit, carefully wrapped in brown paper, tucked under his arm. His mother, Eva, her aging hair bundled at her nape and her fading grey eyes bolstered by the black lustrous brows that she'd bequeathed to all of her boys, met him in the doorway. Proudly, he pulled the suit from its wrappings and held it before her—three sizes too big so's to allow for his last few years' growth—and announced he was quitting school and going fishing for good.

Eva sighed. His was the unsanctioned egg, the one who shuddered from her old woman's body long after the others had been born and grown, and a month after her husband and eldest had been lost to the sea. Too wearied was she to give chase when, the moment he found his legs, he was rattling doorknobs and gateposts and trotting along the beach, bawling to go out in the boat with her third eldest, Manny. And in vain were her protests when Manny, his own chin still soft with baby-down, yet his heart broader than his burly frame and sorrowing for this fatherless youngster, buttoned him inside an oilskin coat that fell below his knees, and hove him aboard his punt. Tying a length of twine with a jigger around Sylvanus's pudgy hands, he shoved off from shore, heading for the fishing grounds. Now, as Sylvanus filled her doorway, grinning foolishly over the suit he held before her, his glut of coarse, dark hair and brows exaggerating a stubbornness fossilized since birth, she merely ambled past him, pulling on her gardening gloves.

Hooking his suit to a notch below the mantel, Sylvanus left the house and sauntered down to his father's stage, untouched since the day of his drowning, and wriggled open the door. It was darkish inside and murky, the air sharp with brine. Filling his lungs, he stood, waiting, watching, as his eyes adjusted, giving shape to the bulks and bundles strewn around him.

CHAPTER TWO

COCKLESHELLS AND TOMMYCOD

THE SUIT NETTED HIM far more than a confirmation certificate. For if it hadn't shamed him to leave such a fine garment hanging on his door, he never would've donned it, now a perfect fit, that Saturday evening four years later and motored in his new thirty-foot, four-horsepower motorboat over to Ragged Rock and the dance Eb Rice was holding in the new addition he was building on his house. Inside was already full of people when he got there, and the door was barred.

Elbowing his way through the boys bunching around a window, he peered in through the paint-smeared glass, and that's when he saw her. She was standing, leaning against the opposite wall, watching others either milling about or dancing to a jig being keyed out on an accordion. Tiny, she was, and pale; yet the whiteness of her skin appeared to usurp the light in the room, enhancing her luminescence and leaving all else as moving shadows of grey.

Despite her being off to herself, she wasn't without attention, he noted, seeing others casting curious glances toward her. Nor was she without conceit, for each time she encountered the eyes of another in the flickering lamplight, she raised her chin, haughtily drawing her gaze away, eclipsing the poor, offending souls once more into shades of grey. And she was proud; he saw that when Rubert Baldwin let his hand graze the roundedness of her arm as he reached past her for his tumbler of brew. Swatted him, she did, and turned her back to him, her face twisting with displeasure as he laughed. Folding her arms protectively beneath the curve of her breasts, she flounced away from him, and upon encountering the chiding looks of some of the dancers, she swung her slender hips exaggeratedly. As though sensing the looks of disapproval following her, she sauntered toward the window Sylvanus was clinging to and smiled, a smile as cool as it was deliberate, yet one that Sylvanus melted into as did Icarus's wings into the sun.

It were as if he had been entombed in a pit and her single ray of light had split him apart, raising him from himself. Others tried to elbow him aside but he held stubbornly to his spot, watching as she was finally persuaded to dance, his eyes clinging to the green, swinging silkiness of her dress as she cavorted into the foxtrot, and then waltzed into his dreams during the night, her siren's song wrestling low the arm trying to jerk his jiggers come morning, taunting him with her dance upon the water, her skin radiant with light and sparkling in the sun. How blue the sea whilst she sashayed, how sweet the pine. And the breeze a gentle fanning for the heat of his brow.

"Syllie, jeezes, what're you gone mental?" cried his brother Manny as Sylvanus leaned against his stage door later that morning, gazing at the sky, a silly grin twisting his face. He shook himself awake and feigned fiddling with the door latch as Manny let himself out of their mother's gate, heading along the pathway toward him.

"Come on over to Jake's," called Manny. "Ambrose just got back from St. John's. He went and bought himself a new boat, a longliner."

"Ambrose? Where'd he get the guts to do that?"

"What, buy a liner?" Manny huffed. "Try sitting aboard a schooner for weeks on end. Not hard to find courage then, you got piles and splinters rotting your arse. Nice boat, too, she is, buddy. Sixty-footer, half the size of a schooner."

"Liners, schooners—all the same to me," Sylvanus replied, jiggling the door to ensure it was latched.

"Sure, b'ye, all the same—big old clumsy schooners, sitting on the water for days sometimes, waiting for a gust of wind for her sails. We'll be seeing the last of them soon enough, now we got diesel."

"Still don't see the difference in them."

"Difference, jeezes, Syllie, schooners got sails, liners got diesel. How's that for a difference? One sits on the water for days with dories doing her fishing for her, and the other nets straight from her decks; one salts, the other sells fresh fish straight to the plants; one got twelve men, the other got eight—"

"All right, all right," interrupted Sylvanus loudly, "like I said, no difference in them. Bunch of men crowding the one deck, hawking and hollering for days on end."

"Diesel, you young fool, diesel, I just said. She'll be motoring home every evening, and full of fish to her gunnels with them nice big nets. Cripes, Father spawned you, all right—you hears nothing but what you wants to."

Manny stood before his younger brother, the baby down that had once softened his chin now coarsened into a thick, grizzled beard that opened onto the same heartening grin as when he used to toss Sylvanus aboard his boat as a youngster, wrapped in oilskins. "Come on," he commanded, walloping his little brother's arm with such a punch that it drew a look of pain, "before Jake drinks all the brew—and watch your mouth, the trawlers tore up our nets agin and he's a bit spiteful."

"A bit! Jeezes, he's full of it."

"Ye-es, floats off him like smoke when he moves," said Manny, starting down the well-scuffed lane. "You coming?" he hollered, as Sylvanus lagged behind, not wanting company just now. "Cripes, why don't you ask Am for a spot on his liner? You're getting like Father, bandied at the knees from straddling a boat."

Sylvanus grinned, giving his door one last jiggle, then trotted after his brother, skirting youngsters and hens squabbling about the door places.

"How're ye all doing?" Manny hailed, rounding the corner of Jake's house. Their eldest brother, along with their buddy Ambrose, was lifting a barrel that lay sideways atop two sawhorses that stood side by side inside the wide opening of a canvased wood-house. Sylvanus kicked a junk of wood upright and sat back on it, watching as Manny hurried forward, helping with the lifting. Built onto the side of the house as it was, the wood-house made a good break from the wind, and with the wide flap that had been ripped out for the opening, fastened overhead for a canopy, a good shelter from any weather being dumped from above. Despite there being no fire lit on this sunny afternoon, Sylvanus rested his elbows on his knees, leaning toward an old, overflowing ashpan that was sunk into the ground, serving as a firepit. The barrel in place, Manny and Ambrose seated themselves around the pit, exclaiming eagerly over the foam capping the mugs of brew Jake poured out of the barrel and passed around.

"By cripes, that's one thing Father taught you, old cock," said Manny, supping back the foam, "how to make a good brew. Here's to your new boat, Am," he toasted, raising his mug.

Jake reluctantly raised his, his mother's grey eyes appearing more aged upon his sunken cheeks with their thorny sideburns. "Something else to rip up our nets," he said, "everybody buying liners."

Ambrose shook his head. "Liners won't come that close to shore," he said quietly. "Midshore is where we'll be fishing—sixty miles out."

"That's right," said Manny, "sixty miles offshore. Lots of room for us inshore fishermen with our trap nets and jiggers. Be all right now, if we could keep the trawlers a hundred miles offshore—or even the three bloody miles that the law says they ought to be out."

"Three miles," snorted Jake. "Some distance, that is, a bloody cannon shot—yeah, a cannon shot," he repeated at the dubious look on Sylvanus's face, "that's how far offshore a cannon can shoot: three miles. And in Grandfather's day, if either a foreign boat come closer than that, they told you to blast the bastards, no problem. Now they even got that took from us—blasting cannon balls up their arse. Don't laugh, buddy," he cautioned at a guffaw from Manny, "because that's what the foreigners are doing, laughing. Our fishing laws are the same as was printed out in Peter's day. By jeezes, shoot a moose—something we governs ourselves—and see what'll it get you—life in the dungeons, that's what."

"Mind now, don't get too worked up," said Manny as splotches of red fired up on Jake's long, bony cheeks. "Christ, b'ye, face like a broody hen. Here, pour me another one," he ordered, dumping the dregs of his mug into the pit and tossing it to his brother.

"Another war, another war," said Jake, his tone rising, "we needs another war and a couple dozen mines out there—that'd keep the bastards off our shelves, if we blows up a few—because I tell you, my son, they never had no problem with no nets when the wars were on and they were all kept ashore; they never had no problem then."

"Ye-es, my son, just what we needs, another war," said Manny with a wink at Sylvanus. "Go on, b'ye, make yourself a bib," he taunted as Jake started to cut in, but belched instead, dribbling brew down his chin, "and get yourself a handkerchief, too, because you'll soon be bawling if you keeps on talking about them trawlers. What do you say, Am—how many's out there?"

"Five hundred," said Ambrose without thought. "Fisheries fellow told me the other day."

"Five hundred. Jeezes."

Ambrose nodded.

"Heh, that made you sit up," said Jake. "You won't be taunting next week you wakes up and finds them moored off from your wharf, you won't be taunting then."

Sylvanus sat up, too. "Five hundred," he said lowly. "Jeezes, that many?" He sat back, envisioning five hundred of the sixty-foot fishing vessels and their thousand-foot nets. He'd never seen their nets, but he could figure the damage even one could do—all thousand feet of it being dragged along the ocean floor, its jaws held open by massive slabs of wood that were heavily shod with iron—dislodging boulders and flattening crevices and outcrops, crushing and burying billions of fish and their habitats in its path as it rolled along, striving to frighten up into its giant maw the bottom fish, including those mother-fish whose bellies were swollen with pounds of roe not yet spawned. Now then, imagine five hundred of them, all ploughing the spawning grounds, he thought, and sat forward again, notably disturbed.

"How much fish are they catching then, brother?" he asked Ambrose.

"A lot of fish, my son. Tons. And they scraps tons. Right over the side. If they gets a load of haddock and they wants cod, they dumps it. If they gets a load of cod and they wants haddock, they dumps it. Tons. They dumps tons of fish. For sure, I seen enough of it out there on the schooners." He paused, bulbous eyes falling shyly askance at each of the men he was addressing. "And then there's the ones they loses, their nets breaks halfways upon their decks, and—whoosh!—everything falls back overboard. Good only for the gulls, then."

"Jeezes, do the Fisheries fellows see all that?"

Jake smirked. "How can you see anything, old man, when you're head's up your arse? If them Fishery people done what they was paid for, they'd banish everything longer than thirty feet fifty miles offshore—or farther. By jeezes, that's what they're doing in other countries then—"

A door slammed, and he grimaced into silence along with the rest of the men as a broad-shouldered woman charged around the corner, her presence like the light of dawn drawing a close to the evening's intimacy.

"They're down hooking gulls with fish hooks agin!" she exclaimed angrily, her lidless eyes glancing off the rest of the men and burrowing into Jake.

"Who? Who's hooking gulls?" asked Jake.

"The youngsters—who the bloody hell do you think?" she snipped, pointing to a huddle of boys farther down the beach. "Go—drive them out of it, else I throws your supper to the dogs!" She hustled back inside the house, banging the door shut behind her.

"Ah, you loves her," said Manny as Jake cut loose with a mutter of oaths. "Ye-es, you do. Go on. Chase after her. Tell her you loves her," he goaded as Jake rose, a dirty look toward his house as he shuffled toward the landwash. Manny shook with mirth. "Pair of sleeves to the one shirt," he said to Sylvanus and Ambrose, "and stun as the gnat, the both of them. Out by Mother's, they was, the other night, trying to dip the moon out of the brook. Yes, they were," he vowed beneath the disbelieving snickers of the others, "swear to gawd. Go ask Mother—she went out and offered them a strainer."

A cry of excitement from the boys and Manny rose. "That one of mine I hears? Little bugger, he's suppose to be chopping wood. Heh, cripes if they haven't hooked a gull." He sat back down, grinning, watching as the boys, oblivious to Jake now marching toward them, fist raised, started pulling in their thirty- to forty-foot length of fishing line and the hooked gull. "Yup, nothing we never done, hey, Am. Remember putting bark on the water and watching the gannets dive for it? Broke their necks every time. Cripes, that was bad. How come boys does stuff like that? You do that, Syllie, put bark on the water for the gannets?"

Sylvanus grimaced. "Break their necks? How'd you break their necks?"

"They sees the bark and thinks it's a fish and dives for it," said Manny. "Dives hard, a gannet do. Can hear the snap when their beaks hits the bark. Oh, now, it wouldn't that bad," he drawled at Sylvanus's look of repulsion. "And we never wasted them—always took them home after for Mother to bake. She never knew but it was a duck after we had it buffed and picked. Here, pass your mug, Am, I fills it. Where's yours? Hey, where you going?" he asked as Sylvanus, shaking his head in disgust, kicked aside his stump and headed toward home.

"That's it, my son, can't hoot with the owls and fly with the eagles, too," Manny shouted after him, "but I must say, you was quite the dandy at the dance last night—all dressed up and watching through the window. Next time come on in, b'ye, and have yourself a dance. Well, sir," he exclaimed as Sylvanus shot him a look, face reddening, "look at that, Am, he's all red. Gentle jeezes, Syllie's blushing! What'd you do, find yourself a woman? Did you, did you, Syllie?" he hollered, rising off his seat, giving chase.

"Fool!" Sylvanus muttered and ducked out of sight around the house. Damned if his ears weren't burning. Melita, Manny's wife, her curly, capped head heightening a round, dimpled face, glanced suspiciously at him as he stumbled over some hens firking at the feed she was tossing them.

"Nice day, what?" he hailed, skirting the flapping, squabbling birds.

"Nice day," she called back, and he shook his head, catching her grin as she tossed another handful of feed around his feet, sending him stumbling through another onslaught of pecking and flapping and squabbling.

"Worse than Manny," he grunted, hopping onto the beach, away from the lot of them. Digging his hands into his pockets, he leaned into the breeze and was soon whistling his way along shore, his nymph from the night swaying before him once more, luring him along some mystic path, beckoning him inside a shanty and seating him beside a fire that warmed his heart as readily as it warmed her hearth. Nothing followed him there—no boats, no fish, no creamy white pods and their wasted spawn—all vapourized by the heat of her fire as it blazed across her bare, naked skin, leaping into his veins and fevering his vision as he wove through the following days, tripping over goats and chicks, and clamouring about his stage, his flakes, his woodpile on weakening legs.

"We needs a new house, Mother," he said irritably one evening, stumbling over mats that had been lying on the floors since he was a gaffer, and peering critically at unpainted faceboards and faded wallpaper.

"It'll last the rest of my years," grumbled Eva, pushing him out of her way.

"There's holes in the canvas."

"Stop your pacing, then, big galoot. I was thinking," she went on as he rested his arms moodily on the windowsill, gazing outside, "perhaps we should take a smoked salmon to the Trapps."

He near cricked his neck, twisting it sideways to see her, but her face was hidden in the bowels of a bottom cupboard. "You talking about a *visit*?" he asked incredulously.

"With all they done for us, wouldn't hurt to pay a visit."

He jammed his hands in his back pockets, studying the back of her head. "Eighteen years ago the Trapps fished Elikum out of the sea, and suddenly you wants go visit them. What're you rooting at in there? Get your head out," he commanded, "and tell me why in the name of gawd you're wanting to visit the Trapps?"

Eva hauled back on her haunches, brandishing a dusty bottle of pickles before him. "You mind yourself," she said stiffly. "They brought your brother home. Least we got one grave marked in that cemetery. Goodness' sakes, can't a body go visiting without all this nonsense?"

"Nonsense! You suddenly wants to visit the Trapps, and my asking why is nonsense? Jeezes, they'd rather sink your boat than let you ashore."

"They've never hurt a soul."

"Enough the way they looks at you. No thanks, the Trapps don't like company and that's fine with me."

"Then I'll get Jake to take me." She creaked to her feet, shuffling tiredly to the bin, polishing off the pickle bottle with her apron. "Besides," she said, "I got something to ask of them. I was thinking on getting one of their girls to work with me this summer in the garden."

"Hey!? You wants a Trapp girl working for us? Oh, come now, Mother—"

"Don't go *now Mothering* me!" cried Eva, turning on him. "I'm not what I used to be, and for all the help you are these days, you might just as well move to Ragged Rock, for that's where your mind's at, well enough."

"Well, sir, is that what's on your mind—that I'm moving off to Ragged Rock?" He struck a fist into his hand. "Bloody Manny! Up shooting off his face, was he? Got me marrying some girl up Ragged Rock. Fool! And, oh, that's a good one, Mother. You'd have me marry a Trapp, instead—sly as dogs—"

"How'd you know that? Nobody ever got to know them."

"That says it right there—a stone's throw up the shore and we hardly knows their names."

"Nothing wrong with keeping to yourselves. We should all be more mindful. Least they're not wanting roads and electricity and to be moving off all over the place."

"Oh, and is that what you're thinking, that I'll soon be getting a girl and burning me boat and buying a car? Well, sir—" and he broke off laughing.

His mother had turned her back, polishing and repolishing the already polished pickle jar.

He sobered, leaning sideways to see her face. "Christ, Mother, you knows I'm not going to move off somewhere—" He lapsed as a dab of water wetted the corner of her eye. Sweet jeezes, she wasn't bawling, was she? "Mother, now, Mother, in the name of jeezes, you're not bawling, are you?"

"Mind your mouth!" she ordered, flapping the dishrag at him as he tried turning her toward him.

"For gawd's sake," and he grabbed her by the waist. "You needs some fresh air, you do. Blow the nonsense out of your skull. Come on," and ignoring her shrieks of protest, he swung her onto his shoulder like a sack of spuds, striding with her out of the house, across the path, and in through his stage. "Now, get down or be flung down," he threatened, lodging her onto the stagehead, steering her toward his boat, bobbing alongside.

"I haven't got time for this, foolish thing," she cried, and started shrieking again as he lifted her off her feet, lodging her down into the boat, rocking it madly as he jumped in beside her. "Syllie, in the name of God, I got bread in the oven, and the goats are wanting—"

"Hey, buddy!" Sylvanus called out to one of Manny's youngsters dawdling along shore, "go tell your mother to go turn Mother's bread! Marry a Trapp," he muttered, pushing her toward the seat in the stern. "Marry a goddamn Trapp!" Shaking his head, he hunched before the engine house, heaving hard on the flywheel. "Yes, now, that's just what I'm about, leaving Cooney Arm," and he tutted over her rebukes as he putted them through the neck, haranguing about her selfishness, that she'd rather have her boy shift in with the sly-looking Trapps over some nice family in Ragged Rock. "Now, there's nonsense for you, Mother, there's bloody nonsense," he chided. Settling himself beside her, he cradled her resisting shoulders, pooh-poohing any and all else that she said. Finally, she settled back, enjoying with him the sun full on their faces, the wind waffling their hair, and the *clip-clop-clop* of the boat hitting on the waves curling toward them off the open seas.

By the time they returned home both mother and son were lulled into quiet. Which lasted about ten minutes after they were ashore. Then Sylvanus was grumbling again about the cramped quarters of his mother's house, its peeling paint and sagging floors. Prowling outside, he started figuring how many quintals of fish it would take to lay a foundation and build his own house—and nearer the shoreline, it would have to be, he figured, sizing up the twenty, thirty feet or more his mother's house held back on land, for wouldn't the woman of his dreams like sitting on her stoop in the evenings, watching the tide washing closer, lifting the seaweed off the rocks and floating it before her like goldenrod, and the starfish fluttering amongst its blooms like butterflies? Her garden, he mused. The sea would be her garden, planting cockleshells and urchins upon her windowsill, weaving her pathways through the eelgrass, baring baby crabs and tommycod playing hide-and-seek amongst the rocks, lulling her with its waves washing up on shore.

Within the week he was feverish with a need to see her, to touch her. Damned were his nights as he thrashed his bed. And damned were his days as he tried to keep rhythm with his jiggers and the rocking of his boat. He paced the shoreline. He threw rocks at the ocean. He scaled the cliffs rising from the neck, trampling over nests and burrows of kittiwake and carey chicks. And he started cursing the head, the coves, and bights that separated him from her.

When, one Sunday morning two weeks after he'd first seen her, he found himself getting out of his boat in Ragged Rock and walking along the path leading to her door, he froze in his madness. What would she think of him—the thick mat of hair covering his body since before he was fourteen, his surly, black brows, his ability to read nothing but the clouds, his bowlegged walk?

He faltered, his knees buckling to his lowliness. Yet it was a thing that had to be done. Doffing his cap, he pulled back his shoulders, grateful for the extra scouring of his armpits with his mother's scrubbing soap, and buttoning his top button to cover the hair curling out of his chest, he tensed his legs straighter at the knees and forced his feet along the rest of the path, raising his hand to rap on her door.

PART TWO

Adelaide

SPRING 1949 TO SUMMER 1953

CHAPTER THREE

DESTRUCTING A DREAM

H ER NAME WAS ADELAIDE and hers was the curse of
the eldest, for from the first that she could remember she was her mother's servant: bathing, diapering, and
feeding the babies, and scrubbing, sweeping, and picking up
after the toddlers trailing behind her. She hated them, hated
their fighting, bawling ways, hated their grubby little hands
forever snatching, picking, and scratching, and she hated her
mother, too—how she was growing shorter and fatter with
each youngster born, and how she hovered and tottered
amongst their squabbling, never knowing where to lay a
restraining hand till, she, Adelaide, leaped into the chaos,
pinching, swatting, scolding till there was thrice the
uproar and thrice the fighting. And it was upon Adelaide,
then, that fault was assigned, and a new ruckus started as
Florry floundered amongst her youngest, warning off this
eldest with the cutting blue eyes and lacerating tongue.

"You always blames everything on me—everything,"
Adelaide was quick to yell, "and them brats gets away with
everything."

"Ah, you're good for nothing," cried Florry forever and a time, "always mouthing and pouting over a bit of work. You'd think, by gawd, you was worked to death— and mind you leaves them young ones alone; they're not yours to knock around. Brazen as the black Irish, is what you are, and mind you takes that cross look off your face because I swear to gawd, Addie, you gets the look of the devil every time you're told to do something."

"No, I don't!"

"Yes, you do—and always hove off in a corner, sleeping and dreaming—"

"I'm not sleeping and dreaming! I'm studying, is what I'm doing. Studying!"

"Studying! How you can study anything up to your knees in dirt is beyond me. Wait, wait, empty the ashpan before you goes," she cried out one morning as Adelaide was rushing around in a flurry, trying to get herself and Ivy and Janie, a good five and six years younger than herself, out the door.

"But I'll get my clothes dirty," wailed Adelaide.

"You'll get my hand if you don't," warned Florry, waddling to the stove, a baby grappled to her tit, and hauling out the ashpan, toppling over with ashes. "Here, name of gawd, Addie, don't go mouthing now—not much I can do with the baby wanting feeding and the others wanting their oats cooked. Hurry on, take the pan, else I tells your father."

"*Tells your father, tells your father,*" mocked Adelaide, snatching the oblong pan by its wire handle and bolting for the door.

Her mother was fast on her heels. "You're spilling the ashes, you young bugger." But Adelaide was slamming the door, carefully holding the pan away from her skirt, her skinny, stockinged knees knocking against each other as she scrabbled carefully across the weed-choked yard, shutting out her mother now rapping at the window, bawling out warnings about telling her father.

"Tell him all you wants!" Adelaide screamed over her shoulder. And sticking out her chin, she flounced along her way, screwing up her mouth at the thought of her father and his ruddy-red face and ruddy-red neck and sickly white body each time he come home from the schooners and stood stripped from the waist up, scrubbing himself at the washstand. *Tell your father, tell your father!* Christ, as if he'd do anything—too wimpy to kick a cat, he was, and she wished to gawd he'd never come home again, crowding up the already crowded kitchen with his big fat gut and whiny, sickly ways as he *whined* at the youngsters and *whined* at her mother and *whined* at arse-up governments and fish-killers and markets. Christ, was there ever a thing he didn't *whine* about?

Ouff! A cloud of ashes blew into her face and she jerked her head sideways, nicking her knee against the tinny edge of the pan. "Damn," she muttered, brushing a smudge off her stocking and stepping more carefully onto the beach. Her lip curled, twisting her tiny, pretty face into a caricature of a cross old woman as she looked about the kelp-cluttered shoreline, looking for a clear path to the water. She hated the water, hated its stink of brine and rot and jellyfish, and hated how all night long it shifted and moaned like some old crone hagged in sleep. And worse, she hated the briny smell of salt fish assailing her from the nearby flakes.

The school bell rang. "I'm going to be late again," she wailed and dumped out the ashpan where she stood, racing away from the smoldering heap, back across the yard, and in through the door. Ignoring her mother's shouts and the baby's screams and the oats burning on the stove, she snatched her books off the plate-piled sink and bolted out the door and down the road toward the school-house and salvation. For it was there her work was tallied, and her excellence in Latin, calligraphy, and reading raised her to the front of the class and above those others sitting and torturing over every simple little test.

Miss Proudy-Pants, she was mocked by the girls for always knowing the answers and sitting up front, tight to the teacher's desk. Miss Stuck-Up, she was hailed by the boys for scurrying past them with her nose pinched as they stood near their fathers' stages, slimed to their elbows in fish guts, cutting out tongues and cheeks.

She cared nothing of what she was called, only of being alone and sneaking into the church. This was where she loved to be—the church. Especially on weekdays when there was nobody about. She'd creep up front then, blessing herself and sitting on the front pew, laying her books beside her. Always she sat in this one spot, revelling in the quiet hush that befell her, for it was here that she dreamed her dreams of travelling over the sea someday to be a missionary and feed starving children. Only there wouldn't be dirty, rotten floors and dishes to scrub, she vowed, or overflowing slop-pails and ashpans to empty. And nor would the youngsters be sour and grubby like her own clan, for they'd be grateful for the hand that fed them and as sweet-smelling as the little baby Jesus who lay in sweet hay at the church altar and was all wrapped in clean cloth, and pretty and pink as he gazed up at his mother and father who were tall and slender and dressed in clean, coloured robes and smiling gently. And perhaps she'd live in a place like this, she'd think, admiring the clean, polished floors of the church and the shiny, lacquered handrail before her, and perhaps, please God, she'd have her very own room, someday, with a door. That could lock.

"Oh, Lord," she'd pray into the hushed silence that always permeated the house of God, even when it was filled with Sunday parishioners, "make me a missionary, make me a missionary." And she'd fasten her eyes onto that holiest of figures, sculpted from wood and painted in the most loveliest, deepest of blues (the colour of her eyes, she once proudly thought), and bless herself with the sign of the cross. Then she'd sit back quietly on her pew, her eyes now lowered, for the church was the one true place in this ratty outport, a shrine of stained-glass beauty and elegantly robed followers, and where the purity of the air cleansed her of baby piss and puke.

And, too, as the years passed by and she grew older, she found that in such a house as the Lord's there was an understanding of her dislike of her younger sisters and brothers, for hadn't Saint Augustine, in that precious book she'd been presented with during her confirmation, said that the only reason babies were innocent was from lack of strength, not lack of will? That if they could, they'd strike and hurt anyone who wouldn't pander to their whims? That even amongst brothers, jealousy and envy rioted within them for the mother's breast, even though milk flowed in abundance for all?

Reason enough to feel dislike, she'd muse, when innocence was scarce, and gluttony and stinginess rampant around her. Fitting, then, that she'd rather serve strangers than her own crowd, for at least in the starving lands of the minister's sermons, it was the failure of the earth that offered up hunger and strife, and not greed and envy.

But in this place of antiquity, where a woman's worth was determined by the white of her sheets flapping on the line like an early-morning flag, announcing the hard-working souls inside, there was little thought for reading and writing and planning out dreams. Other than an act of leisure on a Sunday afternoon and the half hour set aside in the evenings, each moment's study was a thing to be stolen, fitted in between the dishes and diapering, and the mopping and the sweeping.

And as Adelaide grew into those higher grades, and the youngsters kept coming and growing behind her, it became more and more difficult to get that extra time for that extra work the higher grades demanded. And even then, when she was able to worm away from her mother's persistent singing out, and the youngsters competing over her cries, she had the neighbours to contend with. They weren't without wagging their tongues, they weren't, whenever they moseyed through, borrowing a bun of bread or returning a bag of blue, and caught her stuffed away in her room with her nose glued to a book whilst the table sagged with dirty dishes and the youngsters rioted in their half-nakedness and their mother sat amongst them, brandishing orders and suckling her babies.

"Lazy young thing," she heard herself called, if not once, then twice a day, "get up, get up and make yourself useful. Only lords and Old Maid Ethel and her pigs heaves off on a weekday." Lord, how many times was she called after Old Maid Ethel and her pigs! And how many times can you call a beaten man a dog before he starts barking back instead of talking back?

Perhaps that's how it was Adelaide started feeling slovenly. However it was, despite her knowing in her head it was right and proper for a girl her age to do well in school, way, way deep inside, a tiny part of her started oinking. The slovenliness of her mother's house became hers. And at some point she never really noticed, whenever a neighbour nosied by, or a youngster whined, or her mother hollered, she started shoving her books underneath her bed to hide them, and bolt to the kitchen, cleaning, serving, and placating. But not without pay! For the oinking channelled itself into a spite that was forever snapping at her mother and kicking at youngsters coming too close to her heels and slamming about dirty cups and clothes and the like. And throughout it all, she rehearsed in fantasy that coming day when she'd wave goodbye to this shack of a house and its tongue-tattling neighbours, and set off down the road and never, ever, look back on this hole of an outport. Not ever.

LIKE THE BUCKLING WALLS of a card house, her dreams fell in on themselves one fine May morning, two days shy of her fifteenth birthday, when her mother halted her at the door, lifting her school bag out of her hand, saying that the catches were down and her father was scarcely making enough to pay his berth on the schooner, and she was to stay home now, to help more with the younger ones and to accompany her to the flakes.

The flakes! Adelaide stared disbelievingly. Always come spring there was some poor mortal taken out of school to go work on their father's flakes—mostly the Reids and the Dykes. Now, since the war ended, and with the growth of bigger fish-killers and their extended catch taking up most of the shoreline with flakes, more and more women and youngsters were needed to work the fish, gaining themselves extra credit with the merchant. But—make no mistake—no one worked the flakes unless they had to.

Her eyes grew more incredulous as she stared down her short, pudgy mother, to whom the world outside ended at her stoop.

"No! No, I won't," she cried, grasping back her school bag. "You had them. You had them babies—you feed them."

"You mind now, Addie. It's not going to kill you, a few months on the flakes. Do you good, a bit of hard work, and it's only for a summer. You can start back agin in October."

"No, no, I won't start back, nobody ever starts back. You can't make me quit school, you can't make me."

"I already told you it's only a few weeks," cried Florry, her voice rising with warning, "and I'm not changing my mind, so you can stop pouting and get used to it. Not going to hurt you, a few weeks out of school, like I said, do you good, a summer on the flakes."

Adelaide raised a hand to mouth. She was being taken out of school. Her mother was taking her out of school. "You can't," she whispered. "You can't take me out. I won't, I won't!" she then yelled, frightening the baby on her mother's shoulder. It started bawling, its face darkening, wrinkling. Of their own bidding, Adelaide's eyes fell onto her mother's belly. There. It was swelling, again.

That's why she was being took out of school; that right there was the reason why—to help feed them babies that kept coming and coming, and to help with their cleaning and diapering.

"I hates them," she whispered. "I hates them babies." Revulsion twisted her face as she raised her eyes to her mother's.

Florry lapsed into silence, her free hand crossing protectively over her belly as she stepped back.

"You mind now, Addie," she warned as Adelaide bore down on her, hot tears illuminating the startling blue of her eyes. "Addie!" Clutching the squalling youngster to her breast, she scurried across the kitchen, singing out as Adelaide chased after, "You get on now—get on, you young thing."

"No, wait, wait," cried Adelaide, her tone turning into a higher note of pleading as she grasped after her mother. "It's not fair, I won't quit, I won't go. You can't make me." Grabbing her mother's arm, she gave a hard yank. Caught off balance, Florry stumbled, thudding sideways against the wall, near falling, near losing her grip on the baby whose screaming was now frenzied. Adelaide withdrew in fright, watching as her mother caught hold of the corner of the washstand, steadying herself, grasping the baby back up on her shoulder.

"Not fit. You're not fit," said Florry. Spurting across the kitchen, she darted into her room, a last rattled look at her daughter, and shut her door, muffling the baby's cries.

The front door swung open, letting in the sound of the school bell and her youngest sister, Janie. Her cheeks reddened from the cold, Janie grabbed a bookbag from the pile of boots near the door.

"I forgot it," she said and stared boldly at Adelaide. "You got to stay home from school. I told the teacher. And you're not going back, either."

"Get," croaked Adelaide, her throat too tight to speak properly.

"I got to tell Mom something—"

"I said, get!" cried Adelaide, raising her fist as Janie was about to bolt across the room.

"Dyin' jumpin', my dear," said Janie, then ducked back outside as her eldest sister kicked at a boot and bolted toward her. Slamming the door, Adelaide leaned against it, staring out the window, hot tears swaddling her eyes, and the watery shape of the flakes out on the beach blighting what sight was left.

CHAPTER FOUR

THE FLAKES

A STARK DIFFERENCE marked the quiet between mother and daughter as they followed the muddied path to the beach the following morning. Florry, aside from a few guarded glances at Adelaide, tutted at the brisk winds, the gulls screaming like haunts overhead, and looked no farther than the baby swinging off her arm in a basket. Adelaide walked woodenly beside her, eyes glazed upon a face fixed in marble.

Her step faltered as they came upon the all-too-familiar sight of a dozen or more women and young girls, all dressed—like Adelaide herself, this morning—in brown wrapper aprons made from burlap, with white cotton skullies on their heads. Like some kind of rite, she thought, as the women hobbled hunchback over the wooden platforms, ceremoniously laying out their armloads of fish, the wired brims of their skullies shadowing their faces from the sun, and the flaps, sewn along the back to protect their necks, flapping in the wind. Some of the women straightened upon seeing Florry and her girl, waving largely and calling boisterously, "Good morning," and, "A bit breezy. Good for the flies, though."

Adelaide walked stiffly past them, leaving her mother to return the pleasantries. It was like a dream, a bad, horrible dream. She approached with trepidation the faggots—piles of partly dried fish all neatly stacked atop each other—some as high as four feet. They didn't even look like fish, all split open and flattened and shaped like dirtied paper kites.

"Don't be scared of them; they're not going to bite," bawled out Gert, the boss woman, from the middle of the flakes—hired, no doubt, for the foghorn harbouring in her gullet, thought Adelaide. She burned beneath the pairs of eyes turning onto her. Choosing one of the higher faggots, where the fish were already a bit dried and not too soggy with brine, she cautiously picked one up by the tail, grimacing at the coldness of the pickled flesh. It slipped out of her fingers. Picking it up again, she laid it across her arm, grateful for the long sleeves of her blouse, and held the thing arm's length from her chest.

Trampling over the flakes toward her, Gert hollered, "My gawd, not squeamish, is she?" and started piling wet fish onto Adelaide's arms. "There, how's that for a load?" she asked as Adelaide had to stretch her neck to see over the fish. Amidst the spurts of laughter erupting from the women working the flakes, Gert grinned broadly, slapping on a last fish, squishing the cold, wet flesh beneath Adelaide's chin. Near vomiting, Adelaide twisted her head sideways, her stomach heaving from the sharp, fishy smell. Florry, having deposited the baby alongside three or four others sleeping in baskets nearer the flakes, waddled toward them with a look of concern.

"Having a fine old time, are you, Gert?" she said a mite contrarily. "You never mind her, Addie, bad as the devil, she is. Wait there for me, now. We works together."

Gert laughed, "I allows you'll get more work out of that sleeping baby over there than this one."

Fighting back nausea, Adelaide crept away, trying to see her footing over the bundle of fish.

"The other way, the other way, cripes, you'll end up home agin, if you keeps going that way," sung out Gert amidst more spurts of laughter. A figure darkened the entrance to the stage. Suze. Suze Brett. Adelaide groaned. Stun as the gnat, Suze was, and always chasing after Adelaide, till, much to Adelaide's relief, she got took out of school, two, three years ago to work the flakes, and was since married.

"Addie," said Suze. "My gawd, what's you doing on the flakes?"

Adelaide said nothing. Clutching onto her yaffle of fish, she crept toward the farthest end of flakes down by the water, where fewer bodies were hunched. Small wonder, she thought dismally, examining the godfor-saken structure before her. The flakes were rickety platforms made by laying long, skinny birch poles side by side and covering them with a layer of boughs onto which to spread the fish. Beneath them, holding them in place and levelling them against the sloping beach, were stilts of varying heights, with the ones nearest the water's edge being the highest—six feet, thought Adelaide, eyeing them. And with a full tide, as it now was, the flakes extended about ten feet or more out over the water, creaking crazily as the water lapped against the stilts. Along with the women's trampling, the whole thing felt to Adelaide as though it were on the verge of collapse.

"Not deep enough to drown, even if you do fall in," called out Suze.

Latching a foot onto the bottom rung of a spindly ladder and awkwardly balancing the fish against herself, Adelaide started climbing. Boldly, yet shakily, she stepped onto the flakes. They felt knobby beneath her feet, despite the layering of boughs. Her ankle rolled, near throwing her, but she kept steady as she caught sight of Suze abandoning the stage and lumbering toward her. Mannish, Suze looked, with her broad shoulders and broader hips, and by the bulging of her wrapper, it looked as though she might pop a youngster any minute. Yet easily she climbed up the ladder, swinging herself onto the flakes, and propped herself before Adelaide, face flushed with exertion, eyes brimming with light, and berry-red lips stealing away from the shadings of some future moustache.

"Here, give me some of that," she ordered, reaching for Adelaide's fish. "Likes a bit of fun, that Gert do."

"I'm fine," said Adelaide.

"Won't be if you falls over," said Suze as Adelaide stepped precariously close to the edge of the flakes. "And what's you doing here, anyway? Your mother take you out of school? Cripes, brains like you got, I'd keep you there somehow. Here, give me some."

Ignoring Adelaide's protest, she scooped half of Adelaide's bundle onto her own arms and started laying out the fish.

"Like this, skin side up," she instructed, hunching over, laying down a fish. "Head to tail, tail to head," she added, laying down a couple of more fish, hobbling along, "and you does that right to the end of the flake, and then you starts back—skin side up—head to tail, tail to head. Not that hard, hey, maid?"

Without a word, Adelaide followed, gripping the slimy wet fins and throwing down the fish, skin side up, head to tail, tail to head; skin side up, head to tail, tail to head. Florry, halfway up the ladder, toting a yaffle of brine-soaked cod, hailed. Suze, her load mostly laid out, tossed down the rest and hurried toward her.

"Size of you," she called out. "Cripes, don't toddle too close to me, else we'll break down through them flakes," she warned, hand on her belly, eyeing Florry's. "Perhaps we'll keep Addie between us. For sure we won't have to worry about her breaking a pole—skinny as anything, isn't she?"

"She'll pad out soon enough," huffed Florry. "We was all skinny as her once, hey, Nelly maid?" she called to a cumbersome elder, waddling by.

"Make sure they lays them skin side up," Gert hollered to Suze from over beside the faggots.

"Yes, lord jeezes, hard thing to learn, laying out a fish," Suze hollered back. "How long was you in training for that, Gert? Cripes, the mouth on her—foghorn," Suze declared as Gert carried on hollering over the quips and chortles of those others enjoying a good morning's razzing. "What you say, Addie, think she'd make a good foghorn? My, you're awful quiet," she added to Adelaide's silence. "What're you thinking about? Bet you're missing school, aren't you?"

"Perhaps I got nothing to say," said Adelaide, laying out her fish all the faster so's to get some distance between her and Suze. Blessedly, the woman fell silent and hobbled off, leaving room for her mother to lumber into place beside her.

"Lord almighty, the tongue on you," sighed Florry. "The girl's only trying to help."

"Didn't need her yesterday, don't need her today," said Adelaide. "And don't need you, either," she muttered beneath her breath, and watched as her mother stooped off, grunting—like Old Maid Ethel's pigs herself, thought Adelaide, kicking her fish into place: head to tail, tail to head; head to tail, tail to head.

Wasn't the only time Adelaide was to think of Old Maid Ethel that morning. For as she plodded through the hours, hunching and hobbling over the bough-covered poles, laying out the stinking fish and biting down on her tongue as she repeatedly jabbed her hands with bones, she prayed for a hovel, for exile—anything to escape this hell and the stupid, yakking women and the stupid, scratchy skullies and dirty-looking wrappers. And always Suze, working right alongside, seemingly noting nothing of Adelaide's silence as she kept a running commentary on the weather and the water and the bloody screaming gulls and the size of Gert's pipes bellowing over the wind.

The morning crept, the brim of her skully slipping too far over her face as she hunched and hobbled, the flap flapping against her face each time she turned her head sideways to the wind. Yaffle after yaffle, from the flakes to the faggots, from the faggots to the flakes, head to tail, tail to head; head to tail, tail to head. By midmorning, the low of her back ached as though it were cracked. A quick cup of tea on the beach, heated by some of the women building a fire and boiling the kettle, and Adelaide groaned to see a couple of boats returning from their traps, and the fishermen pronging more fish up on the stagehead.

"The day they comes back with none is the day you got no bread," said the eldest Dyke sister, Effie Jean, sitting close enough to catch her groan. Shrugging, Adelaide finished her tea, flung the dregs into the fire, and leaving her mother breastfeeding the baby with two other mothers, she trudged back to the dwindling faggots. Come noon, the faggots were gone, the fish all laid out beneath the sun, and with her back screaming louder than the gulls, she followed the women back to the beach fire. A longer rest this time, with yesterday's leftover bread pudding and a thick slice of uncooked bologna for sustenance. When the mothers had their breasts tucked back inside their clothes once more, and the babies tucked back inside their baskets, she tiredly shoved herself upright, traipsing with everybody else back to the flakes. Starting at the front again, where they'd started out that morning, they began flipping over the fish already laid out; this time, flesh side up, head to tail, tail to head; flesh side up, head to tail, tail to head.

Late afternoon the wind died out and a battalion of black fishflies buzzed in, whizzing about her head. And the mosquitoes, hellish they were, whining and nuzzling around neck, ears, and nose till reason was lost and she was smacking at her face and throat with salt-crusted hands that served to further ignite the dozens of bites that were already stinging and reddening her exposed flesh. But even that was preferable to the beads of fly spit that grew more and more plentiful as the days wore on, all beaded and glistening wet upon those scattered spots of the fish that had escaped salting, and oftentimes already turning to maggots before they were firked off with a stick. Christ, it curdled her stomach, it did, firking off maggots with a stick, and more than once she simply turned the fish, pretending not to notice the spit, caring not a damn for the rot that would set in, spoiling the fish. Rot, for all she cared. It was bloody rotted anyways, from the stench of it. And unlike the low of her back, which strengthened as the days wilted into weeks, and the palms of her hands, which calloused after her first month rolled past, nothing immunized her to the stench of soggy salt fish.

She straightened one morning midsummer, her neck as crusted with salt as her hands from scratching at fly bites, and felt a heavy spatter of rain hit her cheek. Immediately, another one struck, and another, followed by squeals from the women as an unexpected sun shower unleashed itself. Holding out her hands, Adelaide raised her face to its cold, wet sweetness as though it were her first christening.

"Get at it, get at it! Cripes, what's you, addled?" yelled Gert, clipping her on the shoulder. Reluctantly, she joined the scurrying, frantic group snatching up fish to keep them from getting wet and mouldy, and running with them to the faggots, stacking them one atop the other and covering them with canvas. When the last fish was rescued and the babies collected, and all hands huddled inside the stagehead, and those that smoked jumbled in the doorway, lighting up butts, Adelaide kept standing by the faggots, unwilling to leave the cool, clean rivulets washing down her throat, soaking her skin.

She prayed for rain after that. No odds that each rainfall disrupted drying time, which sometimes led to slimy fish and lower prices, or, the worst dread of all, dun would set in: that green, mouldy fungus that can sometimes spread over an entire fish and infect others and send yaffle after yaffle to the dump. What mattered, thought Adelaide, about losing a few fish when the fishermen kept coming ashore twice a day, day after day with boatload after boatload of more and more? Daily she prayed that each fish caught would be the last in the sea, that the flakes would rot and crumble from lack of use, and never, never again would she have to hobble hunchbacked, laying out fish, head to tail, tail to head, firking off spit, firking off maggots, firking off the damn, bloody flies needling her neck, her ears, face, and eyes.

One burly September morning, she looked up from the flakes to see a couple of women hurrying along the road toward the school with their scrubbing buckets and cleaning rags. Her eyes filled with hope. Emissaries, she thought, sent by angels, signalling the end of the fish-drying season, and a scant few weeks more before she, Adelaide, would be hurrying along the road, her books tucked under her arm, for hadn't her mother said she might start back to school again in October?

She snorted, bending back to her work. One truth she knew: a girl never went back to school once she got took out. No, two truths: a girl never got out of the outports, either, without education or money. Unless it was to marry. Or go serving somewhere for her keep. And given how there wasn't a man's hand in Ragged Rock that wasn't soaked in gurry, and doubly worse to be a serving girl in a stranger's house, she shut down her mind from all thought except the work at hand.

Her eyes crept back to the road and chanced upon old Mr. Jacobs creeping down the church steps, the door left ajar behind him, lending her a glimpse of the little baby Jesus lying in his manger and those gloriously robed figures standing about him. The fish slipped awkwardly in her arms, and she clawed them back, staring at her hands, those long, tapered fingers that had so gracefully scrolled calligraphic lettering across the pages of her scribblers. They were all reddened now and scaly from brine and bone bits.

"Addie," her mother croaked from somewhere behind her. She watched as her mother's fat, swollen body shuffled toward her, struggling with a yaffle of fish. "Addie," called Florry, breathlessly, "quick—the fish's slipping."

Pretending she hadn't heard, Adelaide bent over her work.

Gert darted toward them, hollering, "Name of gawd, Ad, what're you in a trance? Sweet jeezes, Florry, time to go home and drop that youngster, don't you think?" she yelled, catching the woman and her armload of fish.

Adelaide continued with her work, any guilt she might've felt buried beneath the anger of a soul forced along another's wake.

CHAPTER FIVE

THE KING NO MIGHTIER THAN SELF

TWO YEARS OF SCRUBBING FLOORS and youngsters
and working the flakes, Adelaide's anger began
wearying itself. Thus, on her eighteenth birthday, as roads
and electricity began creeping through the outports, she
listened with a calm heart to the governing fathers as they
lectured the fishermen to "haul up your punts and burn
your flakes, b'yes, for the midshore fishery and sixty-foot
liners is where she's going to be, and fish plants and
freezers are the new way of curing fish and providing
healthy paying jobs for women as well as men."

Hope glimmered for Adelaide then, when the government encouraged the local merchants to buy a couple of
longliners and build a fish plant in Ragged Rock, pooh-
poohing the old-timers still wanting the flakes. "It's not
the poor Negro markets over the seas you want, my boys,
but the North Americans," they lectured, "and their nice
modern housewives and their want for nice recipes and
fish sticks made out of fresh fish. And just think, my sons,
how organized it'll all be then, with you men bringing fish

straight to the plants, no more salting and drying, and your women cutting and packing them, ready for the markets, and the prices all set and everyone getting regular pay. Can you imagine that, outport housewives? No more working the flakes? Nice indoor jobs all year round with regular pay, and dressing your youngsters in nice clothes from the catalogues, and getting rid of them old oak dressers, and furnishing your kitchens with vinyl and chrome and all those other nice things you'll be seeing on your nice new television sets once we gets you electrified and everything modernized?"

"*Mod-er-nized*," drawled out Joycie-Anne, Gert's girl, huddling to the front of the stage with a bunch of others one morning, waiting for a light rain to hold up. "That's all I hears about these days, getting *mod-er-nized*. I wonder what we're all going to look like when we gets *mod-er-nized*."

"Aah, Joycie, you'll be prettier than a fancy city woman," said Suze, tightening her skully against the rain as she leaned against a faggot next to Adelaide. "God bless their little pinkies—they think that worms lives only in the ground. What you say, Addie, think we'll all have pretty pink fingers then, when we haven't got bones jabbing them to bits? Imagine," she carried on as Adelaide, face held to the drizzle, said nothing, "no more lugging in wood and emptying ashpans. Just flick a knob on a stove and there she'll be—a hot oven for our chickens. I say, sir, we'll have the prettiest pink fingers around."

"I says they'll be pink," cut in the only man amongst them, an old geezer too crippled to haul a net. "And not only your fingers that'll be pink, but your stumps too, because that's all's going to be left of your fingers you works in a plant long enough—stumps! Your fingers froze up and cut off."

"Ooh, jeezes, here he goes," groaned Gert.

"Ah, you'll find out," he wagered, a mock shiver crimping his face. "I tell you, she's not nice, cocky, working them plants in the wintertime, not when you got your hands in icy water, freezing your blood up to your elbows. Cut off your arm then, and it wouldn't bleed—I'm not joking!" he countered the skeptical looks darting his way. "Ask the wife. I sliced open me hand one day and not a stain a blood come out—whiter than the fish, the cut was. No wonder the wife got sick, cooped up on pieces of cardboard all winter long and breeding gout."

"Hey!?"

"That's right—bits of cardboard. Gets so cold they puts bits of cardboard under your feet to help keep them warm. You try standing for hours in a pair of rubber boots on a concrete floor with a bit of cardboard tucked under-neath. Fine thing it was when she did get sick, brother, for another winter would've killed her."

"Cripes, if it was cold that breeded gout, we'd all be crumped up like accordions," said Gert.

"I never said was the *cold* that breeded gout. It's the *hot water* they puts out that breeds gout," said the old-timer. "Ye-es—hot water! They fills up barrels with hot water and puts them right besides ye on the floor to dip your hands in when they're too cold to hold on to a knife. That's what breeds gout—dipping your hands in hot water when they's freezing. Even youngsters knows not to put their hands in hot water when they're freezing. Cold water you puts aching hands into, a good drop of cold water."

"How come your missus didn't know, then?"

"She knows. Everybody knows. Even them that's putting the water there knows. They just wants you working faster, is all, and they don't give a tinker's shit how they does it. Even when your hands is so gnarled up they can't keep a knitting needle straight, they're still coaxing you to dip them in hot water. And you does it, too. I knows because I done it meself, enough times, and now here I got gout along with arthritis. Ye can have your plants, I say. I'll stick with the flakes, cocky."

"Well, my son, if that's your calling, stick with it," said Gert, "because there's always them that'll bide by the old, no matter what good comes along. But I dare say there's a few of us won't mind a real paycheque to buy the odd spud and leave off the gardening, because I can't stand gardening, I can't. Worth a couple of knobs never having to haul a weed agin."

"Hope they does better with the liners than Am's doing, then," said Suze. "He's after warning everybody that they takes too much expense to make a profit. But the government's going right on ahead, building more of them, and bigger plants, and not knowing how it's all going to work out. I says they ought to keep the salt fish markets up, I do. No need to put it all in the one basket."

"And that's what they're doing then, cocky, all in the one basket," said the old-timer. "I hears them on the radio every morning, coaxing everybody off the flakes and into the plants."

"Won't have to coax me much," said one of the nursing mothers inside the stage, "because I can't wait for next summer, I can't, get off them jeezes flakes."

"Me either. Get out from under Mother," said Joycie Anne, a dark look at Gert. "What's you going to do, then, Mother, you got nobody to boss about?"

"Watch your gob. I might still be boss yet. Just because you're *mod-er-nized* don't mean you're not ordered about. All right, back at it," she sang out as the rain feathered off, "before ye all starts rusting. Addie, hold on there a minute. What's you doing with the fish? Full of spit, them ones you been piling in the faggot."

Adelaide heartened as Suze, as she'd done dozens of times these past summers, stood before her, facing Gert.

"Someone's spitting on them, then," said Suze, "because we been working side by side all morning, and all we're doing is firking off spit and flies."

Gert's brow arched disbelievingly. "How do you explain all the spit in that last faggot, then—and that's where she's been piling hers, in that last faggot."

"Middle faggot," said Suze. "We been piling ours in the middle faggot. Check out the old geezer. It's him piling the last faggot. Must be his fingers are too crumped up to hold a stick. Come on, Addie, our turn to get wood for tea." The mere squaring of Suze's shoulders as she marched off defied any further objection, and Adelaide, ducking beneath a cantankerous look from Gert, hastened after her.

"Tongue like a logan, that got," said Suze. She looked back toward the faggots and broke into a grin. "Look, look at her, going after the old fellow. Not spitey now, is she, she got put straight."

"Foghorn," said Adelaide without looking back.

Suze grasped her arm. "Hurry on, we best get out of her sight, because for sure we got her gander up now.

Gawd, I can't wait for next summer, I can't, when they gets the plant built and we haven't got she harping down our throats everyday. Brrr, I can't stand that woman, I can't. And now you owes me a favour, Addie," said Suze, coming to an abrupt stop. Her grey eyes glistened like wet rocks. "I wants you to be the baby's godmother. He's not here yet—or she, whatever it is," she added with a quick grin, laying a hand on her belly at Adelaide's puzzled look. "March. I'm expecting in March. I'm sure it's a boy; feels just like Benji did when I was carrying him. I even got his name picked out, Stewie, after Am's poor old father, God comfort him. Now, say yes. Say yes!" she implored as Adelaide's gaze fell to the wayside.

"Well, I-I just haven't done that before," said Adelaide.

"Silly thing, it's not something you learns, just wear a dress and stand up in church, is all."

"I knows that much, Suze." Adelaide shuffled uncomfortably. Lord, how can you refuse somebody who's always taking your part—whyever she kept doing it. Aside from a few nods and cursory comments, Adelaide was as distant to Suze as she ever was; just accepting, was all, of the girl's persistent presence beside her. And undoubtedly Suze's squarish form made for a good screen between her and the others, for despite her working the flakes for three summers now, and never mind the fact that the house she slept and ate in was overrun with youngsters, Adelaide had never gotten used to being amongst a crowd, forever wanting the comfort of quiet, of aloneness, that sense of a perfect fit she felt only when qualled in a corner with a book, or sitting by herself on a church pew.

"Oh, all right," she said, and pushing away a hug of thanks from Suze, she started gathering wood chips for the fire, raising her eyes to the church steeple just over the way. It looked as doom and gloomy as she felt on this grey morning. Not since her mother took her out of school had she been back. It were as though she had failed it somehow, had become part of the ordinary, her reddened, bone-bitten hands unfit to fold before those lovely gilded figures adorning the altar. Yet its memory still flourished, for in gazing at the doors, imagining herself stepping through, she felt again the cool freshness of that huge ornate room, that hush and the warmth it invoked within her as if it were only yesterday she sat, swinging her legs from the front pew.

But as spring skidded on the heels of winter, and she stood at the font on the day of the christening, with Suze and her new baby boy, Stewie, and her eldest, Benji, clamouring for a closer look, and a host of others crowding around her, she gazed with a sense of detachment at the altar. It appeared smaller with all these parishioners jammed into the pews before it. And that hush that usually reigned beneath those heightened ceilings echoed now with whispers and coughs and rustling. Her chest tightened as all around her faded, revealing a child sitting alone at the front pew, swinging her legs. And as the whispering and rustling and coughing receded, it felt to Adelaide that she was standing at the end of time, looking back to a moment when she had been consumed with hope, with peace, glorying in the blue of her eyes and the blue of the Lord's robe, her carefully written scrolls held up for His approval, her mind full of dreams of far-distant shores. She'd forbidden her dreams since those early days on the flakes, and without their daily feeding, they had starved, the coloured robes fading into memory, the figures becoming wooden.

Dreams! she now thought a mite scornfully as Suze's youngster screamed at the coldness of the christening waters dribbling over its crown, what place for dreams on those long, wind-mauled days of fish, flies, and spit, of the repetitiveness of housework dulling one's senses? And what exactly was a missionary anyway, but one who fed youngsters as she was already doing? And wouldn't there be lots more flies in hot lands, and lots more screaming babies as Suze's was now screaming? Surely they'd be screaming all the harder if they were a starving lot and without the ocean's wind to temper the heat. A sad smile touched her lips.

She begged off the church dinner following the christening. And after allowing Suze to persuade her, instead, to attend the dance Eb Rice was having later that evening in the new addition he was building onto his house, she hurried off home. Miraculously, the house was empty, her mother and the rest of the brood still back at the church. Yet, oddly, as she wandered about, she found no fit in its rare moment of quiet.

Growing impatient with herself, she took out her one good dress, grateful for something to occupy herself, and laying the flatirons on the stove to heat, dribbled water onto the green silky bodice so's to more easily press it for the dance that evening. Beacons, she thought, lifting the curtain and staring through the evening's fading light at the church steeple, that's what those dreams had been, beacons, coaxing her through those hurried mornings as she rushed around getting everyone and herself fed and washed and dressed and out the door for school. Over the seas, indeed. Some chance of crossing the seas when moving a hundred miles to the nearest town was near

impossible—unless you had a nice aunt living there, like
Leah Jacobs did. That little fact she overheard a dozen
times at the overly crowded dance that evening.

Standing against the plywood wall, fighting back
tobacco smoke and the scrooping of a badly tuned fiddle,
she eavesdropped out of boredom on Leah Jacobs, just
back from spending a winter at her aunt's in Corner
Brook, and telling her tales of drudgery incurred whilst
scrubbing floors and making beds and emptying chamber
pots in a cheap boarding house. Nope, thought Adelaide,
ignoring the saucy, flirting grin of Rubert, Gert's brother's
eldest, as he ogled at her through the flicking skirts and
ties of Suze and Ambrose and the rest of the square
dancers, there's no magic in a town simply because it's a
town, not even if you did have a nice aunt living there
on some nice street. Money is what it takes to get
anywhere, or education, or—as Gert said on the flakes
one morning—three legs; always easier to get about if
you got three legs and wore trousers.

Rubert had breached her side of the room and was
now reaching past her for a glass of brew on the
windowsill next to where she stood, his broad, vein-
fissured hand deliberately grazing her breasts. His grin,
she noted, now that he was up close, was drunken. Striking his hand aside, she ignored his hoot of laughter and
marched off, her look of distaste catching the narrowed,
critical eyes of Joycie-Anne and two of her cousins,
standing, gawking nearby.

Cursing Suze for talking her into coming, she
sashayed across the room, exaggerating the swing of
her hips, then grinned as the window mirrored back to her
Joycie-Anne's scathing look scratching her back. Leah was

now dancing, her tales of woe vanquished as she trotted, eyes flashing merrily, after her partner. She'd not leave again, Adelaide mused; she'd be married next year and settled down next to her mother, working in the plant and having babies, that's what Leah Jacobs would be doing, and she, Adelaide, alongside her, if Rubert had his way, she thought, rebuffing his plying grin as he once more made his way toward her.

Then Suze was singing out to her, and somebody, not Rubert, was grabbing her arm, dragging her, without asking, amidst the dancers, and she dully allowed him—to escape Rubert—to swing her into a dance, awkwardly stumbling over both their feet, thinking, bah, dreams. Foolishness; all dreams were foolishness, and she the more foolish for having had them. And prayers, too. And with the growing cynicism that comes when a soul reaches an unalterable conclusion that the four corners of the world are no wider than the house in which one lives, and the king no mightier than self, she tried to make her feet turn in the right directions for the dancer who was now swinging her around dizzily, her eyes burning from smoke, and her head aching from the tiresomeness of repeated thought.

Small wonder, then, the force with which her heart pounded when the Sunday before her first day at the new fish plant, she opened her door to the dark-faced young man standing on her stoop, wearing a finely cut suit, and with no funeral, wedding, or christening taking place for miles around.

CHAPTER SIX

THE EMISSARY

TRULY AN EMISSARY, she thought, an apostle sent by God to bridge that gap between Ragged Rock and the world overseas. And given that she believed him divine, her first impression was the strength registered in the thick of his lips, his skin, the gleam of his tar-black hair, and beneath that darkened ridge of his brows, the never-ending darkness of his eyes sinking into hers. She held out her hand as if to touch him, and he immediately grasped it with his, leaving merely the tips of her fingers showing, and they a ghostly white against the hairy blackness of his. And, oh, the warmth of his skin! Below the clasped hands she took in the sharp edge of his finely pressed trousers, and—and her heart sank along with her gaze onto a pair of well-worn rubber boots peeking out from the length of his well-pressed pant legs.

Lord, what was this?

Pulling back her hand, she stood, noting his fingers curling in the way of all fishermen who hand-lined day after day, and his legs bowed at the knees from fighting for balance in a rocky boat, and his shoulders starting to hunch from reining in jiggers and anchors. She sighed, her hand to her hip. A creature honed by the wind and sea was what he was, fitted only for that which took him from his door to his boat. As though following her thoughts, his eyes dropped and his shoulders hunched a little further; yet his voice, though low, was steady as he raised his eyes back to hers, and in the most sombre of tones, invited her for a boat ride to Cooney Arm.

"Cooney Arm," she repeated, drawing down her mouth as though speaking the name of some dirty relative. She'd been up and down the shore a few times, a dance here, picnic there, but Cooney Arm with its handful of blood relatives, the scattered sheep, and the odd rhubarb patch was never a place she cared to visit. "Isn't that where Bear Falls is?" she asked, dawdling for time. "Winter nights, when it's still, we can hear it," she added as he merely nodded. "I don't like boats. Just a second." A whine from one of the toddlers had mushroomed into a scream. Shutting the door, she turned back into the kitchen. Ivy was dragging the eldest toddler into his room for a nap, the other was sitting on the floor, turning red from holding his breath, and the boys, Johnnie and Alf (or the buggers, as she preferred calling them) were on their knees, barrelling across the kitchen.

"What'd ye do to him?" she cried, darting to the toddler and whacking his back, her hands sticking to a gob of molasses on his nightshirt. "Bloody hell, ye little bastards—they done something to him," she yelled as her mother hurried into the kitchen, the newest addition but a ripple amongst the folds of cloth pushed up over a swollen breast.

"There," and Adelaide sighed with relief as the young-ster caught his breath. "Janie—Janie, you going to wash him?" she sang out over another scream.

Janie hopped down from the washstand where she'd been kneeling and snapped, "I already washed him once!"

"Then wash him agin—and this time change his clothes," she snapped back. Ignoring her sister's sharp rebuttal and the youngster's screaming and the newest member's starting up a wail as Florry fled the room, berating Johnnie and Eli, Adelaide lifted her sweater off the back of a chair and, without word of farewell, walked out the door.

His voice was clear and soft when he spoke, and he smelled clean—of soap. And he lived only with a mother, no youngsters. For that reason alone she agreed to go visit Cooney Arm. She walked the muddied road with him, skirting an ornery baa-aa-ing ram and wincing at the *plink, plink, plink* of a dozen different axes splitting their way through piles of firewood that rose like giant yellow beehives beside each doorway in Ragged Rock.

"This way," she said, leading him off the path and cutting across a weed-choked garden to where the flakes had once stood. In keeping with the governing fathers' instructions, the merchants had, indeed, burned the flakes, making room for the new fish plant and the new government wharf built alongside it. Dismal, the plant looked, with its long, low roof and little porthole windows dotted along its wooden sides. And not a whole lot differ-ent from the flakes, thought Adelaide, noting how half of it extended out over the water on stilts. Bobbing and creaking alongside the wharf was a fifty-foot longliner, its winches and anchors all brownish with a rust that had bled profusely over time, streaking the scaling, yellowed paint covering its forecastle and smokestack.

"The new longliner," she said with a hint of humour. "Ever fish on one?" she asked as he peered more closely at the automated shooting machine that sent a hundred feet of line with dozens of baited hooks interspersed along it out into the sea. He quickly shook his head, sizing up the vertical winch that would automatically haul back the line, leaving the fishermen the tedious job of unhooking the three to four thousand pounds of fish it would catch daily, and then rebaiting the hooks before shooting it back out into the water again.

"Not my way of fishing," he staunchly replied. "I'd rather be the master of my own boat. Good thing for women, though, I suppose—the plant and everything. Lot better than working on the flakes in the rain and all. And the money, for sure they'll like that, making more money." He turned to her, settling into a smile. "Guess there'll be lots of fancy dresses and hats being bought with all that money rolling in."

She glanced caustically at his suit. "Looks like you got the jump on us, there."

"Yeah, well," and he grinned, sheepishly, "gets lots of wear, this suit do. Been a godfather thrice, and best man twice—pallbearer twice, too." He nodded, fingering his lapel. "Yup, gets lots of wear, this suit do."

"Surprise you finds time for visiting."

"Oh, I don't do any of it. Truthfully speaking, I don't like crowds much, so I just lends them the suit."

"You lends them your suit." She eyed him questioningly. "You're asked to be best man because you owns a suit."

He nodded, face serious, eyes intent. "Not many bothers with buying a suit in Cooney Arm. I dare say it got me a walk with you today, as well—or would you rather me knocking on your door in oilskins?" The eyes crinkled. He was grinning.

Not knowing if it was at himself or her, she gave him a cool stare and carried on walking. "You tied on there?" she asked stiffly, pointing to a few boats at the end of the wharf.

"No. Over here." He pointed to the quay over by a fish store, a bit farther along.

She cut through another abandoned yard, picking her way across trampled beds and muddied trenches. He remained quiet, following as she stepped carefully over a knocked-down fence, rotting into the ground.

"Seems like good land," he said. "How come nobody's growing here?"

She shrugged. "Some left off gardening last year when they heard of the new plant coming."

"Don't seem wise to me, letting your gardens go."

"Why not? Not much time for hoeing and planting if you're working on the flakes or in a plant all day long."

"That's something you makes time for, gardening. What happens if you gets a bad year fishing?"

"Not supposed to, with the plants. Not like you needs the sun any more." She crouched beneath a piece of railing, squeezing through a narrow opening of missing pickets. "Anyway, not everybody's giving it up— most keeps their gardens back there." She indicated a stand of pine back the way they had come, at the farthest end of the outport. He shot a glance over his shoulder, then back at the overgrown soil beneath his feet.

"Glad to know they're not all thinking foolish," he said, hopping the fence. "Cripes, up and down like a dog's stomach, fishing is. Always good to have a cellar full of spuds."

"Haven't you heard of Unemployment cheques in Cooney Arm?" she asked with a tiresome look. "No more need for gardening and hunting and birding. If the plant's not operating, everybody's on Unemployment. I'm surprised you're not all in your boats, rowing up and signing on at the plant. Not that far-fetched," she said, annoyed at his unlikely look. "They're moving about everywhere else on the island—resettlement and everything."

"Resettlement." He snorted. "Might be all right for some."

Her annoyance grew as he paused, tossing a critical look back over the bleak-faced outport of Ragged Rock, for it was as its name suggested, a ragged point of land jutting out to sea, its fifty or sixty houses clutching at whatever stony bits of soil was afforded them. Those houses farthest out on the diminishing point appeared to be wedged into rock, some balanced on shores ten feet high, their pathways a muddied black streak that scribbled across the rock face like lengths of cable mooring them to their neighbours' doorways, the scattered garments on their clotheslines flapping like wind-shredded sails.

Her eyes fastened onto his profile as he scanned the outport, arrested by a shifting of his features; yet nothing had moved—the brow, she thought, it was the brow—he'd relaxed it; such a black thing it was, hooding his eyes and rendering the rest of his features dark, sullen-like. And his mouth stiffened with intent; yet his lips so thick and finely sculpted she felt they might tremble ought he to relax them as well.

"And on the seventh day God rested," he said, pulling a smile that registered anything but satisfaction over what he saw. "Yeah, nice place," he added, as she kept her stare, saying nothing.

"You don't think He should've took another day? Thrown in a few more trees? Some gardens, perhaps?" she asked.

"Well, He must've thought it was a job well done, else He wouldn't have rested."

"If that's how you read the words, I suppose."

"What words?"

"The ones you just spoke—on the seventh day, God rested."

"Oh. Well, how do you read them, then?" he asked.

She hesitated, the burden of explanation too much, then quickly said, "It's not God that rested, but those who rest in him. Like when we says 'the joy of a home.' It's not the house we means, but *those* in the house— Oh, never mind," she said carelessly to his blank look. Brushing past him, she ran lightly past the fish store and out on the quay. "Which boat's yours?"

"The grey one with the yellow engine house," he said, catching up. "Why do you think those words—about God resting—mean something other than what they are?"

"Because the Bible's wrote like that. Anyway, it don't matter. That's a nice grey."

"Yeah, well, I got it figured the Lamb of God isn't a bloody sheep," he replied irritably, "but you're onto something altogether different here, with this 'resting' business."

"It's how the saints reads it."

"What saints?"

"Who cares what saints! All the saints. Would you rather just walk and forget the ride?"

With lightning speed, he shifted tones. "Nay, nice day on the water. Come on, I helps you down."

Prompted by the urging in his eyes, and feeling too far committed now to back down, she allowed him to help her into his boat. Within minutes he had them untied and bobbing off from shore. A thrust of the flywheel and the engine caught hold, dotting the air with puffs of smoke. She looked back, always liking the receding shoreline and her distancing from Ragged Rock. Such an ugly place, she thought each time she found herself drifting from its shores—and her house the ugliest one amongst them with its dulled, yellowish paint, blistering like old, fevered skin. The rest of the houses looked no better—bits of colour against grey, barren hillside. Why would anyone settle on such bleakness, she wondered, when all up and down the shore on either side of the settlement were such nicely forested coves and inlets?

The water, was her immediate reply. The biggest piece of naked land next to the holy fishing grounds is where any good fisherman would launch his boat. She glanced sideways at Sylvanus. His eyes were upon her, intent with curiosity, as though she were some prize he was wanting to pry open. Surprisingly, she didn't find the thought disagreeable; yet she felt no such desire about him. A fisherman from Cooney Arm. What could a fisherman from Cooney Arm have that she hadn't already rejected?

An hour's putting, and with nothing but shoreline and grey water all around her, she started shifting restlessly.

"Soon be there," he called out over the drone of the motor. "Another twenty minutes. Pretty place, eh?" he said as they came upon a tidy little cove, all meadow and green, a couple of houses seeking shade beneath a grove of birch, and a cluster of stages and wood-houses hugging its shore. "Little Trite. Only Trapps live there. Never known to be friendly," he added as some of the Trapp youngsters zipped rocks and curses over the water toward them. He motored past, the beachy shoreline giving way to a cliff whose smooth face rose a hundred feet straight up. "And that there's Old Saw Tooth," he said, keeping a wide berth of the jagged ledge, which jutted out of the sea like the unhinged jaw of the rocky face it curled toward, and the waters foaming from its maw. He paused, as if examining for the first time the roiling waters and jagged teeth upon the otherwise calm ocean.

"It's what took Father," he said quietly, his eyes caught upon a molar. "And brother Elikum. Got caught in a gale. Pitched their boat upon them teeth—according to the Trapps. They seen it." He shifted his gaze back to her, smiled sadly, then directed her attention a bit farther along the headland to a narrow channel opening up the rock-walled cliffs. "Through that neck is Cooney Arm. Be prepared—bit rough going through the neck."

Minutes later they were cutting around the head. She gripped her seat apprehensively as he steered them through the neck and the water grew more choppy. He cut back on the throttle as the boat hove up on a swell flung back by a sounder crashing against the cliff face.

"Always rough in the neck," he said again as they sank sickeningly down its other side, immediately heaving upon another. Fright gripping her, she grasped her seat, staring at him accusingly, the blue of her eyes colder than the sea as they swerved and lurched over the catacomb swells. "Almost through," he said assuredly, cutting back further on the throttle, and within the minute they were slithering over the last swell and slipping onto smoother waters. "There she is, then—Cooney Arm." He rose as though it were some grand dame he was announcing.

Grand she was, thought Adelaide, taking in the green-draped hills towering over the cove and the falls frothing white down her front, landing droplets that glistened like sequins onto the meadow grandstanding beneath her. He cut the motor and she rose to the thunderous downpour of the plummeting water and its rush across the meadow into the sea.

"Bear Falls. No wonder you can hear it twenty miles away," she said in wonder. The right side of the meadow, the side nearest the neck and the cliffs of the headland, was bereft of houses. It was onto this side that he steered his boat.

"Yup, the falls is wild now with the spring thaw. She'll simmer down, soon enough. That's Mother's house." He pointed to the first house on the other side of the brook, its coat of paint long since faded into the rotting clapboard, its roof sagged into its centre as its foundation found comfort, many years before, into the thickly sodded soil upon which it stood. A vegetable garden, thrice the size of the house, sprawled off from its back and partway up the hillside, its picket fence winding crookedly around hillocks and ditches, keeping out the goats bleating and hopping alongside with swollen teats. A couple of sheep tugged on patches of chamomile through the wider openings nearer the gate,

fattening themselves from the winter's lean, their thickened fleece ready for knitting.

"And there's Mother," he said, grinning at an old
woman up in the far end of the garden, anxiously shooing
away a goat who must've gotten its snout far enough
between the pickets to nip at her rhubarb shoots. "And the
rest is mostly brothers and kin," he added, and she noted
the pride with which he invited her to look toward the
eight or ten colourfully painted houses that completed the
outport, all differently shaped with add-ons and extended
roofs. Yet, unlike the wedged, shored-up houses of
Ragged Rock, which were precariously balanced on stone
outcroppings, the homes of Cooney Arm were neatly laid
out around a flat, grassy shoreline, their gardens, like his
mother's, sprawling out behind, with groupings of pine
and aspens screening doorways and windows. Not so
different from Ragged Rock was the smoke spewing out of
the chimneys and the host of flakes, sheds, stages, and
outhouses lining the water's edge.

"You hardly sees the flakes and stuff once the grass
starts growing," he said as if hearing her thought. "Up to
your waist, the grass grows. Looks pretty nice then."

"Aren't there youngsters here?" she asked, noting the
quiet as he helped her out of the boat.

"Dinnertime. Always quiet this far up, though.
Mother can't stand youngsters bawling. That's why she
built so close to the falls—to drown us all out whilst we
were growing up, she used to say." He grinned. "I think
she got the sounds of the brook permanently fixed in her
head somehow, for even now she never hears nothing I
says. Or makes out she don't, for she got no trouble
hearing when she wants to, I noticed."

Adelaide walked up over the landwash onto the meadow beside the brook. "How come nobody built on this side of the brook, then?" she asked as, the boat safely onshore, he caught up to her.

"Too close to the neck. Strong winds gust through that channel in winter."

She glanced around the meadow that soon enough would be fraught with grass and wildflowers. "What odds the wind if you lived here," she said quietly. "Everything so quiet—and *nice*." She wandered ahead of him, her feet squelching through the wet sod, her ear tuned to the brook as it pummelled mightily beside her, stripping the turf to the rock beneath, yet its sonata, light, merry, finely tuned to the songbirds flitting amongst the naked, multi-limbed branches of the mountain ash.

The brook deepened as they neared the falls, and she looked upon the tumbling waters with reverence. Despite its being the fountain from which the brook flowed, it appeared as separate from the water gushing from it as it did from the hidden lakes feeding it. Cresting the ridge at the top of the hill, it fell heavily, smashing against the rock shield behind it and foaming furiously downward. She drew closer, leaning a knee upon a spruce that had been ripped from its roots and washed down the incline and was now lying partially submerged in the deep, rioting pool gathered at the bottom. It riots louder than me when I was a youngster scrubbing Mother's floors, she thought, feeling the water's turbulence drumming against the tree trunk and rumbling up her thigh. Rushes of soft, wet air swarmed her face and she drew closer still, as if sucked into the wantonness of the tumbling waters. Gazing above to where the trees split apart at the top of the hill and the frothing white waters blended into the pearly white of a cloud mass, she thought for one wild moment that the water gushed from heaven itself. Just then, the sun brightened behind the cloud, diffusing further the line where sky and water met. And when the cry of a songbird rose over the rhapsody of the falls, as might a soprano leading a choir into its final amen, a hush fell upon Adelaide.

"It's where I'm building my house, starting tomorrow," he said.

She startled back to find him so close, his eyes as rapt upon her face as hers were upon the falls.

He grinned. "I takes after Mother, I suppose—loves the sound of running water."

"Does it calm your mind?" she asked.

"My mind?" He grinned. "There's them who believes I haven't got one. Must be why they kept banishing me when I was a youngster."

"You got banished?"

"Yup."

"Why were you banished?"

"Oh, I was always too serious."

"Did it bother you?"

"Being serious? Nay. I liked boats better than tiddly, was all."

"Being banished, I mean. Did it bother you being banished?"

"Nay. I never chased after anybody that much; liked being by myself too much. Still do. Bobbing on the water in a good stiff breeze, feeling everything big and strong about me—that's what I likes. Drowns foolishness when you sits on something as deep and strong as the sea. Plus, I loves the quiet."

His words rang in her ears like a church bell. And in that moment, with the glory of the falls still rushing through her veins and the sun finally breaking through the cloud, the promise of another world dawned in his eyes, and her heart flared like a struck match.

"It's heavenly," she near whispered. Her stomach quickened as he lowered his eyes onto her mouth.

"What's heavenly?" he asked.

"The quiet," she said.

"Yeah. The quiet." He raised his eyes back to hers, their browns more warm, more molten. "But it isn't quiet, is it?" he said. "The wind and the sea—they're talking all the time, luring you outside, driving you back in. Feels like I'm always fighting or chatting with the weather. Not like that in the woods, though. Don't like the woods much—that kind of quiet. More silent than quiet. Always feels like it's too heavy, that kind of silence, presses in on me." He paused. "Sounds a bit foolish, do I?"

"No. No, I just never thinks of the weather like that." She shrugged. "Either it's raining or it's not. Coming straight down or at a slant."

"Yeah, for sure. Hard knowing weather in bigger places, when there's houses all around you barring it out. Now, a place like this"—he gestured toward the meadow—"you sees it all the time, especially summertime. Like youngsters, the way the wind plays with the grass. And the flowers, too."

She nodded, drawn into his thought, his pretty words, watching as he ran his hand through the coarse, thick hair draping his brow, liking how it fell back again once his fingers left off.

"Yup, heavenly, for sure, this meadow. As good as straddling a boatload of fish. Well, almost, anyway," he added with a grin. "Nothing as heavenly as a boatload of fish. Live and die in a boat, I could."

There it was. The silk purse out of a sow's ear. Barely able to restrain a groan, she turned from him, retracing her steps back along the brook. A window had just been opened for her into another world, a kingdom of princes and castles. And its vision was thrilling, staggering, even, during those moments when she gazed into his molten brown eyes. But no hooded eyes had she. Regal he might be upon his meadow, but it was all a disguise for the beastly fisherman reigning within, waiting, wanting to infuse her body with a dozen squalling infants. And who reigns then, huh? Who reigns in a houseful of shrieking, squalling babies?

Misery, she answered herself. Nothing but misery.

Yet here he was, catching up to her, his fingers strong and warm as they touched her arm, his eyes liquid soft as they invited her to come sit. He closed his hand around hers, all tender and firm as though it were a finch he held, and pointed toward a white speckled rock near the brook, wide and flat enough to sit on. She allowed him to lead her, but he might as well have been the fevered Apollo, for her back was like an oak as she sat, her heart shielded by bark.

Pulling away her hand, she sat, folding her skirt around her. "So, what makes fishing such a heavenly thing for you?" she asked, supplanting his nicely pressed suit with oilskins—a guarantee against forgetting that this was no prince sitting beside her, merely a fisherman, anchored to the sea, and the momentary lapse into fantasy back there, just that, a fantasy.

But it was nice, the quiet of the meadow, drummed into being by the falls extinguishing all other sounds except that of the birds flitting about and the wind playing with her hair. What harm then, given his unsolicited pursuit, to linger a while and loosen a few leaves for his laurel?

"You have pretty hair," he said, stretching out on the grass beside her, reaching out to touch a strand that hung straight as flint across her shoulder.

"Don't do that," she said abruptly, and he pulled back, a deep flush darkening his face. She shrugged, as caught as he was by her reaction, and leaned forward, the fine strands slipping forward, screening her cheek. "Well, then, what is it about fishing you likes so much?"

He lay back, clasping his hands behind his head, squinting contemplatively into the heavens. "Hard to say any one thing," he began after a pause. "It's the whole thing, I suppose. Makes me feel worthy—rich, if you like. Yeah, that's it—it makes me rich." He grinned as she peered at his rubber boots. "Never mind a man's boots. Not always money that makes a man rich. I suppose you'll be buying all kinds of pretty shoes once the plant starts up."

"I dare say it'll be lots of fun," she replied, "getting all dressed up and driving to Hampden, and passing everybody from Hampden all dressed up and driving to Ragged Rock."

"Sounds like you hates where you live." He rolled onto his elbow, his eyes all curious again, watching her. "Supposing, then," he asked, as she shrugged a noncommittal reply, "a house was *so* nice that it made whoever was living in it joyful? If, say—well, you know," he floundered at her puzzled look, "if it made a person *so* joyful, she then rested in God? What I'm saying," he persisted, "is you don't have to be keen on a place so long as you're keen on your house."

"Perhaps. If I could live all by myself somewhere."

"Mother was always singing with the larks, and for sure she had a big enough crowd. Can be lots of room in a house. That's what we always says of Mother, how she kept to herself—despite her brood—and was never surly, no matter how hard she was taxed."

"Maybe it's like you said—she never heard nothing, only bubbling water. Anyway, that's probably what I'd be like," she added, a mite contrite as his mouth tightened.

"Bet I knows what you'd like—the sound of all that money clinking and all them fine shoes and cars it'll buy. That's what you'd like to hear."

She sniffed. "And is there room in your house for that?"

"In my house there will be many rooms," he half quoted. "A man knows from the first when a woman needs a lot of rooms. From the proud way she holds herself and scorns them asking her to dance. Eb Rice's, couple of weeks ago," he replied to her questioning look. "I was watching you through the window."

Her chin jutted out, a gesture of childhood defiance that had become as fixed a feature on her face as her nose. "No wonder you were always banished—sneaking and spying. Well, why'd you come asking me for a walk if you thinks I'm too proud for you?"

"I never thought you too proud for me. Like I said, I mightn't have money, but I'm rich. And proud likes rich. That's what all women aims for, isn't it, to be a rich man's wife?"

"Aiming for?" She gave an absurd laugh. "The only

thing I aims for is to soak my hands at the day's end." And done with his insolence, she rose, brushing off her skirt.

"Hey, wait." He scrambled to his feet as she flounced off toward his boat. "Look, I was just joking—I thought we was joking. Cripes, have you never said a foolish thing?"

"I don't walk around thinking I knows what everybody else is thinking, that's for sure—or calling myself rich."

"Now, that part I wasn't joking about." He leaped ahead, planting himself before her like the spine of a black vir. "It's not poor when you chooses the thing."

Her face hardened. "Where I comes from, a cankered spud is a cankered spud, no matter you chooses it or not. Chooses!" She balked. "As if one chooses one's lot." Brushing past him, she ran down on the landwash, standing beside the boat, waiting for him. He hadn't followed and she glanced back irritably, catching again that wretched curious look of his, and his hands curling by his sides like a youngster fevering to touch a forbidden toy.

"Rich," she muttered. Yet no beggar was he as he shook out the knees of his finely pressed pants and started toward her with the slow, deliberate walk of a lord, despite his awkward gait and rubber boots. Leaning against the boat, she bit her lip in annoyance, begrudging him the truth of his words.

CHAPTER SEVEN

TRADING A MEADOW

SHE KNEW HE'D BE CALLING the following Sunday, and as decided as she was that she wouldn't be accompanying him, she still found herself waiting for his knock. Cruel had been the fates, torching her soul with desire! And the following days as her hands moved mechanically through her chores, she revisited again and again that delectable cupboard of edibles she'd discovered within herself that kept sharpening her senses, igniting her being with the merest touch of cloth caressing a bared ankle, a strand of hair trailing her throat, the tautness of her belly pressed against the windowsill as she leaned against it, gazing outside. And at night, when all was finally quieted, darkness pressed upon her, taunting her with possible worlds and kneading her being with such longing she near cried out with the want of it.

But no matter the mystic murmurings of dreams bewitching her nights, no matter the sudden splashes of colour illuminating her grey fields of toil, she knew them to be barren, to be the passing glory of the blue iris, which blooms with such fever it withers on its stalk at the day's end. But, Lord, how much greyer her fields looked after she had glimpsed a bloom, no matter it hadn't rooted in her. She had seen its glory, had tasted the sweetened nibs of clover on her dream-torn bed.

Thus, when his knock sounded, her hands shook as she jammed the tablecloth she'd been folding into a drawer and dashed across the kitchen, chasing away the mob of younger ones cluttering her way. Her sisters, Ivy and Janie, stood giggling, peering out the window, and she whipped them a look of such evil they cowed, letting fall the curtain. Rooting through the pile of laundry waiting to be sorted, she pulled out her favourite sweater, shook out the wrinkles before donning it, and coaxing strands of hair behind her ears, she opened the door.

As though knowing when they parted the Sunday before that she most likely wouldn't be accompanying him again, at least, not without good reason, he spoke with an urgency the second she stepped outside.

"There's something you must see. Swear to God, I wouldn't have come otherwise."

"As long as you brings me back soon as I says." And waiting not for his nod, she marched straight ahead to his boat, a tinge of guilt over the eagerness with which he followed her. She shrugged carelessly. Had she not bid him a firm goodbye last week? Yet still he came. Fine. By doing so, he buffered any remorse she might have in knowing that it wasn't him she was seeking—at least, not the life he was offering—but merely another morsel for her cupboard.

In just a week, the meadow had changed from a water-soaked bog into a summer's garden, the grass not yet tall enough to hide the sprinkling of daisies and piss-a-beds and buttercups, all swaying in the breeze, as intoxicated as she upon their nectar. And with the wind rustling through the aspens coming into leaf, and the falls more quiet with the spring runoff drying up, it was easier to pry her eyes away from its tumultuous waters and marvel at this bouquet of wildflowers brought to her by this fisherman. Undoubtedly, she thought, casting out her arms as if in dance and breathing deeply of the sweet, perfumed air, it's a different wind that rustles the trees of Cooney Arm, carrying nothing of the salt of the sea, as though laundering itself through the running waters of the falls before folding itself over her.

"You mind if I walks for a bit—by myself?" she asked as he, his boat secured to a rock, came up over the landwash, joining her.

"First, I wants to show you something up on the head." He pointed to the far side of the meadow and a path leading up the wooded hillside and out on the cliffs of the headland and the neck. "Won't take long," he coaxed. "Come on."

He took the lead across the meadow, buttercups, daisies, and clover strangling around his boots. Nearer the treeline, the land sloped upwards with a well-trodden path snaking through the woods. Her sweater hooked on a rotted piece of slab-wood nailed to a tree, the words "Widow's Walk" more worm-chewed than chiselled across its front.

"Mother put it there after Father never come home," he said, carefully checking that his pant legs were tucked inside his rubber boots before bending into the uphill climb. She nodded. Most outports had a similar high peak, one that afforded the best view of the sea, chance someone was late getting home, although none was ever marked.

"She's never said why she marked it. She don't talk about that time," he replied to her thought, grasping branches and shrubs, pulling himself along.

She followed behind, waiting as he climbed up over a rotted stump. Reaching back, he took her hand, helping her alongside, then carried on with his climbing, glancing over his shoulder every so often to ensure she was still following, occasionally reaching down for her hand—as much to touch it, she felt, as to help hurry her along, for the path, whilst steep, was never that difficult. Still, she was grateful for her sturdy canvas shoes, and gasped for breath as the path became more steeply inclined and the wind more strong.

The trail and the evergreens enclosing it gave way to a fringe of junipers that been shorn for decades by screaming winds, till finally they naturally grew into the flattened, entangled brush of the tuckamores. She crouched amongst them, peering out onto the bald, rocky crown of the cliff that narrowed the neck, and at the gulls swooping below eye level, and at the ocean spreading out like an upturned sky, its sun leaking yellow across its surface, and the sporadic breaking of swells like scraps of cloud flung thither by the winds. Old Saw Tooth jutted up not too far off, foaming like a cyclone amidst the breakers crashing around it.

Sylvanus struggled toward the edge of the cliff, his pant legs flapping and his coat tails splayed out like the blackened wings of a cormorant drying itself.

"See there?" he shouted, and she shifted her tear-cut eyes toward where he was pointing and saw a moss-like shrub with numerous clusterings of bright yellow blooms matting the cliff top to the far side. He ducked back beside her, laying an arm around her shoulder, shielding her with his body as he helped her to her knees, this time pointing to a little ways beyond where he'd just been standing. She strained, seeing nothing more than a burrow scarcely visible in a tuft of grass.

"Carey chick," he shouted in her ear, and grinned as she flinched. "Feeding time," he said more quietly as she peered once more, seeing nothing of a bird, surmising the burrow in the grass to be a nest. His arm tightened around her shoulders as he steered her slightly to her right, pointing to another clump of grass nearer the cliff's edge. "Kittiwake," he yelled. "See the chick?"

No. No, she could see nothing, not with this wind moaning at her ears with the pitch of a thousand widows and swiping at her eyes as though spiteful of her tearless cheeks. Clutching the strands of hair whipping her face, she mouthed, "Can we go back now?"

Immediately his arm fell away. This time he followed as she hurried back amongst the tuckamores, through the woods, and with relief down the roughly hewn path.

"It—it was nice," she said breathlessly, finger-combing her strewn hair behind her ears as they came out onto the meadow. "Really nice," she added as he stared at her expectantly.

He smiled, and when it was clear she would say no more, he took her arm, pulling her along, pointing out the heather fringing the meadow with its brilliant yellow blooms. And then there were the blackcurrant bushes, and a thick patch of mushrooms, which he loved fried in butter. "And look, here's some more heather along the brook—Mother's favourite, heather is, and blooming a week early this year. Must be a good summer coming on—everything's early, even the leaves. Mostly middle of June before summer takes hold. See along here—like little stars, them blooms are, strewn everywhere. You like them? So does Mother," he said as she nodded, and she shrank from his eagerness, wondering, as he touched her hand, urging her farther along the brook, what he would do when he ran out of things to intrigue her, for then he'd have no more reason to keep her.

He must've foreseen that. As if by prior knowing, the moment he'd finished showing her the heather creeping around the rocks near the brook, an old woman, as stooped as the junipers, crept out on her step, her black brows the final stand against encroaching greyness, her face weathered by time.

The old woman said nothing. A polite nod, then she withdrew back inside her house.

"That's it, dinner's ready," said he. "Perhaps you can take your walk after, all right?"

She hesitated, not sure of the older woman's welcome, but already he was holding her arm, leading her to where the brook widened the farthest and was most shallow, coaxing her along with more offers of tea and pie after dinner. "Two pies—she always makes two: one rhubarb, one blackcurrant. She bottled gallons of blackcurrants last fall. You likes blackcurrant, don't you? Mother's favourite, and dare say she can make a pie, too, brother. Nobody makes pies like Mother. You can take one home, if you like, to your brothers and sisters—" and as though hearing nothing of her protests, he swung her into his arms and sloshed through the brook.

He came every Sunday after that, using the meadow as his lure. And quick he was to displace himself, referring her eyes instead to a chocolate-winged butterfly perched atop a clump of thistle, or a spattering of water-doctors skittering across an isolated pool of water near the bottom of the falls. But always he was near, curling his fingers around her shoulders as he bade her sit down on the white, speckled rock, encircling her wrist before rolling a handful of blackcurrants onto her palm, then standing back, watching, as she cupped them into her mouth. Once, when she stood eavesdropping on a couple of finches quarrelling on a limb, he rustled amongst some alders and came back with a handful of last year's Labrador tea berries, which he rolled onto her palm. Standing behind her, he cradled the back of her hand onto his palm and held it aloft, his other hand resting warmly on her waist till one, then two of the finches lit upon her fingers, pecking at the berries.

It was always like that—him touching her, drawing her nearer, then standing back, his hands dug into the pockets of his finely pressed suit as he watched her follow his direction. Even when she mocked him, tossing him haughty looks, he never seemed to notice, simply becoming more and more bent upon her comfort, upon searching out and intriguing her with little gifts, upon studying her, sometimes touching her, no matter his mother looking on. And those times Adelaide had been enticed to tea, he would fuss so over the scarcely used china cups, his fingers too thick for the little handles, so's he'd end up holding the cup in his hand, nonchalantly (so he believed) blowing on his tea to cool it and spare his burning flesh.

"I SAY ADDIE'S GOING to marry that fisherman," said Suze jokingly.

Despite the drizzly cold morning, Adelaide was huddling outside the new plant, a scant distance from a fistful of smokers who were sucking back the last of their butts before the buzzer sounded for work. Her mother stood chatting amongst them, and upon hearing Suze's words, tossed a heedful look at her daughter. Breathing deeply of the cool, moist air, preparing her lungs for the closed hours inside, Adelaide hunched deeper into her collar, pretending she hadn't heard. She was used to Suze's forever trying to draw her into the crowd. And given that she, Adelaide, was Suze's baby's godmother (never mind Adelaide had seen the youngster but a half dozen times in the past three or four months since the christening), and given that Cooney Arm was where Suze's husband, Ambrose, was from, and where his mother still lived, and where both Suze and Ambrose spent most of their spare time, knowing as much about the goings on in Cooney Arm as they did in Ragged Rock, it was only fitting for Suze to make such bold statements.

"The hard case, he is, that Sylvanus," she went on as Adelaide appeared not to mind, "but he's some good-looking, hey, Addie?"

"Good-looking all he wants," said Gert, ex-boss woman now turned quality-control inspector, "a gander like all the rest is what he is—when he's not cock-a-doodling in that nice suit. Perhaps that's what you're marrying, is it, Addie, the suit? I say you'll get some fright when he shimmies out of them nice pressed pants. You learns quick enough, then, how good-looking they are after they puts a bun in your oven. Dare say you got that one figured out, Suze," she added, raking her eyes over Suze's hefty bust, swollen with milk. "Bet you wishes now he never left his mother's wing."

"Left her! Right," sniffed Suze. "Just as well he brought the old thing with him. When she's not here, we got to be in Cooney Arm, looking after her. Spends as much time there as we do here. But I still likes him," she ended with a flourish, "and that old thing ought to be dead soon."

"Her lungs filling up agin, are they?" asked Florry sympathetically.

"Wish it was," said Suze. "Might soon drown her if it was. Mostly spite what's choking her, and that's more apt to kill the rest of us before it kills she. But I'll say this for her—she's some help with Benji. Sitting up with him all last night, she was."

"Poor thing. He haven't outgrow'd that old croup, yet?" asked another.

"Nay. It's not croup he got. I always said it was asthma. Could hear him wheezing right through the house last night. Poor little love. And not a sound—only the smiles."

"Little dear."

"Good thing you got the old woman, then."

"Yes, least you're getting some sleep—hard enough as it is, getting up in the mornings."

"Yes, I gets some sleep now I knows," said Suze, "with that little angel sitting up on his pillow all night long, his chest heaving with him trying to get his breath. Sits in the kitchen and cries, I do, till Am comes out and drives me to bed. And then there's the baby to feed. And Am's as weak-hearted as anything. One thing I can say about your man, Addie—kind as anything, he is. Took Benji with him, sir, when he come by last week to help Am fix his boat. He'll be a good one with youngsters when ye haves some—"

Adelaide groaned, relieved as the buzzer sounded loud and harsh above her head, giving her reason to shove in through the heavy wooden doors and away from Suze. Irritably, she hauled off her coat, ignoring her mother, who was shuffling in behind her.

"Ah, you lets everything get to you," Florry scolded, hauling off her coat as well and, along with Adelaide, exchanging it for one of the white frocks hanging on the dozens of nails lining the sparsely painted walls of the dressing room. "You knows she's only joking, sure. Cripes, as if anybody could picture you having babies!"

"Oh, Suze gets on my nerves," said Adelaide crossly.

"Ah, everything gets on your nerves, Addie."

"How can it not when all they all talks about is babies, babies, having a man and having babies," Adelaide flared. "Jeezes, I wouldn't open me mouth if that's all was coming out."

"Haughty! By gawd, you're haughty," said Florry. "Whatever's wrong with you, you been like it since the day you was born. Don't go huffing at me," she warned, stomping her foot in a spurt of anger as Adelaide, her frock buttoned, turned to go.

Adelaide turned back, her irritation vanquished by this childlike mother, staring up at her, all defiant and bristling. "I'm not huffing," she said defensively. "Never mind." She sighed, walking away. "As if I huffs more than the rest of the brood."

"*Brood!*" mimicked Florry and, in a rare show of quickness, leaped ahead of Adelaide, staring her down. "How come you says that now—*brood*. You're not a *brood* to me, you're Addie. And Janie. And I likes Addie so much I got it in mind to call this one coming Addie, as well."

Adelaide's eyes swung in surprise to her mother's waist. Three months? Six? Nine? Who could tell with that short, stubby body, and the belly permanently rounded?

"Perhaps it's wrong to keep having ye when we've no clear means," whispered Florry, her face reddening beneath her daughter's scrutiny. "But I'm only doing what feels right at the time. And even when I looks back, I've no clear mind where it might be wrong. It's only when ye starts growing out of diapers that I'd like to give ye away."

Adelaide raised her hands in exasperation. "Why do you keep having us, then?"

"Because I loves babies, that's why. And nobody else in the *brood*"—she stopped for emphasis—"is all the time mad like you."

"I'm not all the time mad."

"Yes, you are all the time mad, and you always means it, too—whatever it is you're all the time mad at. But that's for you to figure, not me. I wish you would marry, I do. See if it might change you a bit."

Change! From what into what? thought Adelaide dismally as the second buzzer rang, sending fifty or sixty workers jostling around her, assailing her nostrils with the stringent smell of tobacco and black tea as coats and caps got swapped for aprons and hairnets, and dozens of bodies pushed her along, fighting for a dip in the disinfectant water filling the trough before heading onto the floor. Marching past nine work stations laid out side by side before a long conveyor belt, Adelaide stood at the tenth and last, all thoughts about *change* evaporating as she fixed her hairnet in place, tied on the stiffly bibbed rubber apron that hung to her knees, pulled her filleting knife out of her rubber boot, and hauled a pan of fillets off the conveyor belt rumbling along in front of her. Slapping an ice-cold fish from the pan onto the piece of acrylic that marked her workplace, she slit the V-bone from the fillet, trimmed the tail, and hacked apart the flesh too soft or bruised, then flicked each section into a pan designated for different grading. One of the belts rumbling out of the holding room at the back of the plant started a low moaning that quickly accelerated into a shrill screech, sending her clamping her hands over her ears as the sound shivered through her teeth.

"Shut it down, shut it down!' hollered somebody. 'Sweet Jesus, shut it down!" The demonic sound subsided, and Adelaide let go her breath with relief. Four weeks! Four weeks she'd been standing here, and never had her nerves been more jagged. Hell is what this plant was, bloody hell with its ten stations to each side of the conveyer belt, and another belt rumbling behind her with another twenty stations, making for forty stations and forty women, arguing, cackling, and shrieking over the belts rattling along its pans of fish from the filleters to the skinners to the trimmers (of which she was one), and then on to the packers where it was wrapped in five-, ten-, twenty-pound boxes and nailed shut and jammed into freezers, steel plates clang-ing, doors slamming, steam hissing from the web of pipes snaking barely a foot over the tallest head. And despite its being the loudest, the station closest to the skinners and the holding door was the one she chose to work at, sparing herself the added aggravation of having to shout back at Suze or Gert or her mother or a dozen others all working around her, bellowing to each other over the ruckus of the machinery.

Most mornings she worked three hours steady, up to break time, without a word, without looking up. Yet, hellish as it was, she rested assured she'd never have to scrape another maggoty fish, for not even a mosquito ventured into this low, oblong cell of harsh overhead lights, of walls shaking from the clanging, vibrating generators, of air putrid with gut and gurry, and fishermen out-shouting each other over the clanging of the motors and winches as they tied up at the wharf in their longliners and skiffs and motorboats and punts, unloading their thousands of pounds of fish into the holding station.

Yet, despite the growing complaints of those working around her for more air, longer tea breaks, and a place to sit and have lunch, she liked it just fine to stand straight-backed, not hunched; to have her world reduced to a piece of acrylic with a light beneath it and five pans in an arc around it; to have her daily wardrobe consist of an over-sized rubber apron dragging past her knees and a hairnet that rendered her and the rest of them—men and women alike—to caricatures of old women. What need to expend five minutes of caressing the yellowy petals of a buttercup, of gazing through the honeyed haze of the sun, of feeling last evening's raindrops slide coolly down one's cheek—of what use was anything when most of daylight's hours were spent standing imbecilic amongst the maniac roar of machinery, hacking apart flesh already eating itself?

Marry the fisherman in the fancy suit? Humph. Not as if she didn't think of it. Divine were those visions of grass and finches and clean, running waters. And she gorged herself upon reliving the sweetness of lazing beside the falls, her cheeks cooling to its mist, and the grass cushioning her bed, and the breeze lifting and fondling her hair with fern-scented combs. But to conjure the meadow without Sylvanus Now was like conjuring the brook without the falls, for dark was his figure upon that mantle of grass and wildflowers, and his presence, no matter how much he held himself behind her, was as commandeering as the foaming white waters plunging down the hillside.

Loneliness is what he evoked in her, a great, starving loneliness. She had always banished those around her, scorning their foolish games, seeking aloneness. Now he had violated that aloneness, pried apart the four corners of her world, inviting her to step outside, filling her with other needs and trading his meadow for them.

She winced, and not solely from the conveyer belt starting up again with a shrill whine, but from where her thoughts had taken her. For just as beauty of face goes no further than to bring attention to the person beneath, so was marriage a sham, bringing attention to silly things like rings and veils and nice kitchens, distracting the mind from fancy pressed suits getting exchanged for oilskins, and babies swelling out bellies, and the eternity of days to come, ravaged by the deadening detail of domestics.

A blast of cold air struck her, and she shivered, laying down her knife and buttoning the top button of the sweater she wore beneath her frock. A side door opened beyond the faulty conveyer belt, letting in a flash of light that vanished instantly the door shut, like a star sucked from its nebulae and extinguished in a dark hole. Which was exactly how she felt walking to work each morning: like a body forced through light, then sucked inside a dark hole. No wonder she needed to be sanctified. No wonder her thoughts kept turning to the desiring eyes of Sylvanus Now. She conjured again the sweetness of his meadow. Even those times he carried her across the brook to visit his mother were nice, no matter the old woman's quietude—or aloofness, for she appeared that, Adelaide thought, aloof and a bit disapproving of her son's bringing home a girl from up-along somewhere. But no matter. That was the very thing Adelaide liked about her: her keeping to herself, knitting in her rocker and watching out the window as the kettle's humming filled the room around her.

Sure, once, when Sylvanus had gone to fetch something, and she, Adelaide, had been sitting back on the daybed, nodding hypnotically to the clicking of the old woman's needles, her cheek fanned by the same breeze as was fanning through the window onto the old woman's fissured cheek, she, Adelaide, had actually slept.

Another scream from the broken conveyor belt and Adelaide quailed, her knife falling from her hand. Picking it up, she wiped it clean against her apron and cursed this hellish hole that wouldn't allow even for a waft of thought on this cold, drizzly morning.

CHAPTER EIGHT

THE LAST SCHOONER SAILS

"ELECTRIC WASHER," pleaded Ivy that evening as Adelaide and her mother trudged wearily into the house, still wearing their frocks, and staring aghast at the sorted bundles of dirty clothes spread out over the floor, boots strewn about, and plastic balls and smatterings of pebbles spilling from an old sun-bleached plastic bucket. "Can we? can we *please?*"

"Name of gawd, can we *what?*" cried Florry.

"Get an electric washer when we gets electricity."

"Praise the Lord, is that what you're waiting for? How come you got nothing done?" wailed Florry, eyes anguishing past the dirtied clothes and onto the dirtied dishes covering the sink. "And where's the youngsters—where's all the youngsters?"

"I sent them out so's I could get some washing done, but then the sink plugged—"

"In this weather? You sent them out in this weather—praise the Lord, and what're you doing, starting the washing on a Wednesday—and this late in the day?"

"Because I can't do it tomorrow. I'm going to Carol Ann's," she ended pleadingly. "Her father's showing the new western show and she said I can stay and watch. That old sink's always plugging up. If we ever gets electricity—"

"Electricity!" scoffed Adelaide, picking her way across the kitchen, shrugging out of her frock. "What's that going to do for a plugged sink? And who'll be taking care of the house whilst you're watching shows in the middle of the day?"

Ivy faced her. "Think I'm just going to run off and leave everything?" she yelled defiantly.

"Might as well for all you got done today."

Ivy pulled a sour face. "You stay home, then. See how much you gets done!"

"Yeah, think she's just going to run off and leave everybody?" snitted Janie from across the room. "I'm helping her look after them—if that's all right with you," she ended brazenly.

Adelaide snorted, brushing a pile of clothes off a chair and sinking onto it. "You'll take care of them, all right. From the looks of this place, it takes the two of ye to fold a pudding bag. Oh, don't bother me," she ended tiredly as Ivy started toward her, howling in protest.

"And don't you bother we, either," yelled Janie.

"Well, she's always at *us!*" said Ivy as her mother held up a fist of warning at Janie. "And I was taking Johnnie and Alf with me to the show, so it's only the small ones Janie was looking after. Oh, what odds," she ended in a wail, kicking a bundle of clothing aside, "I never get a chance to go anywhere."

"Big mouth," said Janie, fishing a ratchet out of the

drawer and glaring at Adelaide. "Perhaps you're jealous and wants to go yourself."

"Mind now, Janie," said Florry, "be none of ye going nowhere we don't get this mess cleaned up. What're you doing with the ratchet? You got something dropped down the sink? What you got dropped down the sink?"

"We got nothing dropped down the sink," both Janie and Ivy cried at once. "It's just plugged, is all, like it always is," continued Ivy, "and if we had hot water, we could run it down the drain and cut through the fat."

"Fat!" said Adelaide. "You got fat poured down the drain?"

"I never said I poured fat down the drain! You never hears nothing I says. Everybody else is getting their houses wired. How come we're not getting ours wired?"

"Oh, for the love of the Lord, don't bring up nothing else," moaned Florry, sinking into her rocker and easing her feet out of her rubber boots. "Go out and find the youngsters, for gawd's sake—go on, and no more saucing. Who's that talking outside the window? Addie, take a look. Well, sir!" she exclaimed as Adelaide, her boots kicked off, rose and walked past the window without a glance. "Was that too much to ask—take a look through the window? Cripes! Go see, Janie, go see who's outside the window. Janie? Well, sir, what's she at!" she cried as Janie, halfway inside the cupboard by now, started hammering at the pipe with the ratchet. "Wait, hold on. That's not how you uses it; name of gawd, it's not a hammer! Get it from her, Addie, quick, before she breaks the pipe."

Adelaide was pouring hot water from the kettle into a faded plastic pan at the washstand. "Watch out!" she yelled as Ivy, hauling on a coat, barrelled past her, near causing her to lose her grip on the kettle. "Trying to bloody scald me," she yelped, then huffed in exasperation as Ivy flung herself out the door, leaving it wide open behind her. "Born on a bloody raft," she muttered, kicking it shut.

Immediately the door popped open again, and thinking it was Ivy ducking back for a last retort, Adelaide drew in front of it, holding out the kettle threateningly. It was her father, Leamond. Still wearing his sou'wester, his jowls blackened by a month's growth, and his eyes a brighter blue than she remembered, he stood squinting into the room as though he were still searching out horizons from the bow of a schooner.

"Leam!" exclaimed Florry. "Well, sir, I thought 'twas you I heard out by the window. My gawd, Addie, stand aside and let him in. Sir, what're you doing home middle of the month?" and kicking aside her rubbers, she lifted herself out of the rocker, skirting her way around the assorted piles of dirty clothes toward him. Adelaide stood aside as he edged his thick frame through the door, his shoulder bent painfully beneath the strap of a heavily stuffed duffle bag and a pair of logans dangling by their laces from around his neck.

"Lift it off, lift it off," he croaked impatiently, nudging his bent shoulder toward her. Adelaide pulled back, a constrained look on her face at his odour of schooners and rust.

"Squeamish, Lord, how squeamish is she!" cried Florry, as Adelaide hooked a finger beneath the strap of her father's bag, giving it a little tug. "Get away, here, get away," said Florry, grabbing the strap from her daughter and yanking it off Leamond's shoulder. "Gentle Mary, what've you got in there, rocks?" she exclaimed as it thudded to the floor. "How come you're home, my son? What's wrong, haven't got yourself hurt, have you?"

"Nothing, there's nothing wrong," Leamond replied in that whiny, quarrelsome manner Adelaide hated, as though he was always caught in argument. And in effect he was, she thought, eyeing him as she laid the kettle back on the stove, for he reminded her of a tuckamore, forever beaten by the wind, his limbs gnarled in protest, his trunk thickened and stunted, and his scruff of hair flattened mat-like atop his head—as was Sylvanus's, she recalled, that day on the cliffs, standing bowlegged as he leaned into the wind, pointing out to her the nest of a carey chick. Her heart lurched sickeningly as she now watched her father crossing the room with a bowlegged gait.

Ooh, were you once dark and tall? she cried silently. Were you once the upright juniper, now dwarfed by the wind? Ooh, and unable to deal with such a thought, she rooted through the dirty dishes in the sink, looking for the soap that was forever missing from the washstand, listening intently for her father's reply, as her mother never gave pause with her haranguing.

"Then what's you doing home? You only been gone a few weeks. Name of gawd, Janie, stop clanging at that pipe. Take that ratchet—or the wrench, whatever the hell it is she got in her hands—away from her, Addie. Didn't I tell you to take it from her? Here, sit down, Leam, before you falls, and don't tell me you're not sick, else you'd not be home in the middle of the season. Mind now, Addie, you don't hurt her," she cried as Adelaide, her sleeves shoved up and about to immerse her hands into the pan of hot water, now trod impatiently across the room, grabbing her younger sister by the ankles.

"My Lord, they got me drove foolish," Florry carried on as Janie let out a series of yelps, clinging to the pipe and kicking at Adelaide trying to drag her out, "I wish you would stay home, Leam, I wish you would, for the older they gets, the worse they gets. Janie!"

"You can't just hit at it," yelled Adelaide as Janie kept kicking and clinging to the pipe.

"I'm not just *hitting* at it. I'm loosening it."

"A bit more and you'll have a sink full of water drowning you!"

"I got a bucket to catch it, you idiot. You think I'm stun like you?"

"Hear them? Hear them? That's what they're like all day long," said Florry, "like savages. I wish you would leave the boats, Leam, or else take the whole brood out to sea with you. Now, that'd be a blessing, that would, all of them floating on a boat for the rest of their days."

Leamond huffed, as though deciding between sitting at the table or joining the ruckus over the ratchet. "What boats! Neither one left to float on," he said testily, choosing to sit and scratch at his weather-reddened neck. "Nothing, sir, nothing! Last schooner sailed today—the last one. Goddamn arse-up governments," he muttered, oblivious to Adelaide and Florry, who both turned to him in astonishment.

"What's that—what's you saying?" asked Florry, shaking her head as if she never heard right. Pulling up a chair, she sat, leaning toward him as he spouted off more about the last schooner sailing, and goddamn arse-up governments.

"Catches on to something new, the first thing they does is get rid of the old. You wouldn't know, bejesus, fresh fish was God's gift to Peter, never mind we salters who been eating it and working it since before the Ark."

"Well—not for good," said Florry, still struggling to understand, "you don't mean the last schooner sailed for good."

"You knows that's what I means," shrilled Leamond. "What the hell do you think I means? The last schooner sailed! She's over. Everybody's getting liners and selling straight to the plants—goddamn stuff!"

"Aah, not that bad, now. They can't sell everything to the plants, not that many around to sell everything to."

"No, not yet, there's not. Give them another year and we'll see what's out there—more plants than flakes, I guarantee you that! Soon won't see a flake, you watch." He grunted. "Not that it matters, price of salt fish low as it is. They'll never get it back up this time—and they're not bleeding trying, either, arse-up governments! They wants everybody off the flakes, they do, and into them plants, you watch and see if that's not what they're scheming for—getting rid of salt fish and working only with fresh."

"Ah, you worries about nothing," said Florry. "Always be markets for salt fish. And I don't mind the prices going down. Up and down like a dog's stomach, the price of fish. Been like that since I can remember. Gawd, the stink of you, knock a cat off a gut-wagon. Take off that shirt and get over here," she ordered, shoving herself to her feet and trudging wearily to the washstand. "Hurry up, I gets a wash myself. Lord, I'm dead on my feet this evening. Oh, what's the matter now?" she cried out as Adelaide, the ratchet wrestled out of Janie's hand, let out a yelp as her father, stripping off his shirt, headed for her pan of water. "Name of gawd, Addie, you can let your father have a wash, can't you?"

"Women and youngsters," spluttered Leamond, dipping his hands into the water and dousing his face, "that's what spoiled our salt fish markets—letting women and youngsters working the fish" *splash splash* "bringing down quality" *splash splash* "and it was the big fish-killers that done that; bringing in more fish than they could handle. Goddamn fools" *splash splash splash* "can't keep up quality with women and youngsters working the fish. Where's the soap, Flo, where's the soap—got any soap?"

"Ah, you can't keep it, sir, for the youngsters forever running off with it. Janie, what they got done with the soap? Love of God, Addie, you going to stand there all night pouting? Get that halibut I brought home for supper. Scrub your neck, Leam—I knows now, women can't work a bit of fish."

Adelaide slammed the ratchet into the drawer. "More than one maggoty fish I let go then," she said loudly, then turned to find her father's eyes stricken upon her, water dripping from his whiskers.

"I like to have them here now!" he roared at her. "You'd be eating them for supper if I did, you slovenly thing!"

"Mind now, she never meant that," said Florry, blotting the water off his face with a towel. "Best worker in the plant, she is. Here's the soap—hurry up and scrub. She's the crooked thing, she is, if she can't have her wash—and you mind now," she yelled as Janie delivered a kick to her sister's shins and darted for the door.

Leamond twisted away from Florry's scrubbing rag as Adelaide let out a yelp and darted after Janie. "Jeezes, I got to listen to this agin," he yelled. "like youngsters, young women acting like youngsters."

"Mind you, don't start now," Florry exclaimed with a extra hard scrub. "Enough I got with them all the time at it. Janie, touch that door I'll break your fingers—go make your father some tea. Show, is that Ivy coming with the young ones? My gawd, you can't see a thing," she complained, brushing aside the clutter on the windowsill so's to peer out. "What's that? Is that your oilskins?" She pulled back from the window, eyes widened with surprise, clamping a little, round hand to her mouth. "Leamond Ralph, you quit the boats!"

His eyes popped. "Jeezes, isn't that what I been saying!?"

"I never thought you *quit* quit!"

"I never *quit* quit. The boats quit. I knows you don't listen, brother."

"Well, sir, I never thought I'd see the day you'd quit the boats. God's sake, Janie, don't split the cup," she cried out as the younger girl stirred her father's tea, the spoon clanging all sides. "Now, isn't that something, your father living home. What's the youngsters going to think of this? Sure, they hardly knows you. Addie, look out the window and see if that's Ivy I hears coming. Blessed Lord, here they comes then," and the door burst open and two young ones, couple of years out of diapers, raced in, their shrieks a mix of fear and excitement as Johnnie and Eli bolted after them on all fours, butting at their behinds with their heads and neighing like horses. "Blessed God, Johnnie, leave them be—the mess they're in! Get their boots off,

Janie. Where'd Ivy go? Where's she gone too? Addie, fill
up the washpan, I gets myself a wash; hurry on now, I gets
your father's supper. Did you find that halibut? Well, sir,
that's going to take some getting used to, your father
home."

"Supposing they gets rid of the salt fish trade?"
asked Adelaide through a yawn a few mornings following.
They had put ashore near a mussel bed around the bend
from Little Trite. Sylvanus, an old felt hat shading his eyes
from the sun, stood knee-deep in salt water and kelp, his
pant legs tucked inside his rubber boots, his jacket sleeves
rolled up to his elbows as he bent over, feeling amongst
the seaweed and rock for mussels.

"Always be markets for salt fish," he said airily, tossing
a fist-sized mussel into a pot of salt water by her feet.

"How come they're burning their flakes in Labrador,
then? The last schooner sailed last week."

"What makes you say that?"

"My father said it—the last schooner sailed last week
and he was on it. Now he's not. Now he's home for good,"
she added with a downward twist of her mouth.

"Fits right with me. I wouldn't feed a dog what they
cures down Labrador, much less send it abroad."

She bristled against that cocky manner of his. "They
been doing it for years. Can't be that hard to get right,
curing a fish."

"Heh. You'd think they'd be putting out more than
cullage, then. Because that's all they been putting out
down there for years—bloody cullage—brittled and
yellowed as jaundice from salt. That's what's costing us
our markets, cullage. I wouldn't barter a fish if it weren't

high grade, damned if I would. That's what got you soured this morning, is it, your father being home?"

"I'm not sour."

"No, you're not. If it weren't for gritting your teeth, I wouldn't know you had any. How come he went down to Labrador every summer?"

"I dunno. Likes it, I suppose."

"He could've fished offshore here, on the schooners, and been home every two to three weeks for a few days if he wanted to. No need to have gone to Labrador all summer long."

She shrugged uninterestedly. "Perhaps he liked not coming home," she offered, and silently thanked God that he hadn't, as she fought back another yawn, reminding her of the extra twenty minutes she'd spent standing over the stove every morning since his return, flipping pancakes as he wolfed them down, slurping noisily at his tea whilst ranting and whining about prices and longliners and arse-up governments.

"Wonder what that'll do to the shores of Labrador," Sylvanus was saying, "no more schooner fishing off their banks. I say lots will just stay on, build there. Settle with them that's already settled there. Perhaps they'll start putting out some good fish, if they goes working for themselves and not the big fish-killers."

"Oh, for gawd's sake," she interjected, "you sounds like Father."

"Then he knows something of what he says. I don't mean that you can't turn a fish, Addie. I just means you don't have the same interest in drying high-grade fish as somebody working by himself, for himself. And all this cullage that's being put out is what's bringing down the markets. A man shouldn't fish no more than what he can rightly cure and dry himself. Try telling Manny and Jake that. They went off last week and bought themselves another cod trap and are now netting more fish than they can rightly cure. Now they got to have their women and youngsters working their flakes for them."

Adelaide rose, impatiently kicking together some driftwood as he switched back to prattling about the liners again, and the midshore in full swing, and the government giving away more and more money for them who wanted a liner built, and how there would soon be as many liners on the water as there used to be schooners, and fishermen ought to be watching out because there wasn't as much money in owning a liner as there was in owning cod traps, and everybody was getting into debt for nothing—no different from her father's prattling since he got home. Ugh, fish, liners, and governments; fish, liners, and governments, she thought. Was there ever a place that never smelled a salted fish, never saw a cod cheek, a cod tongue, and wouldn't know but that britches was a man's garment? Small chance of that when even Jesus sucked their bones. She inwardly groaned and, piecing together some flat rocks, built a pit for their fire. "You never did answer me," she accused after he lapsed for breath, still rooting through the water.

"Answer what?"

"What you would do if fresh fish puts an end to the salt fish trade."

"Like I said, not going to happen."

"If it did!" she stated emphatically. "I'm asking—what would you do if it did?"

"Not something that's worrying me. Forty million pounds a year, that's how much salt cod we sends over them seas a year, and a hundred mil of fresh. Figures like that don't change overnight. And it's not just a way of preserving a fish, either," he said more strongly, pointing at her with a mussel shell. "That's where you're getting it wrong if you thinks it's all about preserving fish. It's more than that—it's the taste. People *wants* salt fish because they wants the taste. Cripes, if I had to go a week without a scoff of drawn butter—" His words fell off, his face grimacing as he fathomed such a thought.

"You still never answered," she said hotly. "I asked what would you do *if*—ooh, never mind. I knows exactly what you'd do. What everybody else is doing is what you'd do—switch over to fresh and sell straight to the plant. For sure you'd never give up your precious boat. Not even listening," she muttered as he sauntered through the kelp-twisted waters, effortlessly ripping from the roots those vines that didn't flow with him. Like a frigate, she thought resentfully, settling down on her patch of grass near the pot of mussels, stalwart as a frigate when he was on or near water. She was starting to prefer the clumsy gait he took whenever he was too far from it, like traipsing behind her on the meadow or along the roads of Ragged Rock, feeling unsure of himself and keen on pleasing her. Least then she stood a chance of persuading him of something.

"Ooh!" A fist-sized mussel plopped into the pot, splattering her bared ankles with ice-cold water.

"You just going to watch?" he called out, now the defrocked priest with his shirt collar white against the dark of his throat, and his shirt-tail hanging below the black of his jacket, and his forefinger jabbing wickedly toward her.

She wrinkled her nose. "Wriggly tails."

"Wriggly tails!" He examined the wet, black hair matting his forearms, checking for sea lice. "Thinks I'm lousy, do you? Bet that don't feel too good, huh, dining with a lousy fisherman? Bet you would've stayed home, had you known this, huh?"

"Had I somewhere else to go, I would've," she said contrarily.

He fell quiet, his eyes losing their revelry, and she flushed at her forthrightness. Sloshing ashore, he stomped the water off his boots, his mouth twisted angrily.

"If I hated a place as much as you, I'd crawl out," he said evenly. "Must be why you hates babies so much—they reminds you of yourself."

"What's that suppose to mean?"

"Means you sees in their helplessness your own. They can't get about without nobody leading them, and neither can you, it seems. Else, as you just said, you'd be gone."

He looked away as her eyes sharpened onto his and, searching through his pockets, pulled out some matches. Kneeling beside the firepit, he struck a match, cursing softly as the flame died, and struck another. Two more matches met the same fate, and he leaned closer to the pit. A flicker of fire started, and he sat back, feeding it birch rind and wood chips till he had a good-sized blaze going. Placing the pot of mussels on top of two sticks he'd criss-crossed atop the firepit, he squatted, watching her through the rising film of heat and smoke.

"I didn't mean what I said," she offered.

He nodded. Picking up a stick, he idly poked at the fire. Laying down the stick, he clasped his hands around his knees, his face troubled. Finally, in barely audible tones, he spoke.

"I'm not much of a chance for you, am I? No, that's fine," he said more deeply as she opened her mouth to protest. "I knows what I am. I'm like the bull I hunts, always walking into the wind. The second I gets whiff of someone, I skelters. I was in Corner Brook just once. Not for me, cities aren't—people milling about everywhere, and impossible to get near the water for docks and freighters. All for being by myself, I am. And you're the other way around."

"Don't know how you can say that when I'm always hankering to be by myself."

"City crowds is what you'd like. People everywhere but nobody knowing you—and no flakes and fish for a hundred miles. You hates it—fish and flakes."

"Throw in babies," she said, and felt contrite beneath his pained look. "What do I know what I likes?" she then asked. "I might be a great dancer or dressmaker for all I knows. The closest I ever got to a wonder is the falls in Cooney Arm."

"Then you should find yourself one," he replied. "Hunting—that's a wonder to me; how it's always taking me somewhere different in my mind, figuring this, figuring that, the time of day, the time of year, the wind, old habits, new tricks by me and the bull alike. Same with fishing—tides, currents, habits." He shook his head. "Everything—warm water, cold water, where they're feeding, when they're not, where best to moor. It gets in your blood, thinking and figuring like that all the time. Even when you're cutting logs during the winter, you're figuring next spring's tracking, mooring, when the caplin might roll. Nothing else gets in my blood like that. Nothing I hears on the radio, unless they're talking the price of fish, or the new nets coming out, or the markets. You got to lose yourself in something, Addie, and that's when you finds the wonder of it." He lapsed at the far-distant look in her eyes, as though she stood watching him from another shore.

"It's something that you even find time to gather your thoughts like that," she said after a while. "Even when I'm sleeping, there's a youngster bawling out for a bottle, his piss-pot, or a piece of jam bread. I can't remember a thought that's mine."

"Let me build you a house," he urged, his eyes sweltering through the heat of the fire now leaping between them.

She shook her head, raising her hand as though to keep him at bay as he practically leaped the short distance between them, his feet scrunching through the rocks as he lowered himself beside her, nudging her aside for more room on her patch of grass.

"I'll build it on the meadow, right next to the brook. You love it there, I can tell."

"No, it'll be the same."

"No, no it won't. It'll be your house. It's a different thing then; it'll *feel* different."

"You said it yourself—it's when you chooses a thing it makes you rich. And now you're just choosing for me, like everybody else."

"What about me? Would you choose me?" he asked, his hands heavy as he laid them upon her shoulders. "Would you have danced with me, had I asked? Would you?" he half whispered, rubbing his cheek against hers. She closed her eyes, liking the roughness of his skin against hers, the heat of his chest breeching her blouse.

"Like holding on to a finch," he murmured, circling both arms around her, his breath warm against her ear. "It's a wonder the wind don't up and blow you away. If I built you a house near the neck, I'd have to tether you to the porch."

She struggled to protest, but the air was full of him, his arms bands of heat that suddenly she would be cold without.

"You won't ever have to touch a fish agin," he said thickly, "or even see a flake—I grant you."

"No, because I'll be too busy having babies," she cried, making a feeble attempt to free herself. But in that moment her defiance became a grace that overthrew his timidity, and he pulled her to face him, his lips softening, trembling as she knew they would.

"We don't have to," he whispered urgently, "as long as I can touch you, is all; as long as we can do this," and a tremor shot through her as he touched his mouth to hers, his fingers stroking fire through her belly. And as his desire created desire within her, that other thing was created: the need for someone. And who more better than he, now lying back upon the grass and pulling her atop of him, his chest cushioning her breasts and his hands roving her back, pressing her, pulling her, tightly, more tightly against him.

PART THREE

Sylvanus

SUMMER 1953 TO WINTER 1955

CHAPTER NINE

A GREATER MAN

H E STARTED BUILDING her a house on the meadow, door facing the woods, windows facing the neck, and a solid wall facing the houses and flakes of Cooney Arm—not that she asked for a wall with no windows. No, sir, she never said nothing about that, but he knew how she hated the sight of the flakes, how she liked being by herself, feeling alone, and no doubt if he'd asked, she would've wanted it. Foolery, tut-tutted the folk, building so close to the neck, and twice as foolish placing one's door direct to the wind. And what of this—a wall with no window? Sure, how you going to see anything?

Cup after cup of tea was poured and emptied as the women sat through the fall at Eva's table, peering out the window as Sylvanus, with the help of Manny and Jake and whoever else had time that day, sawed, hammered, and nailed, and she—the girl he married—all the time traipsing through the meadow or sitting by the falls, stuffing her mouth with a steady supply of blackcurrants she kept in her pocket. Glad they were that Eva's clumsy galoot of a youngest had found himself a girl; but, gawd, she was standoffish. Aside from a few dalliances around the outport when Sylvanus first brought her home, she hardly poked her nose alongshore; a quick cup of tea with Manny and Melita, once, and not even that with Jake and Elsie.

"Got to go," Adelaide had said one evening, standing on Elsie's stoop, "Sylvanus is waiting."

"Come as far as the door and wouldn't come in," said Elsie to her neighbours afterwards, "and she with the look of the devil then when she ran off, as though it were spit I offered and not tea."

Sylvanus is waiting! they scorned. Yes, for sure now, Sylvanus got some say about where that one goes or don't go, the way she dragged him off to the United Church in Hampden to be married, and the both of them Anglicans. And inviting not a soul, except Suze Brett, for a witness. And Sylvanus, then, foolish enough to allow it. Yes, brother, he got himself a good one, there. Like Jake said now, she might have nice knockers, but that sickly white skin don't hold promise, and they'd see how well she'd do, living by herself on the other side of the brook, her back to them all. And Sylvanus! Poor fool, they charged when one day after Adelaide had wandered up through the woods, he threw his hammer down and gathered a bunch of holly and heather, speckled with the pale yellow blooms of the honeysuckle shrubs growing beside the brook, and laid them on the rock where she always sat. And with the men watching. Foolish. He'd gone foolish.

Sylvanus nodded, knowing their talk and thinking nothing of it. Adelaide told him what she overheard Jake saying that day she'd walked away from his wife's invitation to tea. "Weaker than a cripple," he'd said about her, and even though he hadn't seen her standing in the doorway, Elsie had. Yet Elsie had said nothing to explain to the rest of the outporters why her guest had so quickly departed. Which left Adelaide arguing with Sylvanus that Elsie must think her weaker than a cripple too, and if Elsie thought her weaker than a cripple, then for sure that's what everybody was thinking and saying. And for sure they would've heard the doozy stories from the folk up in Ragged Rock about how she was always lying about, up to her throat in dirt—no matter she worked like the dog on the flakes all them summers.

"But they never heard no such talk," protested Sylvanus after she went on so. "At least, I never heard any talk about you, and for sure I'd have it heard from Melita or Elsie by now, if they had. You always sounds so mad, Addie, when you're talking about people."

"That's what Mother said, how I was all the time mad, and why wouldn't I be with everyone calling me lazy because I'd rather work my mind than my back? Ooh, don't bother with it, Syllie, I knows it's mostly in my head, but a lazy, grubby girl is how I feels when I'm amongst women, and that's that."

"How come you thinks yourself higher, then? Yes, you do think yourself higher," he argued as she opened her mouth to protest. "I hears it every time you talks about everybody else."

"Perhaps that's what comes out of staying home and minding your own business, it makes you think yourself higher. For sure the lowest kind is them you sees out snooping through other people's houses, sniffing out dirt and then going home yarning about it. Oh, don't argue with me, Syllie, I knows how people's talk takes on. They starts out on one thing, ends up on another, and plies everything in the middle to fit what they wants it to—which is fine if they're trying to make you look good. But we all knows if it's not shocking, it's not interesting. So, believe me, it's not 'good' they spends their time talking about. And"—she gave a short laugh—"everything they bad-mouths against is things I'd rather be doing myself than sitting with them. Besides, I likes being by myself, simple as that."

And that was her final say on the matter. No odds. She was quick to start talking about something else. Sure, he'd've liked it if she was more friendly with the folk in Cooney Arm, cut down on their talk. But aside from feeling like a misfit amongst neighbours, she really did like being alone, and what could he say about that when all he himself ever wanted was to be alone in a boat, jigging cod?

Yup, she suited him fine, his Addie did. She had given over thought of living in a town to become his wife. If he could, he would've passed her the sun in return. Instead, he painted the walls of her kitchen yellow and heaped pots of creepers around the window, mimicking the green outside for those shortened fall evenings already starting and the meadow lying in darkness and she alone in their house as he worked late, making fish.

A kitchen, bedroom, and porch 'twas all was needed to bide them till the following summer, and he worked with glee, studiously following Manny's instructions and those of others taking time to show him about measuring, sawing, and hammering, and about joists, ground pins, and heaves, and about all those other things it takes to build a house. He brimmed with satisfaction as he saw it taking shape, feeling the worth of his being in those walls and floors and ceilings wrought by the calluses of his hands. It was the same as he felt that year he quit school for good and claimed his father's stage as his own, stepping inside and rummaging amongst the coils of ropes and nets, and clamouring over barrels and puncheons and assorted boxes of jiggers and bobbers and oakum, and medleys of chisels and anchors and other half-rusted tools and objects that rested there. He had hunted out those pieces and bits, fitting one object into the other, into the other, till an order was woven. And now, with his house finally built, with the last plank laid and the last nail driven, he stood with the same full chest as he had had during that first fishing season when he worked his inter-related system of jigging, splitting, salting, and curing upon the sea and shoreline. Then, as now, he had stood looking around at his creation, seeing that he, Sylvanus Now, was its centre, the overseer of its harmony.

His brothers chided him when, that first summer as a married man, he turned down their offer to buy into a third cod trap with them. With a woman to keep and youngsters soon on the way, they figured he ought to take the opportunity to make more money and spend less time at sea. Plus, it was safer to be fishing with two other men in a larger boat.

Brushing them aside in that same lofty manner that provoked them as much as it provoked Adelaide, he ignored their taunts and shoved off from shore alone, as he always did, his jiggers at his feet and a satisfied look upon his face as he motored across the arm through the neck, a lingering look back at his house sitting proudly on the meadow. Cripes, it felt good. With a brimming heart he rounded the head, passed Old Saw Tooth, Little Trite, and the Trapp youngsters skidding rocks toward his boat. Motoring up to Pollock's Brook, he anchored where the river poured out of the estuary into the sea, and he stood, a greater man than yesterday. Today he had a house. Triumphantly, he wrapped the twine around each hand, tossed his jiggers into the sea and, planting his feet onto either side of his boat, started jigging: right forearm up; left forearm down; left forearm up, right forearm down; arm up, arm down; arm up, arm down; the twine glistening wet as he yanked it up from the water; legs stiffening against the rocking of the boat; hips loosely held, yet dead centre, rigid; shoulders erect; and twine-laced hands fisted toward the heavens; up down, up down, up down.

His left line tugged, becoming taut. Slipping the other onto the thole-pin, he whistled, pulling in his line, hand over hand, till he was looking into the popped eyes of a good-sized cod. Dinner. His first dinner in his new house, and what better delicacy than this bird of the sea?

He wished he could bring her here. He wished he could show his Addie how, in the beginning, when he was just turning a man, his father's stage had beckoned him inside, sweetening him with its sharp, pungent smells of brine and fish. And then how, through his labours of jigging and gutting and curing, he had gained the grace of flight with his bowed legs. Perhaps then she wouldn't be so quick to turn up her nose at a fish and at him as a fisherman. He wished she were standing alongside him right now, facing the estuary, seeing how, just as no man is an island, so an inlet like this one is the lungs of an ocean, inhaling the rising tide through its mouth, swishing it along the lushness of the shoreline, then filtering it through swaying eelgrass before exhaling it back out with the ebbing tide, enriched, cleansed. She'd see then what a thing it all was, that even as the tide was flowing inland, the rivers and brooks continued flowing outward into the sea, stirring up the ocean floor with its undertow, and flushing crab and shrimp and brittlestars and flounder into its upswell so's to feed the cod that were feeding his jiggers till the belly of his boat was glutted and the table laid for tomorrow's supper. She'd see then how this house he had built contained the land and the sea, as well as himself. And were she to constellate this piece of architecture onto the heavens, she'd see how he, Sylvanus Now, formed the swan in the Milky Way, his bowed legs its wings, and that luminous field of innumerable stars and nebulae surrounding him the milt upon which his creation was spawned. She'd want then a window on that back wall, he wagered, and a big one, too, if she were to see all he continued to make out here in his stage and on his boat, dressed in his father's oilskins and sou'wester. Yes, sir, she'd want it then.

He grinned, the mere thought of her looking out a back window and watching him engorging his loins. Tossing his jigger back into the sea, he followed himself home, stripping naked in the porch and posturing a bit as he lowered the length of himself into the tub of hot, soapy water she kept waiting for him in the kitchen each evening, the stove crackling out heat, and her fingers cool upon his nape as she streamed heated water through his hair, soaking his scalp and trickling hotly through the black, silken hairs of his chest, before gathering in a fevered pool within his naval. No doubt there was talk about how he wasn't allowed into his own house without stripping and bathing the length of himself with the cold-water hose in his stage, each and every evening after a hard day's work. But bugger their talk. He found nothing wrong with scouring his hands of blood and gurry before setting home each evening. And what man amongst them wouldn't love to lower himself into a tub of hot, soapy water after sitting cold in a boat all day, and luxuriate in a figure such as hers, laying the table for supper, her hair neatly bowed at her nape, and her waist all trim and smart in a skirt he'd watched her learn to cut and sew for herself. What man wouldn't?

Sometimes she leaned over him, towelling his hair, her skin scented with evening's dusk, and he desired to pull her closer, to lay his mouth upon that throbbing hollow at the base of her throat. But she was skittish about some things, even though her eyes often lingered on his, and she'd lean unbearably closer sometimes, her hands slowing as she towelled. It was in the bedroom where she allowed him to touch her. Despite her wanting it dark, he managed to keep a lamp burning softly outside their door, allowing just enough light to trace the curve of her brow, her cheek so perfectly fitting the round of his palm, the darkening of her eyes as her pupils widened onto his.

"Like a bird," he'd whisper, the width of his hand encircling a wrist, his thumb pressing against its frailness. And heaven was when she smiled as he sought out with his mouth the shadows flickering across her nakedness.

He worried about babies. Not that he would've minded a youngster or two, but he knew how much she hated them.

"I don't *hate* them. Lord, I don't know that I hates

anything," she said one afternoon to Elsie, who had invited herself for tea and was sitting, scrutinizing the polished floor.

"Perhaps you hates that they'd dirty up your floors," Elsie mused. "I was only joking," she added when Sylvanus threw her a dirty look. And he heard in her impatient tone that she had been only joking. But he didn't see his Addie believing any of that, and he smothered a grin, watching his strong-shouldered sister-in-law shrink beneath the cold blue of his wife's eyes.

"Joking about what—my shiny floor or my hating babies?" she challenged. "Didn't I just say I didn't hate anything?"

Elsie reddened. "I just heard Suze say once how you hated babies."

"Suze!" snorted Adelaide.

"I'm sure she was only joking, too," said Elsie. "But I wonders now if you don't hate them," she added, keen enough, "given how mad you're getting."

Adelaide sighed. "Well, I don't hate them," she replied. "Mother was always having them, is all, and they were always in the way."

Elsie's eyes popped. "You don't say—a youngster getting in the way. Now that's shocking, that is—a youngster always in your way."

Adelaide wasn't taking to the humour. "Not *my* way," she said quite seriously. "It was Mother who had them. They could get in *her* way all they wants—"

"So, you don't want youngsters because they'll get in your way."

"They won't be in my way because they'll *be* my way, once I haves them—if that makes any sense to you.

Anyway, you want more tea?" she asked as Elsie locked her brow in puzzlement.

"Did you mean that, Addie," Sylvanus probed after Elsie had left and Adelaide was gathering up the dirty cups, "about not hating babies?"

"Don't mean I'm looking for them," she replied. "But when that day comes—and it will—I'll be fine with it. Like I said, least they'll be of my making and not somebody else's. Besides," she said with a grin, "the trick is to have lots—that way the eldest feeds the youngest and the mother just gets to sit, ordering them about. That much I learned from Mother."

He appreciated her grin and her saying that, but he felt the weight in her tones and practised diligently the tricks he'd learned so's not to have babies. He might've done and said more, but she was skittish talking about those private things. So he left it alone, filling his time with loving her instead.

Over supper one evening, with the fishing season closed and him leaving the house in the dark hours of early morning to work cutting wood and not returning home till nightfall, he worried she might be lonely, being by herself all day long over here on the other side of the brook.

"No!" she exclaimed, her face hardening as though unjustly accused. Then, shaking her head, she broke into a laugh, laying the tips of her fingers onto his hand. "Remember what I said? I likes being alone more than anything. It's a joy having a place all to one's self." And he saw that it was—in the way that she'd pat a loaf cooling on the bin and raise it before his heartening glance, and how she relished keeping her kitchen as neat and tidy as could be with the arms of her chairs and centre of her table covered with every spare piece of cloth or rag embroidered with the coloured thread she begged of Eva. Hanging above the large picture window he had brought out from Corner Brook and built into her southern wall were bunches of aster and hawkweed, their mingled smells perfuming the kitchen—and killing his fishy smell, she said one evening as he jokingly complained the outer world was taking over their inner.

He minded not. Her little quirks and wants endeared her further, giving him more ways with which to please her. And as for the wall with no window, shutting out the rest of the arm and his stage and his boat and his flakes— what cared he? A different room is what his stage and his boat were, and he'd promised her different rooms. What cared he that she preferred some more than others? They were all within his house, even that small corner she'd curtained off for herself.

She never told him about it, but he felt its presence the first time she pulled out a little well-read book about some saint she didn't like to talk about and became lost in its pages for hours, sometimes brooding, sometimes smiling, oblivious to his lying and pacing about, wanting her attention. And, too, he was told by others often enough that she sometimes slipped into their little clapboard church during *week*days, glancing about first, as though making sure no one was watching her.

"Can't think what she's doing there on a *week*day with no minister or nobody about," Elsie tut-tutted to him once, her eyes relishing the hint of another of his Addie's oddities. He merely shrugged, saying something about God keeping no specific hours since the day creation was finished. Yet shamed as he was admitting it to himself, he was a bit jealous that she was doing things sly of him. And he'd brood a bit then, thinking perhaps it was the house, not him, she had married: a means of escape from her own wretched life. But so deeply did he feel himself a part of the walls encircling her, he figured that curtain would soon crumple, and she'd stand with all of herself bared before him. Besides, she always seemed so much more impassioned after one of her church visits, or after a good hour's reading from her little saint book, that he started figuring the books, the church, and God were a prelude to that coming good moment.

Brushing aside jealousy then, he bent himself to his loving her. Nothing mattered then, not a hundred curtained corners if she so desired them.

Her comfort was all he wanted, and she seemed comfortable. Even when their first winter together came, and ice entombed most of the falls and the brook, and snow buried the meadow, she appeared as contented as he, listening to the wind yodelling outside, the stove crackling cheerily, and nothing but a handful of dishes waiting to be done. Truly, his heart nearly burst one evening when she looked up from her supper of corned beef hash, a startled look widening her clear blue eyes, and told him he had become her first best friend. Later that morning, as she sat beside the southern window, laying back her head and closing her eyes to the white of the hills against a full blue sky, he crept toward her, knowing how she disliked such foolish things, and leaned his cheek so close to hers he felt the heat of it without touching it, then allowed the softest flutter of his lashes against hers, like filaments of velvet brushing her lid.

"A butterfly kiss," he whispered as her eyes sprang awake.

"My Lord, how do you think of such things?" she exclaimed, and tutted as he strolled back across their tiny kitchen, his chest taking on that fullness it always took whenever she attributed to him some simple little thing, as though he were its creator—which is what he felt like sometimes watching her putter around the kitchen, polishing the kettle, the doorknobs, the leaves of her wandering Jews, her windows—her creator, taking her away from mind-numbing wretchedness and building her a house that pulsated with a life of his making.

'Course, creators need souls to realize their works. And thus far Adelaide had complemented him wonderfully. And were things to have remained stationary, great harmony might've persisted in that tiny household. But as Sylvanus might well have known from his days fishing on the water, nothing is stationary, but always in a state of change, either for the better or the worse. And undoubtedly, given the omen preceding the news of Adelaide's first pregnancy, he prepared himself for the worst.

CHAPTER TEN

STATE OF CHANGE

S PRING CAME EARLY THAT YEAR, breaking up the
frozen water of the arm and sending it drifting
through the neck and dispersing around the head. Soon
as the arm was cleared, Sylvanus launched his boat, some
dinner stogged in his cuddy, and his rifle and a shotgun
resting alongside. The sky was creamy white, making for
pearly-grey waters in the windless morning. A perfect
day for spotting the rippling black V of a young seal's
nose cutting through the water as it swam on its back.
Outside the neck, Sylvanus opened his throttle, heading
out of the bay.

Several times he spotted the slick black coat of an old
harp sharply outlined upon a pan of white ice. But, nay, he
wasn't wanting to cut speed just yet; not this, his first day
on the water since October past, and the wind softened by
a touch of warmth. He loved it, he did, the openness and
the sense of freedom he gained from motoring on those
soft, calm days with a warm southerly.

A good twenty miles out, the headland rounding into

Cape Ray neared to his right. Several motorboats dotted the water, all a fair distance from one another, motoring easily in various directions. Sealing, they were, and as he watched one boat of hunters cut their motor and drift silently into the pathway of a black snout rippling toward them, he thought to cut his motor and join in the hunt. But something else caught his attention, something white and big appearing above the ridge of Cape Ray like a huge iceberg. Which is what he thought it was at first, but as it moved steadily forward from behind the cape toward the open waters, he felt his mouth drop. It was a ship—unlike nothing he'd ever seen, or could've imagined—thrice and thrice more the size of trawlers and ocean-going freighters, its smokestack bigger than the boat Sylvanus was sitting in.

He gave a low whistle. Must've got caught in pack ice, he thought, and took refuge behind the cape. The massive ship rounded the headland and would've swamped a dozen trawlers had they been in her path. About three hundred feet long she was, and a thousand tons for sure, he was to tell his brothers later, and flying high above her smokestack was the British flag, and scrolled along her hull in huge white lettering was *The Fairtry*. But it was the net rigging on her stern that was most astounding. A fishing boat?

Nay. Not possible. Not possible that this leviathan of the seas could believe itself a fishing boat. He shook his head in wonder as it cleared the headland, heading out to the open waters, black smoke belching out of its stack and the deep braying of a horn warning of its arrival. In minutes it was vanishing, the white of its deck houses pluming white against the spring sky, its stern gliding effortlessly through the water.

"Jeezes, where you been at, brother, you never heard tell of she?" said Jake, after Sylanvus had motored home and ducked into his brother's stage, telling of what he had seen. He listened with both awe and foreboding as his brothers, busy with mending nets and gear in preparation for the summer's fishing, told how the British ship—just this year put to sea—was a plant and freezer all in one, filleting and freezing thirty tons of fish a day, and how it could stay on the water for eighty days without putting ashore.

Thirty tons of fish a day for eighty days. Sylvanus tried, but couldn't figure such a thing. He thought of the trawlers, five hundred sitting on the sea a number of years ago, and their colossal thousand-foot nets catching upwards of fifty thousand pounds of fish or more from just one hour's dragging, and did so about six, seven times a day, storing the tonnage in her hold before heading back to her homeland. And he thought of Ambrose—and others, since—telling him of the waste: the split nets, the dumping of unwanted catches. Christ, and his breathing tightened, how heavily carpeted would be the waters with this leviathan beast fouling her nets and losing or dumping her load? And more—much more than fouled nets and dumping—how heavy a price would those mammoth nets extract from the spawning grounds? And that was what sickened Sylvanus Now—that something too big for a mind to figure was out there fishing the spawning grounds.

There's talk, too, his brothers were saying, about the Russians having hoodwinked the British out of the blueprints for the factory ship. But the Russians had no fishing fleet yet—small worries there. It was the ones already out there, the French, Spanish, Portuguese, Americans. Jeezes, there were more colours out on the fishing grounds these days than on an old woman's quilt, the brothers agreed.

"Yes, sir, buddy, the foreigners caught more fish out of the sea this past year than we did," said Manny. "First time that's ever happened, sir—the foreigners catching more fish than all of Canada."

"They did?" asked Sylvanus with surprise.

Jake, hunched over his skinning table chiselling out a thole-pin, threw him a look of disgust. "Jeezes, douse some water in his face, wake him up," he said to Manny, "else the trawlers will be tying up to his stage, carting off his fish."

"Aah, marital bliss," said Manny. "That'll end soon enough. Better get yourself home, my son, there's something waiting for you."

Sylvanus was unhearing. All his life he'd been listening to the old fishermen talking of their fathers and their fathers before them, pleading and begging and petitioning governments to scourge the ocean of the trawlers that pillaged and pillaged again the belly of the sea, leaving destruction and waste in their wake, and that threatened the extinction of a way of life—*his* way of life. And he heard again and again the placating response of those governing fathers since time beyond: "Sit back, my boys, for as vast as the sky is the ocean, and more plentiful than the stars are her fish. So worry ye not about a few trawlers when the fish is so thick ye can walk on water, and worry ye not about the ocean's floor when a good trawling is necessary for thinning her beds and thickening her growth."

"Look, Syllie," said Manny, pausing before him with an armload of netting, "there's always going to be bigger and better ways of doing something, my son. You just got to jump on board, buddy, and ride it to the end."

"And we all knows what end that's going to be," said Jake. "Fished out, that's what. They seen it in Father's day after the First War, and we're seeing it now after the Second—the same goddamn thing. Another war is what we needs, blow the bastards off our waters—"

"Yes, my son, yes—another war," cut in Manny, heading out of the stage with his load of netting, grimacing over his shoulder as Jake blustered into his well-worn tirade about the buildup of trawlers on the banks before the First World War, and how the catches went down, but grew again during the war with the submarines and mines keeping the waters free of fishing vessels, "and we seen the same bloody thing with the Second War," he argued, following Sylvanus who was following Manny outside. "Dozens of trawlers out there fishing, catches go down, and along comes the submarines blasting everything off the water, and what do you know—the catches start rising agin, fish coming ashore in droves. So don't bloody tell me you can't overfish. All the proof they needs right there. We can be overfished, plain as day, plain as the jeezes day."

"Yes, b'ye, plain as day," said Sylvanus.

"And now they got a boat bigger than a plant sitting on the spawning grounds. You watch and see, buddy, if the fishing's not going to go agin, you damn well watch and see. Another war is what we needs, and by jeezes, if they tears up another one of my nets, that's what they're going to get, and it won't be no jeezling cannon shot from shore, either. You can snicker, buddy," he threw at

Manny, who was shaking his head and grinning as he spread his netting over the beach, "but I ain't laughing, I guarantee you. I won't mind picking off a few of them foreign bastards—and our own government along with them—they keeps tearing up my nets."

"Yes, b'ye, go blow them up," said Manny. "Syllie, get your arse home. Didn't I tell you there's was something waiting for you? Never mind what, just get the hell home," he hollered.

Sylvanus grinned. Hard to feel glum around Manny. He dodged toward home, sidestepping a swarm of screaming youngsters racing thither, shaking his head at wisps of his brothers' arguing brought to him by the wind.

The instant he set foot on his stoop and his mother swung open the door, he sobered.

"Addie's pregnant," said Eva. "Quick, get in and close the door, she's sick. Here, take this to her. Well, take it," she said, shoving the towel into his hands as he stood there, gaping stupidly.

He moved woodenly toward his bedroom. Adelaide was leaning over their bed, retching into her chamber pot.

"I don't remember Mother being sick," she gasped as he entered. "I-I just don't remember her ever being sick."

"Seven youngsters, she never had time," said Eva, bustling past him with a cup of what looked to be brandy whipped with egg. She paused, turning back to Sylvanus. "Here. Help her drink this," she said, shoving the cup into his hands. Snatching back the towel he was holding, she passed it to Adelaide. "Syllie, are you listening?" she demanded as he simply stood there, watching his Addie pulling her hair back from her face as she continued retching.

He nodded and sat on a chair, his eyes fraught with concern as Adelaide weakly sat up and took a sip of the brandy he held awkwardly to her mouth.

"Not as though we didn't know about babies, is it?" she said, her voice all a-tremble, yet her eyes grappling onto his as she lay back on her pillow. "So stop your worrying right now—unless you thinks I'm the princess finding her first pea. Is that what you thinks," she asked as he stared at the paleness of her skin, the half-filled chamber pot, "that I'm going to start screeching and bawling like a youngster myself? That I'm without reason?"

"No, no," he mumbled, clinging to the sparkling blue of her eyes, trying to shut out the damp, limp hair, her tiny shoulders. Lord, she was scarcely a wrinkle beneath the mound of blankets, and when, as if struck with a sudden rash of heat, she pulled the blankets aside, he stared at the narrowness of her shoulders, her tiny waist, her hips no more than two hand spans apart—

"Stop that!" she cried, struggling to sit up. "I'm well fitted for a dozen babies. Mother's proof of that."

"I promised you'd never have to."

"Promises!" she scoffed. "Only fools make promises. You listen to me, Sylvanus Now, I already told you I'd be fine once this day come, and now it's come. Ooh, Lord, and I would be fine, too, if my stomach ever stops heaving. Figures Mother never once puked." She put her hand to her mouth and appeared she might throw up again; but as if by sheer will, she slid off the bed, holding her stomach as well as her mouth, calling out, "Eva! Eva, it's bread I needs."

He trailed behind, holding back from laying a steady-ing arm around her shoulders as she shuffled into the kitchen, her naked toes flitting amongst the folds of her cotton nightdress. Plenty of times during the weeks that followed he strived to hold himself back as her morning sickness persisted each and every day, sometimes well into the evenings, and she fought to stay upright, cooking a few meals and polishing her kitchen.

"Oh, bugger it, Sylvanus, I won't be caught doing nothing. They already thinks I'm a cripple," she argued of her in-laws and those other outport women coming to visit, as he tried to coax her back to bed.

"Oh, now, Addie, you're not still thinking about Jake's foolishness."

"Jake or no, that's how I feels with all them sitting around and me in bed—like a cripple. I told you all that before, how they makes me feel grubby, even when I got the place all cleaned up. Take a nap themselves if that's all they got to do, flick around other people's houses."

"Cripes, Addie, you can't look down on people who're only wanting to help."

"Help?! Help me do what—throw up? And that's just what they does with their sitting around, chatting, looking for dirt—makes me throw up. Ooh, don't argue with me, Sylvanus, I knows I'm not fit to listen to, it's mostly that I'm sick, is all, and everything's getting on my nerves, especially when there's a bunch of women flocking at the table, hobbling and pecking like hens over the slightest little thing—" She whipped her hand to her mouth, gagging. "Ooh, see? One word about hens and all I sees is runny eggs."

He traipsed after her, watching helplessly as she bent over her chamber pot, retching.

"Just go on out somewhere," she cried one Sunday morning, sitting at the table, pushing away a cup of tea he was offering her.

"Some bread," he urged. "It'll settle your stomach."

"Nothing settles my stomach—and get that stuff out of my sight," she groaned, brushing aside a clutter of little brown jars and glass bottles that were sitting in the centre of the table. "No wonder I'm sick, drinking all that old stuff they brings me—ginger wine and castor oil. Turns my stomach just to smell that ginger wine. And that sweet spirits of nitre? If you never had cramps in your life, you'd have them after a cup of sweet spirits of nitre. *For the baby, for the baby.* Cripes, that's all I hears. How am I suppose to have a healthy baby if I'm poisoned with their tonics? Shoo—is that somebody coming? Lord, make out we're going to Ragged Rock, Syllie, and that I'm in the room getting ready."

"It's probably Mother."

"Go let her in then; the stoop's nothing but mud. Where'd the summer go, Syllie? I don't remember nothing of the sun for ages, and it's not your mother I minds, even though I know it's just you she's checking on. Don't argue with me," she cried at his protest. "Why else do she bring supper every evening, unless she thinks I'm not feeding you?"

"She's making sure you're eating."

"How come she never brings breakfast, then, only supper when she knows you're coming home? And how come she's always bringing turnip when she knows I hates turnip?"

"Oh, Mother don't think like that; she loves turnip, is all."

"Bugger it, Sylvanus, it's enough I got to keep a bit of porridge down and not to be smelling boiled turnip. And that Suze, ugh, I rather sit down with Old Maid Ethel and her pigs. Worse thing I ever done was stand to her youngster. Now she thinks she's my mother—here most every day, preaching, *Move, move, you got to move, Addie, else the baby will grow onto your insides.* Mother of Christ, what do she think I does, lie in bed all day long? Certainly, that's what they all thinks, anyway."

"That's a sin, Addie. She's always trying to help and you does nothing but mock her—shh!" He rose as Suze pushed in the door.

"Not stopping," she said, poking in her head, a rush of wind instantly drafting the kitchen, "just seeing if you're going to church this morning. I thought I'd walk with you."

Adelaide flashed a false smile. "Not this morning," she said brightly. "But you'd better hurry on, else you'll be late."

"Phooey, I worries about being late now. Old Pastor Reeves is preaching this morning. I allows I'll be asleep before he gets through his first prayer. How you doing, Syllie, b'ye? She got you wore off your feet yet, doing for her?"

"I does for myself," cut in Adelaide.

Suze gave a loud laugh. "Not like me, then, when I'm carrying. I drives poor Am so hard he don't know if he's Angus or Agnes half the time. Well, then, you're sure you're not coming? Well, sir, you're the strange one, going to church when there's nobody there and staying home when she's full."

"Rather my own preaching on a Saturday than sleeping through the parson's on a Sunday," said Adelaide.

"Well, come in or go, then," she added. "The draft's blowing out the fire."

Suze's smile faltered. "Well, I'll see you, then," she said, a flush tinting her cheeks. "See you, Syllie."

Sylvanus nodded, a brief smile touching his lips as he helped close the door behind her. He turned to Adelaide, his mouth tightened with anger. "Cripes, no wonder they thinks you haughty. She was only wanting to walk to church with you. Nothing unreasonable about that, is there?"

"If my head wasn't hung over a piss-pot, it mightn't be. What the hell, Syllie, everybody knows I'm bloody sick, yet they still all keeps coming," she ended up shouting, "and that's your mother I hears coming there. Did you fill the buckets yet? How am I supposed to make her tea when you won't fill the water buckets? Nothing unreasonable about that, is there, me wanting the water buckets filled?"

Clamping shut his mouth, he opened the door to his mother and slipped outside, carrying the empty water buckets.

SYLVANUS WAS TO LEARN lots about reasoning that fall as the fishing season drew to a close, pitting him more and more into the company of his ailing wife. Truth was, he no longer felt himself the creator of his own path, but more the lowly subject of another. Undoubtedly, since the first moment he saw her, he'd been tripping over terrain where laws unknown to him determined reason. But never had he felt so lost as during those first months, watching her sickness grow along with her belly, hollowing her cheeks and rendering those luminescent eyes to mere bruises upon her shrinking face.

Ordinarily, fighting his way through brush, struggling through knee-deep snow, couldn't hold him as did standing in his boat and rolling on the wide, opened seas, listening to the ocean's murmurings as she lapped around his boat like a coddling old mother. But after his boats were hauled up, and jiggers and puncheons stored, and close to a hundred pounds of fish soaking in brine for the winter's eating, he eagerly sought the shelter of the woods, anything being preferable to her growing sullenness and the silence engulfing them both. Thankfully he still carried the newness of providing for his own house, and it was that—setting out his snare line, tracking caribou, and cutting firewood, along with his daily logging for the sawmills—that helped set his course through those darkening fall days, preparing for this, his second winter in his own house. For sure, it would be a lean winter indeed, if not for his prowess, he consoled himself one morning, smacking a surprised bull moose between the eyes with a bullet. After gutting, skinning, and quartering it, he cut a few meals off the carcass for himself and his mother before hanging the rest of it to freeze in the woodshed, then set off for home, feeling more calm than he had in months. And in the days to come, filling his Addie's pots and roasters with the grainy brown meat of the boo birds and turrs (which she loved), and all those other saltwater ducks that flew low over the ocean and that he brought home by the boatload, and the plump white breasts of the partridge and grouse he shot in the back woods, and the eels he caught in the brook and pickled by the dozens, he started feeling again a sense of worth. Cripes, times he even felt himself lord of his manor again.

With great affection, then, as the winds came and the snow started piling up outside, he would stand beside Adelaide, calming her as she watched in fright the windows drifting over. He'd go outside then, trampling the snow so's she could see the blue of the sky and the grey of the ocean, assuring her that all was fine; just a bit of snow, was all, and she could go visit Eva, her mother, or anybody else she cared to anytime she wanted.

"On that?" she once asked, staring at the wind-frenzied waters in the neck, crashing sheets of spray sometimes thirty, forty feet high against the cliffs. "Suppose somebody got sick, real sick, and needed the doctor?"

"Woods road, silly," he replied. "The lakes are all froze; easy to cross over. Wouldn't take more than an hour on horse sled. Or Alex's dog team—faster than a horse. And parts of the bay will be catching over soon enough. She'll freeze straight up to Ragged Rock—a nice sled ride."

"I'm always scared walking on ice."

"She freezes too thick to be dangerous. By the middle of December, it'll take a half hour to chop down through to the water. Addy, you getting nervous? Perhaps you'd like to stay with your mother this last month."

She turned from the window. "Nope. Nobody else leaves their house to have a baby, and I won't either," she replied, resuming her reign, leaving him fumbling behind as she shuffled through the days, her sickness never abating, her belly growing bigger and bigger, and her groans increasing as her hair grew limper and thinner, filling her hairbrush and coating her pillow in the mornings. It frightened him, it did, this ballooning weight upon her tiny frame, hunching her shoulders and crippling her lower back, sometimes making her hobble about the house, her hand rubbing her neck and spine. Yet other times she drifted ghost-like, the blue of her eyes lost in a shadow that foreclosed light as she wafted through it. Even her kitchen dulled, despite her attempts to keep up her daily polishing. But when finally she grew into her last weeks, and her horrible nausea appeared to be increasing, she became truly despondent, withdrawing to her bed.

"It's the smells. Everything bloody smells," she cried as he came home from the woods one evening, chilled from a wind-driven rain that had lashed him all day, and cuddled up next to her on the bed. "And you, too, Sylvanus, your hair's sticky with myrrh. You never bathed, did you? Oh, don't argue with me," she cried weakly as he protested his hair was still damp from a soaking. "It's curdling my stomach, the stink of it. Go wash it agin—and soap it good this time."

"And I would if there was warm water," he muttered, springing upright and heading back to the kitchen.

"Kettle's on the stove—not much I can do if it won't boil," she called after him.

"You might fill it with water, Addie. It'd boil soon enough, then."

"Oh, don't argue with me, Syllie, I can hardly lift a thimble, let alone a dipper full of water. Why don't you wear a cap to keep the myrrh off your hair—the stink of it."

"I wears a cap every day, and myrrh don't stink."

"Bloody hell, it don't stink—worse than gurry."

"Perhaps you'd rather I sleep in the stage," he said childishly, and checking that she wasn't looking, he quickly ran his hand through his thatch, sniffing his fingers.

"If you're foolish enough," she said. "Else take yourself off to Jake's—for sure he's hovering over his pit and drinking by now."

"Oh, you likes me smelling of smoke, do you? Perhaps I will, then."

"Matters not if I likes it. That's what you smells like all time these days anyway, a smoked mackerel. Must be some fun, hogging around a fire all night, smoking and drinking."

"I don't smoke," he snapped.

"Same difference if the fire's smoking you. Ooh, go away from me, Syllie. How'd you like to be lying here sick as a dog and somebody arguing with you?"

His eyes widened in disbelief. "It's not me who's arguing," he yelled. Seizing his cap out of the boot box, he swung out the door into squalling winds.

CHAPTER ELEVEN

THE BACK WALL

"**B**EST TO NOT GO near them when they're like that," said Manny.

"Best not to go near them no time," said Jake over the rain pelting the canvas canopy above their heads. "Foolish as hens, women are; cluck, cluck, clucking, and half the time not knowing what they're clucking over."

"Ye-es, my son. Don't suppose it got something to do with the rooster crowing in their faces, do it?" asked Manny with a wink at Sylvanus. "Jeezes, Syllie, get your face off the ground. Cripes, if that's what you looks like around the house, no wonder she's kicking you out the door."

Sylvanus tried for a grin. "Who owns that new long-liner tied up by the plant?" he asked distractedly.

"Fellow from Hampden," said Manny. "That's three liners now, coming out of Hampden. Lot of new people getting into the fishing," he added with a shake of his head.

"Well, you knows, old man, the way the government's praising the fishery these days," said Jake. "Cripes, everybody that left years ago is now coming back for work in the plants and on the boats. Some good now, trying to make the outporters better off when there's more people moving back by the droves, taking the jobs. Too many people, too many people getting licences and buying boats. She's won't last, buddy, watch and see, she's not going to last. I say, if we're going to get that trap, we better get at it," he ended, nodding at Manny. "The way the berths are going, soon won't be room on the water for another net."

Manny nodded tiredly. "Yes, b'ye, might as well. We're buying a third trap," he said to Sylvanus.

"A third!? Christ, how you going to keep up with hauling all them nets?"

"We're getting rid of the flakes," said Manny. "Sell straight to the plant in Ragged Rock. Easier, my son, it's easier," he quickly added as Sylvanus shrank back, looking like a youngster being abandoned on shore. "That's what everybody is doing, giving up the flakes for the plants. Foolery, anyway, drying fish when the weather is always flying in your face. And besides, more money in selling green fish. Salt fish is going to the wayside."

"Before you starts," said Jake, holding up his hand to block the protest already registering on Sylvanus's face, "we're asking you to come with us— Give me a chance to bloody finish!" he said loudly. "It's no good you out there jigging all by yourself. Mother's always on edge, and you might want to start thinking about her getting on in years. She won't always be able to run to your flakes, covering up the fish when a sudden rain takes on, and for sure you'll never get that one you married out on the flakes, not from what the women says—"

Sylvanus near choked. "What the hell you talking about, Mother turning my fish? I pays your boys to do that."

"The boys!" snorted Jake. "Up the woods all the time, building camps, that's all the boys are good for. Most times it's Mother running to your flakes."

"By jeezes, it's time somebody told me that, then," roared Sylvanus, rising. "Them little bastards! I been paying them, and Mother doing the work?!"

Manny waved him back down. "Just hold on," he said impatiently. "Melita and Elsie been helping her—and no, they're not going to say nothing to you about it, not with Mother threatening them."

"Oh, jeezes, don't tell me no more," cried Sylvanus.

"No more to tell," said Manny. "Forget about that now. There's no problem with turning your fish; the women's fine with it. It's the future we're talking about. Things are changing with the fishery, and we got to change too if we wants to stay at it and do either bit of good. The youngsters are all growing up, and by jeezes, their wants are starting to outgrow them. Other fisher-men are doing good without their flakes and selling to the plants—from what they says. And anyway"—he paused, patting his younger brother on the knee—"that's what we got figured, and going off the head talking about it won't do no good. So perhaps you can think about it for a while before you makes up your mind."

"Already did," cut in Sylvanus

"Yup, like Father," said Jake. "By jeezes, you're his spit."

Manny shook his head irritably. "Just never mind all the arguing," he said. "Nothing wrong with flakes and curing fish if that's what a man wants to do. But," and he lowered his eyes onto Sylvanus, "I'm getting out of it. And you're welcome to come with us if you wants. And that's all I'm saying." He raised his mug of brew. "Come on, raise your jeezling mug," he bawled out as Sylvanus took on a sullen look. "Brother, if them eyebrows keeps growing in, we'll have to tie them up in ponytails so's you can see where you're going."

"Like the pothead whales, that's what he'll be like," said Jake, showing a rare moment of humour, "all the time running aground." He halted, a dawning look widening his eyes. "By cripes, you don't suppose that's why they throws themselves aground like that every year, do you?" he asked Manny. "They got eyelashes stuck in their eyes and can't see where they're going no more?"

"Nay, suicide, my son—their women drives them to it," Manny ended with a groan. "Because I tell you, buddy, women could drive a sunken boat to shore, women could." Raising his mug, he washed back his words with a good dollop of brew.

Jake stared at him keenly. "Hey, you cast out, too?" He broke into guffaws as Manny gave a mock shiver. "Aah, go tell her you loves her, b'ye, that's all you got to do, go tell her you loves her!"

"Shut your mouth," said Manny. "Women is good in all ways—except when they're looking my way. And that's when I scuttles out the door like the dog. But I don't be hanging my head over it all night, either," he charged, leering at Sylvanus who was staring glumly into his brew. "What's you pouting about now—the flakes or your wife? Bend over, my son, I kicks your arse. Go dig a hole, Jake, we buries him. Where's that shovel? Go on home, b'ye, if that's what you're going to do all night, sit there and mope. And if it's the wife you're pouting about, you haven't got a worry. Like the pup, she'll be, cuddling all over you when you gets home. Yeah, that's right," he said as Sylvanus looked at him disbelievingly, "that's what all women are like after a fight—nice and cuddly. What odds she just scratched out your eyes like the coyote, right, Jake? That's the trick, right, Jake, telling her you loves her?"

Jake threw a mangy look at his house. "And never mind they throws your supper to the dogs."

"Nay, don't mind that stuff. Only because she likes dogs, she feeds them your supper, and that's why you cuddles up to her like a pup, because she likes dogs. Guaranteed, my son. You listening, Syllie? Better be, my son, you wants to tame that woman of yours. You sees how Elsie is tamed, so you knows what you got to do now."

"Yes, b'ye," said Syllie.

"Yes, b'ye," said Manny. "The Nows keeps their women happy because that's what keeps us happy—when our women's happy, right, Jake?" Manny broke into a hard laugh as Jake snarled back something undecipherable. "Look at him, look at him," he roared to Sylvanus, "too goddamn joyful to talk. Yes, my son, yes, we knows your joy, we sees your joy all over your face, right, Syllie? All over his face. Come on now, let's sing 'er up," and grabbing Sylvanus's hand, he held it to his heart, bellowing in a deep base, *We got the joy, joy, joy singing deep in our hearts.*"

"Jeezes, you'll have her yodelling through the window, you keeps it up," shouted Jake. "Shut your mouth, shut your bloody mouth. Jeezes! Screech owls, the both of ye," he carried on as Sylvanus, along with Manny, buckled into laughter.

The flakes were forgotten as the evening wore on, and the brew kept flowing, and Manny kept up a steady tirade of nonsensical things. And with the fire warming his bones, and his face broadening from laughing, Sylvanus soon forgot his fight with Addie. Was late, real late when he found himself leaning closer to the fire, all the time nodding and grinning; even when nothing was being said, he was nodding and grinning. Time to go home, he thought, and stood up. His legs wobbled like rubber beneath him, and he wondered how long he'd been drunk.

"Now, enter like the lamb," cautioned Manny as he set his sights onto the corner of the house and started staggering toward it. "Remember that—like the lamb."

"Thought it was the pup."

"Noo—yeah—noo, that's later you cuddles like the pup. First, you got to get through the door, and that's how you does it—enter like the lamb. Gets them right off if you bleats like the lamb."

"That right, Jake? Bleat like a lamb?" asked Sylvanus, kicking his eldest brother's foot as he stumbled past him. "Can you show me, Jake? Can you bleat? Just show me how you bleats," he begged, and yowled as a boot in the arse from Manny sent him stumbling into the winds blasting through the neck.

Nice fellows, he thought of his brothers, weaving his way through the dark, nice fellows. "Bejesus, I'm not riding your back this night, hussy," he muttered as the wind delivered a slather of spit from the sea against his face, "bejesus I'm not," and he hurried his step toward home, yellow patches of light from the houses on his left divining his path, and his outstretched hands seeking an invisible railing against the seawater broiling a greyish white out of the abyss to his right.

His mother's house drew near, and he saw her face in the window, watching out for him. "Been doing it since you was three. Don't ask me to stop now," she'd shushed him once, after his wedding night, when he'd complained about her still doing so. And she hadn't stopped, either, still treating him like the youngster, he thought, and he stood grinning, waving at her as he passed by, trying to keep a straight line so's she wouldn't think him drunk and worry. The night turned blacker past her lamp-lit window. He staggered, trying to keep to the path and figure out the outline of his house through the darkness before him. His ears picked up the brook over the roar of the falls and the pounding of the sea, and he headed toward it. A window, he thought, weaving off the path and stumbling to find his way back, we needs a window on that damn back wall, that's what we needs. What harm to have a little window to light the way home sometimes, especially if we're to have youngsters, he thought solemnly. Yes, they'd have to have a window. He would tell her once he got inside—a window, we needs a window, Addie, a window to light the way home. That's what he would tell her, then; but not in the rambunctious manner of the ram—*"Addie, we needs a window!"*—but real quiet like, "Addie, we needs a window on the back wall, just a small one so's when we haves a youngster, it won't go drowning itself in the brook, trying to get home— Heeyy!!" And he let out a cry as his feet slipped from beneath him at the same instant his mother opened her door, letting out the lamplight and showing him, too late, the brook broiling up to greet him.

"Christ!" he cried out as the icy water flooded his boots. Then, scrambling back up the little incline with the water squishing through his toes, he stood shivering, waving his mother back inside.

"Syllie! Did you fall in?" she called from her doorway.

"Naw! Get back inside."

"Syllie!"

"I'm here, I'm here on the other side!" he roared, waving wildly. "Go on in. Go on!"

"Did you fall in?"

"No, cripes, Mother, get your head inside. Go on." And as her door closed, he grunted, balancing himself awkwardly on one foot while pulling off the boot of the other and emptying it.

A gust of wind hit him full and he stumbled backwards, landing on his arse, cursing as he held his boot in his hand, trying not to let his socked foot touch the ground, while all the time wondering why not when it was more soaked than the ground he sat upon. "Might as well be riding your back, hussy," he muttered, letting his foot flop down into the mud and hauling off his other rubber, "might as bloody well." And clambering to his feet, he gulped as a squall of wind snatched at his breath, slathering him with another dose of spit.

"Blood of a bitch," he cursed, and rising with his boots in his hand, he stood facing the wind, laughing as he staggered toward home, pitching and rolling as might a ship upon a stormy sea. Orange sparks flared out of his chimney and he knew by the sudden bursts Addie was digging at the fire with the poker and he sobered, his heart sinking. Was she cold? Was she scared of the wind screaming like the haunt through the head? She didn't like the sea. She'd told him that. And now here it was roiling like the hag upon the shore, the froth of her fury gnashing like teeth just a few feet from her window. More flankers flared and he started running, his feet slipping and sliding beneath him. He made no more headway than when he was walking, but still he ran, no longer knowing how much of his gait was due to the brew, the wind, or his slipping and sliding on the muddied path. And all the time thinking as he ran, she's cold, and she's scared, she's cold and she's scared. Breathlessly, he arrived at his stoop, and remembering Manny's words about the lamb, he paused, forcing a calm to his racing heart. Catching his breath, he pulled off his wet socks, his coat, his workshirt, and piled them in a heap beside his boots. Flattening his hair back off his forehead, he rubbed his hands on pants that were more soaked than the garments he'd just hauled off, and quietly pushed open the door.

It was warm inside. She sat quietly rocking before the window facing the neck, her feet propped upon the windowsill, a shawl around her shoulders, and the lamp burning steadily beside her as she read from that little red book about some God-hungry saint.

"Put in some wood, Sylvanus," she said quietly, scarcely looking up as he entered. He gazed over the back of her chair onto the crown of her head, and at her little ankles propped upon the windowsill, levering her rocker back and forth, and the rest of her all snuggled inside a wool wrap. So small, she was, without her belly showing, like the little girl they would soon have (he was sure it was a girl), and his chest broadened, and feeling mammoth from his blustering in the big wind outside, he crouched now within this tiny kitchen he'd built for her and laid his hand upon the arm of her rocker.

"Addie," he whispered, and she near startled out of her chair at his sudden nearness.

Her creator, her protector, he felt in his drunken stupor, and his eyes filled with tears as he laid his hands on her little ankles, whispering fervently, "I won't let you get cold agin, I pledge to the Almighty. I'll never let you get cold agin."

"Cold? What's wrong, Sylvanus? I'm not cold."

"Never, never"—he shook his head, tears rolling down his cheeks—"swear to God, Addie, you'll never be cold agin."

"But I'm not cold. Are you crying?" and her voice rose in alarm. "Is it Eva?" she cried, half rising. "What's the matter, Syllie?"

"Shh, I knows, I knows you can take care of yourself," he said, easing her back into her chair. "Everybody knows Addie can take care of herself. I'm not saying that—"

"What?"

"Nothing, nothing. I don't want you worrying, that's all. I knows, I knows"—he raised his hand placatingly—"you thinks I'm foolish to be worrying about you like this, but that's just what I'm saying—I'm going to take care of you, I just wants you to know that, that's all. I'm—I'm going to take care of things."

She had pulled back, staring at him in astonishment as he stuttered his way through this last speech. When he'd done, she said blandly, "You're drunk."

His eyes widened into a hurt look. "Now that's a fine thing to say. I says I'm going to take care of you and you calls me drunk. Well, sir." He rose all in a huff, hating that he lurched, hating that she watched him wavering toward the bedroom. Jeezes, the wind still had him and he clutched the door frame as it swerved before him. Taking good aim, he then fell onto the bed. "Aah, it's warm, so warm," he murmured, burying his face into its comfort, hearing her as she called out something—what was that? The wood? Put in some wood? Was she saying put in some wood? And he would, his dear, lovely Addie, he would put in some wood, he would stog that stove to its tops, he would redden its cast-iron front with heat, he would never, ever leave her agin, his Addie, his lovely Addie—

"Nice fellows," he murmured as he opened his eyes a bit later, feeling her tugging at him, scolding him about getting the bedclothes wet. "Nice fellows."

CHAPTER TWELVE

TOKEN FROM GOD

H ER WATER BROKE two weeks before her time. A cold snap had fallen, crystallizing the air and sending everyone chopping the ice from their wells, two, three times a day. Not wanting her to be alone or his mother trekking through the snowbanks, Sylvanus laid down his axe and saw and stayed home that week. When she cried out to him from the kitchen one mid-afternoon, her tone fraught with fright, he threw down the shovel from where he'd been shovelling off the door place, and ran, pummelling along the footbridge to get his mother. Practically lifting her off her feet, he half carried, half walked her back across the brook, shoving her inside his kitchen. Snatching the scarlet red cloth off the table, he tore back outside, furiously waving it—a signal he'd set up that the midwife was needed.

He met her a hundred yards to the other side of his mother's house, looking like a lost janny with the dark woollen blanket wrapped around her bony old shoulders, and the skin of a beaver tied around her head. It wasn't

how his Addie had planned it—this old thing with the wisps
of hair scarcely covering a splotchy scalp, and the fat
stubby butt forever stuck to her bottom lip; but too late
now for the young thing in Ragged Rock who was doing
all the birthing these days. Coaxing and pleading for the
crone to hurry, hurry, please hurry, he kept two steps
ahead of her, not wanting to pick her up and run with
her as he had his mother. When finally she made her
examination and determined that it would be hours,
perhaps days, before the baby was born, he bent to
Adelaide's begging looks, and layering himself in woollens
and skins, he raced Manny's horse and sled through the
woods, across the ice-covered ponds and down the hills
into Ragged Rock.

But the young midwife was gone—up to Hampden to
deliver a child there. He bounded back into his sled and
was well on his way to fetch Florry instead when a sudden
dread fell upon him. Pulling back on his reins, he stopped
cold. And with foreboding weighing his limbs, he pulled
the horse around and started toward home. Suze came
tearing out of her mother's house, a scarf wrapped around
her head and dough still clinging to her fingers as she
hauled on a hooded parka.

"She's started, haven't she?" she yelled out, bolting in
front of the horse. The horse snorted, jerking sideways
around her, but she clung to the grip on the sleigh, pulling
herself up without him even stopping. "Where's Florry,
then? How come she's not coming? My gawd, you'll break
our necks," she cried out as he whipped the horse, near
tossing her off the sled as they sped down a bank, jolting
up the other side and over the roughened hobbles of a
frozen brook. He said nothing, saw nothing, giving the

horse his head and the whip to hurry the hell up and get him back home.

"She already sent Melita and Elsie home," said Eva, meeting Suze at the door. "I don't allow she'll be wanting you, either."

Leaving Suze to fight it out with his mother, Sylvanus pushed in through the door, quailing at the sight of the midwife's clawed hand upon his Addie's naked belly and the other probing at her most private part.

"No place for a man," the crone whined, her mouth all sunken without the habitual butt sitting upon it.

But he wasn't budging. "Not to worry," he crooned into Addie's ear as she cringed beneath the hag's claw. "Mother's keeping the fire going good and the water heated, and she's done enough birthing herself to know a few things."

Adelaide nodded, her face pale, pensive. "I don't want nobody here," she cried, hearing Suze's voice through the door.

"She'll stay in the kitchen, but you'll not get rid of me, lady. I'm sitting here till that baby's bawling in my arms."

And thus he sat through the evening, his head close to hers, mindful to keep his breath off her face because of her not liking smells, and coaxing her through what must've been Dante's frozen circle of hell, for never had he felt a night so cold, and never had he witnessed a body writhing and locked into such pain. A horse, once; he'd seen a horse scream and pound the ground to bits with its hooves as it sprawled on its side, eyes bulging with exertion, nostrils splayed, and every muscle taut to the point of tearing as that strong, lean beast screamed and pounded its way through the night. When finally, in the light before dawn, a weakling foal was expelled from its innards, the horse lay convulsing into death. And, Lord, how his heart now feared for this sprout of a woman who would not scream, and who would not moan or pound her pillow despite her taut and jerking body, and who held her breath despite everyone telling her not to and gritted her way through paroxysm after paroxysm of pain with mere little gasps escaping her tightly clenched teeth.

But as the night wore on, minute by minute, hour by hour, and morning dawned and she lay sweltering in sweat, her face more stark than the wintered land outside, and her eyes more wild than the waters of the neck, her moans started making themselves heard. Only she was too tired now to manage more than the slightest sound, and he stood behind her, silently cursing the woman Eve for believing such a thing as a venial sin, and helped push his wife, his suffering sinner, into a sitting position as she grunted and pushed and grunted until finally, as a pale glimmer of sun glanced in through the window, she pushed the thing into being.

He wept in his relief, trailing kisses across the terrible damp of her forehead as she fell back, depleted, onto her pillow. "See, see," he choked, "it's over, all over. Everything's fine, just fine."

But all was not fine. It wasn't fine at all. At some point during the night, while heavy frost was chilling the waters of Cooney Arm, the baby's umbilical cord settled across the mouth of Adelaide's womb. And as a thin sheet of ice caught over the waters of the arm in the false light of dawn, choking the flow through the neck, so the unborn, with its own weight pressing against the cord, began choking itself of blood and air. And now, this morning, as the blue of the sea fused beneath a thin cataract of ice, so too, was the blue of the newborn in the midwife's hands fused within the shroud of its own caul.

"What is it? What's wrong with it!?" Adelaide cried.

"It's dead, my dear. Your baby's dead," said the old midwife.

"Dead? Eva!" But Eva was crossing herself, her eyes closed, her head bent in prayer. Adelaide struggled to sit up, to see. "Syllie!"

"Shh, don't look, it's—it's all right," he said, holding her back, his eyes as rooted as hers onto the thing in the midwife's hands, all white and shrouded; the membrane of an egg that ought never to have been seeded.

"It's a caul," said the crone, her little rock eyes aglow in the lamplight as she brought the thing closer. "It brung you a caul. A precious gift is a caul—will save your man from drowning like his father and his brother."

"No! No, don't touch it—don't touch it!" cried Adelaide, and she squeezed shut her eyes, screaming, "Eva, stop her, stop her!" as the old midwife started pulling on the white film.

"Mother's got it, shh, Mother's got it, Addie," soothed Sylvanus as she coiled into his neck.

Eva crossed herself once more and, leaning forward, took the thing from the crone's hands.

"Addie, listen to me," said Eva. "You too," she said sharply to Sylvanus as he shook his head, gesturing toward the door for her to be gone. "It's only a film. It's a pretty baby underneath. You need to see that, Addie, you need to see your baby—Addie," she pleaded as the girl cringed deeper into Sylvanus's neck.

"Addie." It was Suze, her voice a tremulous whisper. "You should look. It's not awful at all."

Addie stiffened at the sound of Suze's voice. "Why's she here?" she cried, near hysteria, and tearing away from Sylvanus, she latched onto the pair of frightened grey eyes staring at her from across the room. "Get out!" shrieked Adelaide. "Get out, get out!"

"Addie, stop it," pleaded Sylvanus, and held her tighter as she recoiled against his shoulder. The crone approached, taking her arm.

"Cursed! You'll be cursed," she hissed, "sending back a token from God. Ungrateful woman."

Sylvanus pushed away the crone's hand. "Get her away," he cried out to his mother and buried his face in Adelaide's hair as she sobbed hysterically.

Taking the midwife's arm, Eva led her from the room.

"Shh, be still, be still," he pleaded with Adelaide. "Don't listen, nobody listens to that old hag. Borning babies is the only good she ever done. Mother's taking care of things. Please, Addie," he begged as she shivered against him. He continued holding her for a while until she became quiet.

"Leave me be now, Syllie," she whispered.

"Addie." He touched her brow. It was cold, clammy. She pulled away, her face now lost to him.

No, don't you turn from me, Addie, he wanted to say. But said nothing. Rising, he stepped softly out of the room.

"Close the door," she said quietly.

A lasting look at her still form beneath the blankets, her averted head, and he closed their door.

PART FOUR

Adelaide

WINTER 1955 TO SPRING 1960

CHAPTER THIRTEEN

SUZE'S GIFT

S HE REMAINED STILL, her face hidden in her pillow for the rest of the morning and throughout the day, unwilling to sleep, unwilling to speak, unwilling to have anyone sit with her. The next morning, however, Eva came into her room with a small coil of oakum, as nicely combed out as you could get the tarry hemp, and closing the door, helped her sit up and undo her nightdress. Locking eyes with herself in the mirror, Adelaide watched expressionlessly as Eva first wrapped a piece of red flannel around her bared upper body, pinning it, and then started lacing the oakum tight around her swollen breasts, so tight she could scarcely breathe, the rough sticky hemp scratching those little bits of flesh the flannel didn't cover, the stink of tar bringing water to her eyes.

"There. It'll take a few days," said Eva sympathetically after she had finished and was helping her rebutton her nightdress, "but the milk should dry up after that. Not too tight, is it?"

She shook her head, and after Eva had left, she pulled the bedclothes over herself, forbidding anyone to enter her room, even Sylvanus. Yet when he came home with a roll of white cotton, she wouldn't allow her door to be shut. Half turned into her pillow, she followed his hands as he wrapped the stillborn, with no knowing of its gender, in layers and layers of white cotton till it looked like a misshapen wing. Laying it into a wooden box he'd fashioned himself, they buried it with the shortest of ceremony in the little cemetery in Cooney Arm. Most everyone came, but as Sylvanus had once said to her of the people in cities, they all muted together the way trees blend to make a wood. She felt only the numbness of her hand curled into the warmth of his, her eyes, glazed by tears too chilled to flow, and the dark beneath them, pressing in like bruises, and as stark, no doubt, as the uncovered earth upon that field of white.

The days following the funeral she would find herself sitting forward in her chair, looking out through the dried hawkweed hanging in her southern window, her arms wrapped around herself, her legs tightly crossed, and the most pensive look straining her face—like sitting on the edge of one's seat, awaiting judgment, she sometimes thought, and wondered if perhaps she was. Token, the old midwife had said, the caul was a token from God. But, nay! Tokens! Old women's foolishness, she kept telling herself, turning her attention instead onto her visitors. They all came, the ones from Cooney Arm. Even from Ragged Rock, they came, risking the newly frozen waters of the bay to pay their respects and bring bread and cookies or some other small thing. She watched them as they sipped tea and munched on the cookies and cakes,

searching for those things unsaid, but might lurk within
their eyes, like the tsking, slanderous eyes of her mother
and her mother's neighbours those times they'd caught
her hove off on the daybed, reading books when the house
was filling with filth. For that's how she felt since the
morning of the delivery, since the moment the stillborn
with its caul was raised before her, and the beady, hard
eyes of the midwife were raking over her—befouled. Too
lazy and haughty she had been to take note of those good
medicines brought to her, and in her neglect, she had
rendered herself unfit to bear a strong, healthy baby. And
then her fretting, selfish ways had expelled it before the
breath of God sounded it.

A tightening of her chest brought her hand to her
heart. It had started upon the old woman's pronounce-
ment of the caul—this tightening of her chest—and
appeared to have dug in deeper as Eva had strapped her in
oakum. Plus, a lump of sickness sat in her stomach. That,
too, had been brought on by the caul—the sight of it, all
sickly white and slimed, and the sickness kept growing
within her.

She brought her hand to her mouth as she felt it
now, shifting deep within the pit of her stomach, and
she peered more closely at those women she sat with at
her table who were nibbling on the cakes and jellies they
had brought so's to put fat on her bones, and giving
testimony about the moors of raspberries to settle one's
insides. A part of her had always blamed them, her
mother's neighbours, her mother, others, for making
her feel like a dirty, grubby girl. Yet they hadn't been
standing in her room during her hour of birthing,
shaking their head in abhorrence at the malformed

infant. Still, she had lain there long after the midwife
had gone, feeling just that—a dirty, grubby girl, as when
she'd been caught reading books when the sink was
sinking with dirty dishes. Perhaps Sylvanus was right,
she now thought grimly; perhaps nobody can make you
feel a thing that you aren't. Perhaps 'twas because she
was a dirty, grubby girl that her mother's neighbours
could make her feel that way. Perhaps that grubby little
girl, now looking into her neighbours' faces, searching
for favour, was a creature of her own making, after all, a
creation as defiled as the thing she had given birth to.

The thing in her stomach rolled, frightening her as
much as it sickened her, and she hunched closer to the
circle of women, forcing herself to listen to their shared
stories of troubles past—Melita, Elsie, the missus from
farther along the arm, her mother, Florry, and two others
from the fish plant. Even Gert had made the trip this
evening, subduing her tones to that solemn quiet a group
of women can take on when sharing reverence, even when
all were talking at once. Some of them had just met, yet
she saw the ease with which they leaned from one into
another, the alphabet they played out with their hands,
touching, patting, folding, impressing their collective
sorrows and comforts upon each other till it was the one
heart beating for them all, thus easing the burden of the
one most bereaved. For someone looking on, watching as
they poured themselves into Melita as she brought forth
her story of miscarriage during her first year of marriage,
it'd be a hard guess as to whose moment of sorrow the
occasion was hosting. And despite their sympathetic
glances at Adelaide, their pats and touches and caresses, it
was how Adelaide felt, sitting there with this group of

women—like someone looking on; the dead at their own wake; present, but too cold to feel their mourners' touch.

With little hope, then, she rose on the same unspoken cue they all rose to an hour or so later, and stood like an expectant child, searching into the softening of their eyes, their faces, as they turned their goodbyes onto her, waiting for this thing, the collective heartbeat, to enter her and share the lump of sickness in her stomach, the tightening in her chest. But peace isn't for the taking, and so far had she dwelled outside the lives of these neighbours, their goodwill had less effect upon her heart than a tepid kiss upon a wintery cheek.

"Why? Why can't I feel anything of what they says?" she cried out once to Eva after Melita and the missus from down around the arm had just left, leaving behind nothing of the warmth they'd brought. "Feels like they're talking to somebody else, even when they're looking at me."

"Some things only the heart can hear," said Eva, busying herself at the sink.

She scoffed. "Even when the heart's the part that's hurting? My, Eva, you says the strangest things." And like a youngster, she grew impatient with all them visiting and offering her things she couldn't reach, and she turned a haughty ear upon their talk, wishing them gone so's she could curl into her rocking chair instead and moodily watch the waters rioting in the neck. Point of fact, she always felt worse after they left, the tightening in her chest deepening, the cursed sickness rolling in her stomach. Impatiently then, almost angrily, she opened her door to Suze one afternoon about three weeks after the burial.

It'd been almost two years since they had stood at the font, christening Suze's baby, yet she was still waddling in her baby fat, Adelaide noted a mite disdainfully. She checked herself for her nastiness, but she was still mad about Suze showing up at her birthing and seeing that— that *thing* that had been such an intimate part of herself. She'd no right, no right to have been there, seeing that. And perhaps that's why everybody was all the time coming, visiting, she muttered silently; Suze had them all worked up, yarning about it.

She bent closer to the warmth of the stove as Suze, kicking off her snowshoes by the door, bustled inside, the kitchen shrinking around her oafish frame as she skimmed out of her hooded parka and mitts.

"Brrrrr," she blustered, an explosion of shivers emitting pockets of cold into the room as she stood, rubbing her hands for warmth. Snapping up the room with glistening grey eyes, she took a seat at the table, smoothing back bristly black hair that immediately sprang forward, encircling cheeks bursting with red as she quickly divulged her story of snagging a ride across the ice with Dicky Bennet and his horse, bringing over the mailbag. "You knows I'm frightened to death on ice," she said loudly, "but 'twas the only chance I had to get over for a while, so I left Stewie with Mom, even though he's not weaned yet, and I dare say he's bawling his head off by now, for he's been crouped up all week. And you can't feed him enough! No sir, he eats everything you throws at him, and still bawls for the tit—and he almost two years old now. I told Dicky Bennet, poor Mother will be tearing her hair out by the time I gets back." Suze paused as Adelaide sat before her. It was the first time she'd sat alone with Adelaide since the birth, and now that the moment had settled itself, she glanced around uncomfortably, almost shyly.

Adelaide, irritated beyond will, stated perfunctorily, "You shouldn't have left him, then."

"Oh, well," and Suze gave an exaggerated shrug. "He shouldn't be on the tit anyway, the mouthful of teeth he got. Can't get the little bugger off—bawls like the devil, he does. Anyway," and she took on a sympathetic air, "it's not the baby I come here to talk about."

"How's Benji?" cut in Adelaide, pushing back the pending moment of condolence.

Suze went silent.

"Is something wrong with him?" asked Adelaide.

"Oh, same old stuff—his asthma; but I never come here to talk about that."

"As well to talk about your problems as mine," said Adelaide shortly. "Tell you the truth, I'm done with people feeling sorry for me. Was he up agin last night? Oh, for gawd's sake, what's wrong?" she demanded as Suze's eyes filled.

Struggling to overcome her emotion, Suze inhaled deeply, half whispering, "They had to take him away yesterday morning. He's—he's fine, though."

"Took him away, where?"

"The hospital in Springdale. He—he was half dead, he was—" and the overwrought girl burst into tears. "I found him in the snowbank," she whispered convulsively. "He'd had an attack and gone to sleep. H-he always goes to sleep with asthma, makes him sleepy, it does. And then the snow drifted over him. I thought—I thought he was dead when I found him, God help me, I thought he was dead—" and now conscious of her words, she gulped back her sobs, wiping the tears off her face. "I should be grateful," she whimpered, looking through tremulous eyes at Adelaide, "after everything you been through, but I keeps thinking about the way he looked when I first seen him—all white—and now he's took away to the hospital, and me not with him."

"How come you didn't go, then?" cried Adelaide. "For sure there's enough around to care for Stewie—and like you said, he's not a baby if he's almost two."

Suze nodded, sniffling into a handkerchief she'd pulled out of a pocket. "I should've, I suppose. But Stewie's sick, too. I couldn't leave Mother with him sick like that—and like I said, bawling for the tit—and she's not well, either, Mother's not. My Lord, seems like everything always happens at once. But it's not nothing that won't set itself right." She shook her head, noisily blowing her nose. "Anyway, what's I doing, sitting here bawling over my own problems when it's yours I come to sit with. I suppose," she said, wiping at the tears that refused to ebb, "it's sitting here, feeling what you're going through that makes me softer, harder to hold back. My, Addie, I don't know how you're holding up. Gawd, I just never thought nothing like this would happen to you."

Adelaide shifted uncomfortably. "Why wouldn't it happen to me?"

"I don't know. You're always so proper, the way you does stuff. I just never expected you to have trouble, I suppose."

"Proper!" Adelaide gave a ghastly laugh. "Lord, I never done nothing proper in my life. What makes you say that?"

Suze shrugged, wiping her face. "You always seems proper to me, the way you keeps to yourself, and never talking about nobody, and not showing things—how you feels."

"Well, I don't know if that's what you calls proper. Perhaps I don't think of anybody long enough to talk about them. Proper is what you're doing—coming over to visit somebody you think needs the company. I never done that in my life—go visit somebody needing company." This last she spoke more lowly, as though to herself.

Reaching across the table, Suze patted her hand. "What's you doing now, then," she asked, "if you're not listening to me go on and on, with everything you're going through these days? Addie," she leaned closer, her eyes doubtful of what she was about to say, her hand closing more firmly over Adelaide's, "Addie, I knows it takes a long time to get over something like this, but you should've looked. It wouldn't feel like such an awful thing if you'd seen—"

"I'll not talk about that," cried Adelaide, snatching back her hand. "And I'd appreciate it if you wouldn't no more, either—to nobody!"

"I haven't—I wouldn't," protested Suze, her face flaming, "but I got to tell you something—"

She drew back as Adelaide stood up so fast she near knocked the chair over behind her. "Nothing! I'll hear nothing about it, do you hear?" And looking hard at the stove, she marched toward it, asking in a highly agitated tone, "You want some tea?"

Suze shook her head, her cheeks flaming.

"You might as well, I already got the water heated." In quick snappy movements she took down the tea things, noisily clinking the cups in their saucers as she lodged them on the table, hating the fresh bout of tears on Suze's face, hating knowing that she had caused them. "I can cut some bread," she offered, a mite contrite.

"No—I—" Suze cleared her throat. "Dicky give strict orders, ten, fifteen minutes, no more," she said quietly. "And it's been that now, for sure. Last thing he wants is getting caught in the windstorm coming on. So I'd better go."

"You'll hear him when he's ready. Here, have some tea." She poured the hot liquid into Suze's cup and sat back down, floundering for want of something to say. Rather the old buoyant Suze and her steady stream of chatter keeping everything light and mindless than this silence now squelching them. "And Benji's getting on fine now?" she asked.

Suze nodded, gulping back a mouthful of hot tea.

"Did somebody go with him?"

"Maisie went."

"That's good, then. Benji likes her, don't he?"

Suze nodded. "My, yes. Loves her, he does—bawls after her, so I knows he's fine. Anyway, I think that's Dicky Bennet I hears now. I'd better go. Addie." She leaned forward. "I didn't mean to say anything just now."

"That's fine. I'm a bit testy, I suppose."

"Dare say you are. Perhaps you should bar your door and keep us all out. For sure we knows you likes keeping to yourself, you do."

Adelaide nodded, relieved at the old bounce creeping back in Suze's tone. "Let me wrap you up some cake to take home," she offered. "I'll never eat all of what they brings me."

"No! No, I'm big enough now," said Suze with a quick laugh as she rose to leave. "Oh, I almost forgot," and she crossed the kitchen, fumbling amongst the folds of her parka, bringing forth a loosely wrapped paper

package. "I got you something. Yes, take it," she urged
as Adelaide pulled back. "It's because it suited you so
well that I got it—won't look no good on nobody else."
She let fall the paper wrapping and held out a shawl, a
satiny shawl of the deepest blue interwoven with
silvered threads that, within the shaft of sunlight striking through the window and shimmering over it, jolted
Adelaide back to the figure of God at the church altar,
whose blue-coloured robe she had once vainly likened
to her own eyes.

"What? Where'd you get that?" she gasped, aston-
ished for a second into thinking that it was such a robe.

"The old Jew peddler, Liney Bullis. He just come
down from Hampden yesterday, right after they took
Benji. Chance I seen the shawl through the door—I
couldn't go look at his stuff, I can't do nothing that feels
like fun, not with you over here going through all this.
Anyway," she added, her discomfort dissolved, her tone
tendering, "Mother let him in, though. Can't turn him
away, he'd think you had something against him, you
turned him away—soft-hearted as anything, Uncle Liney
is. So, chance I glanced out and seen it—the shawl—and
my gawd, Addie, it's the same colour of your eyes. You
knows you got that different colour blue in your eyes."

A chill crept into Adelaide. Slowly her fingers touched
upon the cold blue of the shawl. She pulled away her
hand, staring into the warmth-filled eyes of this woman
who had abandoned her child not yet weaned and braved
the wind and ice to see her; a woman whom she had
repeatedly cast lower than Old Maid Ethel's pigs, whose
soul she had shunned because it couldn't read a prayer
book, whose comfort she had just now scorned, and who,

despite all, was still standing before her, expectant grey eyes bubbling fat tears onto her cheeks as she stood, smiling, waiting for Adelaide to take her gift.

Tiring, Suze tossed the gift onto Adelaide's lap. Nay, it was not Suze tossing the garment onto her lap, but the God she, Adelaide, had built out of her vanity as a child, Who, she believed, existed only on the cleanly swept altar of her weekly visits, and Who looked only upon her carefully written scrolls, and blessing her shiny blue eyes, exactly the blue of his garment. Clearly, despite the child having grown, she was still shrouding Him with her inflated notions. And now He had torn her adornment from His shoulders and flung it onto her lap.

"My, what's wrong with you," tutted Suze as Adelaide drew back from the shawl.

"It's—it's for you, not me," cried Adelaide. "You take it!"

Suze tutted again. "Look some good on my dumpy shoulders now, that would. And like I said, it'll look right nice with your eyes."

"No. No, yours are nicer. Please—I—it must've cost you a fortune."

"Money!" scoffed Suze. "What's the use of that? It couldn't keep Benji from getting sick or save you from what you went through. I should be shamed to bring it over, but Lord, you looks so white, Addie. If it brings a little bit of colour to your face, it's worth it. And now I'd better get going, Dicky's probably out there waiting for me—he said no longer than twenty minutes, and for sure it's been that now. No, don't get up," she said with a no-nonsense shake of her head, thick hands clamping Adelaide's shoulder as she was about to rise. "Stay off your feet as much as you can, that's what you can do. I knows me way out."

"But," and her voice dropped to a low whisper, "I don't deserve this."

"Oh, pooh," said Suze, climbing back into her snow-pants. "We don't know half the time what we're giving others. Might be a strange thing to say, but when I was missing Benji too much last evening, I thought about you and what you're going through and it made me feel better. Might be the devil working through me, but there's a comfort knowing others are suffering worse than you right now. Makes you think about them rather than your-self. I hears others say the same thing, so it must be the way of it if others are feeling it too. And I expects if anything happens to Benji tonight—pray sweet Jesus that it don't—I expect you'd feel better because of my misery. It's a hard thing to say—somebody else's misery bringing comfort to another—but like I said, I'm not calling it, just naming it, is all because I hears others say the same thing. Strange how God works, isn't it, maid?"

A hard stirring was taking place inside Adelaide. "Suze," and she followed her guest to the door. "Thank you," she said quietly.

Clenching the shawl, Adelaide crept to the window after Suze had let herself out. She stood watching her snowshoeing through snow so soft it sent clouds of flur-ries around her feet as she lunged forward, step after step, toward the frozen waters of the arm, Dicky Bennet, and his horse, black as tar against the white. A tear cut her eye, enflaming further the garment in her hands. Raising it before her, she bowed, trembling into its folds.

CHAPTER FOURTEEN

THE ABYSS

SHORTLY AFTER SUZE'S VISIT, Adelaide started working toward a commonality with her neighbours. Crossing the brook almost daily, she took tea with Melita and Elsie, baked cakes for the old midwife, who was seemingly always down with a flu, and helped scrub the school floors and desks every Saturday. On those Sundays the weather was good, she made the trip to Ragged Rock, rocking Benji and chatting with Suze (always wearing the shawl, although after that one first time, Suze, as though sparing Adelaide the painful thank-yous, never noted it again), and visiting with her mother. She even attended a card game at the church, once whilst she was there, nodding to her father's uproar with a bunch of other fishermen about the Russians showing up in St. John's with a factory freezer built from the plans they "stole from under the Limeys' stinking noses."

"And now here's our own government spending thousands, waltzing them straight across the country, wining and dining them," whined her father, fidgeting with his cards as her mother trumped his ace. "Ve're not here to vish Canadian vaters," he mimicked in a bad Russian accent, "ve're just here to vatch." And Adelaide grinned and nodded along with everybody else, and nodded all the harder as Gert's husband, Ro, latched on to her father's talk, and with his eyes snarling onto hers over the kitty, exclaimed all the louder, "You hear the likes of that? 'Vee got lozs ov vish, b'yes; jez zopping by to visit, is all.' You ever hear the likes of that—our government listening to the bleeding Russians *and believing them?* They'll be back, you watch and see if them damn Russians won't be back, hey, Leam, b'ye?"

Ending off the card game with a round of handshakes to all, she settled into another game with another pair of opponents, listening and nodding and sometimes adding commentary of her own about the fishing and the long-liners and the trawlers and the factory freezers. Even chatting with women over tea became an exercise she faithfully greeted; smiling and thanking them as they exclaimed how well she was starting to look, no matter the paleness of her skin, and praising her house, its tidiness, and what a good worker she was—had always been, some testified, recalling those long, laborious hours of working the flakes and the assembly line at the fish plant.

Nice. No doubt everyone had their ways, but mostly she found everyone nice. And who knows but that she might've learned to enjoy this new rapport—the fussing her mother made each time she came, bringing bread and buns, and the ongoing bantering of the others as they furbished her table with thoughts and anecdotes—maybe she could have, had her second pregnancy brought forth a child.

But, no. Her second baby, born two years after the
first, lived no longer than the minute it took to show
the blue of an eye before dying upon her breasts. Two years
again, and her third was readying itself for birth. This time
Sylvanus insisted she travel the four-hour trip by train to
the hospital in Springdale. Three days after a healthy
delivery, an infection running rampant in the nursery rid it
of life. She returned home, stone-faced and cold, the small
white box in the coach behind her. She ordered Ambrose
to motor it to Cooney Arm, while she motored with
Sylvanus. And there she ordered it be taken to the church,
whilst she sat at home, waiting for the service. Not once
did she visit that little white bed. Not once did she look as
it lay at the altar; nor when they lowered it into the ground
before her, did she look at it fully. Frozen. Her eyes were
frozen, and her blood ran cold as winter's rain. For she
still wore that thin wrap of vanity, the one stripped from
her shoulders and flung onto her lap through the hands of
Suze. Why else had she come to believe that the hideous
birthing of the baby wrapped in caul was a summons
toward her own salvation, and that a few jaunts across the
bridge, caring for the sick, and a few hours rocking Suze's
youngster, were sufficient installments of retribution for
her past sins? And come now, surely her second birthing
would be the sweet, pretty baby of penance. And she
would be smiled upon as she herself had smiled upon that
flawless Mother of Divinity at the altar of her youth.

But there was no salvation, only her neighbours. And
salt onto a fissure were their sympathies, for far was she
from the grieving mother they thought her to be. Rather,
it was the Christ child she grieved, believing it him she
had sullied, first with her vanity, her haughtiness, and now

with her self-serving nature. For her hours of rocking and scrubbing and serving the sick were never from a true sense of goodness; they felt more like bribes now, no matter she'd honestly wanted to make things right, to make folk like her. It was to save herself from this awful sorrowing that she really wanted them to like her, as though their affections could validate her goodness before the all-knowing God.

"Make them stop," she whispered from her crumpled pillow to Eva one morning. "Make them stop coming."

"It'll just be another thing you'll fret about, if I do," said Eva, straightening her bedclothes around her.

"Why? Why do you say that?"

"Because these days you'll fret over anything. I could say you're sleeping, I suppose, but then you'd only be straining to hear what they were saying over their tea."

She would've asked, had she the will, how it was the old woman knew so well the workings of her mind. But she already knew what Eva would say—that you don't grow old without learning some things, my maid—so she said nothing, accepting the woman's quiet administrations, trusting the gentleness of her hands as she quietly let herself in and out of her room, and grateful for her lack of need for words.

Yet she rose, her face stricken with fear one morning as Sylvanus crept in with her morning cup of tea, and cried, "I've never felt life, Syllie. Not even when they were readying to be born—almost as if they were already dead in the womb." Her hands shook so bad he laid the cup on her night table.

"They're not, though, Addie," he said soothingly, coaxingly. "We knows that—at least with the last two—"

"I feels the same dead now, like there's no life inside of me. It's a godawful feeling, Syllie," she said shakily. "It's like my soul was expelled, too, this time—or maybe I only thought there was a soul—but what holds you up if there's nothing in there?"

"Oh, Addie, the will of God is what holds you up. The simple fact you wakes up tells you that. Don't—don't think of such things," he pleaded.

"How can I not?" she cried out, "when all the time I'm dreaming of a tombstone at the foot of our bed—and I wants to know the name on it, but I'm too afraid to look, scared there's no name written—that it's waiting for the next one, my next baby." Her voice had risen, but she saw he couldn't listen, couldn't hear what might be madness, and she sank into herself as he buried his face in her breasts, pleading with her not to think about such things, that dreams were dreams after all, and like Grandfather Now always used to say, you'd lose your mind if you read them religious books too much; that life's to be lived, not thought about, and religion is what you carries in your heart, and she'd nothing to worry about there, for her heart was as pure as those babies she lost.

"And never you mind nothing else," he argued as she cried out in protest. "Good health is all you needs to pray for, and I'll do the rest. Strong hands, I've got, and a strong mind when it comes to caring for you, so stop thinking about those things."

She wished she could. She wished he could rip apart with his bare hands that hidden chamber within that was beckoning her more and more with each passing death. For as the days wore on, and her depression settled like lead, she despaired of ever finding her way out, that her worrying and penance and guilt were all for naught, that there never was a soul shoring her up, that God was simply the makings of her own creation, and the kingdom of heaven a construction in her limited world of thought, a ceiling onto the four corners of the room that contained her.

She nearly cried out to Sylvanus then, but could find no words, no thoughts defined enough to share. Instead she watched, his step heavy with his own thoughts, his hands busied with fixing things around her. She marvelled at the strength that built and buried those little white boxes, that kept their larder filled, that kept the fire burning in their stove. And it was nice, those gifts he kept bringing her, of snow crab, and scallops bigger than tea plates, and handfuls of last summer mint tea buried beneath the snow, and the paths he kept well shovelled so's she could take walks around the house, along the brook, or across the footbridge to sit with his mother. He did well with all of that, as he'd done in the past, as he'd done with listening to her trite little tales of high marks and passed grades and fallen ashpans and wretched skullies and aprons and fly spit.

But some things she had never shared with him; some things were too deeply forged within to bring to the outside—like her sitting alone as a youngster before an altar, admiring the holiness of colour and quiet, the divinity of mother and child, and the lure of dreams before her co-conspiratorial God. Beauty. Those moments, those dreams had been the beauty in her young life, the magic, despite her subsequent judgments and brandishing of all else around her. And as does a snowflake dissolve upon touch, so does fantasy dissolve upon a tongue. So she hadn't shared them with Syllie; had kept them in her private chambers. And now, with this darkness fallen upon her, and her thoughts so— In fact, there were no thoughts, not since the moment she had blundered into thinking there might be no God or Divine Mother or babe that had lain in a manger. The fright of such a discovery, or fear of its being, had struck all thought from her—even the tightening in her chest, and that wretched sense of befoulment sickening her stomach, had been struck from within her, forsaking, leaving her with a huge emptiness that sucked her attention inward as though it were a maelstrom, and leaving her as disconnected to Sylvanus and her outer world as if she were a babe in her own womb. Who can speak of such things?

Thus, she burrowed into her pillow, getting out of bed simply to wash and relieve herself, or to peck at whatever small morsels of food Eva was able to persuade her to eat. And only Eva. She was back to wanting no other around her, not even Sylvanus.

But to remain so was to bury Sylvanus as well. Those moments when he sat beside her bed, the brown of his eyes awash in the black of his pupils, and so deeply pitted with fear of this place she had gone, she felt him drowning in his effort to follow her. Eight weeks, then, after she had birthed and buried her third child, she started coming out of her bedroom, spending small amounts of time sitting at her table, delighting Sylvanus, delighting Eva, Suze, her mother, and all those others whose names she was too tired to think of, who traipsed through her kitchen, bringing stews, bringing buns, bringing salads, and their sweet spirits of nitre, and their ginger wine and tales of trite and woe. And grateful though she tried to be for their well-meaning gestures, she wished them gone, wished to be alone.

But, nay, nobody listened to her pleas of "I'm going to be fine now, I can do for myself. Yes, yes, it's time I started doing for myself."

"Nonsense, nonsense, you're not fine, you're weak as anything," they rejoined. "Here, sit down and let me get you some tea, some sweetbread, and take off that night-dress; time to get it washed, and your sheets and pillow-cases, too, and look, over there by the washstand, some nice clean towels for your wash." Even Sylvanus was hanging around the house all day long, leaving only to bring in a bit of wood or a piece of meat.

One morning, early spring, after the ice had freed the arm and he ought to have been fishing, she crept into the kitchen as he stood making breakfast, her hands trembling as she pulled the kettle onto the front top.

"I'm fine. It's been well over two months," she said, as he tried to steer her back to bed.

"But you've still a lot of bleeding—Mother said."

"Only normal. I wonder you haven't started fishing yet?"

"Bit early still."

"Others have been fishing the past two weeks."

"I got a hundred quintal on salt in the stage, Addie. That's a good start on the season. I can take a week if I needs to. Sit down. Will you please sit down and let me make you some tea?"

She sat, watching him as he emptied the dregs from the teapot into the trash box behind the stove, refilling it with more tea and water, and settling it on the damper to steep. A small dipper of water was boiling on the front top, and to it, he added a cupful of oats, gently stirring. His step felt fatigued, she noted, and his hands heavy. She averted her eyes, not wanting the burden of what his thoughts must be these days about her, her illness, the babies, the deaths.

"If it's me you're staying home for, I'm telling you I'm fine," she said quietly.

"You says you're fine. That's not what everybody else says."

"Everybody else!" She sighed, sinking deeper into her chair. "Oh, if they'd all just stay home. I'd get better faster if I had the place to myself."

"Not for a while yet, then, you won't have the place to yourself," he said, laying a cup of tea before her. "Not till we sees some colour on that face."

"Then I'll put it there," she cried, sitting forward with a burst of strength, pinching her cheeks. "There. Do I look fine now? Oh, I knows I'm still a bit under, Syllie," she added at his pained look. "It's just that, well, I'm fine for what I'm going through. It's normal to be pale and tired and—and—all the rest of it." She shook her head, sighing as he started back, stirred her tea, hearing nothing of what she was saying, seeing nothing of what she was doing, only that her tea needed stirring and she was weak and pale, and her body still bleeding. Was there nobody listening?

Or perhaps she wasn't saying the words, she thought. Perhaps she was only thinking them, for that's what it sounded like each time she spoke—her voice far away, distant. Cripes, perhaps that's why they weren't listening, merely nodding and smiling as she pleaded with them, "I'm fine, I'm fine, really, I am, and ye ought to be home, caring for your own crowd. I can wash a cup and make a stew, yes I can, yes I can."

"Do you hear me?" she asked abruptly.

He glanced up, pushing the oatmeal to the back of the stove, his eyes mirroring the hurt of a forgotten child. And she was immediately burdened—doubly burdened—by her own load, and now his, unwittingly laid upon her.

"Oh, never mind." Pushing herself up from her chair, she took the bread knife off the sink and started cutting into the loaf he had laid out. Her wrist buckled as though it were hollowed.

"You've been through a lot, Addie," he said quietly, taking the knife from her hand.

"But I've got to start doing things," she said. "How can I start getting better if everybody keeps doing everything for me?"

"They're just trying to be helpful."

"I don't want their help! Let them stay home if they wants to help. Gawd, Syllie, everyday there's two or three bodies sitting around my table, gabbing and yakking about the damn old weather and their gardens and never once talking about youngsters so's not to upset poor Addie, poor Addie. Gawd, I hates their *poor Addie* look. I'd rather they were all busy making fun of me. Yes, I would," she exclaimed as he looked at her skeptically. "Least then I didn't have to sit, talking and smiling all the time. Bloody pretending, is all it is, and I hates it; I hates pretending right now."

"Pretending what?"

"Pretending that I'm nice, that they're nice, and everything's nice," and she broke off, stunned to find herself still hating and wanting to curse everyone after all she'd been through, and was still going through; that she was still the same old Addie, hating everything and everyone excepting for her own house, and she was starting to hate that too now with everybody coming, all the time coming, and talking and supping. Gawd! Her thoughts trailed off and she stood appalled by them.

"Oh, never mind," she said as though she had spoken them out loud, and giggled as Sylvanus continued looking at her with a growing perplexity. And worried that he now feared she was losing her mind—as she very well might be—she threw down pretense and trudged despondently toward the window, looking out over the sunless sky, the dreary grey cliffs of the neck, and the grey waters of the arm. Leached. Everything leached of colour—the little dirtied bodies—at least the two she had seen—the first had been hidden beneath that awful caul, and her chest constricted in fear as the old midwife's words shot through her mind: "Cursed! Cursed!'"

"Addie." She sprang from his touch. "Addie," he whispered, placing both hands onto her shoulders as though to keep her from escaping him. "I'll stop them coming if you want. Let me take care of you for a few days." His arms went around her, steadying, strong, and she rested against him, allowing him to rock her. In this manner, at least, he could be that pillar upon which she leaned. She gazed up at him, managing a smile, as tremulous as it was grateful.

He stopped rocking, his eyes having found hers again. And there in the bright morning light, in the sobriety of her solitude, they begged from her an intimacy that even when they had lain together as lovers she was able to enter only under the diffusion of shadow. And now, with her body cramping from a third dead baby, and the air sickly with the smell of blood, she tried to turn from him as he brought his mouth down on hers.

"Oh, gawd, Syllie," she groaned, twisting from him, "how can you even think—" and she buckled onto a chair, her hands to her stomach, her mouth lined with self-loathing, which, from the sudden reddening of his face, he no doubt believed was for him. She reached for him, but he was lunging out through the door, leaving it swinging behind him. "Syllie!" She rose, stumbling after him. "Should've left me rotting in that damn plant," she cried out, as though he were standing on the other side of the door, listening. Standing on the stoop, she watched as he hurried over the footbridge, past his mother's, half walking, half running, like the fool who, unlike the wise man building his house on rock, had built it on sand instead and was now fleeing from the fall of it.

"Should've left me rotting," she whispered more quietly. "Should've left me rotting."

CHAPTER FIFTEEN

WIDOW'S WALK

STUMBLING BACK INSIDE the house after Sylvanus shut the door to his stage, Adelaide clung to the table edge and lowered herself onto a chair. Fatigued. Every bone, fatigued. A sound from outside and she raised her eyes—it was him, come back. But, no. It was Eva, a knowing look in her eyes and a commiserating murmur as she entered, giving Adelaide permission to sink back into her state.

"Perhaps you needs to get out and walk a bit," said Eva, flitting about the kitchen, gathering the bread pan and flour can and yeast crock from a bottom cupboard.

"Oh, it's just my stomach," lied Adelaide, wishing that it was her stomach, wishing even for that lump of sickness back; anything over this hollowed-out emptiness, this nothingness!

She watched listlessly as Eva pinched butter into the flour, adding warm water to a bowl of sugared yeast.

"Walks are always good," said Eva. "After the drownings, I always went off by myself, walking."

The drownings. First time Eva had ever mentioned them. Adelaide watched as she poured the yeast and a dipper of warm water into the buttered flour, and stuck in her hands, folding and mixing and kneading, the mixture turning the thin gold band on her gnarled finger a filmy white. Something that Suze said that time she gave her the shawl came back to her, something about another person's misery bringing comfort.

"Must've been awful," she exclaimed. "The drownings, I mean."

Eva said nothing, her eyes dissolving into the glob of flour and water that was becoming a sticky ball of dough beneath her strong hands. Adelaide glanced away, shamed by her continuing self-serving notions, which sought now to feed on another's grief so's to alleviate her own.

"Perhaps I should walk," she said, half angrily. "I got to do something—but then everybody will be calling out, wanting to go with me," she added wearily, the mere notion of expending such energy already defeating her.

"I used to like it up on the head," said Eva.

The head. Adelaide turned to her. She hadn't been up there since that time with Syllie, looking at the carey chicks. "It's like it's haunted up there," she said, and again, regretted her thoughtlessness, remembering that rotting piece of board with "Widow's Walk" carved across its front. Eva carried on punching, turning, and kneading.

"Nothing wrong with haunts, my maid," she said, a bit winded. "They're only lost souls, like ourselves sometimes."

"Widow's Walk. That's a hard name," said Adelaide, quietly. "Why'd you name it that?"

"We raise stones in the earth to mark souls at rest," said Eva. "Why shouldn't we mark the steps of those still labouring?"

"You mean your soul, Eva?"

"That's what I means, my maid. And every other widow watching out for her man's remains."

"Do you ever stop? Watching, I mean."

Eva shrugged. "No doubt there's them that never do. They wakes up simply to watch. And wait. That's when you gets in trouble, when all of your life becomes the one small thing, the widow." She held up a handful of flour from the flour can. "See this? Nothing ever comes of it, long as it's sitting by itself." She threw it into the pan. "So, thinks the head's haunted, do you?" And with a grin like Syllie's when something pleased him, she sprinkled a last handful of flour over the dough, now shaped into an oval loaf, and dotted the sign of the cross across its centre.

"There, that's all you got to do to ward off haunts: flaunt the cross before them. They'll leave you be then, unless you're a restless soul like themselves."

Long after Eva had left, Adelaide sat, watching the dough rise beneath the blanket she had wrapped around it. When it was time to knead it back down, she rose, peeled back the blanket and started punching, mauling, and squeezing the soggy mass. Standing back, she stared breathlessly at the deflated dough, punched flat into the pan. Hearing footsteps, she quickly tucked the blanket around the pan and ran to her room, pretending to be asleep should it be anyone but Eva.

"The haunts from the head," she muttered as no knock sounded. She trudged back into the kitchen, all senses sharp for a footstep, ready to flee to her room.

Hell, why wait? she thought despondently. Wrapping herself in layers of wool, she hauled on her boots and stepped outside. The falls were churning madly from the winter's thaw, spicing the air and spurning the brook wildly across the meadow. She yearned toward its wantonness; but Suze would come running with blankets and the rosary if she happened to glance through a window and saw her sitting by the damp of the falls, she thought grimly. Heeding Eva's words, and wondering how she'd get the strength, she set off toward Widow's Walk.

Pulling herself along by the branches of the evergreens, she climbed slowly and steadily, pausing every couple of minutes to catch her breath. Twice she thought she'd faint from the exertion, thrice she sat down, leaning against a tree trunk, winded. But finally the steep path broke out of the woods onto the tuckamores, the bald crown of the cliffs, and screaming winds. Cowering, she held tight to her scarf and cap and half crawled, half ran toward a suitable clump of tuckamores with a good rabbit run hollowing out the thickness in its midst. Lying beside it, she burrowed her back into this midst, the interlocking branches overhead forming a canopy that protected her from whatever might fall from the heavens.

"There, scream all you wants," she bade the wind and the haunts. "And if I goes mad, I'll scream with you." Digging farther into this womb, she fashioned her shawl as a pillow and that's how she spent the morning (and many others to come), lying comfortably amongst the tuckamores, sometimes dozing, sometimes gazing unseeingly out over the cliffs, immune to the moaning of the wind flying about her, to the roar of the sea below, to the smell of rot as the earth gave up those things entombed within it, to the acrid taste of salt upon the air, to the wet of the scattered raindrops falling heavily on her cheek. Cocooned. She felt cocooned, with no desire for anything outside herself and no will to act upon what others desired for her. As when a body lies still with fever, its energy consumed by the forces battling within, so she lay; a slight figure with a starkly white face, bundled in heavy woollens and tucked out of the wind amongst the tuckamores, staring vacantly out over the sea.

Several weeks, she managed to get in, several full weeks of solitude, of nestling on the head, of leaving the house soon after Sylvanus left for his fishing grounds and Eva had done her routine morning check-in. Most times, up there on the head, looking out over Old Saw Tooth and the expanse of sea, she saw Sylvanus motoring back around the headland from Little Trite, on his way home from the fishing grounds. She'd scrabble home then, throw some dinner together—leastways, those days she saw him. Sometimes she slept. Didn't matter. Eva was always there with a hot pan of something made for all their dinners.

Having dinner ready for Sylvanus wasn't the problem. It was his trailing about the outport, looking like a lost pup those times he motored home and she was still up on the head, that became the problem. And that piteous look he was taking on—was it for his own exile, she wondered, or hers? For certain he must be seeing her as something broken, a dandelion fluff waffling in the wind. And with Melita or Elsie or Suze, no doubt, taking advantage of his hungering ear, planting seeds of worry about her disappearing from her house each morning, he was starting to plague her about the size of their house, that maybe it wasn't big enough, that she should have more room, and perhaps he should add on a piece come summer—yes, that's what he would do, add on a piece, a nice sunroom with lots of windows so's to cheer her and grow more things come winter. And when he wasn't planning an add-on to the house, he was building upon his other little tasks of pleasing her, bringing more cups of tea to her room, mint berries, delicacies from the sea, the woods.

But as happens when unselfish deeds are offered by a self fraught with fear, everything becomes uncertain except one's own needs. And Sylvanus gave but for a short while, she noted, before he was trotting behind her like the lost pup again, wanting his ears stroked for his good-ness. Receiving nothing but an impatient sigh or vacant look, he'd amble off again, pushing off his boat and spend-ing long hours at sea, puttering about his stage till late in the evenings and then loafing around Jake's firepit, drink-ing brew and bemoaning his fate to his brothers. Or, perhaps he didn't complain to his brothers, she thought. Perhaps it was at his mother's table that he sat, bemoan-ing himself. Whoever. It was Eva who sounded the call.

"Awful late thaw this year," said Eva. "Should've had the seeds in before now." She stood, gazing out through Adelaide's doorway, sniffing the rot of last year's meadow as though gauging its providence. It was middle of June, four months now since the third burial, and four weeks since Adelaide started abandoning her house for the tuckamores.

"I can do that," said Adelaide as Eva lifted the broom out of the corner and started sweeping off the stoop. Her tone was without conviction and Eva carried on sweeping. Comfortable as an old robe was Eva as she puttered around the kitchen most mornings, washing the few cups and sweeping the floors, and Adelaide had grown perfectly content with lolling in the old woman's early-morning visits before donning her garments and slipping out of the house for the head.

This morning, as Eva opened the door, sweeping the crumbs and bit of dirt outside, Adelaide was feeling more listless than usual. She watched moodily as Eva stood on the stoop, tossing a water-sogged doormat over a junk of wood to dry off. The falls trumpeted loudly from the spring thaw. Eva stood for a moment, staring intently at the swollen waters of the brook sluicing past, as though caught in its urgency. Adelaide remembered when she, too, stood in the doorway, carried away by the strength of a morning.

A stream of sunshine flowed through the doorway, gathering in a pool of warmth around her feet. It would be nice upon the cliffs. Eva ought to be leaving soon; it was already past the time she usually left.

"Yes, easy enough to smell the ground these mornings," said Eva, breathing deeply. "Finally. Thank the Lord, I was starting to worry we'd never get the seeds in this year. Can you smell that ground?" she asked Adelaide. "Yes, sir, that's the sign to start hoeing. Abruptly, she stepped inside and, shutting the door, crossed the kitchen with quick, little steps, as though having spoken the thought, it was now a deed to be accomplished. "Promising to be a good summer after all, don't you think?" she added, shaking out the tablecloth into the wood box. "Be good to start gardening again, feel the air. Is your tea all right? I can make more." Sweeping up the few more crumbs falling from the cloth, she opened the door again, flicking them outside, and started wiping down the bin she'd already wiped and filling the teapot she'd already filled.

Fussing is what the old woman was doing, thought Adelaide impatiently, and never one for fussing was Eva.

"Snow got part of the fence knocked down," she was saying, rooting at the ashpan with the poker. "Syllie ought to fix it soon. I don't allow Melita or Elsie can help with the planting this year—they're taking over the old midwife's garden. Too old she is now to be stooping over all day." Eva grunted, straightening out her back. "Feels like I'm getting old myself," she said, hanging the poker off the side of the stove. "Getting harder to bend over."

"I could help, I suppose, ready the soil," said Adelaide absently.

"That's good, then. We'll start day after tomorrow— give it another day to dry up. You want some bread toasted? I might have some bread toasted."

Adelaide jolted. Was it time? Time to be well again? How long hadn't she been well—six weeks? Twelve weeks? A hundred weeks? She couldn't remember this dispiritedness having never been there, could hardly imagine its ever leaving her.

"Suppose everyone's calling me lazy by now, are they?" she asked childishly.

"You've a right to grieve, child."

"Yeah, ten, twelve weeks, right? Like a bout of arthritis." She flushed as Eva paused, slicing the bread. "I gets a bit impatient sometimes," she mumbled apologetically.

"You're holding on better than most of us," said Eva, laying the sliced bread in the oven.

Most of us? Who's us? thought Adelaide, leaning sideways to catch the old woman's face. But was it ever possible to read that startling mix of light grey eyes and black brow? "Eva, will you sit down," she near snapped as the old woman circled the bin like a bird searching out a roost.

A child's shriek, followed by a loud laugh from Suze, sounded from outside, sparing Eva a response and bringing a groan from Adelaide.

"Swear to God, I'll cut out that wall myself," she cried with such misery that Eva looked to her, startled. "Oh, you can never see who's coming or going."

Eva snatched the toast out of the oven, eyeing her sympathetically. "Go to bed if you wants," she said quietly, "and make out you got the cramps. Morning, ma'am," she said pleasantly as the door opened, letting in the rush of the falls and Suze. Her eldest, Benji, stood reluctantly on the stoop, his boots muddied and his face hidden beneath a mock sou'wester.

"Go on, get in. You're not shy as that," chided Suze. "Here, don't go off the mat, take off them boots, my gawd, the mess he's in. And how're ye, the day?" she asked the room at large, face flushed from the exertion of walking and eyes bright as lanterns. "Caught you this morning, didn't I?" She grinned toward Adelaide. "Wherever it is you been going in the mornings. Go ahead, eat your toast before it gets cold. My, Eva, you're spry as a lark. No getting old with you—not like Am's old mother. Cripes, I told Am we might as well move down here to Cooney Arm because she's getting flightier every day and won't leave her house at all now. Certainly, we might all be moving yet, if you paid attention to the news. Sir, that relocating—or location program, or whatever they're calling it—that's something else, that is, relocating people all over the place. Here, fall back on the floor," she ordered her youngster. "I hauls off your boots."

"Resettlement, that's what they're calling it," said Eva, hurrying for the mop. "Let me wipe the water off the floor. This dirty old weather should clear up soon. Silliest thing I ever heard, people floating their houses from one place to another."

"The government's paying a good penny, maid. And like they says, they can't be building roads and light poles to every cove and cranny on the island—and they're promising lots more work for bigger places. I'm surprised there's not more of it going on around here. For sure there's enough people dotted about. Cripes, how hard you got that boot jammed on, my son," she cried, giving the youngster's boot a harder yank. "There! Now, take off that cap. You looks like old Wessy Noseworthy. My, look at his hair, frizzier than mine—better to look like Wessy, I think. Go on over with your aunt Addie—he loves to rock, Addie. How you doing, anyway, my love? My, she looks a lot better, don't she, Eva? Getting some colour back in her face. Lord, no, Addie, don't take him up like that; he stands on the rocker, that's all. Well, sir," she ended as Adelaide pulled the cumbersome boy onto her lap.

Easier to feign a smile and a rock than the cramps and endure more fussing, Adelaide thought resignedly. She tossed an appreciative look at Eva, who ordinarily was wrapping herself in scarves and heading for the door herself at the first sign of company, but who was now making tea for Suze and popping the lid off a cookie tin, offering Benji a gingersnap—as she should, thought Adelaide as sullen as she was grateful, for she'd be safely cocooned upon the head by now had the old woman stopped her fussing and gotten on her way earlier this morning.

With much coaxing and admonishing from his mother and Eva alike, the shy youngster finally whipped out a thick pink pad and stole a gingersnap, snapping it shut in his hand as his mother now coaxed him into saying thank you.

"You'd think, by Lord, somebody was going to snatch it back from him," exclaimed Suze fondly, as the boy hid the cookie inside his pocket. "Great big baby, he is. Mommy's boy, like his dad." She rolled her eyes. "Up with the cough all week, Am was, and my Lord, it don't take much to bring he down, I tell you. Slightest bit of a cough and he's dragging the mattress out of the room and throwing it on the floor beside the stove, and that's where he lies till he's better. That's right—bed only ten feet away, and he's dragging out the mattress to get closer to the stove. Perhaps he thinks it's the stove and not the heat that warms him. I allows he'd be crawled up me arms like one of the youngsters if I let him sometimes. Boys is worse than girls, I dare say. What you say, Eva? You had enough boys—you should know."

"Lots of times I rocked the boys," said Eva.

"And when he coughs! Oh, my dear, his old body shakes—one little cough and it's like he's having convulsions. True! A hiccup from somebody else is a full-bodied sneeze coming from Am. I suppose Sylvanus is the other way, is he?" she asked, turning to Adelaide. "Don't show a thing."

"He don't show much," said Eva, answering for her. "Hard to tell with the strain he's under these days with the markets dropping like this."

Adelaide, who'd been half listening, glanced at Eva, but the old woman was busy serving Suze tea and the buttered toast, nodding to another tirade of Suze's about poor Am worrying himself to death over the trawlers or freezers or some darn thing.

"My Lord, I can't even think about figures like that, can you, Addie?"

"What figures?"

"About what they're hauling out of the water, maid, you was always the smart one. My Lord," she exclaimed as Adelaide drew a vacant look, "I don't believe she knows a thing were talking about. The trawlers, maid, and the factory freezers—and the three hundred tons they took from the water last year." She paused, looking doubtful of her words. "Anyway, I'm sure that's what they said. It's all you hears on the radio these days: how much fish the factory freezers and the trawlers are catching in a year, and now the Russians are out there with two or three more factory boats. Frightened to death, Am is, that they're sucking the grounds dry. He don't say nothing, mind you, but he's not good with hiding things, he's not. Like he says now, once something like this gets started, there's no stopping it. Am's right nervous about it, he is, although he's getting his catch! That's not what they're saying on shore—the inshore fishermen are always the first to feel it. How much fish did Syllie get on hold last year?" she asked Adelaide.

Adelaide blinked. "On hold?"

"In brine, maid. They always got fish in brine all winter. How's they going to dry them they catches in the fall of the year when it's all the time raining?"

"I knows that, Suze, cripes! I don't know how much. Syllie don't talk about them things."

Suze tutted. "Not something you *needs* talk about— something you *knows*, isn't it?"

"Something *you* knows maybe. My father fished on the Labrador—and it's not like I hung around stages. A hundred!" she quickly threw out, remembering something of what Sylvanus had said a few weeks ago. "He got a hundred pounds on hold."

"Pounds!" Suze grinned. "Not *pounds*, maid, he'd have *quintals* on hold. Well, sir, she don't know a thing. Where'd you grow up?"

"A hundred quintal, then," said Adelaide.

"He got none on hold," said Eva.

Adelaide stilled, watching as Eva fussed at the sink, her comment hanging loudly in the air. A sense of disquiet filled the kitchen, and for once Adelaide was grateful when Suze's clacking—if not her rashness—started up again.

"Well, maid, I don't allow Syllie would burden you with his fishing problems. Enough you got on your mind as it is, and I don't worry but that he'll soon have his puncheons filled. Although he got a late start this season—but that's it now; some things can't be altered, hey, Eva?"

Cursed tongue, scorned Adelaide, sliding the youngster off her lap, her hand to her stomach. But there was no fooling those aged eyes now standing before her with the teapot, offering more tea, and no misreading their pointedness as they stared deeply into Adelaide's whilst she said, "Syllie's to himself, no doubt, but there's some that needs to be rocked more than others, and I always felt that he was one."

There. That's what you've been on about all morning, is it? asked Adelaide silently, drawing her hand away from her stomach and proffering her cup. Looking away from the old woman's eyes, she settled back in her rocker, Suze's voice droning in her ears as she prattled on and on about gill nets and how Syllie should get one, seeing how he likes working by hisself, "because for sure he'd get more fish with a gill net than hand-lining, and they're lot easier to handle, maid, a gill net is, because you can move them around to where the fish are. How come he won't go get one, then, when things are getting so bad?"

This last question was directed at Adelaide, who was now rubbing her brow, a tight band forming around her head as she tried to think of something she'd heard Syllie say the other day—no, not Syllie, the radio, it was on the radio, she heard someone talking about gill nets. Oh, that's right, she remembered now, it near sickened her what they were saying about how they hung like curtains in the water, catching fish by the gills in their mesh, and how they were made from a modern kind of fibre, from nylon, and never rotted—which was a good thing, except that they were always breaking from their moorings and then floating about for years in the sea, filling up with fish till their weight sank them to the bottom, and how, when all the fish rotted or were eaten by other fish, they rose again, fishing themselves full, till their weight sank them again, and again, fishing and rotting, fishing and rotting, and entangling other things in their mesh like sharks and seals, and becoming a floating larder for other fish to feed on as they drifted by with their fresh and rotting carcasses. It had nearly turned her stomach, it had, when some fellow came on saying how he come upon one, floated ashore, once, with a half-eaten shark in it, and hundreds of fish, their bellies bit out by seals. She had hurriedly turned off the radio as he started telling how the fish that was still living in the net was flicking and strangling amongst the dead and rotting ones, and how he and his buddy got enough live ones to make up a quintal that morning just by walking on the beach.

"They're not fit," she now said with a shiver, no longer faking the illness in her stomach. "Nobody should be allowed to use them awful things."

"Unless it's the only way left to them," said Eva, and again Adelaide felt undone. She was spared a response by the door swinging open and Melita poking her dimpled face inside. But there were no smiles deepening those dimples this morning, rather a pinched look, as though she was being unnecessarily chafed.

"Should've known where you were!" she exclaimed to Eva, glancing sideways at Adelaide. "You let your fire go out. Elsie is over there now, lighting it. We can start hoeing your garden after dinner, if you wants."

"No, never mind. Work on your own gardens," said Eva. "I'll start day after tomorrow. Addie's working with me."

Melita raised an eyebrow. "Like I said, we can start right after dinner."

"Carry on, carry on," said Eva, shooing Melita back out the door, "and tell Manny to look at my fence when he comes home," she called after her. "The snow got it buckled in."

Suze tutted as Eva shut the door. "My, she was looking some cross at you, wasn't she, Addie? What's you doing, robbing her eggs?"

"They always looks at me like that," said Adelaide. "Hope they don't think you're here because I'm asking you to, Eva."

"None of my business what others are thinking," said Eva, fastening a bandana around her head and slipping her arms into her coat. "I'll see you later this evening. I got a marrow bone broiling for supper. And goodbye to you, little man," she said fondly to the youngster who was occupying himself by the stove, constructing tiers of squares out of splits. "Why don't you bring him by for some molasses candy?" she invited Suze.

"Perhaps I will, maid. Addie, you should go take a nap. You looks tired." Lumbering to her feet, Suze gathered up Benji's coat and boots. "Mommy's little man, that's who he is," she called out to her youngster. "Loves playing by himself, don't you, my love? Come on, then, we goes to Grammy Evie's and gets some molasses candy. Good for your asthma, that is. No, stay where you are," she said as Adelaide made to get up. "We knows our way out. Come on, Benji, hurry on now. Put them splits back."

"No, that's fine, that's fine," said Adelaide, getting up anyway. "I can put them back, looks nice seeing that a youngster was playing here. No, don't worry about that," she hastily added as Suze's face melted into a pained look of sympathy. "For gawd's sake, I didn't mean nothing."

Finally the women were out the door, the youngster straggling behind. A quick check to ensure they truly were crossing over the footbridge, and Adelaide donned her coat and scarf and boots. Downing the last swig of her tea, she let herself out the door, another backwards check to ensure nobody was watching, and she darted across the meadow, all muddied and swamped, and started up the path leading to the head.

CHAPTER SIXTEEN

ROCKING HER MAN

T HAT NIGHT, after Eva and Suze's visit, she took
Sylvanus's hand after he crept into bed beside her,
and laid it on her breast, pressing it tighter as he tried to
pull it away.

"I want to," she said as he whispered, "Shh, no, it's all
right, Addie, it's all right."

Curiously, feeling the warmth of his hand on her
breast, she did want him, wanted him now, and the closer
she moved into the warmth of him, the smell of him, the
more urgent her need became to feel his body around
hers, warming her, cocooning her. And once he had
himself knotted around her and was easing himself inside
her, she lay back, motionless, as might've the bride of
Adam before her first breath of life, for lo, she must've
been dead! For now, with his penetration, it felt as though
life was being stirred once more within her. Nothing of
passion. She'd long since blown out the lamp in the
hallway, obliterating any flickering shadows that might've
prompted his tongue over her skin in their old, exciting

manner. But life—to feel life again, even if it were his. And greedily she raised her haunches for more, wanting passion, too, now. Why not? Why not passion? And she strove harder and harder to reach it, hating his coming release, hating his shrivelling and dying within her as had so much else.

Later, as they lay back together, bodies quivering, hearts pounding, she thought with a grim satisfaction, There, now, Eva, your son's been rocked. Yet, despite her momentary resentment about everyone coming to her, no matter her never asking nor wanting nothing from no one, there had been, in that moment of lovemaking, the stirring of something when she had thought all was dead.

His quiet drew her toward him, and she saw the tension with which he held his face from her and onto the whitish hue of the moonlit window.

"Looks nice outside," she said.

"It's cold," he replied tersely.

"Not in here, though."

"Feels like nothing in here."

She was silent. "Then you knows what nothing feels like," she said, and rolled onto her side of the bed.

"Is that what you feels like, Addie, like nothing?"

She never replied.

"Suppose you got pregnant just then?"

"Suppose I did?"

She felt him move closer. "I won't put you through this agin," he half whispered.

"You? What makes you think it's *you* putting me through this?" she asked, twisting just enough to see the shape of him over her shoulder. "Perhaps there's more than you and me living in this house, Syllie. Perhaps there's a God that reigns here, and it's through them dead babies that He's talking. You ever think of that?"

He half rose in astonishment. "You think you're being punished—that's why our babies are dying? Christ Almighty, Addie, you've never done nothing to be punished for!"

"A thought's as good as a deed!"

"Then we'd all be hanged if we were tried for our thoughts. That's crazy. That's plain crazy thinking, Addie— No, you listen to me," he said urgently as she dropped her head back on her pillow. "You acts like it's just you having and losing them babies. Well, what's He punishing me for, if it's you He wants? You never thinks that, do you—that they're my babies, too? That I might be sick at heart, too?"

She bunched the blankets over her ears, not wanting his words, wanting only the oblivion of darkness, despite the flicker of life she'd just now felt, despite the tinge of hope such life must bring, and oh, sweet Jesus, she needed hope, she needed so very much to feel hope right now. But he was tugging too hard, wanting her back, saying things.

"Addie, I touched them, I touched them babies. One looked like Janie—your sister Janie—her cheek was cold."

"Oh, gawd, Syllie!" She dug deeper into her pillow, her hands over her ears as he carried on saying things— things she'd not hear, not hear. "Stop it! You stop it right now!" she cried out, rising in a frenzy. "Don't say no more! No more!"

"No more about what—no more about what?" he persisted as she dove back into her pillow. "The babies or me? What is it you don't like talking about? Goddamnit,

Addie, I've a right to know how you thinks about every-thing—about me!"

"It's not about you," she cried. "Go away, Syllie. It's enough I rocked you already tonight."

"Rocked me! What do you mean, rocked me? You mean—Jesus Christ, Addie, what kind of way is that to put it? And it was you wanting to—I never wanted to."

"Ooh!" and she clung onto darkness, hearing nothing more of his words, only those still floating through her mind, *Like Janie, like Janie, one looked like Janie—*

Forgive! At some point during the night she awoke, the word resounding through her being. *Forgive!* Forgive what, she near exclaimed out loud, struggling to stay awake, forgive whom? She struggled for a while with the thought, then faded once again into darkness.

PART FIVE

Sylvanus

SPRING TO FALL 1960

CHAPTER SEVENTEEN

STAYED IN HABIT

MISERABLY, SYLVANUS WATCHED her coil away from him, bury herself within her blankets. He lay back with a groan, yearning to lie closer, to wrap himself around her tight little body. But never had she felt so distant. A great loneliness consumed him, more terrible than those wretched days after first seeing her through the window of Eb Rice's partition, and he had paced the beaches and cliffs, pining after her. At least then there had been the anticipation of her. How he longed for her quick tongue, the startling blue of her eyes, the woman who once quivered beneath the passion of his touch. At some point during the night, he felt her stir, awaken, and he shifted a mite closer to feel something of her warmth through the blankets. But he might as well have slept with the folk on the other side of the brook—Tantalus, dying of thirst with the sweetness of a cool spring water forever welling, but never cresting his parched lips.

Unwillingly, his mind trailed back to that wretched morning in the kitchen, weeks ago, when she had leaned against him for comfort, and he had started kissing her, wanting her, and she had pushed him away, staring upon him with loathing. Even now, in the darkness of his room, his face reddened as painfully as it had that morning he fled from his house. Shutting himself up in the dusky light of his stage, he had sat on an overturned puncheon, snatched a tangled pile of fishing line from the summer past and started pulling it apart. Jabbing his finger with a hook, he cursed, then prayed for a thousand more jabs so's to stave off the sight of himself trailing behind her like a love-starved dog, moping about her stoop like a scorned youngster, pining upon his pillow like the rejected lover, and then his boring down upon her in the kitchen like that—and he had jabbed himself again hard, almost deliberately, obliterating with pain the image of him, him, always him, battering himself against that door she'd barricaded herself behind.

He smothered his face in his pillow, cringing from the rawness of the memory, only to be besieged by those others: his moping, his begging, his pining repeatedly, one image spinning behind the other like the quickening ripples in a whirlpool dragging him farther and farther down till he was gulping for breath. Pathetic. He was pathetic in his need. Yet the following morning he was as helpless as a hungering babe at staying his eyes from her as she moved about the kitchen, washing her face, making tea.

She pitied him. He saw that as she kept glancing at him, wringing her hands as she trailed out of the house behind him, watching after him as he crossed over the footbridge on his way to his stage. Once inside, he peered through the doorway, watching as she trudged lifelessly back to the house, and he started feeling the same pity for her as he felt for himself. A fear colder than yesterday's cinders gripped him, for in leading her out of bondage, he had imprisoned himself, and he bent beneath the weight of it, sometimes forgetting the things he held in his hands as he stood jigging his lines, leaning into the wind. Job's comfort, he thought, glancing at the empty belly of his boat despite half an hour's fishing. Normally he'd have thirty to forty pounds jigged and split by now. Things were wrong, horribly wrong this past year. He'd lied to Adelaide about the hundred quintals he had on hold. The fish had stopped running two weeks earlier last fall, leaving his puncheons bereft of the winter's holdings. And he'd lied about his taking an extra week before starting fishing this spring, too. He'd already been a few mornings, and there were no fish running. None! And other inshore fishermen up and down the bay were reporting the same. No fish.

"She's good midshore," Am had said on the wharf in Ragged Rock a few mornings back. "All the liners are making good time, getting lots of fish." He shook his head. "Hate to think I'm taking it away from ye fellows on shore, though."

"Nay," Sylvanus was quick to reply. "No harm with liners. Shooting trawl lines is not going to hurt the fishery. It's them offshore killers, that's the ones," he added disdainfully. "The trawlers scraping the bottom, getting the mother-fish and all them not yet spawned."

"Yes, b'ye. Agrees with you there," said Ambrose.

"And the bloody factory freezers," Sylvanus went on. "Jeezes, multiplying like caplin, aren't they? Soon be more of them out there than trawlers."

He looked toward the plant, all a charm on the inside

with the clanging and banging of machinery, and noisier still on the outside with the half-dozen liners thudding alongside, shouts from the men unloading their fish, and the gulls swooping and screaming. Overtime. Everybody was working overtime this evening, he was told. Making more money. Now, that was a different thought—working overtime. He worked till his fish was done, sometimes long after dark in the fall of the year. He never thought of it as overtime. *Overtime*. He sniffed. What the hell is that, overtime? And so's not to hurt Am's feelings, he bade him good-evening and motored off from shore, staring back skeptically at the dozen or more fishermen, all running and hopping about within an arm's reach of the other, singing and bawling out, making a game out of sneaking off for smokes, and one old-timer finding it funny how he fished every day but hadn't touched a fish in weeks. An industry. They had been made into an industry: these men who had once worked their own lives were now paid to work *overtime* on another's. "When the hell did they work their own lives, then?" Sylvanus muttered scornfully.

Turning his back on the lot of them, he had motored homewards. Back last fall, when the fish had stopped running two weeks early, a score of inshore fishermen in Hampden and Jackson's Arm, and other fishermen up and down the bays, who, like him, were seeing the signs of overfishing, had started up meetings. They were too distant for Sylvanus to travel to, but he paid attention to the news and the few radio programs allowing the fishermen their voice. And he signed the petitions and letters that were circulating, calling for governments to do something, to bloody do something about the trawlers and factory freezers.

Thus far, they'd done nothing. Coddled them, was all. Travelling to a few of the bays, harping the same ole song, "Now, my boys, a bit soon to be calling it overfishing. We all knows there's different lines of fish running out there, different fish swimming the offshore waters, different fish swimming the midshore waters, and different fish again swimming the inshore waters. Yes, we're almost sure of it—and yes, undoubtedly, there's them that swim the gauntlet, but not enough to make the difference to your catch. It's the cold water this year that's ruining the inshore fishery; you must know the cod don't like cold waters. Give her time to warm up, lads, and she'll be ashore, if not this week, then next. Fishery's always been up and down, up and down; but she'll be back, she always comes back, and worry you not about the foreigners. We're working with them—not easy to police, you know, the North Atlantic waters; but we're talking to them. Every day we're talking to them and their governments, figuring what's best for all, and in the meantime we're building you more plants and boats to ensure you get your fair share of the catch. She'll be fine, lads, and the fish will be running soon enough. Watch and see if they don't, watch and see."

"Watch and see," muttered Sylvanus on this cold morning of watching his Addie trudge lifelessly back to their house, and the belly of his boat still empty. Watch and see what? The day when there's no fish to jig? What's the point of watching, then, when there's no fish left to jig?

The sea rose and fell beneath him, but he was unable to be lulled by her murmurs this morning, unable to lose thought to the upward, downward jerking of his jiggers as he trawled her depths. Scared. He was scared that that's all he'd be doing till the day's end, standing and jigging with his hooks trailing uselessly through empty waters. He raised his eyes to the sun already rising, and his morning's work not yet started. What was wrong with it—the sky? The thought jolted him when it hit. There were no gulls. Where the hell were the gulls? Christ, and he gave a short laugh. Of course there would be no gulls. Why would they beg breakfast from empty waters?

His jigger hooked. Jeezes. His knees bent in relief, and he sat, hauling in his line. A cod, a good-sized cod. Before he'd chance to bleed it, the other jigger hooked, and a tremor of excitement shot through him. Scrabbling, he hauled in another fair-sized fish, holding the wet, shimmering body before him and near planting kisses on that puzzled, gulping mouth. And then there was another. And another. They were running. Thanks be to Jesus, they were running, and he silently repeated his prayer of gratitude. Left arm up, right arm down; right arm up, left arm down; up, down, up, down, another hook, another fish, another hook, another fish, and he jigged and he jigged, and after fifty pounds or more, he leaned more comfortably into the lop. She was back. The mother was back. And shamed he should be for doubting her doting old ways. She changed habits sometimes, was all, he chided himself, she changed habits. And what harm was that? What harm with Addie wanting to leave the house for a few hours each morning, taking a stroll upon the head, getting a different view on things? Everybody can't be stayed in habit like me, he thought, not even fish.

He grinned his relief up to the heavens for the mother's return. One thing he ought to be sure of by now was that the mother would be forever fertile, and the salty taste of her depths would forever dampen his lips. He checked his thoughts, thinking of his Addie, how she looked this morning, trailing out of the house behind him, her face the paleness of a winter's moon—Addie, his Addie. And as though he had uttered her name out loud, he lowered his head with the shame of his wanting her.

IT WAS A WEEK or more after they'd started running he noticed the pattern of the smaller fish. Scarcely anything over a ten pounder in either of his fishing holes. Hauling anchor, he sought out a different run of cod, the larger blackbellies nestling in the undersea gully of Woody's Inlet. When it, too, yielded smaller size, he motored to the shelves and crannies of Gull Rock, a shoal that rose out of the water at low tide and formed part of a rugged ridge that ran deep into the ocean's floor. From there he chased down the vagrants at Peggy's Plate, and the cosmos at Nolly's Shelf, and the scrub cod that favoured the smooth, sandy surface of Petticoat Falls. Then finally he made the two-hour run to an old settlement, long since abandoned, and jigged the ridges and plates off its shores.

Nothing over a ten pounder. And nothing over a ten pounder up and down the bay, either; nor midshore; and according to word from the trawlers, there were no big fish offshore, either. Gone. All the big fish gone, sucked into the bowels of the colossal leviathans that were starting to crowd the offshore as thick as the trawlers were crowding the inshore.

Blisters popped up on Sylvanus's hands from his wearying hours of jigging. The smaller the fish, the more hours to jig a quintal. And harder it became to toss back those undersized fish, those that had yet to spawn. But, by

jeezes, he would toss them back, he muttered one
morning, unhooking the fourth underweight that past
hour from his jigger. Tossing it back into the sea, he
watched it vanish beneath his boat. Tomorrow's catch, it
was, and God's speed, for what was he without tomorrow's
catch? Without the milt of this mother who now rocked
his boat as he stood trawling her belly?

Cloud shadowed the sun and a stiff breeze veering
out of the sou'east shivered inside the open neck of his
oilskins. It would blow before the tide let out, but as long
as the fish were feeding, he'd cling to this spot. He
couldn't afford not to. Another hour he jigged, his catches
becoming fewer, his stomach emptying, and his legs trembling for release. The tide was starting to ebb, taking with
it the food holding the cod to shore. Still, it was another
two hours' fishing before the tide was fully out, and as long
as his boat remained half full, he'd stand here.

Twenty minutes of jigging with no hook, he pulled
anchor and motored to Gregan's Hole, a quarter mile up
the shore. And with his legs now buckling from a growing
lop and his stomach gnawing from hunger, he set ashore,
hurriedly building a stone pit. Lighting a fire with bits of
dried grass and driftwood, he rummaged through his fish
for the smallest of the small, gutted and cut it into bits,
and tossed it into a cast-iron frying pan with some onion
and soaked hardtack he always took to sea with him.
Setting it across the firepit with some water from a nearby
brook, he lay back on the beach, arms cushioning his
head, and closed his eyes against the greying sky, relishing
the ache falling from his bones. Sleep slackened his mind.
Ten, fifteen minutes later, he awakened to the sumptuous
smell of stewed fish, tack, and onions.

Lifting the pan off the fire, he dumped the brewis onto a clean, flat rock, hungrily fingering the food into his mouth. A cup of tea, strengthened with blackstrap molasses, a pork bun, and he was back, bucking in his boat, his stomach full and warm, and jigged for another hour, his back to a breeze that would be full-blown before noon. Hopefully, he'd be ashore by then, save his mother from worrying. He was usually home long before this with his boat heavily laden. Thirty pounds more and he sat down, still jigging, his shoulders slouching forward, his hands smarting. The tide was almost out by now, the fish scarcely biting. And the wind was building. Time to haul anchor and motor home. Not so bad, he thought, eyeing the fish in his boat. Not so bad. Just taking bloody forever, was all, to get a decent catch.

Back on shore he forked his fish onto his stagehead and loaded them inside the stage. Slapping one after the other onto his skinning table, he commenced slitting bellies, gurry flying from his skinning knife, down the trunk hole and into the water, feeding the gulls waiting and squabbling outside. As he worked, his knife became more sure, his hands more hurried, creating a rhythm that needed only the feel of his fingers to execute. Once the fish was gutted, he reached for a different knife, one with a more rounded blade, and started at the fish again, this time cutting it more deeply behind the backbone, slitting it from gill to tail, further opening it till it laid out flat, shaped like a butterfly. This done, he scrubbed them each with sea water from a large trawl tub, quickly and carefully cleansing off bits of blood and entrails and any other thing that could rot or spoil its look, and then laid them out in puncheons, layering each with salt; more on the thick part, less on the thinner parts, and always the least amount needed without risking souring. For it was the more lightly salted fish that got the highest grade, and no matter the fatigue foiling his fingers as he stayed on his feet, sometimes till one in the morning, working the double load of littler fish, it would never be the business of Sylvanus Now to work a lesser grade.

More than his legs and fingers were fatigued that summer. For as the season wore on, his mind crippled, too, with the onslaught of figures he'd never had to think about before with regards to fish: hundreds of thousands of tons being fished from the sea by countries he'd never given thought to; the Germans appearing on the banks with thirty or forty brand-new factory freezers; and the Spanish not content with the hundred trawlers she had out there, but now building more; and the Japanese starting to come on board with the largest fishing fleet in the world; and Poland and Romania and Greece and Belgium and the Netherlands and a whole host of others preparing to set forth onto the banks. And now this latest, the fishermen cried, the stinking Russians had dropped their mesh size, scooping up millions of the smaller cod as they targeted one different species after another—herring, mackerel, squid, caplin—fishing each to the point of exhaustion, not to mention the extra two hundred trawlers they'd brought along, complementing their thirty-five brand-new factory freezers. And all the rest of them, the Spanish, the Portuguese, the French, and half the bloody globe were hunkering in colossal ships over the fishing grounds two hundred miles from shore, the sea lit up like a starry sky; spring, summer, winter, and fall, sucking, sucking, sucking the mother dry.

Late one evening, about the middle of summer, Sylvanus putted ashore to the unlikely sight of Jake and Manny waiting for him on his stagehead. Noting his fish already gathered off the flakes and stacked into faggots, he rose, a sudden consternation overtaking him.

"Face on you, this evening," called Manny jovially, as Sylvanus tossed him his painter. "Jeezes, you gets blacker every time I sees you."

"What're ye at?" asked Sylvanus,

"Jigging for tommycod. About as big as what you got there, for sure," said Manny, peering down at his catch.

Sylvanus grinned, relaxing a bit beneath Manny's easy tone. "Probably easier to catch, too. What's up, b'ye, what're ye at?" he asked, gesturing toward his cleaned flakes.

"Slack as you're getting, we figured we'd give you a hand," said Manny.

Jake snorted. "Slack as *he's* getting, he means," he said to Syllie. "Cripes, got to drive him with a whip these days. Good thing we got clear the flakes when we did. Slower than Father's old sawhorse, he is these days."

Manny grinned. "Not surly, is he? Don't mind him, this evening, Syllie, b'ye. The tap broke off his barrel and he lost half his brew down the dirt."

"Lost it! Old man, I wouldn't've lost nothing if you weren't so stun—trying to catch it in a leaky bucket. That's right," he said incredulously to Sylvanus, "instead of rolling the barrel so's the tap's pointing up and stemming the flow, he leaves it as is and tries catching everything flowing out with a bucket—forty gallons of brew in a gallon bucket, and a leaky one at that! Jeezes, no trouble getting you to dip the moon out of the water, buddy. I believes it now, the time you thought your horse was drowning through his arse. True story, sir," he argued over the loud protest from Manny. "His horse's hind legs and arse broke down through the pond ice, and he"—Jake pointed at Manny—"was dancing all over the place for us to quick, quick, haul him out afore he drowns. Fool!" scoffed Jake. "One of the old-timers was after telling him a horse takes in water through his arse."

"Not just any old-timer," said Manny, "but old Pete Warford never cracked a smile in his life, the old bastard; face like a mourner. Whoever thought he'd crack a joke? Only time he talks is in the confession box. Go on with ye," he gave over as his brothers kept chortling. "But I'll tell you one thing," he said, making a last attempt to get inside the joke, "that horse looked like she was with foal when we got her out, she was so full of piss. Old man, you want to see a horse piss; all night she was pissing—Mother remembers that—the old horse, pissing all night. We had to take her down on shore, flooding Mother's garden, she was. Laugh all ye like now, but that horse was pissing for two days after we dragged her out of that water, so perhaps she was taking it in through her arse; perhaps there's something to it, after all. And besides, that old bastard Pete wouldn't know a joke if it was up his arse. He must've seen something like it before."

"Right, he did," said Jake. "He seen a horse swim across a pond once and take a piss right after, and that's the size of it. And then he told it to you—" Jake broke off as one of his boys sang out to him from down the shore.

"Yes, go on, go on, get started!" he called out. Turning to Manny, "We're going to have to hurry up, b'ye; the boys is waiting."

"The boys," scoffed Manny, bringing an extra pitch-fork out of the stage. "They can wait all they wants now. I'll be there when I'm ready." And leaping down into the boat, he started helping Sylvanus prong the fish up on the stage. "That's the third camp we've helped them build this year," he said to Sylvanus. "Gets into fights, they do, and one tears it down on the other. Jeezes, they're like savages. What's you, lame?" he goaded, pointing to the empty fish-basket beside Jake's feet.

"You're both going to be if ye don't get the hell off my stage," said Sylvanus, leaning on his fork, eyeing the two brothers suspiciously. "What's into you this evening? What're you doing in my boat?"

"We're buying a skiff and we wants you with us," said Jake.

Manny never faltered with his forking. "That's right, Jake, my son, nothing like buttering him up, first. By jeezes, you missed your calling, you did. A priest, that's what you should've been; you'd have everybody converted by now. Anyhow," and he leaned on his fork, looking soberly at Sylvanus, "that's about the short of it, brother. The government's offering money for a smaller-size longliner—skiffs. Thirty footers. Half the size of a liner. Better, much better—not so much overhead, and they're safe enough for midshore fishing. And anyhow, like Jake said, we're getting one."

"You'll be foolish if you don't throw in with us," said Jake, as Sylvanus, hearing Manny through, went back to pronging up his fish. "Nothing left of the inshore. Bit of plankton for the gulls, that's all the inshore's going to be soon enough, unless we haves another war. Cured the problem before," he argued as Manny rolled his eyes.

"Blow the bastards off the water for a few years, that'll do it, that'll bring the fish back. Father and them seen it with First War, and we seen it too, after the Second—"

"Yes, b'ye, ye-es, for jeezes sake, don't take us through that, agin," groaned Manny. He turned back to Sylvanus, who hadn't broken stride with his pronging.

"She's changing, Syllie, my son, everything's changing."

Sylvanus nodded. "Heard it all before. When you scrapped your jiggers for the traps, I heard it, and when you scrapped your flakes for the plants, I heard it. What're you going to do when you got nothing left to scrap, that's what I'd like to hear."

"Beg at your table, I suppose," said Manny dryly. "From the size of them fish you're catching, I don't allows you'll have any problem feeding us. Syllie!" He laid his hand on his brother's arm, stilling it. "It's staring us in the face. Them small fish you got there is the first sign—nay, not the first, the second; the first was the season getting shorter. And now we got smaller fish— that's the second big sign she's being overfished. The big ones is all gone, and the young's not getting a chance to grow old."

"Yes, that I knows," said Sylvanus quietly. "And I appreciates your offer. But I'll stick with her. She's been running good the past few weeks. Maybe it'll right itself, she always do."

"Think about it, buddy. That's all I'm asking from you—think about it."

"Already did. And like I said, I'm sticking with it. If I changes my mind and wants in, ye'd be the ones I'd go with." He nodded up to Jake appreciatively, then started back pronging.

Jake grunted. "Oh, you'll be wanting, make no mistake, you'll be wanting—but it'll be too late then, when all hands is gone."

"Comes to that, I'll go with somebody else."

"I'm not talking about the boat. Brother, listen here, there's things happening that's not going to be too good if you don't start thinking ahead."

"Always going to be things happening," said Sylvanus.

"You're not listening," said Jake. He paused, getting a warning look from Manny. Muttering something unintelligible, he started scooping the fish his brothers had tossed up near his feet into the fish baskets stacked alongside.

Sylvanus cast a suspicious look at Manny. "What's he on about?" he asked.

"Nothing," said Manny. "Trying to figure things out, is all. We're going to use gill nets when we gets the skiff. I don't like trawl lines. Perhaps that's what you ought to get, a gill net. Make it easier on yourself."

"Gill nets! You mean ghost nets." Sylvanus stuck his fork in his gunnels, shaking his head at his brother. "Old man, I wouldn't put something that dirty out in the water."

"They're only dirty if they breaks from their moorings. We'll make sure ours won't break."

"Won't break! How the jeezes can you help that when the trawlers are forever ripping up the nets? That's uglier than trawlers, them gill nets are."

"Yup, like Father," grunted Jake. "Thinks he's better than everybody else, and too bloody stuck in his ways to listen."

"Oh, to hell's flames with Father," cried Sylvanus. "You're no better than the stinking foreigners if you joins in with them, buying bigger boats and bigger nets. And if you thinks that's going to solve anything—all hands going midshore—you got your head up your arse."

"Which is where yours is, buddy, if you thinks standing on shore, blathering, is going to get you somewhere," said Jake, his voice rising. "And I gives a fat shit now about what you or anybody else thinks when I got a family to feed, and *dick* is all your mouthing is going to do, when all hands is too busy fishing to listen."

"Simmer down, simmer down. Syllie didn't mean it like that," cut in Manny, but Jake was riled, his bony cheeks a scratchy red. Kicking aside the basket of fish, he wagged a finger at Sylvanus.

"And I'll tell you something else, too, brother. I'll take the last goddamned fish out there if I got to; rather me than them. And if you ever gets a youngster, you'll be out there no different than the rest of us, trying to scrounge up a meal. So stick your preaching up me arse because if that's where me head is, I've a better chance of hearing you."

"Listen to them, listen to them, like the dogs," cried Manny as Jake shoved back inside the stage, Sylvanus near snarling after him. "Imagine hauling nets with the two of ye in the mornings. Cripes, you'd have the Virgin Mary gnashing her teeth." He sighed, the stage door slamming as Jake let himself out on the other side. "Listen, brother," he said more calmly, as Sylvanus, his mouth a grim line, pitched the last fish up on the stage. "It's fine if you don't come with us, but you can't keep going like you are, either—jigging. Not by the looks of them boils on your wrists. And what time did you get off the flakes last night— two o'clock? I knows because Mother was watching."

"Give it up, Manny," said Sylvanus wearily. "I'm doing what I'm doing till there's no more doing, and then I'll think of some other way. But I'm just not packing it in first sign, is all."

"First sign?" Manny sat back on the thwart, looking up at his brother in resignation. "Fine," he said. "Fine. Just let me say this—I'll just say it once!" he yelled as Sylvanus grunted in exasperation. "It's not all that bad, all right. Getting rid of the flakes is not all that bad. Just hear me, all right, just hear me. Since we started selling straight to the plant, I sees a big difference in a day. Don't have to be out in the stage all hours of the night, gutting and scrubbing, and the least bit of rain sending me running to the flakes, or else a whole bloody load of fish is spoiled. You don't have to hang on to all of it, Syllie. There's a comfort, brother, in hauling your nets and passing your catch straight to the plants—especially now, with other things that might be coming. Anyway." He rose to leave as Sylvanus's eyes brooded onto his.

"What other things?" asked Sylvanus. "What's this other thing you keeps hinting about? Well, you might as well tell me," he hollered as Manny brushed him aside, leaping upon the stage. "What? Is bloody Noah floating by on his ark? Oh, I knows—he can't find a pair of codfish, so he's after mine, is that it, brother? Noah wants me fish—oh, and me stage, too?" he asked as Manny turned, jabbing a finger back at him. "Oh, Jesus Christ, Noah wants me stage."

"Bang-o, buddy. I didn't know how to tell you," said Manny. "Better tell him to hold off, though, because the first load of fish me and Jake catches in our new skiff, we're dumping right here on your stagehead. That's right,

bawl all you likes, now," he said over Sylvanus's scoff, "but
that's just what we're doing—giving you our first catch.
So, start hauling up your bleeding boat before it's too late
in the evening and you're out on the water in the dark.
Got Mother drove off her head, worrying, you have."

Sylvanus threw down his prong. "Now, you listen
here!" he said angrily.

"Nothing left to listen to," said Manny. "Come over
after you've done, and have one of Jake's new brews. He'll
be fine, then. Don't give me that," he said threateningly as
Sylvanus snorted. "Mother don't like goings-on like this.
And look, there's a fish beneath your boot, not even bled.
Getting slack, my son, getting slack."

Sitting back on the thwart as Manny vanished inside
the stage, Sylvanus picked up the missed fish, his hands
shaking. Making Mother worried, he mocked. She'd be
more bloody worried seeing me off to sea with Jake in the
mornings. She'd be worried then!

Pulling his skinning knife out of his boot, he slit the
fish's throat, imagining it his own should fortune send him
aboard a thirty-foot skiff, hauling in gill nets for hours on
end, listening to Jake's ongoing sputtering, and the
arguing and spitting and farting of two or three others
crowding around him, spoiling the quiet of a morning.

"Not a bleeding chance," he muttered out loud, "not
a bleeding chance." Climbing out of his boat, he angrily
cleared off his splitting table, trying to figure the one
thing making him the angriest—the overfishing or
arguing with Jake. Attacking his small pile of fish, he
started gutting and splitting, gutting and splitting, his
hands creating a rhythm that eventually hammered all else
outside, no matter he was missing that sense of comfort

that always came when he centred himself amongst his labours; no matter his half-emptied puncheons were stealing his sense of worth; no matter the dying babies and how desperately he lay beside his Addie, wanting her; no matter it took him sixteen hours to do what normally took twelve. His mainstay was making fish. And making them proper. And when the last one was gutted and split and carefully laid out in the puncheons, he rose with a grim satisfaction and stepped outside, taking a stretch and a breath of clear air.

It was growing dark. His mother's lamp was already lit, her face peering through the window—and was that Addie? Yes, it was Addie, letting herself out through his mother's gate, picking up some rocks and whipping them at a couple of crows having a late-evening feast on some garbage rotting near the side of the yard. She was most times at his mother's since she started helping in the garden. She glanced his way, her features lost in the hour just past twilight.

"Are you finished for the day?" she called out.

He nodded, feeling a warmth as she stepped into his mother's lamplight and smiled, the shadows playing over her face. She started toward him, and he sucked in his breath, cursing that he stood in his oilskins, streaked with blood, and with the stench of gut upon his hands.

Backing into his stage, he called out, "I'll be home in a minute." Closing the door, he glimpsed through the window, watching as she stood there for a minute before turning homeward. He glanced about his stage, dimly lit by an old kerosene lantern, its mantle partially blown. After pumping more air into the lantern for more light, he skimmed out of his oilskins, and whereas in the past he had scrubbed his hands and face before going home, this evening he stripped proper—sweater, shirt, pants, and underwear—and stood naked in the shadows. Unclamping the cold-water hose, he hosed the length of himself, then started lathering the broad expanse of his chest, the length of his arms, digging deeply into the black, hairy crux of his pits. He bent over with a grunt, soaping his navel, his loins, his heavily muscled thighs, his bowed knees, his calves, all hairy, black. "Like the beast," he grunted, "like the mute beast."

His teeth chattering with cold, he hosed himself off, then scrubbed himself dry with a ratty, threadbare towel and hastily climbed back into his dirty clothes. Holding down his head, he hosed his hair, the cold water numbing his scalp. Flicking it dry, he finger-combed it back in place, and getting a tidied view of himself in a cracked piece of pane, he stepped back outside, feeling somewhat heartened, and hurried home.

CHAPTER EIGHTEEN

OLD SAW TOOTH

ONE LATE AFTERNOON, and the tide already partway in, Sylvanus shoved off his boat with a heavy heart. He ought to be out on the water by now, already jigging, not just pushing off from shore. But with the small fish he was hooking these days, it took forever to catch his morning quota. And by the time he'd cleaned and salted them, and laid out those in the faggots and turned those on the flakes, well, it felt like he was always racing the tide to get back out for the evening catch, and then racing against the falling light, now that fall was taking on, to get back to shore.

It was not just the lateness of the hour that was deflating him this afternoon. He was getting used to that, fishing all hours of the day and evening. No, something a whole lot worse he'd just heard on the fishermen's broadcast was causing the sickness in his stomach. The haddock fishery was at the point of collapse. Collapse! A fish that was as abundant upon the sea as the cod near gone. Fished out. Fear swept up and down the shores like fire.

Didn't we say, Sylvanus silently cried out, standing in his boat, steering his way through the neck, didn't we bloody say? And the cod won't last, either. This shows she can't last—not when the spawning grounds are being fished out. What kind of fool can't figure that? What kind of fool can't figure we're farmers, not hunters; that we don't search out and destroy the spawning grounds, that we waits for the fish to be done with their seeding, and then they comes to us for harvesting? What kind of fools can't figure that what's happening to the haddock will happen to the cod? That's it's already starting with the smaller fish and shorter seasons? That what's happening on top of the water is a sure measure of what's happening beneath? That with the mother's immeasurable depths and complexities, a fish once lost can never be found? What kind of fools—what kind of *fools* can't figure that?

And that's when a great silence fell upon him. Any man could figure that logic. What truth, then, was this?

They knew. The weight with which this thought struck him forced him to sit. They knew. Of course they knew. Everybody knew. Governments. Corporations. Merchants. Even the fishermen working the big boats knew. But they would keep doing it anyway, like a youngster gobbling down the profits from his jelly bean business—knowing the difference, but unable to stop.

Sickened, he anchored two stone's throws past Pollock's Brook and tossed his jiggers into the sea; left arm up, right arm down; right arm up, left arm down. Left, right, left, right. Two hours went by with a quarter of the bites he was used to getting. His stomach knotting with hunger, he rowed up to Gregan's Hole and went ashore. There, he kicked together a pit and skinned the smallest cod in his boat, throwing it into his pan with hardtack and onions.

"Government," he grunted, stoking the fire so's to stew the fish faster and get back to jigging, "a bloody government is what we needs, one who's not afraid to stand up and stave off this glut off our shores, who's not scared to go out and do what Jake says, blow the bastards off the water. And never mind talk; talk don't do nothing because nobody's listening to talk. And for the name of jeezes, don't give us another ten years of research because your last ten years proved to be wrong, and now you needs another ten to figure why. A limit is what we needs, a goddamn two-hundred-mile limit like the Chileans got so's to protect the spawning grounds—our spawning grounds!—and drive all them foreigners the hell home to fish out what's left of their own shores."

Fingering back the last of the fish, he shucked the bones to the gulls and started back out to sea. Anchoring over Gregan's Hole, he stood wearily, left arm up, right arm down, right arm up, left arm down, right down, left up, left down, right up, his mind tiredly playing over and over the rest of the broadcast he had heard that morning, the governing fathers responding to the accusatory voices of the fishermen after the announcement of the collapsing haddock fishery.

"Yes, b'yes, no doubts you've seen things, learned things over time, and no doubts your bits of lore might have some truth," they had said placatingly, "but it's not weighty enough to be sorted—not like the research our experts are doing on the trawlers and the factory freezers. No, sir, there's still lots of fish in the sea. We know because we're catching them—and it's what you need to do, too, as we keep telling you. What you need is a better means of catching them, a better way of processing them, and better markets to sell them to. And forget this *blasting boats out of the water* business; you can't go blasting boats off the water, not when most of them have been fishing out there longer than you have, and not when they've families to feed, just like you. But a boundary, yes, you've a right to a boundary, and we're working on getting one, the day is coming, b'yes. Just give us time, give us time."

"Time," muttered Sylvanus, tossing his jiggers back out into the water, "time for what? For us all to starve?"

He jigged for near on two hours. Still his catch was far lower than what it ought to have been. Raising his eyes, he checked the clouds—feathered whites, racing a bit hard, but it was a blue sky with lots of light left yet, and the sun nice and warm for late September. Instead of heading home with the belly of his boat not quite fed, he heaved on the flywheel and putted another thirty or forty minutes out on the open waters of the bay, jigging the undersea gully of Woody's Inlet, searching for the larger blackbellies.

The fates were with him, and he hooked a fish within minutes after tossing his line—not the size he was hoping for, but, hell, he was starting to be appreciative of a tommycod these days. They continued biting, and he felt some of the tension leave his body. Not all bad, I suppose, he thought. Stories drifted daily up and down the bay about the lone fisherman forced into trap fishing, the liners, or the plants. Some poor bastards were forced to move, not just by the lull in fishing, but by their wives and youngsters, too, buying into the bloody nonsense resettlement program the government was pushing more rapidly

these days. He shook his head. It didn't make sense to
him, moving people from a smaller place to a larger one—
easier to build roads, no doubt, and drive poles for electricity. But not to find fish. You had to go farther along
the shore to find fish—a cove or arm or headland where
nobody lived—then hunt out different spots, different
runs. That's how they'd always done it in the past, and it
made more sense than this crowding families into the one
cove and the fishermen out on the same shelf, especially
when those already settled there had the best spots. It was
not as if you could drop anchor beside somebody else's
boat and start fishing their hole. Nor were there signs
planted on the water telling everyone where the plates and
ridges and shelves were located, and where best to find a
good run and the kind of fish that fed there. Not an easy
thing to move and start figuring the belly of the sea
around you. Might as well give yourself the best chance if
you did have to move, and go where nobody else lived and
get yourself first pick.

Some of the morning's gloom started leaving him as
he slowly filled his boat. As bad as things were getting, he
was lucky, he supposed. Least nobody else hand-lined in
Cooney Arm, which gave him lots of room to move about
and lots of holes to fish. Perhaps it was taking him longer
on the water to get lesser catch than he had before, but he
didn't mind the extra work, as long as she held out the rate
she was—as long as she just bloody held out!

Despite the late hour, the sun grew warmer. He threw
off his oilskin, feeling its heat burning through to his skin
like a strong liniment. Right arm up; left arm down; left
arm up; right arm down; up, down; up, down; right, left;
left, right. He yawned, starting to feel the length of the

day. Times, he swore, if it wasn't for the fish hooking his lines, he could pass himself off as a horse and sleep standing up. And perhaps he did sleep, he was to tell himself later, and that's why he stayed jigging as long as he did that evening. He should've known better—he did know better; smaller boats fished inshore, not midshore, not offshore. They fished inshore because there was always time to get the hell home if a bad wind started up, whether it was a full-on blowout, a die-down easterly, or the savage nor'westerly that, without warning, screeched out of a sunny-lit sky like twisters, skidding into the sea, and sending drifts of water ten, twelve feet in the air before they spread out like a black cloud overhead, falling back into the water like a heavy rain. And it was this, the savage nor'westerly, that first got him.

He rode it just fine. Spiteful as they were, there were saving graces in nor'westerlies. Their squalls were isolated gusts, never measuring more than five to ten feet wide when they struck the sea, and they were sporadic; a squall here, a squall there, never more than two striking at once, and then, never less than hundreds and hundreds of feet apart. Which gave Sylvanus lots of room to figure where the next one *wouldn't* hit. Yet, instead of grabbing a paddle and rowing to where the first squall had just now purged itself, he stayed where he was, pulling in a hooked fish.

"Christ!" he muttered as another squall skidded into the sea a direct line behind him, raising a sheet of water and sending it hurtling toward him and his boat. But hell if he was going to lose this fish! Madly hauling in his line, he hunched down in his boat, wishing to jeezes that he'd had time to haul his oilskin back on. A gale of iced water sluiced against him, drenching him, knocking him sideways. He swore and clenched more tightly to his line, gripping the thole-pins as his boat rocked and bucked like a overwrought ram.

"Son of a bitch!" he swore again. But no matter. His boat was sound, and the squall was gone as quick as it hit, sucking up its venom for another strike some distance away, leaving him sitting on a patch of sea that within minutes was calmer than a duck pond. And the sky still blue.

Flicking aside the fringe of black hair now plastered to his forehead and streaming salt water into his eyes, he finished hauling in his fish and bled it. His hands—his whole body—were becoming chilled from the water seeping through his garnsey into his bones. Tearing off the garnsey, he pulled on an old workshirt from the cuddy, hauled it on over his wet undergarments, and donned his oilskin. The squalls were pitching more frequent than he liked, stirring up water first to this side of him, then to the other, till it felt as if he were sitting on a giant checkerboard, waiting to be hurtled to the wayside.

Time to get the hell home, he silently muttered, then cursed as a black ridge out on the open waters, past Cape Ray, caught his eye—the nor'westerlies were circling about into a full-out blow coming from the east. It was possible to sit through a nor'westerly, if you had faith in your boat, but only fools attempted sitting through a full-out blow in a motorboat loaded down with fish and a half hour from shore. Coiling his lines, he lunged for his motor, cursing at the bloody nemesis keeping him from a decent hour's fishing this evening. Studying the sky once more and seeing dark clouds moving in from the east with dark fog trailing below, he opened his throttle, avoiding the dead straight route to the head, and steered toward shore instead. In twenty minutes the winds would either be full pitch and levelling off, or building for a stronger blow. Better to be close to shore than caught going through the snarling waters of the neck in a full-out blow.

Ten minutes later and the wind had outraced the fog, bumping his boat along on choppy waters. Half hunkered beside his engine, he leaned his elbow on his knee, watching the cold, galloping winds and the dirty-grey clouds outstrip the warm sunny evening. Dismal. The only time he didn't like the water was when he was being shuttled about by the easterlies with damp grey sky pressing down on him. The wind was battling harder now, and he nosed himself a bit more in alignment to the shoreline so's to keep most of the wind at his stern and not be broadsided. It was easier motoring into a wind than having it push at his rear like this, threatening to swamp him with a far-flung breaker. Little Trite popped out from behind a bend, its windswept shoreline bereft of souls, the lamp-lit windows like little suns through evening's falling light. He tightened his throttle. Good place to put ashore—but, hell, the fish had to be cleaned, and he was a dirty mess, and swear to gawd, he could smell roasted mutton trailing from Mother's door. Besides, another ten minutes and he'd be rounding the head—but, hell, in this wind the neck would be broiling beneath its breakers. Still, he'd seen his brothers put through in rougher waters than this.

He released his hold on the throttle, steering himself farther offshore. He'd run it. Besides, it might ease off yet. Few minutes later he started doubting himself. A swell rose ahead of him, foaming a sickly white as it slapped against his bow, near cresting his gunnels. No, sir, this was one gale that wasn't going to reach its peak after twenty minutes' building. She was going to blow long and hard into the night, and she was building fast. He glanced back and was startled to see the silent wall of grey almost upon him, a tentacle of which crept out, circling cold around his neck. He shifted around uneasily and saw the black, rocky ledge of Old Saw Tooth coming up before him, foaming like a mangy dog through the half light. Jeezes, now, how'd he let this happen? He swore and steadied himself as the wind started picking harder. The bow of his boat rose up on a swell, and he sickened to see that it was part of Old Saw Tooth's undertow. With a growing fear, he watched helplessly as it took him off course, steering him toward the black, jagged rock ledge. He sank down the other side and was immediately lifted by another, his bow pointed fully at Old Saw Tooth now, a sheet of spray shooting over the molars upon which he imagined his father and his brother clinging, their boat bashing about them.

A hoarse cry sounded on the wind, followed by another, full of warning, and he cried out himself as his bow rose higher, higher, on the swell and he lost sight of land, of Old Saw Tooth. Immediately it crested and he dipped downwards, his innards relieved as Old Saw Tooth reappeared, still some distance ahead.

The cry sounded again, "Hey! Hey!" hard, hoarse cries, and he stared around in fright, searching the sea, dreading the sight of his father's drowned head bobbing out of the water and screaming before him. "Hey! Hey!" and he rose, shouting, screaming, "He-ey, He-ey," back into the wind.

Two straight-back figures appeared on shore, racing along the water's edge, waving frantically with both hands, shouting, "Hey! Hey!" It was the Trapps. Another hard gust hit him. He lurched sideways and quickly hunched down by his engine, cutting back further on his throttle. Grabbing the tiller, he cut her too sharply shoreward and was near broadsided by the wind. He straightened a bit, smelling for the first time Old Saw Tooth's foul breath of rotted kelp and gull shit. He steered farther toward shore, fighting from veering too sharply. Another hard gust, another swell, rendered his rudder useless, and he could see Old Saw Tooth's palate. Jesus Christ, and he was full of crazed disbelief at how he'd let this happen, at how sudden, how bloody sudden it all was.

"Screw you, you bastard!" he roared, and seized by fear, he shut down his motor, jarred his tiller as far leeward as he could, and grabbed his paddles, plunging them into the sea. Minutes. He was minutes from Old Saw Tooth's maw. He plied on his paddles with the might of a madman, his shoulders tearing against their bones. Another swell and his boat rose awkwardly on her side. He was fully broadside to the wind now. "Turn! Turn! Turn, my baby, turn!" he roared at his boat and was fisted in the face by a slather of sea froth burning his eyes and filling his mouth. He spat and cursed and kept rowing, blinded, knowing nothing of his course now. He dipped powerlessly down the hollowed sea and wiped at his eyes, seeing for one sweet second his bow veering shoreward. A groundswell. He was being nudged by a groundswell. With a cry he grabbed back his paddles and, half standing, plied them with a fierceness that near broke his thole-pins. Another man! Christ, for another man to start his motor! Now, now, he needed his motor! He plied his paddles, frightened to let them go.

The shouts on shore grew louder. "Here! Here!" He stretched out his arms and pulled, his hands gripping the oars like the talons of a great bird—twice, thrice, and then he dropped the oars and lunged for his motor. Jabbing the start button, he lunged onto the tiller, shoving it ninety degrees shoreward. He felt it, felt his boat take him, moving him—not the sea now, moving him, but his boat. And his rudder, he felt it, too, dig into the sea. She was taking her course; his boat was taking her course. His bow turned full side to the wind as he plunged through the lengthening swells. Good, good, rather drown upon a sounder than be smashed against your brazen molars, he silently screamed at Old Saw Tooth. Almost ashore now. Almost ashore. He'd wait another minute before cutting his motor and running aground. Another minute and he'd cut his motor. He could almost see the whites of the Trapps' eyes. He jabbed off the motor and grabbed the thole-pins, bracing himself. The keel of his boat dug into the beach rocks, and he lurched forward, painfully wrenching his shoulders. The Trapps were immediately beside him, one on either side, up to their knees in water, taking hold of his gunnels and dragging the nose of his boat ashore. He leaped out and sank to his knees, near kissing the rocks. But, no, he'd save that for later, he thought, staring up at the grim-faced Trapps staring down at him. Climbing weakly back up on his feet, he nodded his thanks.

They nodded back and dragged his boat up on shore. Finding strength, he held on to his gunnels and hauled with them.

"We'll keep watch on her," said one of the Trapps, as the other climbed aboard and threw out his anchor.

Ensuring the drag-line was tightly tied to the stern, they dragged the anchor just above the landwash.

Sylvanus stood watching. It surprised him how weak and quivery his legs felt.

"That's good. She'll be fine there," he said as the brothers wedged the anchor between a couple of big rocks. He nodded his thanks. Closest he'd ever been to a Trapp, aside from the odd passing in boat. Good-looking bunch, for sure, their faces clean of hair, their features nice and smooth. But there was a grimness to their jaws, as though they were locked onto a maddening thought.

"Supper's on, if you wants," said one, the elder by the looks of his crinkled eyes.

Sylvanus looked toward their houses. Gone were the little yellow suns. Up this close, it looked more like cold blue moonlight spilling from their windows.

"Nay, better get home," he said. "Mother's off her head by now."

The younger one pointed at a cut in the treeline. "Over there's the road," he said.

Sylvanus nodded, wondering if they were the two who fished his brother out of the sea and brought him home. He turned to his boat, his fish. "Be back in the morning, I suppose," he said. "Appreciate your help." A last nod of thanks, and he set off onto the footpath that took him up over the hill and onto the old horse road that would take him near to the head.

CHAPTER NINETEEN

EVA

Sʏʟᴠᴀɴᴜꜱ ᴡᴀʟᴋᴇᴅ ʜᴀʀᴅ, grateful for the light left in the sky and the trees sheltering him from the wind. He was cold. With the sluicing he'd taken, his pants and undergarments felt like wet blankets draped around him. The path steepened, and his legs, still quivering from fright of Old Saw Tooth, were now aching with fatigue. Was a long day since five o'clock this morning, he thought wearily, and raised his arms over his head, stretching, trying to shift about some of the wet clothing that was starting to chafe his skin. Ten, fifteen minutes of walking, then another five to ensure he was definitely over the head, he cut off the path into the woods. Fighting dead sticks and boughs, he held out his hands, shielding his eyes against the bared limbs, invisible in the near dark, snapping at his face. Cripes, he hated the woods.

Finally he broke through, his relief shortened by the wind lashing him back. Thank Jesus he judged it right and was on top of the cliffs of the head—the far side from the path leading down through the woods and home. He bent into the wind, and thought to drop on his knees and scuttle across the bald cliff top like the dog. And he might've, if not for a black shape sifting out of the woods and floating toward him. Already spooked this evening, he now froze, the hair rising on his neck. The wind snatched at the spectre, tearing back its shawl, and he cried out with relief to see his mother, her face severe in its anxiousness as she fought against the winds, trying to reach him.

"Jesus Christ!" he swore, leaping forward and grabbing her outstretched arms. "What the hell you trying to do, frighten the shit out of me?"

She crumpled against him, her thin arms holding tight to his waist, her face digging into the wetness of his garments. He hung his head, knowing full well why she wept.

"Jeezes, Mother, you knows I'm not going to stay on the water in a bad blow."

She pulled back, raising her fist, shrilling like the she-devil. "But you did. You went off too far, didn't you? And couldn't get back in time!"

"You knows I got back in time. I'm here, aren't I?"

"By the grace of God! By the grace of God, you're here."

"For God's sake, Mother—"

"For my sake," she shouted, and her voice fell, barely audible over the moaning of the wind as she pleaded, "For my sake, you stay off them open waters. Promise me you'll stay off them open waters—else, go fishing on the skiff with Manny and Jake."

He balked. "Oh, cripes, now don't start with that—" But she was turning from him, bending into the gale, hobbling toward the edge of the cliff, her shawl flying off from her sides like darkened wings.

"Mother—Mother, where you going?" and he leaped after her, taking her roughly by the arm before she was blown off the cliff. She fell to her knees, her shoulders stiff to his touch, her hair all loosened and whipping about her face. He held tighter as she leaned forward, staring out over the cliff and down to the sea. The woods were fully dark, the sea, a leaden grey, its swells oozing greyish as they broke up on the backs of another and up over Old Saw Tooth.

"I saw him," she whispered.

He leaned closer to her, wrapping his arms around her, trying to edge his body between hers and the winds squalling around them.

"Saw who?" he asked.

"Your father. I saw him. I was crouching here, watching—just as I was watching for you—and I seen it happen—his boat carried on a swell."

"Oh, jeezes, Mother."

"It capsized. They both went overboard—I saw them. Your father come back up, clinging to Old Saw Tooth. He was staring up at me. He was late. He knew I'd be here, watching. He saw me—I know he did—I held him—with my eyes, I held him. I would've held him for all eternity if he hadn't looked away. But he had to look away—to search for Elikum—"

He struggled to breathe, his arms holding her too tightly, trying to shut out with his mind what his eyes had already seen.

"Elikum," and she moaned. "I seen him—just once. His head come up, and then his hand, his arm—like he was waving goodbye to me—or else reaching out for me to save him," she ended harshly. "Then he was gone. When I looked back, your father was gone, too."

"God, Mother," he choked, the wind colder against the tears wetting his face as he looked out over the sea, seeing his father clinging to Old Saw Tooth, and Elikum reaching up from his watery grave, grasping for the hand of a mother who could not save him. And she had stood here, this mother, reaching down from a wind-torn cliff, battling the sea with the strength of her eyes to heave back her man, her boy. And he heard her screams as Elikum sank beneath his last farewell, and he heard her screaming again as Old Saw Tooth grinned wickedly up at her, licking his chops over the feast of her man.

"I stayed a long time, watching," she whispered. "Watching—and waiting—waiting for them to come back up. Pray to Jesus I never got to sit here, watching for you agin," she ended bitterly, pulling back to lash her eyes onto him. But the light was nearly gone, and he caught just the faintest gleam of her tears.

"I won't drown! Swear to God, I'll never drown." He wept, pressing his face against hers. She trembled and he held her more tightly, infusing her body with what warmth was left in his. "Lord, how could you keep this? You should've told me, told somebody."

"Eva."

The softly spoken name shivered through his ear like a snippet of wind, near jolting him out of his skin. It was Adelaide, kneeling beside him as if she'd been there for some time, her face barely discernible in the fallen light, her tone full of anguish as she spoke again,

"Eva," and her voice caught on a sob. Reaching her arms around the old woman's shoulders, she pressed

herself against Eva, trying to warm her as he himself was
doing. "You should've told somebody, Eva, you should've
told," she said tightly. "Carrying this all these years."

Eva was still staring out over the sea, giving no indi-
cation she heard or was aware of the younger woman's
presence. Presently, her hand crept out of her shawl,
patting Adelaide's.

"Would've been harder for the boys." She pulled away
from them both, her tone surly once more as she looked
to Sylvanus. "I only tell now to save you from your own
foolhardiness—if only to spare your mother extra
burden."

Adelaide's eyes were on him. "What were you doing
out there? Why'd you wait so late to come home?" she
flared. "Lord, Syllie, you keep your mother worrying like
this."

He touched her shoulder lightly. No matter her
words. He heard the fright in her tone, and he felt her
tremble as he had his mother. A shiver cut through him,
more from the cold wet of what must've been his mother's
pillow these past years than from the night's chill and his
wet clothes.

"Let's get home," he said, and slowly unfolded
himself, standing, buffering them both from the wind as
they rose alongside him.

"I don't know who's the more foolish," Adelaide
admonished, tucking her arm through Eva's and hurriedly
leading her across the cliff toward the trees. "Certainly,
it's the both of you," she chided, "for being out on a night
like this."

"Pay attention, Addie," said Sylvanus as she near
stumbled. Keeping directly behind, he held out the flaps

of his oilskins like a tent, shielding them as much as he could. It was much darker in the woods, the path barely visible. "Here, let me get ahead," he said to Addie, but she shushed him back.

"I've walked this way enough times," she said, carrying on feeling out the path with her feet. She paused as Sylvanus, in his tiredness, tripped over a tree root. Cursing, he grabbed a branch, catching himself from pitching headlong and tumbling over them both.

"You'll be the death of us yet this night," cried Adelaide, reaching back to help steady him. Her hand was soft and warm as it found his, and he relished her squeezing his fingers for a second before relinquishing it and grabbing onto a branch to keep her own footing. He relished her chiding as well, for there was a warmth in it, like the relief of a distraught mother whose negligent children have wandered off and are found, cold but safe. And after they had reached the foot of the hill, he followed obediently as she ordered him home while she trekked across the footbridge with Eva.

He watched after them, worrying for his mother's crimped figure leaning heavily against Adelaide. As if feeling his concern, Eva looked back. Waving him inside, she stood a little straighter—making herself look strong so's he wouldn't worry about her, he figured, as Adelaide tugged her along. "Cripes, Mother," he groaned.

Trudging inside, he skimmed off his clothes and fell into bed, without washing, without supper. His eyes closed wearily, only to be emblazoned again with the images of his father and Old Saw Tooth, and of Elikum. And his mother—that she had seen, that she had seen. He listened now to the roar of the ocean crashing against the head, and for the first that he could remember, he hated this jealous bitch of a sea mother who would snatch babies from a land mother's breasts and hide them in the massive rolls of her own. He turned, tormented, upon his pillow, trying to shut out her rumbling as she tore at the shore-line, and the moaning of her dead tucked into her bosom, forever fitful in their slumbers, forever rolling upon different shores, seeking the beach upon which they were spawned, and heralded by a wind endowed with the cries of their grieving loved one.

He drifted toward the sound of his mother's voice calling to him. He raised his head, trying to see her, to answer her; but an explosion of water hit him, toppled him, and immediately the sea bitch was upon him, pawing him, dragging him under, muffling his mother's screams calling him back. But he was too far afloat, too buoyant, with nothing to grab hold of, sinking, sinking, the sea mother wrapping him in her cold, wet blanket, heavy, heavy, the weight of it too heavy and cold, numbing him, sinking him—sinking—

"Syllie!"

He tried to breathe, to fight—couldn't—couldn't move. The cry sounded again, calling him back, holding him. He tried moving but couldn't, couldn't move, couldn't move. The voice called again, more faintly now, and he strove harder toward it—just a bit, if he could move just a bit, a hand, a finger—the voice was weakening, weakening, drowning amidst the frightening roar of the sea mother.

"Syllie!"

He thrashed, jolted. Something had him, was tugging him, pulling him up. He gasped for air, his eyes, unseeing, his chest stricken with fear. The hag, the hag had him; her fingers, tentacles of cold, damp fog, encircling his throat, choking him, her face appearing before him, fused, twisting grotesquely behind the thin white membrane of a caul.

"Syllie, for gawd's sake!" It was Addie, his Addie, leaning across him, grasping at him, shaking him as he wrenched at the folds of her white cotton nightgown.

He sat up, his chest pounding, sweat running in rivulets down his face. He wiped it off, hating the wet, clammy feel of it. He tore off the blankets, hot all over, wanting nothing, nothing, touching him.

"You're making me scared, Syllie," Addie cried, and he was scared too, despite his eyes opened, despite his knowing where he sat, and he grasped the blankets back to him as if they were a buoy and he about to be swept away again.

"Syllie?"

He turned to her, her face wan in the partially lit room. She'd left the lamp burning outside their door, as she used to do when they'd first married. It softened her, the dim, gold light. Softened the room. He started breathing more deeply, slowly taking in the room, Addie. Holding his head into his hands, he let out a long, slow breath.

"Jeezes," he croaked. "That was a bad one."

"I thought you were dying," she cried. "A heart attack or something, a fit."

He pulled her to him, lying back down. "Nay," he said. He tried to say more.

"I couldn't wake you up. The sounds—you were making godawful sounds—not human, swear to gawd, Syllie, they weren't human."

He let out another long, slow breath, patting her, afraid to close his eyes, afraid of it coming back, the hag. "How's Mother?" he asked, wanting her voice.

"You got us all scared to death this night, Syllie, damned if you don't."

"I never meant to."

"You ought not to have scared her like that."

"I never meant to."

"But you did. She'd been coming back and forth all evening. If Manny and Jake weren't off buying their new skiff, she would've had them on the water looking for you."

"They would've known I'd put ashore."

"You saying it can't happen—you can't drown? That old water's always drowning somebody—for sure you knows that."

Her tone was again that of a distraught mother. He turned his cheek to hers, gazing into her eyes, wanting to sink into their blueness as might a dying sun into the sea. He was afraid. Afraid of the dark, afraid of fear.

"She saw them," he said to keep himself awake, to keep her talking.

"Don't say it, Syllie. Oh, I can't think of it—what she seen up there, watching."

"Gawd, she saw them!" The tension from the day snapped, leaving him crumpling like a baby. She slipped her arms around his neck, cradling him. "Addie," he whispered, the grubbiness of his cheek imprinting itself against the softness of her breasts, "Addie, I didn't wash—I—"

"Shh," and she cradled him tighter, her fingers stroking his hair, the back of his neck. "I'll heat some water in the morning and pour you a tub."

"Addie, were you scared, too?"

"Yes!" And she sobbed out loud, then muffled her mouth into his hair. "Don't you ever stay out in a storm agin. It's damn foolishness getting yourself drowned."

"I won't," he whispered.

"I couldn't be without you. I know you thinks I'm all to myself—and perhaps it's not fair—"

"I don't think that."

"Yes, you do, but I can't help what's been happening to me—leastways, not all of it."

He nuzzled deeper, closing his ears to her words, despite his need to keep her awake. It was *his* fear tormenting him now, not hers, and he wanted the night to be his.

"But you'd think me mad if I were to tell you my mind these days," she cried out, her body stiffening, her arms slipping away from his neck, taking with it her breasts, his pillow.

"Wait," he groaned, tightening his hold, wanting her back, wanting her breath all soft and sweet upon his face, but she was disappearing, back into that room where he had no place.

This time, though, she jarred the door, clenching his hand, saying, "I feels your sympathy, Syllie, I always feels your sympathy, and even though I hates it most times, it keeps me from *feeling* that I'm by myself, even though I am." She gave a short laugh. "There, now you hears how mad I can be. That's why I can't talk to you about most things—you'd lock me up. Yes, you would," she cried as he tried to soothe her. "Better left unsaid, some things— like I'm forsaken, I feels forsaken. Oh, Christ, I couldn't bear you gone, Syllie. I couldn't bear it if you thought me mad, either; renounced me. There, now you knows how mad I am. But don't worry, I likes being in the garden with Eva. I'll not go mad. And I'll stay off the head if you'll stay off them goddamn waters when there's a wind on. You listening?"

She wrapped her arms around him again, but in the fashion of old: her arms clasping him to her, her body pressing urgently against his, her breathing almost halted, as though she were listening, searching, waiting for his life's breath to enter her so's she could breathe again. As much as he loved it, he hated it, how she clung to him like that, rendering their lovemaking to something inside of her, outside of him. But he understood her now, her fear, her need to cling to something living, strong. And he clung to her in the same desperate manner, his buoy against the sea mother still out there, still rattling her emptied arms across the beach rocks, searching. He shivered, wondering how in the name of Jesus he'd ever get himself out in boat again.

CHAPTER TWENTY

SHOAL BENEATH FULL TIDE

THE FISHING SEASON was all but done the morning Manny and Jake slipped by on the water in their new thirty-foot skiff. They sang out to him, but he carried on walking alongshore, pretending not to hear, knowing full well what they wanted—or were offering.

"Get the hell flames over here," Manny sang out.

Without raising his head, Sylvanus waved them onward.

"Come on, b'ye. Day in the skiff do you good," yelled Manny. "Jeezes, for fifty quintals of fish, the least you can do is help haul it aboard."

"I'm not taking your fish," said Sylvanus.

"No, you're not, then. You're not the only one who'd give away your arsehole and shit through your belly-button. Now come on. Jump aboard."

They were coasting the shoreline, Manny leaning over the bow with a paddle, steering the boat alongside, and Jake leaning on a paddle in the rear, pushing them forward. Shaking his head, Sylvanus swung off the path, ducking behind his mother's house, shutting out Manny's vexed sputtering and Jake's harangue that he was "just like Father, just like Father."

Leaning over the fence, he watched Adelaide straddling a drill of carrots, pulling them up by their tops and dropping them into a sack she was dragging alongside her. He was continuously surprised by how well she had taken to gardening. Cripes, even when the rain was pissing and wind walloping, she pulled herself out of bed, hauled on her planting clothes, and nibbled a piece of bread on her way to his mother's. Like most anything with Addie, she never talked about it, except to say it was fine, everything was fine. He had given up arguing with her, for he was as guilty as she, these days, keeping things to hisself and saying, "Oh, it's fine, the fishing's fine, everything's fine," whenever she asked. Cripes, enough she'd settled for a fisherman and Cooney Arm. He wasn't about to start whining that she'd settled for a fisherman without fish. And if truth be told, since the night of the storm, he was starting to be more appreciative of her keeping things to herself, for undoubtedly she was hearing from his mother, from Elsie, from Melita, and others that things weren't fine. But she wasn't coming onto him about it—like Melita was onto Manny these days—worrying and fretting. And for that he was infinitely grateful. It was his to worry and fret and keep his pantry filled. Enough for her to worry and fret about her own things.

Yes, sir, strange thing to talk about, fear—fear of a dream, fear of nothing, fear of fear itself. It was like she said, some things just can't be told. Enough to understand that it wasn't about him, and to leave her alone so's to find her own light and vanquish the dark from that inner room she still remained inside of, brooding.

She had worked her way to the end of the drill and was about to drag her sack, bulging with carrots, up the mound of the root cellar at the farthest end of the yard, when she glimpsed him standing there. Laying down the sack, she started toward him. With her hair scrimped back and clipped, baring that wan, little face that had become a mite tinted over the summer, he swore he could count every fleck in those luminous blue eyes. And as she drew nearer, raising a hand and loosening a scarf she wore around her neck, he well imagined the throbbing in the hollow of that long, graceful throat.

"You ought to have gone with Manny," she said almost scoldingly, coming before him, "even if you won't take his fish."

He grinned. It felt like she was always scolding him since her fright that night. "Why would I go, then, if I don't want his fish?"

"Lots of reasons. You've never fished midshore in a skiff. You ought to try it before you shuts it down. Perhaps you might like it, and God knows, it's lots safer, and it'll get you more fish. And it's not going to hurt you, either, to take the load of fish he's offering you this evening. Not when you needs it and he already got enough."

He was too stunned at first by her knowing of his deeds to calculate the sudden surge of anger darkening his face. "Elsie up shooting off her mouth agin, is she?" he yelled, glaring around the yard as if expecting to find the mouthy sister-in-law hiding behind the cellar.

"You think I can't figure some things? You think I needs you figuring everything for me?"

"Then you knows I can take care of my own larder and I don't need anybody else's handouts."

"No, you only had Elsie and Melita turning your fish every day—oh, you still thinking Jake's young fellow is doing it, do you?"

Sylvanus sputtered in rage. "But I had it out with the little bastard. Don't tell me he's been slacking off agin!"

"You hold on there," demanded Adelaide, catching hold of his shirt sleeve as he slewed around, about to charge off. "You just never mind that crowd—lazier than their mother, they are. And that's why for once Elsie didn't go shooting off her mouth about who was turning your fish—because her youngster was getting paid a nickel for it, a nickel for nothing."

Sylvanus pounded his palm with his fist. "I'll throttle that little bastard!"

"Yes, and I'll throttle you if you spins one more yarn in my face about puncheons and quintals. You listen to me, Sylvanus Now," she said with an anger matching his, "for sure I haven't been much good to you in the past, but you could've told me some things. Cripes, better than having Melita and Elsie and everybody else looking down their noses. And I don't mind work. For sure I turned enough fish in my days to handle the few you got—and if I got to handle them, I got a say in what we does, too—like taking fish from Jake. So you can stop acting like you're a king and me your little hussy."

"Hussy!" He near choked. "Jesus Christ, Addie, where the hell did you get that—"

"Well, that's what a hussy is, isn't it, something holed up in a bedroom?"

"Addie, I haven't got you holed up in no bedroom."

"No, you just got me petitioned off from everybody

else with that damn wall and no window, so's I won't have to feel a part of anything."

"Well, that's what you wants, isn't it," he cried out, "never having to see a flake agin?"

"Not when you got the likes of Elsie breathing down my neck, scorning me for having to do my work. I'll work a thousand flakes rather than having that calling me cripple. And I don't give a shit if she was saying it or not saying it, that's what I felt like, finding out they were doing my work—a cripple! Especially your mother, hobbling around the garden all day long and then running to the flakes, first sign of rain."

"Don't talk to me about that," he choked. "I'm going to kill that little bastard, and for sure you could've figured some things out, Addie. It's not as if you don't know the life of a fisherman."

"And maybe I should've, but you sure made it easy not to look. Ooh, don't argue with me, Syllie," she cried, throwing up her hands, "and don't bother bringing up anything to Jake's fellow or Elsie or your mother—I've taken over turning the fish when you're gone. Don't ogle like that—I've been doing it all summer. So, it's not only you who can yea or nay anything Manny's offering. If you don't take his fish, I will."

His sharp intake near cut his throat. "Bloody hell, you will!" And he stepped forward, clenching his fists.

She drew back, startled. And with the blue of her eyes colder than the mother on a winter's morn, she walked back to her bag of carrots, her back stiff as a picket.

Oh, fine, just bloody fine. Not enough he had everybody else on his back, but now she was climbing on board, too. He'd thought it was too bloody good that she was minding her own business and letting him stick to his; but, no, bloody sir, that couldn't last long. She had to start going against him, too—and about his own work! A vein popped on his neck. He expected slurs from Jake and Elsie and others with idle tongues; but this rebuke from the one whom his strength and abilities sheltered did more than nick his pride; it erected a feeling of dread for his next encounter with her, because for damn well sure she wouldn't give up on a thing once she got started with it; he knew her well enough for that. And his mother turning his fish! And Elsie and Melita! Christ, why hadn't somebody said something? And now she, Addie, hobbling around on his flakes, doing what he swore she'd never have to do again—and all behind his back. Anger choked him.

Swinging himself inside his stage, he kicked a puncheon, caving in its side. Catching sight of a coil of new white jigging line that needed dying, he seized it and lunged outside. Chasing off a couple of boys lurking around, looking for mischief, he kicked together enough driftwood and slabs for a fair-sized fire. Dragging out his father's old iron bark-tub from the stage, he laid it atop the two sticks he'd criss-crossed over the now blazing flames and half filled it with sea water, yelling hell's flames at the boys attempting to edge their way back.

How did she know about Manny's offer of fish—unless Manny was shooting off his mouth about it? But, no, Manny wouldn't do that—Jake would! Elsie would, and she'd be sure to run, yarning about it. Or perhaps Jake never said nothing, either. Perhaps Addie had taken to snooping about his stage, spying on everything he was saying and doing. Cripes, that's what Elsie was always doing, snooping and spying—and he hadn't ruled out her foul tongue yet. No doubt she'd been up spouting off to Addie and threatening her not to tell.

But he knew the unlikelihood of that, no matter how much he would've preferred it. The opposite of anything Elsie said is what Addie would do, simply because Addie was as spiteful as Elsie in her own way, which served all their purposes because there was nothing nobody liked better than seeing Elsie getting the short end of something. He sighed, and lifting a bag full of pine cones out of the stage, he dumped them into the water just starting to boil, and watched dismally as the brown dye from the cones started muddying the water worse than his anger was muddying his thoughts. And all this time his Addie was turning his fish.

He grunted. Yet no matter his displeasure, the thought stayed with him—Addie turning his fish. It started warming him—like when he'd watch her ironing his shirts sometimes, gently smoothing and patting his sleeves as though it were him she was smoothing and patting. He grunted again. But why hadn't she let him know? Why the bloody hell hadn't she let him know?

He shook his head. Of course she wouldn't let him know. It was just her way to say nothing—not that he wasn't making his peace about her always keeping things to herself! No, he was starting to be fine about that. But this was different. This was *his work* she had took on and kept to herself.

His anger was starting to ebb. Mad as he was at her butting in about Manny and the fish, it was starting to feel fine that she'd taken on working his flakes and not telling him. Not one for rubbing his nose in his dirt, Addie wasn't, he'd give her that. And not one for complaining either, no matter that she'd settled for a fisherman in Cooney Arm and even that was turning out all wrong. Took everything, she did, laying nothing on him.

With a sigh, he tossed his fishing lines into the dyed water and sat, arms crossed over his knees, staring moodily as the boiling mud decimated the whole of what was white, yet leaving the matter beneath unaltered. Unlike his Addie. Everything was altered within her since he'd met her. Yet despite his attempts to understand her, she was starting to feel more of a bulwark than the defined structures of his stage and boat these days. For with the downturn in fishing, all was shaken beneath him, and he was more uncertain of his life with the mother than he was with the woman sharing his bed.

What if the foreigners and bigger boats did take it all? What if, come spring, nothing ran, not even the scrub cod? What then? Thus far, his house had wanted for nothing, despite his shortage of fish the past year. The bit of coin he'd saved had seen to that, and she hadn't felt a thing, hadn't known but that his puncheons were bursting to their brims. And for certain he'd keep them in meat again this coming winter. But his coin was gone, all used, and no amount of hunting would put flour in the larder, or butter on the table, or clothes on their backs. It was the fish that provided him with coin. Logging brought some relief, but not enough.

The grimness of the thought sobered him. He'd take the bloody fish, then. He'd take whatever the hell would help him through this winter, and he prayed to the sweet Jesus Lord that the coming spring would favour his jiggers as well as it was favouring the gill nets and the trawlers—

and not just for money, either. Fish was his mainstay mentally and spiritually as well, for he had built himself upon that cursed sea, and he was only a part of himself without her.

Upon making the decision, a weariness crept over him, comforting almost, like the soothing that comes after a hard knock to one's bones, and he felt like balling his oilskins into a pillow and crawling into the crux of his boat and going to sleep. But, no. The harshness of his loud-mouthed threats and his clenched fists summoned him back to the garden, to putter around, fixing the back-bridge or something, pretending all was fine and rendering the harshness of his behaviour a common thing, else it'd be harder and harder to go back, making it a thing that would then have to be spoken of. And he didn't want that. Hell, he didn't need that, he thought, hanging his head ashamedly.

Hanging the dripping line up over the rafters in the stage, he kicked beach rocks onto the fire and trudged toward his mother's yard like an old soldier. And that's just how they were as they battened down their house, moving into winter, like two old soldiers wearied from battles fought on different soils and now picking through the foundations of what had been common ground, careful lest they trip a land mine and harm their respective solitudes, which kept the flag of truce between them.

CHAPTER TWENTY-ONE

OCEAN OF ANCIENTS

CURSED. HE SWORE he was cursed, as winter brought with it screeching winds and snow, and ice storms that befogged even the old-timers' memories. Cripes, how he longed for the openness of the sea as he pushed through brush, suffering the snow creeping coldly down his neck, branches scratching at his face like a surly cat, and ice-blasted winds snatching at his breath. Even sunny days were wretched as the sun glittered off the white, searing his sockets, and warming the snow just enough to suck him thigh-deep into its banks. And the silence! There was always that silence when the woods were blanketed with snow, a heavy silence that bore down on the trees and the land with the stillness of death. Separate. All sounds became separate in that silence—the creaking of a boot, the rustling of his garments, a cough—all separate and spreading out in time so's time itself became a thing that had to be ploughed through. No, sir, the woods couldn't take him as did the sea, rocking him upon her breasts, fanning his face whilst he straddled her belly, plumbing her depths, his hips swaying to her heaving and ebbing beneath him, her bodice spreading so far out that it was impossible to see where water and sky separated.

Come midwinter the snow was banked twelve, fifteen feet deep in most places, making logging and hunting near impossible, and driving him mad as he prowled the limited space of his house, worrying about the meat, the larder, and the cursed knowing that all the while he sat, snowed in, the draggers, the trawlers, the factory freezers, and all else built around a diesel were sitting out there on his banks, sucking in his fish, day in, day out, day in, day out.

She wasn't doing much better, he noted, grimly, chancing the occasional sideways glance at his wife. Any lightening of mood her absorption with the garden might've brought had certainly vanished with the summer sun. Yet, unlike him whose foot tapped impatiently as he stood pressing his face and hands against the frosted windows like something held captive, she was strangely calm this winter, her broodiness well contained within her.

Cripes, he envied her that as he paced and prowled, shovelling the path between his house and his mother's every day, sometimes twice a day, bringing water when the buckets weren't even emptied, and overflowing both their wood-boxes with splits. And when that was done and morning not yet over, and his peep-holes in the windows steamed white with his impatient sighs, he'd start back to prowling, working extra hard to clamp shut his eyes so's they wouldn't cling to hers like burrs whenever she drifted by—at least, that's what it appeared like to him, that she *drifted*, her eyes seeing and resting on nothing except when ensnared by his.

She'd exclaim impatiently over his impatience then and seat herself in her rocker facing the window, her back to the room so's to escape him. She could sit for hours like that, facing her window, her feet propped on the sill, levering her rocker to and fro, to and fro—no different than when she was immersed in her little red book when they'd first married. Not that he ever bothered trying to bring up the subject of those little red books, for they were directly connected somehow to her brooding, their babies, their dying. Cripes, no. The mere mentioning of anything to do with the babies, and she skittered from him like a cat in cold water. Didn't matter to her how he ached, building those little boxes. Didn't matter to her how he had wept upon every nail hammered, that he walked around as emptied as her belly after each burial, that each unfulfilled expectation tore a deeper hole in his heart than the ground into which he had buried them. Hell, no. Too caught in her own grief, she was, to give notice of his.

He'd catch himself then and hang his head, recognizing in himself that wounded dog limping around for a pat, whereas his brooding had nothing to do with her; nothing to do with the burials, even. Truth was, as the long winter days pressed on, he started not giving a damn about any of it: her brooding, his brooding, whatever the hell it was they were all brooding about. Getting back to the sea was what was driving him, and filling his boat and his puncheons, and covering his flakes with fish, and gaining back some comfort in knowing that the mother was still there for him, that she hadn't abandoned him, and that he could resume the life she had once so generously given.

Middle of March the winds died, and the sun started cutting through the snow. He was out the door like a singed cat, sawing the blade of his bucksaw through the spine of a black vir oozing with sap, and axing off its limbs, wood chips flying, and a ringing sounding through the woods like church bells. First of April he was setting snares, tracking moose, and chopping open ponds for a blessed meal of fresh, pink trout. Christ, what relief to be swinging his arms and legs over bogs and lakes, and envisioning that day when he could finally start caulking his boat and readying his jiggers and gearing up for another season.

His first day on the water, and he near trembled from the want of it. Yet it was the mother's nervousness that took his mind. He felt it, swear to God, he felt it: her constant shifting, even on the dullest day; her quick leaps from a breeze to a near gale with no warning; her uncalled-for storms up to the end of April; and those long mornings of glassy stillness throughout the latter part of May. He knew the wind to be her accomplice, but it were as though the sun and moon held vigil, too, for it was a queer light on the water these days, and he kept searching skyward for a reading of something to come. More precisely, it was what *didn't* come. Two weeks, three weeks, four weeks into the season before a small stream of cod, half the size of four years before, swam wearily to his jiggers.

He near wept. No wonder she was tossing and fretting beneath him. No wonder she was reluctant to yield to his jiggers. He caught sight of a dragger that had crept but a quarter mile sou'west of him, and two more sitting a few miles farther out.

"Bastards!" he spat, watching the one closest to him steaming even closer, two miles farther in than she ought

to be by law, the bright orange bobbers of some fisherman's net quickly sinking beneath its hull. When he
thought the beast would swamp him, it cut its engines,
engulfing the sea with quiet. The creaking of her winches
sounded over the sea, and a mumble of voices as the men
aboard milled starboard, leaning over the bulwark. She
was raising her net. Lifting his paddles, Sylvanus rowed
within a few hundred yards of the mammoth beast,
shading his eyes as the iron-shod slabs of wood rose dripping out of the water, thudding heavily against the wooden
side of the trawler as the clanging chains winched them
upward. The ocean beneath started broiling, foaming
white as the net breeched.

"Jeezus!" He knew from talk the size of a trawler's
nets, but he'd not seen one, and he stared in awe now, as
the thousand-foot netting rose out of the sea, its bulbous
shape gushing back water and vibrating with its thousands
of fish all crushed together and bulging, strangling, wrig-
gling out through the mesh. The cranking of the winches
grew louder as the net rose abreast of the gunnels. A cry
cut forth from the men, and Sylvanus stared disbelievingly
as the net split dead centre and its cargo of fish—redfish,
mostly—started falling, slowly at first, as though the hand
of God held it mid-air, but then with a turbulent swoosh,
back into the sea.

"Jeezes," and he stared disbelievingly as the mass of
redfish floated on the surface like a bloodied stain growing
bigger and bigger as the waves took them, spreading them
farther and farther outward and toward where he was
now standing in his boat. Loud, angry cries grew from
the men abandoning the trawler's gunnels. Black smoke
spurted out of her stacks, signalling the trawler's return to

the open sea, leaving in its wake the drowned redfish spreading like a ruptured sore upon the face of the sea.

Within minutes Sylvanus's boat was encompassed by the fish now drifting on their backs, their eyes bulging out of their sockets like small hen eggs, their stomachs bloating out through their mouths in thin, pink, membrane sacs. Gulls flapped and squawked frenziedly, clutching onto the bellies of the fish, jabbing at the pink sacs till the membranes broke, spilling out the guts. The sea of red broke, and Sylvanus clutched his side sickeningly as he took in the spread of creamy white pods now floating before him. Mother-fish. Thousands of them. A great, speckled gull perched atop one of the pods nearest him, jabbing at her belly, weakening it, rupturing it, till the mother's roe trickled out like spilt milk.

Who, who, Sylvanus silently cried, would accept such sacrifice in the name of hunger? And he sat back, bobbing in his little wooden boat upon the giant expanse of blue ocean, his pitiful few fish at his feet, and he felt his smallness, his minuscule measure against a sphere where thousands of fish can be flung to the gulls thousands of times and count for nothing. He thought of the mother-fish he'd saved from his jiggers over the years, and her sacs of roe, and he drew his eyes now back to the frenzy of the gulls jabbing at her belly, spilling her guts, her unlived life, into the sea, and he weakened, seeing in the mother's fate his own. He rose, churning with anger at the stupidity, the *stupidity* of it, and shook both fists at the pillagers, roaring, "Bastards! You goddamned bastards! You stupid, goddamned bastards!"

In destitution, he closed his eyes to the hideous sight surrounding him, reopening them onto the hooded eyes of government, replying, "Yes, yes," to the angry cries of the fishermen who were forced ashore in droves, "we hear you, and we'll soon have our boundaries, and we're working with foreign governments; but let's not be hasty about blame. It's as we told you before, there's a cold front out there these days, and we've been telling you and telling you that cod don't like cold water and that's probably the reason she's not swimming ashore. And, too, we got an overabundance of seals this year, feasting on your catch; and it's the worse year yet for slub, despoiling nets up and down the bay; and it's your spirit, men, it's your spirit—you haven't really given over the ways of the old; still too many of you clinging to your fathers' day and not taking on the more modern means we're equipping you with—what of the new fibre gill nets? We're giving them to you, free—more competitive they'll make you inshore crowd, more competitive. About twenty thousand we got out in the waters by now, and those fishermen are hauling in the cod, and they like them, they do, they like them."

SYLVANUS SNORTED, nearly punching the radio one afternoon a few days after he'd witnessed the colossal waste of fish, and heard for the second time that day the government urging gill nets onto the fishermen.

"No, no, we don't like the bloody things," he exploded. "We hates them, we bloody hates them. For the love of jeezes, stop giving us what we don't want and give us what we wants."

He broke off as Adelaide darted in from the clothesline, a startled look on her face. "Bloody government," he muttered, switching off the radio, shoving back his chair, "heads up their bloody arse. The more they learns about fishing, they better they gets at catching them, not sparing them." He dug a tumbler of water out of the water bucket and stood drinking it back, thudding the emptied glass on the bin. "Nothing, Addie, nothing; just fishing stuff, is all," he added, brushing aside her worried look. "Seen my cap? Where's my cap? Cripes, the bloody thing is never where I lays it."

"On the table." She pointed out as he rooted noisily through a box of woollens behind the stove. "Syllie, what's got you going?"

"Nothing you haven't heard a hundred thousand times," he grunted, pulling on his cap and heading for the door. She stood back, the size of her no bigger than a bean sprout, trying to bar the doorway, the blue of her eyes tinged with concern. "Look, it's nothing to concern yourself with. Bloody governments, that's all."

"What about them?"

"What about them?" He stared at her incredulously. "Cripes, Addie, you knows some things, don't you?"

"I knows a whole lot more than you thinks I do," she quickly replied. Her tone softened. "Syllie, perhaps there're other ways besides jigging. We can talk about it, can't we?" she pleaded as he balked at her words.

"Talk! I'm sick of talk. Sick of the government's talk, sick of the fishermen's talk, sick of my own. Jeezes, how much can a thing be talked about and still remain the same thing? Now, stand aside, else I dumps you over my shoulder and lugs you out on the fishing grounds—you'll know enough then, about fishing and talk." And ignoring her cry of protest, he clamped his hands around her waist, lifting her to the wayside. Dropping a kiss upon her cheek, he started toward the footbridge, fuming over the news he'd just heard on the radio, that the Russians were now building another seventy factory ships and two hundred more trawlers, and the Germans were knitting thousand-foot nets with built-in sonar for spotting fish up to two miles away, and still more countries were preparing to come on board.

He cursed upon reaching his boat, realizing he'd forgotten his hardtack and onions. Hell's flames with it, he muttered silently, hauling out his oilskins. Be more than his belly empty if he didn't get his arse out to sea; his puncheons would be empty too. And by the look of things, no doubt they would be without their winter's hold again this year. He sighed tiredly. Still, there was another good six weeks left yet. Who knows what six weeks would bring, he said more to encourage himself on this lacklustre evening of grey skies and squally winds. He pushed off his boat and climbed aboard without courage. He felt tired. Half the fish and half the work he was used to, yet he felt tired.

It was a fatigue that had pursued him throughout the season. By summer's end, with his prolonged hours on the sea, his persistent jigging and the continuing decline of his catch, he was starting to feel older than the hills.

Stuffing his lunch pack into the cuddy one cold September afternoon, he turned a keen eye to the wind. It was a full-out blow, meaning it would either reach its full pitch in twenty minutes, in which case his boat could easily handle it, and he would then be able to drop anchor and jig; or else she'd keep on building, in which case he'd turn back or run ashore. It was already late in the afternoon, and he was feeling the pinch too hard to stay ashore, wasting twenty minutes waiting to see how hard she'd blow.

"Hey, what're you at, old cock?"

He looked up in surprise as Manny lunged down onto the landwash beside him.

"How're you doing, buddy?" he replied, pulling his oilskins out of the stern. "What the hell!" he yelped in disbelief as Manny grabbed him by the front of his coat, throwing him against his stage.

"I asked *what're you at?*" yelled Manny, clenching his coat tighter. As quickly as he'd grabbed him, he let go, his breathing heavy, his face darker than the rain clouds threatening overhead.

Sylvanus stared at him, stupefied. "What in hell's flames do it look like?" he cried. "Never seen a jigger before?"

"Not sticking out of a man's arse, I haven't—leastways, not yet. But by jeezes, I'll see one before the day's out, you tries getting in that boat in this wind!"

"The wind? You think I won't turn back if she keeps building? Cripes, I'm not that stun. Manny!" he shouted as his brother grabbed him again, shoving him hard against the stage.

"Yup, and that's what I'll tell Mother," Manny shouted back, "when she's climbing up on the head, watching out for you agin: 'Bugger off, Mother, he's happy as a lark, snuggled in onshore somewhere.' You think that's going to save her a night of hell, you little shit!" Hauling back, Manny struck him a clean one across his chin.

Stunned, Sylvanus stared at this brother, whose bearded face, always softened with laughter, was now hardened with rage, his mouth a thin, angry line, his eyes full of fear, and full of—of what?

Haunts, he said softly to himself. Full of haunts. "Mother just told you about her seeing the drownings," he said simply. He turned from his brother's pain, turning a bleak eye onto the bleaker face of the sea.

"How come you never told me?" said Manny. "First, she keeps it to herself, and then you."

Sylvanus shrugged. "I don't know, brother. I figured it was hers to tell."

Manny drew a raspy breath. "Should've told us a long time ago, keeping all that to herself. Bloody hell of a thing—" His voice broke, and Sylvanus kept his eyes on the sea.

"Wish I'd lived through it with ye," he said to give Manny time.

Manny wiped at his face. "You did," he said brusquely. "Probably closer than we all did—inside of Mother, like that. Anyway, fighting with the missus, that why you were putting off this evening? Go on, b'ye, everybody fights with their missus," he carried on as Sylvanus never spoke. "No need to drown yourself—not right off, anyway. Get drunk first. Come on—Jake's got a fire going."

Sylvanus shifted moodily. "I'm not fighting with the missus."

"Well, what else would send a man out in a gale, then?" And as if finding the answer to his own question, Manny let go with a wearied sigh. "Looking for a fish, right? Jesus Christ, man, if it's come to this—pushing off in a storm—it's time to do something, isn't it? Look, Syllie, there's other things coming. You're going to have to start thinking differently."

"What other things?" asked Sylvanus. "Manny?" And a different kind of worry knotted his stomach as Manny looked beseechingly to the hills, as though begging for words. "What the hell, Manny? Jeezes, you're not dying or something, are you?"

Manny scoffed. "Not that I knows of. Look, you just got to give up your stubbornness, is all. Just give up your blasted stubbornness!"

"Stubbornness! What the hell you talking about, *stubbornness?*"

"Yeah, that's what I'm talking about—stubbornness! And don't fly off your head at me," he warned as Sylvanus groaned. "See! See, that's just what I means!" he said as Sylvanus turned from him impatiently. "You don't listen, Syllie, you don't listen to nothing or nobody."

"What things—what bloody things? In the name of Jesus, say something and I'll listen," yelled Sylvanus.

"Nothing! I'm not trying to say nothing! No sense talking to the likes of you about nothing when it comes to fishing!"

"Right, right, just like Father, just like Father— whoever the hell Father was," and he wiped at his mouth, near frothing he was so bleeding mad.

Manny grinned—a hard grin, one that was more a curse than a grin. "My son, you're the case," he said. "Boundaries, b'ye, that's all. We finally got them—just heard it on the radio. Twelve miles. Perhaps that'll change everything. Come on, let's go to Jake's."

"Boundaries? Hell, that's not what's up your arse this evening. Boundaries!" he spat, as Manny swung away from him. "Some good now, to make boundaries when the fish makes their own. Horseshit, is all that is, horseshit!"

Manny spun about. "Yeah, well, why don't you go have a little chat with the fishies," he said, jabbing hard at his brother's chest, "and when you gets everything

straightened out between them and the wops and the
limeys and the krauts and all else who's out there, you give
me a shout and we'll have another chat, all right?"

"Oh, bugger off!" snarled Sylvanus, knocking his hand
aside. "Bugger off!" he warned as Manny, enraged, curled
a fist. "By the jeezes, you won't get away with that agin."

"Manny! Syllie!"

They both turned at their mother's voice. She came
running, her winter shawl weighing down her thin shoulders and her boot laces all untied. Adelaide hurried
behind, pulling on a coat, her hair whipping with the
wind.

Manny stove his fist behind him. "For gawd's sake,
Mother, get back in the house," he yelled.

"What're ye fighting over?" cried Eva. "Manny?"

"Nothing, we're not fighting over nothing," said
Sylvanus. "Take her back, Addie. Jeezes, she's freezing,"
he cried, draping an arm around her shoulders to shield
her.

The old woman broke clear of him, her brow as dark
as her boys'. "I'm not so lame I needs to be led. Did you
tell him?" she asked Manny.

"No. No, look, Mother, go on inside."

Sylvanus raised his hands to the heavens. "Yup, here
we go agin." Turning appealing eyes to his mother, he fell
before her on one knee, his hands mockingly clasped in
prayer, asking, "In the name of Jesus, will you tell me what
it is ye haven't told me?"

"They're moving us." It was Adelaide who spoke.

Sylvanus rose, looking to her. Her face was white with
cold, her lips blue. "Who?" he asked, despite his incom-
prehension of her words. "Who's moving us?"

"The government," she said.

Manny's voice was strained. "You're the last one to hear it, brother. The government's moving us—everybody. Resettlement," he added almost irritably as Sylvanus kept looking from one to the other with a blank look. "The whole shebang—except for them who won't go. But from what I hears, there's nobody saying no—except the old midwife, probably. And Mother, if you don't go," he added as an afterthought.

Sylvanus stared speechless at his brother, an awful dawning opening his eyes as he heard, finally, what his brother had been trying to tell him for some time.

"How long have you known this?" he asked, then lapsed a second before falling back as though struck. "You're all for it. You're all for it," he repeated, as though to convince himself of his words. "And Jake—no doubt Jake's for it—he's talked you into it, hasn't he, hasn't he, Manny? Yes, he has, that son of a bitch," he yelled as Manny shook his head. Again Sylvanus lapsed into silence, his eyes beseeching his brother to tell him no, no, it isn't so, that he, Manny, wouldn't go along with no government plan to shut down Cooney Arm, shut down their homes, their fishing. No, no, not so, nobody would want this, to shut down Cooney Arm, to be moved.

A sickness crept into his heart, leaking into his guts, his testicles, weakening him, and he stared disbelievingly at this brother who was now shifting uneasily, dragging in deep breaths for words of persuasion.

"Stick it," said Sylvanus in the awful quiet of a voice whose anger has been shorn by its source. "Stick anything else you got to say. It'll sicken me to hear it." He turned to his mother, her aging face sinking into the hollows of her skull, her eyes pleading with his to be fine.

"I knows it's hard, Syllie," said Manny. "But we can come back whenever we like, keep our houses for a summertime place—"

"Screw you! Screw you, a summertime place! And you knows dick if you thinks this is going to fix anything. How long have ye known this?" he asked his mother and Addie. "Bloody hell," and he punched his knuckles into his palm as his mother's eyes fell away.

"Only yesterday," said Adelaide. "You haven't been home long enough to say nothing to."

She reached out to touch him, and he shrank from her. "You knows the way to the stage," he said stealthily. "You wouldn't have gotten dirty poking your head in for a minute."

She flushed red and he was surprised by his cutting her. He was surprised too, as if he'd just awakened, at the sight of his mother standing there in the freezing winds, wearing only a shawl.

"For gawd's sake, take her back in," he said to Adelaide, and then turned to Manny, grabbing his shoulders, his voice strong, "Manny, jeezes, b'ye, we don't have to follow through with this. What the hell, Manny, *move*? Everybody *move*? What the hell, brother, we don't have to move."

"Not just for we, buddy, for the youngsters, too," said Manny. "They'll have better schools and roads. We're too small and too out of the way to get some of the things they're getting in Ragged Rock, Hampden, places like that. Look, b'ye," he said as Sylvanus turned from him, "it's not what we wants, all right? It's all that's left for us, that's all. The whole goddamn thing's turned around. They don't need we salting fish no more, not with the factory freezers on board. And you can't help but see the truth of it. Might not be what we wants, but it's a better way, simple as that. Freezing fish is a better way of keeping them than salting. Bigger boats is a better way of catching them. Simple as that. And if we don't go along with it, we're out in the cold."

"Bullshit! That's bullshit," Sylvanus snorted. "That's just what they wants you to think because it's too bloody much trouble to keep after the markets, is all, and they all wants the new stuff—the new markets, and them big, pretty boats, and everybody wearing aprons and looking white and clean and modern—*modern!*" he mocked. "That's what they're always saying, isn't it, that we got to be modern, that we're backwards with no vision? Shamed of us is what they are, shamed of a bloody sou'wester and a punt.

"Well, you better watch out, buddy, because they'll have you trading your skiff for a trawler next, and your sou'wester for a derby, and next thing you'll be all nice and modern on the deck of a freezer, doing to us what the rest of the bastards have been doing for years now—wiping us out. Vision!" he spat, his mouth contorting with anger. "There's more vision in the eye of my dick than what's in their heads. Ye go, then, along with everybody else listening to their crap. But I'm not. I'm bloody not, youngster or no youngster."

He couldn't bring himself to look at Adelaide as he spoke this last. Lowering his head, he lurched past her, past his stage, and onto the shore, hunching his shoulders against the sky already darkened with low, heavy clouds, and the winds swooping off the land, and scuds of foam flitting along the beach from the fevered sea.

Move. A sickness churned in his stomach, and he stood still against the squalls as though to feel the steadiness of the rock beneath his feet, to assure himself that it, too, wasn't about to erode. It started to drizzle, the wet scenting the air with a fleet of smells that, under this threat of moving, were already alien with nostalgia. He'd been breathing them since the day of his birth. He hadn't noted them a separate thing from all else around him. Pine smoke, birch smoke, green vir—cripes, he knew whose chimney they were pouring from: Manny hated vir; Jake burned only vir; Ambrose, as he himself, loved the nice clean smell of birch.

Blind. He could walk blind through this place and know the exact pebble he stood upon simply from the smells. There, roasted squid; only Ambrose had dried squid this early in the year. And that sour smell was from the old midwife sloshing dirty dishwater outside her stoop for the past thirty years. And there, the smell of Melita's chicken coop; never cleaned it, she didn't— though it was the only thing not spruced to a shine around her. And the wet of Manny's sawdust heaped beside his wood-house, the seaweed rotting minerals into his mother's potato beds, the strong trouty smell of the brook water, the freshness of the falls, the sweet smell of grass from the meadow luring him more quickly toward the footbridge, leading home. And if the wind was off the sea, smothering everything with the smell of brine, the sounds would guide him along: the muffled voices behind the doors, each of them distinguishable in their familiarity, the hens clucking, the *baa* from his mother's goats, the rushing of the brook, the deepening roar of the falls.

He strolled off the beach, crossing over the footbridge. The brook was wild beneath it, and with the esca-
lating roar of the wind, the falls, and the sea, it felt as
though he were caught in a full-out storm. He paused
before the back wall of his house. Even if there was
anybody inside with the fire going and lamp lit, you'd
never know it, he thought grimly. From this vantage
point, it always looked emptied, abandoned.

Bending into the wind, he veered off the path leading
to his door and trekked instead down over the meadow to
the beach and up toward the neck. The sea was a dirty
grey crashing upon the rocks. Soon, with the failing light,
and aside from the sparkles of plankton rippling like stars
along the catacomb shoreline, she would be black. But he
didn't need to see her. Like the land, she, too, had been
imprinted into his brain. He knew her every fit, her every
calm—from her ripples as she stirred with the first breath
of morning into wavelets as the breeze taunted her
further. Best of all, he knew her laziness beneath an easy
wind, how her long, slow swells lent a greater buoyancy to
his boat. And he knew, too, how quickly those swells could
deepen and be whipped into twenty-foot peaks by
squalling winds, and how to get the hell home afore those
peaks crested and toppled, toppling him and his boat, too,
if he were too heavy with fish. And when she stirred too
deeply, when she scraped her floors and hurtled herself
forward, and her whole surface darkened beneath the
white of her spit, and ships disappeared in the length of
her troughs, and her fury reverberated through the rocks
of the head as she thundered and crashed against them—
well, he felt then the strength of this mother, and he
wondered at his fear of overfishing, that mere man could

hamper such a powerful, massive thing as an ocean.

He wondered, too, at his resistance to leave the shores of Cooney Arm, when it was the same sea that washed upon all shores, for it was the ocean that mattered, never the land upon which she cascaded. In his grandfather's day, the hills had no names, for it was toward the sea that they looked, and her shelves and ridges that they named. But, no, not so for him. It was the headlands and harbours that graced her shores that he was just as beholden to, most especially this arm, Cooney Arm, onto whose land he was born. Like a homespun blanket, it was, whose four corners held firmly to the bedpost, despite the ripples, bulges, and protrusions caused by the growing, squirming souls sheltering beneath it.

He had stood, once, amidst the ruins of an abandoned settlement. He had seen the stumps of the homes that had once been; the well, all emptied and dried; window frames and doors flung hither by the wind and rotting into the ground; mounds of dirt and grass covering the floors like graves. And he had felt cold, standing there, listening to the moaning of the trees as though lamenting the loss of the souls they had once sheltered, and the grass bending to and fro with the wind, searching for the children who had once adorned the fields like daisies.

He rose from the rocks upon which he clung, looking back through the darkening settlement of Cooney Arm and the little patches of yellow light stitching her shores. Now she, too, was threatened with death, her homes mutilated to stumps, her wells parched, and the wharves and flakes left to rot. For without the breath of her home-steaders sweeping through her grass, without their blood trumpeting down her hillside, carousing across her meadow, without their hands moulding her seedlings and touching their tongues to her fruit, she, too, would die.

No, he thought. Not him. Maybe others could up and move, but not him. He was as rooted into this strip of land as were the woods around him.

A burst of flankers poured from his chimney, its fiery orange burning through the evening. She was home. Had she spoken? Had she protested his thought? He paused as a patch of yellow lit up his window. His shoulders sank as he heard his brother's accusations that he was stuck in the past, still living in his father's day. Was she accusing him, too? And was he? Was he so embedded that time swept past him? That he was no more than the mute beast in the field? Is that what she, his Addie, saw—one of his mother's goats, mindlessly chomping back feed all day long whilst the rest of the world grew modern around him?

It was a sickening thought, yet almost immediately his answer was no. Undoubtedly, as a feathered creature shapes and grows into its habitat, so was he woven into the fabric of this land. But it was when he lifted his head at the day's end that he differed, when he saw the all of what he'd done and what he had become. For he was more than the land and the sea. He was an accumulation of all that had come before him—his father, his grandfather, his great-great-grandfathers who had coddled and had been coddled by these waters since time began. A repository, that's what he was, a casket into which the old put themselves. No, not a casket, a sieve whereby they continued to flow through him, and those others who, God willing, would come from him. An ocean of ancients is what lay behind him, and he, little more than a drop of rain before his immersion into that great sea.

Perhaps she did see him as a mindless galoot covered in gurry. Perhaps the whole damn world saw him as that. But he knew different. And to remove himself from the very thing that sustained him would kill him as it would kill it. Yet that was the very thing being asked of him—no, not asked, told—that he go pour himself over the outgrowth of another. And for some, that ought to be the way of it, to pull their past forward and combine it with the newness of another to make a different thing.

But ought not there be some things that remained the same, as with the trees and rocks around him? Ought not some things stand still for those others caught in the cyclone of change, should they need to return? Even he, this lowly man clinging to a rock, could see in the buildup of the offshore fishing fleets the germ of their own demise. What then? Had it been for a better thing, merely because it was bigger, newer?

The patch of yellow beyond which Addie had sat dimmed. She was standing now, blocking the lamp, her hands cupped against the pane, staring out, looking for him. He should go in; she might be worried, he thought. Since the night she'd led him and his mother off the head, she had become edgy whenever he was a bit late.

She pulled away from the window, and immediately his house vanished into darkness. He half rose. Had the lamp run out of oil? No, no, he could see its flickering now through the bedroom window, a faint flickering, as though she had set it down in the hallway near the bedroom door. She was taking herself to bed. His stomach sank a bit further. He felt cold without the warmth of her light, without her watching out for him. His eyes trailed along the dots of light around the arm.

But it was hers he kept coming back to, kept wanting for comfort.

Immediately, his window lit up. She was back, lifting the curtain aside, her light spilling out through, and with it another part of the awful, beautiful truth he'd already learned that evening: that just as those from the past continuously flowed through him, so, too, were those in his midst a grid through which he himself had to pass. And who more than she? Had he not built himself around her as he had the sea? No doubt he could resist a faceless government, tighten his belt and live as he always had, but could he resist her should she start packing? And even if he could persuade her to stay alongside him on a deserted beach with a failing way of life and where never a gadget of modernity could reach her, would he?

He sank back down, shaking his head. No doubt, in true Addie fashion, she probably would stay beside him, alone in Cooney Arm, and never once complain. But, cripes, how long could he continue living alongside such favour without searching her eyes for reproach each time she glanced his way? He'd already persuaded her once to live with him in Cooney Arm, promising her she'd never have to turn another fish. In that, he had failed her. He failed her again in believing that a nice house of her own would bring her joy, despite her telling him on that first day they had sat upon the meadow that it were those within a house that brought it joy. And no doubt the cock crows three times, he thought with a wretched sigh, shifting back on the rock as a rogue wave crashed heavily at his feet, for during her deepest times of need he'd failed her again in not guarding her solitude, in trying to supplant her need with his. But she sure as hell stood guard over his, hadn't she, turning his fish, protecting him from further intrusion of his collapsing world.

Another sounder crashed before him, dampening his brow with a cold spray, rattling up over the rock, snatching at his feet. The mother was getting too wanting. Raising his eyes onto that yellowed window of his house, he rose wearily, climbing back over the rocks toward home and a decision he hadn't been aware he was making.

She was sitting in her chair beside the window when he entered, reading, he noted, from her little red book.

"Next time you're visiting your mother, pick a spot where you wants to build," he said upon entering. Without waiting for her response, he went into their bedroom, dropped his clothes and climbed into bed. Strangely, he felt good, as might one who makes a gift out of sacrifice. More strangely, he felt rested, ready to start building another house, another world, anywhere of her choosing. Wonder what God did on the eighth day, he thought idly, punching his pillow for comfort.

PART SIX

Adelaide & Sylvanus

FALL 1960

CHAPTER TWENTY-TWO

A WELL-LAID PLAN

SYLVANUS HAD FEIGNED SLEEP the night before as Adelaide crept into bed beside him. She left him alone, simply because she wanted it that way as much as he did. There was much to be said, but she wasn't sure yet what those words might be. And this morning he was up and out the door before she was awake.

She stepped carefully across the footbridge, nearly slipping on its muddied planks; then, pulling back the hood of her long green raincoat, she studied the sky. It was cold and dreary, with a contrary rain that couldn't decide whether to pour outright or dry itself out. A sharp breeze cut across her face, reminding her of the frost soon to come. Quickening her step, she neared the garden, spotting Eva already hunched over a bed, uprooting potatoes. A loud thump sounded from the stagehead, and she paused, catching sight of Sylvanus through its open door. Lingering at the gate, she watched, as she had several times this past summer. Black and formless, he stood in his oilskins, fading in and out amidst the shadowy interior of that fisherman's grotto, his feet moving lightly amongst the rubble around him, his skinning knife flashing glimmers of silver as he slit open and split the meagre catch his morning's efforts had brought him. Deftly he flicked the gurry down the trunk hole, the tongues into a bucket at his feet, the britches into a pan alongside the cheeks, and that fleshy poundage of fillet into a well-scrubbed puncheon, already partially layered and salted with his morning's work.

Decisively, she pushed away from the gate, made a rare trek along the path leading to his stage, and stood quietly in the doorway. With the light so dim he didn't see her at first, busy as he was, laying out fish in brine and noisily lifting and sliding things around. But the murkiness halted nothing of his work, as though his hands and feet knew where each and every thing was strewn, and needed no light to retrieve and place them proper—like her in her kitchen, she thought. Hoisting onto his shoulder a coil of rope with a huge iron anchor attached, he stepped out onto the head of his stage, his eyes squinting into the light, his brow fiercely dark; and yet, curiously, that finely sculpted mouth was all set and calm this morning, as though nothing of the night before had touched him.

Bending at the knees, he lowered the anchor by the rope into his boat, bobbing some four feet below. Stalwart as a frigate, she remembered thinking of him once. And he continued being that, consistently (if not patiently) tied to her landing, waiting. Even his uncertainty around her, his moping, had been a strong mooring, tugging against those times she might've strayed too far within that labyrinth of darkened thought.

Guiltily, she noted the tap from which he scrubbed himself before coming home every night, and shivered from the dankness of the air around her—and around him, undoubtedly, as he had stripped on those cold, easterly nights before coming home to her. Perhaps she should put one by the footbridge so's to scrub her own grimy hands and knees, she thought grimly, glancing at her broken nails and the faded, stained knees of her trousers, and her hair forever scraggly with the wind.

Walking resolutely through the stage, stumbling over things made indistinguishable by the dark, she stepped out on the head, squinting, as he had, into the light.

"It matters not to me where we lives," she stated clearly. "So you don't have to worry about moving from Cooney Arm."

He glanced up, a look of surprise on his face. "Now, aren't you the prettiest thing to lean against a blubber barrel?"

She stepped aside, and seeing nothing of a blubber barrel, looked to him, catching the ghost of a grin. "Oh, joking this morning, are we?" she said dryly. "Did you hear what I said?"

"Yup, and that's nice of you, Addie. Am's taking Suze to Ragged Rock in the morning. Why don't you go and get a ride to Hampden? Take a look around. Nice place, Hampden—good fishing, logging. Not far from Deer Lake, Corner Brook. Good place to build. We'll take Mother with us," he added, turning back to the anchor he was fiddling with.

"Yup, and that's nice of you, Sylvanus, but I doubt Eva's moving anywhere after I asks her to stay on here with me," she said calmly. "And if you plans on moving by yourself, you might want to know this—the government's paying only them that's moving to Ragged Rock, so you won't get money by moving to Hampden, Deer Lake, or anyplace else you got in mind."

He struck his finger on something and swore vehemently. "Jeezes, don't get me going on that," he warned, rubbing at his hand. "I'll eat with the gulls and then eat the gulls before I gives another man the right to tell me where I builds my house. You just pick a spot, and I'll worry about how we gets there," he ended angrily, tugging at the anchor.

"And I suppose you never heard what I already said twice now, did you—that I'm staying in Cooney Arm? Will you look up from that stupid thing?"

He rose, facing her, his eyes dark slits beneath an encroaching brow. "Like I said, it's good of you, Addie. But you'd be living in a place with no minister, no lights, no roads—"

"Never needed lights and roads before."

"Or schools—and yes, we will have need of them," he said quietly.

She hesitated. "Then you knows more than I do, Sylvanus Now."

"Then I knows more than you do." He bent back over the anchor, tugging on a piece of rope beneath it. "And I knows, too, that you wouldn't be satisfied for long," he carried on, his voice straining as he shifted the anchor aside, freeing the rope, "living here with everybody gone. And I wouldn't expect you to be."

"Still thinks you knows what I'm thinking all the time, do you? Tell me something, Syllie, if I'm so bloody easy to read, how come everybody's thinking something different of me, then? How come there's them that sees me as the grieving mother, and them that sees me as the dirty thing, or the spoiled thing, or the sweet thing, the poor thing, or—or the good worker and whatever the hell else one soul can think of another. Which serves me fine," she said, holding up a silencing hand, "because most times I don't know myself what I'm thinking. So God bless you for thinking you do, and I hope you're right, my son, and you can keep on telling me and saving me the bother of figuring for myself." She turned and marched angrily back into the darkened stage.

"Not as if you're chasing after me telling me what you thinks," he yelled after her.

She stumbled again, this time nicking her ankle on something pointed. Biting back a cry, she hobbled back out on the stage, her voice sharp with frustration. "Oh, you wants to hash up all that old stuff again, do you? A load equally carried, I say—you the dying fish and me the dying babies. Now I just told you what I wanted, and I've no doubt it's what you wants, too. The only question is whether we *can*, and that's for you to figure, Sylvanus Now—how to keep them bloody puncheons filled."

This time silence followed her footsteps back inside the stage. Skirting the damn things in her path, she exited through the other side, exhaling the dank air out of her lungs. Ignoring the questioning look with which Eva greeted her in the garden, she marched to a drill of cabbage and started yanking heads.

An hour drifted by, perhaps two, then Eva was calling her to have tea. She straightened up, rubbing her lower back as the old woman stepped off the stoop and started back along her furrows, still munching on a biscuit, having already drunk her tea. It was always that way: Eva leaving off her work, making tea and biscuits for them both, then calling out to Adelaide after she'd eaten—as though the crows would fly off with their seeds if they both left the garden at the same time, thought Adelaide. But Eva was like that: wanting quiet as much as she herself. During those first days that they had hoed the ground together, working loads of rotten sawdust and sheep manure into the soil, scant words had passed between them. And as they spent the better part of the day working on opposite ends of the yard, Adelaide had started feeling the same sense of seclusion as she had tucked amongst the tuckamores up on the head.

Only she hadn't felt like the fugitive down here, crouching amongst the furrows, screened by the broad rhubarb leaves flourishing alongside the fence, hiding her from the neighbours. They'd left off visiting anyway, once she had started working the garden and was no longer seen as the grieving mother—aside, that is, she would think resentfully, from her sisters-in-law, Melita and Elsie, who dropped by Eva's yard to check up on her. But she made sure they'd have nothing to snit about, and as time passed and they continued seeing her out working the beds before they themselves even had their faces washed—well, their visits fell off as well. Except for their chats and cups of tea with Eva, and she gave them that as long as she was left alone. And gloriously, she *had* been left alone, embedding herself into that cool, dark earth, seeing only the seeds that rolled off her palm, feeling only her knees pressing into the grit of the furrows as she straddled the drills—like an opened grave, this unearthed soil, and she entered it willingly. Her thoughts she plucked like weeds, embedding them along

with the seeds till all that remained were her hands,
directed by purpose.

Daily she had seeded, weeded, and trenched, her back
long since strengthened by the habitual turning of the fish
on the flakes. When finally the planting was done that
first summer, she couldn't help but feel a sense of satisfaction overlooking those deepened furrows running neatly
beside their beds, and the drills perfectly peaked and
running as straight as corduroy across their field of brown.
And she wasn't too surprised when at some point during
the latter part of that first summer, and now during these
past summer months, she had felt her fingers, once
numbed by the coldness of death, begin warming themselves in the earth along with the seeds she planted. Other
parts of her started warming, too, as though the wind, its
vengeance expelled against the cliffs of the head, were
softer, more yielding as it swept over her down here in the
lowland. And in time, as the glaze melted from her eyes,
she'd seen the soft green of the first seedling push its head
above ground and quiver upon the slightest breath. And
she loved the creamy white petals of the potato blossoms,
even more those tinted that delicate mauve that were so
like the wild mallow she wondered they were without
scent, and she would lower her nose instead onto the
yellow lobes of the dandelions sprouting madly from her
beds. It were as though she had planted herself, those long
summer months, with Eva, and was now regrowing into a
world with colour and with song, a world into which she
could once again touch and be touched by gentle winds.

She wondered, as she finished uprooting another drill
of carrots this dreary, wet morning, why none of her anger
or resentments followed her into the garden, even though

she'd been summoned there the same as she had to the flakes. Most likely it was because the garden had saved her from her too-friendly neighbours, she supposed. Plus, work, no matter its stature, was sanctioned.

Nothing like a good worker to earn the praise of the neighbours, she now thought scornfully, emptying her sack of carrots through the gaping black hole of the root-cellar door. She straightened, remembering that old choking anger she used to feel when reprimanded by her mother for lazing about like Old Maid Ethel, when it was studying she was doing and not lazing about at all.

Eva was making her way up the hillock, dragging two sacks of potatoes. Her eyes were seeping water from the cold and her nose reddened with the sniffles. Tutting impatiently, Adelaide went down to meet her.

"Here, give me that," she said, taking the sacks from the old woman. Dragging them to the cellar, she lifted the door, emptying them down the hold. "You sure we didn't wait too late to start uprooting, Eva? There was a bit of frost last night."

"Nothing to hurt a root vegetable," replied Eva. She shivered, glancing up at the sky. The drizzle had ceased, and the clouds were thinning. "Might get some sun after all," she added, wiping her nose with a rag she pulled from her pocket.

"You taking anything for that cold? Here, let's take a rest," said Adelaide, laying the burlap sacks on the cellar door. "Perhaps we should go inside and sit; too damp for you to be out."

"Nay," said Eva. She eased herself onto the sack. "Old fall weather, dirty as anything," she grumbled, the cold siphoning a steady stream of water from her eyes. "We'll go in in a bit," she said impatiently as Adelaide kept fussing above her. "Sit. Sit down."

Adelaide grunted, sitting beside her. "You'll wish you'd listened, you ends up with the flu. Glass of hot brandy is what you needs, and a warm bed."

Eva sniffed testily and Adelaide left her alone, looking down over the garden that, with most of its lush green foliage plucked, was back to looking like a grave again.

"Did you get any sleep last night?" she asked as Eva yawned.

"But for the wind beating at the door, I might've. And all this moving business. How's Syllie this morning?"

"Stubborn. Like he always is."

Eva said nothing, her silence prodding Adelaide into a shrug.

"I don't know what he's thinking. I just told him I'd stay here in Cooney Arm, if that's what he wants." She paused. "He don't believe me. Don't blame him, I suppose. For sure I would've jumped at the chance years ago. But now—" She paused again. "Perhaps you grows into a place like you grows into a name, eh? Is that what happens, Eva?" she asked with a quirky grin. "I've grown into place like a turnip top?"

Eva smothered a cough. "Elikum was like you," she said, clearing her throat, "always off brooding on his own, even when there was nothing to brood about."

Adelaide's surprise at Eva's mentioning her drowned son's name was overthrown by the slight she felt in the old woman's comment. Surely she'd had lots to brood about, hadn't she? And yet she'd found great comfort working in the garden these past two summers.

"Always going to be leaving and working on the lakers the following year," Eva carried on, her sight set upon the fog rolling through the neck. "I heard him say that for years: he was going on the lakers. He drowned saying it. That's a problem with the young around here," she added with nettle in her tone, looking at Adelaide, "too timid to go after something they wants."

Adelaide pulled back, feeling a sting. "I'm not harbouring desires, Eva. There's nothing out there I wants to go after."

"Nothing now, perhaps. But there's something gnawing at you. I seen that the first time you laid foot on my step. Same look about you as Elikum had—and not just Elikum, either. I had it in me once."

"Had *what* in you?"

"Wants. And it don't have to be a thing or a place, either. Most times we never knows what it is we wants— like Elikum. Wasn't just a job on the lakers gnawing him. If it was, he would've went after it—not that hard to get a job on the lakers. But whatever it was, he took it with him. Perhaps that's one of the things that don't let me rest now, not having listened hard enough to him."

Adelaide snorted. "Cripes, if you got any quieter, we'd have to write a letter to reach you. And you seems awful rested to me. Is that true, that you're not rested?"

"Since I got my garden, I am. That was the one thing I craved, getting my own garden. Mightn't sound very lofty," she added defensively, "but if you was raised on the downs like I was—nothing but rock and tucka- mores—a garden seemed a precious thing. More than one hour I whiled away planning that garden. Nothing but flowers, I had it figured, and perhaps a rose bush.

Lord above," she sighed, "as if roses could grow out of rocks. But I'll tell you something, my girl—that first summer I got my garden, I was out the door before sun-up every morning, looking to see how much everything grow'd the night before. Swear to gawd, when time come to pull up all them pretty green plants, I wept over the hoe."

Addie grinned. "You wept over your hoe."

"Indeed, I did."

"Yeah, well, I was going to be a missionary and sail the seas."

Eva paused. "That's lofty. How'd you come by that?"

"Some Sunday school lesson once. Sounds foolish, but I always had dreams of it happening," she added with a silly laugh.

"It's not foolishness once you carries it out, my maid; it's a well-laid plan then. Like I said, that's the problem with the young, too timid to go after something. By the time they figures they can do a thing, they got a brood of youngsters holding them back."

Adelaide sniffed. "That's because they're discouraged from doing anything but scrubbing floors and having babies and working fish."

"I don't say it's easy," said Eva, "but wisdom is greater than might, the Scriptures says. So follow along with everybody and scrub till sundown, if you wants. But if you don't see godliness in cleanliness, then what's the use of your shiny floor?" she ended on a deep, wet cough that broke into a proxy of sneezes. "God above," she gasped, rooting for the rag in her pocket.

"That's it. You're going in," said Adelaide, taking her by the arm. "Come on," she insisted as the old woman protested. "That's the problem with the old—never knowing when to take care of themselves." And tightening her hold on Eva's arm, she partially led, partially dragged her down the hillock and across the uprooted beds. Once inside, she bade her into her rocker, stoked the fire, and went hunting for the brandy in the small pantry off the kitchen.

"You got none left," she called out, holding up the empty bottle.

"Or sugar, either, I don't think," sighed Eva. "Oh, wait—down in the cupboard in the corner, there's a bit of brandy there."

"I got it. My, you're down in everything. Perhaps I should go up the store. I needs everything, too. Am's taking Suze in the morning, Syllie said. Perhaps I'll go after all— far as Ragged Rock, anyway," she said mostly to herself. Pouring some hot water and the few grains left in the sugar dish into a couple of glasses, she mixed in the brandy and brought one of the glasses to Eva. Slouching in an old worn-out armchair nearer the window, she sipped her own toddy, watching as Eva held her glass to her nose, breathing deeply of the vapour before taking a timid sip. Leaning back in her rocker, she cast a look of displeasure over her floors.

"My, I haven't scrubbed the floor in days," she said.

"Looks cleaner than mine," said Adelaide, taking in the canvas, scuffed clean of its paint in places, and the floorboards, uneven from their years of settling into the bedrock beneath them, now worn through in some places. "Not enough you're sick, you got to start worrying about your floors, too, now, do you?" she chided.

Eva smiled, laying back her head, stroking the fringed ends of the shawl she had wrapped around her shoulders, her rocker creaking beneath her. Nothing much got her goat these days, thought Adelaide, when the rocker ceased creaking and it appeared the old woman dozed. But ought not something be stirring on that gentle, resting face over this threat of upheaval, of leaving her house, her precious garden?

"You seems awful calm about this resettlement plan," she said quietly as Eva fluttered awake.

"Hard enough it is on Syllie. He don't need to see me bawling."

Adelaide was about to chide her again, but paused, caught by the old woman's eyes, their light grey faded almost to transparency as they gazed at her, her dark brow the only remnants of colour remaining on that thin, papery face. Leaning forward, she asked with sudden concern, "How old are you, Eva?"

Eva sighed. "Not good getting a fright at your age, my maid—" and broke off in a fit of coughing.

"My age indeed," sniffed Adelaide. "If the old was that smart, you'd think they'd take better care of themselves— out hauling turnips, damp weather like this." A smattering of rain struck against the window, followed by a sudden downpour. "Well, sir," she exclaimed, lifting the edge of the curtain, "that's not going to end for a while. That settles it, then, no more gardening for you today. Why don't you lie down, take a nap?"

Eva was leaning back, her eyes closed. Yawning, Adelaide, too, sat back, relishing the comfy old chair and the rain drumming the window.

"It's nights like this he comes back," said Eva quietly.

"That who comes back?"

"Never nice out when he comes. Always raining or storming. No, I'm not going daft," she murmured, her eyes still closed, seeing nothing of the startled look on her daughter-in-law's face. "He comes back, is all," she added, slowly. "Not so's I see him. He comes late. And he sits here, in this rocker and rocks for a bit. Used to be I'd creep out from my room, a bit scared, when I first started hearing the chair creaking. But there was never nobody there, just the chair, rocking a little, like someone just got up."

She paused, only the rain sounding on the window. "I don't come running no more now when I hears him. I leaves him alone. I figure if it's me he's coming for, he'd stay. Or else visit me in my bed—or the yard. But it was always his to sit up alone and watch out the window on stormy nights—like he was keeping watch for us all, I used to torment him." She opened her eyes, catching Adelaide's startled look. "It's not a ghost story, Addie. Lord, he'd be the one spooked seeing me after all them years." She grinned, running the tips of her fingers over her fissured cheeks.

Adelaide shifted, uncertain. "Well, what is it, if it's not a ghost?"

"A spirit, I suppose, maid. Ghost haunts. A spirit don't haunt. Most times a spirit is haunted himself, and that's why he comes back. He's looking for something. Or perhaps just to give comfort."

"Well, if he's not coming to comfort, what's he looking for? And how do you know it's him—and not Elikum, I mean?"

"Because there's always a little drop of water after he leaves. Right there," she added, leaning forward and glancing at the floor beneath her feet.

Adelaide shivered. "Oh, my, Eva!"

"Nothing to worry about, my maid. He was never laid to rest like Elikum. Never given the Lord's blessing. That's why he's haunted, why he's not at rest."

"Well, you could've still given him the Lord's blessing—said prayers for him."

"I could've," said Eva lowly. "I could've given him prayers. Marked his grave. Everyone wanted to. But—ooh, I don't know, girl. For the longest time I kept hoping he'd walk out of the woods someday—like Syllie done that evening. Even though I seen him go." Her eyes flitted restlessly around the room. "Then I kept seeing him underneath the water somewhere, like a lost salmon, trying to find the river water that spawned him. Not a morning for years I didn't prowl that shoreline, looking for him. Then, by the time I got used to knowing he'd never come ashore—well, then he started his visits. And I couldn't give that up, either."

She leaned forward, her hands clammy, shaking as they clutched Adelaide's. "That's why, when I dies, I wants you to bury my man, too—to stand over his grave and say prayers," she whispered. "Listen to me. No, really listen," she said strongly as Adelaide nodded reassuringly. "I got his coat—his one good one. And his gun. I want them put in the box alongside of me, then say prayers over us both. It's what I request from you—bury us both, then have Syllie mark our grave with a cross for each of us. I can't say this to anybody else—they'll think I've gone daft, taking a gun to my grave—and they're welcome to think what they wants, as long as I'm not around to hear it. So, you promise me now, Addie, promise you'll make Syllie bide by my wishes. He'll listen to you."

Held into place by the urgency in the old woman's

eyes, Adelaide could do nothing but nod. "Not much to promise, is it?" she asked, her words thick in her throat.

Eva kept hold of her hand. "I won't go far from this house, Addie. I'll winter it out in Ragged Rock for the boys' sake, because for sure they won't go nowhere without me. But soon as the ice breaks, I'm coming home. Coming home and keeping his house going, so's he got something to watch out for."

"Well, sir, I'm starting to think I'm a haunt myself," gasped Adelaide. "Don't nobody hear nothing I says? Didn't I say I wasn't moving? And here you got us all paddling through the neck."

Eva shook her head. "Be no place here for you when everybody else moves."

"Sounds perfect to me," cried Adelaide. "I'd be happy as a clam with nobody nosying about."

Eva sighed. "Addie," she said, her voice nearly spent, "just listen. I'm moving in with Manny, I already told him. Please, listen," she begged. "It'll be hard on Syllie. But that's where you steps in. He hates Ragged Rock, and so do you. So, go on, somewhere—up Hampden. Find a nice place you—" She lapsed, overtaken by a spurt of coughing.

Taking advantage of the moment, Adelaide rose, helping her to her feet. "It's you who ought to be taking it hard," she scolded, "not we, the young and in good health. Take on anything when you're young, I learned that from the flakes. Thought I'd die that first summer, but I survived it and would've survived the plant, too, if I'd had to. But not you. Different with the old. Something about the mind, I think. After it's lived in a place long enough, it starts becoming part of all else around it. Least, that's what it feels like to me. And it makes for a bad fit, then, when you're wrenched out of it and put somewhere else. For gawd's sake, will you lie back," she commanded, as Eva, sitting on the edge of the daybed, kept trying to talk over her coughing. "No, I won't listen, you've talked enough. Now, lie back and stop worrying, I already told you I'm not leaving the arm, either, so you got nothing to worry about."

Eva lay back resignedly. "Be nothing to worry about soon," she said, patting her heart.

"Lord, now she's burying herself!"

"A well-laid plan, like I said."

"A well-made bed is what you're getting—leastways for the day," said Adelaide, tucking her shawl around her, pulling it up to her chin.

"Don't smother me, for gawd's sake."

"Oh, now, Miss Fuss. Lie still. I gets some Vicks and rubs it on your chest. You got some flannel?"

Eva was dozing off by the time Adelaide had found a piece of red flannel and the Vicks bottle. Scrawny as a bird, she thought, gently loosening the old woman's dress and tugging it away from her chest. After she'd rubbed on the strong-smelling salve and covered it with flannel, she tucked Eva back in again and sat back in the chair, sipping her hot toddy.

"A well-laid plan, eh, Eva?" she asked quietly as the old woman slept. She gazed at the rain plinking against the window, thinking back on the skinny-kneed girl, sitting, dreaming on a church pew. Now, why hadn't she, smart as she was and full of dreams, figured something as simple as a well-laid plan?

CHAPTER TWENTY-THREE

THE SEEDLING MOTHER

THE FOLLOWING AFTERNOON Adelaide stood in her mother's kitchen for the first time since the last burial a good two years earlier. Florry was finishing chopping the last stalk of rhubarb and scraping the pile already chopped into a pot. She laid down her knife, wiping her hands in her apron.

"Janie, get some water for the pot and put that rhubarb on the stove," she said. "And don't go picking it apart, either."

Janie was searching through the bottom drawer, pulling out a rolling pin. She rose, lanky as a young colt and standing a head taller than Adelaide, took the pot of chopped rhubarb, and dumped them on the table instead.

"Now, what did I just say?" cried Florry, but she was immediately distracted by a youngster's ball smacking against the window from outside. "Young buggers," and she scurried out the back door, hollering at the boys hooting and singing out in the backyard.

Making a sour face at their mother's back, Janie gave Adelaide a shy smile and continued discarding the small and thick cubes, tossing the medium-sized ones back into the pot. Adelaide gave her a sympathetic look, struck by the resemblance of her sister's oval face to her own, her deepened blue eyes pitted with impatience, and the defiant, uplifted chin. Women, thought Adelaide with some surprise, her sisters had become women.

She glanced across the kitchen. Ivy stood before a mirror over the washstand, plying her dark, shiny hair into a ponytail that trailed down over one shoulder, her breasts fully curving the front of her knit pullover, and ochre lips staining a face smooth as ivory. Mimicking the same sour face toward their mother, she joined Janie sorting the rhubarb, whispering something that brought a flush of red to Janie's cheeks.

"Janie's got her eye on a man," Ivy whispered loudly to Adelaide.

"Oh, right," said Janie, pulling another sour face and slapping her sister's hand playfully.

Adelaide grinned. "I'm surprised you're not married," she said to Ivy. "You must be all of twenty."

Ivy gave a mock shiver. "I'll be far from here if I ever gets married. I'm trying to get Janie to quit the plant and come with me to Deer Lake. I knows we can get work at Croaker's Inn," she added with emphasis, looking to Janie. "We could get a room between us."

"Nope, you can go make all the beds you wants, but I'm not," said Janie. "Rather work the plants."

"Rather make Jordie's bed, she means," said Ivy aside to Adelaide.

"All the sweeter," said Janie with a tilt of her chin.

"Too scared to live by yourself in a city, that's why you wants me with you."

"Right," said Ivy. "I spent enough time there this past few years to get my bearings. For sure people don't bother me; fishermen and loggers, that's all you'll find on this island, fishermen and loggers. A few fancy people strutting around, but they're eating salt fish for breakfast, just like the rest of us. Bet you'd come with me if you weren't married, wouldn't you, Addie?"

Adelaide glanced away from her sisters, her smile more shy than Janie's had been earlier. Her sisters. Yet she felt a timid stranger before them, despite their quick glances and asides, including her in their chatter. Her chest swelled with an overwhelming gratitude. Feigning interest in the mounting shrieks and cries from the yard, she turned to the window, absently watching the ruckus outside, feeling undeserving of her sisters' intimacy when, only a short time ago, it was she, Adelaide, out there ranting, and they, Ivy and Janie, the most likely recipients of her fury.

"Bet it's nice," she said. "Deer Lake. Not on the water, no flakes and fish plants."

"Yup, real nice," said Ivy. "And the cook's from Hampden. She'll get me on soon, watch if she don't. I told her I'd keep her going in decent fish if she gets me on. Christ, you should see the bad fish they gets—buys it from Corner Brook, and nothing but cullage. I wouldn't eat it, sir. And them businessmen, they haven't got a clue they're eating cullage."

"There you go, two jobs," said Adelaide. "Trading good-grade fish from Cooney Arm to stores in Deer Lake and working in the inn as well."

Ivy grimaced. "Enough flies around me now, without dragging around quintals of old salt fish."

"Then get somebody else to drag it for you—somebody with a truck. All you needs is a well-laid plan, my maid," Adelaide added with a grin, her mind back on the hillock, sitting beside the cellar door with Eva.

Janie laughed. "It'd have to be a well-laid plan if Ivy was going to make it in business. She fared worse than me in school. You was the only smart one in the family," she ended, blue eyes flashing at Adelaide.

A burst of shrieks from outside interrupted them, followed by a loud obscenity from one of the boys. Both Ivy and Janie grinned, and as the rising tenor of their mother's cries overrode the youngsters', they rolled their eyes and groaned in unison. The back door flew open, and Florry bustled inside, shivering from the late-September air.

"The young bugger, that Johnnie is," she cried, kicking off her slippers, dirtied from the wet grass. "Brazen as anything he's getting, and making Alf the same as hisself. Well, what's she doing? Now what'd I tell you," she sang out, toddling across the kitchen like an oversized youngster at the sight of the rhubarb spilled out on table. "Foolishness, foolishness, that's all that is. Here, put it in the pot, all of it!" she ordered, scooping up the rhubarb.

"No! Wait—stop it!" cried Janie. "I won't make them, I won't make no pies," she warned, standing back helplessly as her mother kept dumping the rhubarb into the pot.

"It's all the same, I tell you, young, old, all the same. You mind now," Florry called out as Ivy muttered an oath across the room. "It's only foolishness, is all. Mother never picked apart a bit of rhubarb in her life."

"What *Mother* done, what *Mother* done," mocked Ivy. "Who gives a shit what *Mother* done?"

"You mind now," cried Florry as Ivy flounced off, a twist of repulsion marring her face. "Brazen as anything, you are. Here, give it back," she cried as Janie snatched the pot from her hands.

"Just leave it alone," said Janie in exasperation. "For the love of God, Mother, what odds how I makes a few pies when you're not the one eating them?"

"No, old Jordie Noseworthy, that's all you're thinking about," said Florry, "and he scrubby-looking as anything, and Milly Rice crawling all over him."

Janie's cheeks stained red. Turning a murderous look onto her mother, she smacked the pot into the sink and marched to her room.

"Go on, you foolish thing," Florry called after her.

The same red staining Janie's cheek was staining Adelaide's as she stood, confronted by her sister's discomfort. "What difference do it make how a pot of rhubarb is cut?" she asked.

"Don't *you* start! Bad enough with Mother flapping her gums," flared Ivy from across the kitchen.

"No, I was asking Mother. Janie should do what she wants ..." Adelaide trailed off, her words unheard by Ivy, who was now bellowing, "Janie! Janie, get your clothes on. We gets the jeezes out of here."

And why wouldn't she think the worst? thought Adelaide dolefully. For sure I was quick to cast blame and pounce on them both in the past. She sighed resignedly as Florry, throwing up her hands, overrode them all with her well-worn rant: "Ah, all of ye stop it, crowd of young women acting like babies. I wonder where ye gets the energy for it, I do. Here, where do you think you're going, my lady?" she asked as Janie came out of her room, hauling on a long, wool coat. "You watch out now, Janie, you're not following Ivy to no Deer Lake. Gawd knows what she's doing there."

But Janie was swinging through the door after her sister, buttoning her coat up to her chin. Twisting sideways, she managed a tremulous smile at Adelaide, and with a quickly whispered "Bye," she was gone, the door shivering on its hinges as she slammed it.

Through the window Adelaide watched as a buttery yellow car pulled up and some curly-haired fellow reached over, pushing open the door for Ivy. Janie climbed in next, her face a blur of white through the side window as the car drove off, a glaring glance back at Florry, who was now hanging out the door, waving her hand and hollering and threatening, "Get back here, you get back here!"

"Trouble, nothing but trouble, that's what they're going to bring home, you watch and see," said Florry, coming back inside, rooting at a boot that was blocking the door from shutting. "I allows her father will skin her alive she goes chasing after Ivy, because that's the trollop, that Ivy is, and she'll bring trouble on us yet. Watch and see if she don't, prancing around the way she does and always driving off to Deer Lake. The worse thing they ever done was put that road through." She toddled back to the table, sinking breathlessly onto a chair, her fringe of bangs scruffed off from her forehead, and strands of thick, cropped hair sticking to her face with the sweat she'd worked up.

Adelaide sat, anger working its way through her limbs. "You treat them as if they were still girls," she finally said.

"Janie's near nineteen. Why wouldn't you just leave her alone, make her pies whatever way she wants?"

"Ah, now, don't you go starting, Addie, because that's who they all learned it from, you—all the time fighting and bawling out."

"I'm not starting nothing. I just wants to know why you wouldn't leave her alone, is all. Why wouldn't you just leave her alone?"

"Because she'd never get nothing done if I left her alone. Always up to foolishness, Janie is. And that Ivy, that's worse again, that is. Lord above, Addie, wait till you gets a house full of youngsters and see then what happens when one wants Pablum for breakfast and another wants eggs and another wants boiled fish. Come back and tell me then what housework gets done if you leaves them alone." She sighed in an overplayed moment of weariness. "More than once I wished they were babies agin. Only time they had any sense is when they were babies. That's what I was always telling my own mother—give me the baby to look after, and you look after the rest. Swear to gawd I never touched a youngster after they was two till I had my own."

Adelaide stared at this dumpling of a mother, her thoughts tripping in astonishment. "Did you never think we'd grow?" she asked incredulously.

"Like any mother with a house full now," Florry replied, "if I had given thought, I wouldn't've had any of ye. My, Addie, sit back; you're like the cat about to pounce. As if anybody had time for thinking with a crowd of youngsters all the time bawling out! Cripes, by the time I learned to think, I was already carrying you. Too late then for thought. What're you wearing the long face for? Would you rather you was never born?"

"I've sometimes wondered," said Adelaide absently.

She was immediately drawn back by her mother's own sense of frustration as she cried out, "Name of gawd, not that big, is it, you'd rather not be born than stew a bit of rhubarb all together? You knows you got to keep it simple, maid. If it weren't for keeping things simple, nothing would ever get done. What's you wanting to make a thing hard for when you can keep it simple? There's no more difference in rhubarb than there is in grass, providing it all come from the same patch. Any fool knows that. Oh, my," she wailed as the ball struck against the window again, hard. "Swear to gawd, I'll tear me hair out yet. I bet you remembers that day, don't you, when I fell on my knees in front of you, threatening I'd tear me hair out? That's how bad you was one day, Addie. Swear to gawd, I almost done it, too. You remember that?"

No, thought Adelaide grimly as her mother creaked back in her chair, her feet scarcely touching the floor as she rocked, her chins sinking into the pudgy stem of her throat, some things may have escaped me, but their meanings haven't. Sickened, she turned back to the rhubarb on the table.

The ball smacked against the window again, and Florry was on her feet, tutting and huffing as she toddled to the door. Adelaide watched through the window as Johnnie, a good head taller than she last remembered, dove ahead of the younger ones, grasped the ball and ran with it, the others screaming after him. They stalled as Florry appeared, shaking her fist.

"It was Johnnie, Johnnie," the younger ones cried.

"Go on, you little liars," cried Johnnie.

Catching Adelaide watching him, he grinned, swaggering toward where Eli was studiously kicking at a clump of weeds. And ignoring their mother's ordering them inside, they both broke into a run, their heels kicking at their behinds as they shot onto the beach, out of sight behind their father's old stage, racing upon the road again, a little farther on, their shoulders almost touching, as Janie's and Ivy's had when they stood sorting rhubarb.

A daring glance back at their mother, and the boys ducked behind the church. The church. Where she had fled. Alone. Finding her camaraderie amongst its quiet, its order, its sanctity, and in her need for acceptance, had reduced the altar to a world of her own making, and God into a cloth of her own fit.

Her mother came huffing in from bawling at the boys, saying something about the yard and her father. Mumbling something about getting home, Adelaide looked about for her coat, an anxiousness growing within her.

"Well, sir, I suppose you can say more than that," said Florry, visibly offended. "It's not every day your father offers somebody his yard!"

"His yard?"

"Well, sir, she don't hear nothing. He's offering you his yard to build on. There's not much room anywhere else to build, leastways not near the water. And knowing Syllie, he'll want to be near his boat. So your father's offering you the backyard." She sank into her chair, trying to catch her breath, pointing to the water bucket. "Give me some water, Addie. Swear to gawd, I'm wore out. Hector Rideout got his mother's old place up for sale. Last year he wouldn't have got a bed of spuds for that—boarded up for years. But he's asking a nice price now, with all ye moving here. Who's that? That's your father now I hears. Look out the window, see if that's your father. You can go talk to him about building a house in the yard."

The dread of such a likelihood was offset by its offering. Glancing through the window, she saw her father dragging a gill net out of his shed, its mesh all cluttered up with the greenish-black slub that was a fisherman's curse these days. Spreading it out over the beach, he kept hollering at the youngsters who were stumbling around awkwardly as they helped with the spreading. The smallest—Gilbert, or Gilly as he was called—darted across the net, getting his foot entangled in the mesh halfway across. He fell with a yelp. Adelaide more felt than heard her father's oath of impatience, as he threw down the net and stomped toward Gilly. Swinging the youngster up over his shoulder, he lugged him, screaming and kicking, into the yard, dumping him into the soft mound of sawdust beside the woodpile. Like a shot, the youngster was on his feet, racing after his father, grabbing his leg and shrieking for another horsy ride, another horsey ride.

"When did *he* start disliking us?" she asked curiously.

"Who? Your father? Your father disliked ye? Well, sir, who said anything about anybody *disliking* ye! I just said ye were harder to get along with, that's all I said! Sir, she's like the robber, stealing your words, then making them her own. There was nothing your father never done for you when you was small. The little doll, he thought you was, and more than once wished he never had to go off on the boats all the time, or in the wood camps. Like coming home to strangers, he said often enough, with all of ye growing up, and he hardly ever seeing ye."

Adelaide sniffed disbelievingly. "I don't remember many horsey rides."

"Well, sir, I just told you he was never home. Sure, the five years between you and Ivy I hardly seen him. Never thought I'd have another youngster. As if I was never married, I told him once. He started coming home more after that. But I tell you he never had much patience when the others started coming. He wasn't around ye long enough to get any, I always told him. Like we'd all be, I suppose, if we weren't used to a thing. But he's been good this past while, especially with the younger ones. Ivy, now they're at each other's throats worse than you and he ever was. Certainly, that Ivy is at everybody's throat, she is, wild as the cat."

Adelaide watched a moment longer. He had swung the youngster over his shoulder and was lugging him back down on the beach again to where the others were scampering all over the net, picking off the slub.

"What's he doing with a gill net?" she asked. "Don't he work in the plant?"

"Nay. He quit that a few weeks ago—got on his nerves, working in all that racket. He was midshore for a while with Hector on his skiff. But he couldn't even handle that—being fifty, sixty miles out on the water in a small boat. Nerves is gone. So he's on his own now, if he can keep himself going in nets. That's the third one he got this year. Them trawlers keeps tearing them up. Good thing the government's giving them away."

"He's getting enough fish with the gill nets?"

"He's not doing too bad with it, although he'd like to be working alongside somebody. Not young now, your father's not."

She turned back to her mother. "What'd you mean, the government's giving them away?"

"Out at the fish store. They just gives you one whenever you wants."

"But what about ghost fishing—all them fish it catches and rots."

"My gawd, don't get your father going on that. They took away his schooner and his flakes, and they're letting all them foreign boats in here, robbing us. The gill net's all he got left, and if they takes that away, he'll be nothing more than a hangashore, because for sure you won't catch him back in the plant agin. Anyway, like I tells him, them nets can't be that bad, else the government wouldn't be giving them away like they are. They're not as stun as all that, are they? Go on out and talk to him. He'll want to know about the yard, seeing's you were here."

"I'll—tell him I'll talk to Syllie. I got to go—Suze and Ambrose is probably waiting by now."

Her father rose as he spotted her leaving through the back door, cutting across the yard. She gave a half-hearted wave and kept on walking, feeling a sudden need to be home.

CHAPTER TWENTY-FOUR

A LESSER GOD

C LIMBING OUT OF THE BOAT in Cooney Arm, Adelaide waved to Suze, and leaving Ambrose to unload and sort out their purchases, she started homeward. The wind was against her, rakish, and it swayed trees and saplings alike, rippling through the grass and battling with her skirt and hair. The graveyard appeared to her left, and her step faltered, her eyes fastened upon the three little mounds of dirt, all sodded now, with shorn grass, and with three wooden crosses looking over them, and seashells, bleached white by the sun, scattered about. Put there by Sylvanus or Eva, no doubt, for she hadn't ever been inside except for the burials.

"Addie!" It was Suze, catching up with her. "Nice, isn't it?" she said, glancing at the graveyard and the sun-bleached seashells. "Syllie put them there yesterday," she added, dispelling Adelaide's sudden notion that perhaps it had been she, Suze, who put them there. "It's for the garden service on Sunday. Addie, you should come. No, wait," she implored as Adelaide turned, brushing her away, "I think it'll help you. I knows you don't like me talking about this—and Am thinks I shouldn't, either—"

"Then don't," cut in Adelaide, that old tightening back in her chest. Bending into the wind, she ploughed forward, trying to shut out Suze, who was chasing after her, her pipes bellowing louder than Gert's.

"Perhaps I am interfering, Addie, but some things I just feels, and this never visiting their graves, I don't think it goes well, especially since you're their mother. They were awful pretty babies, Addie—even the one in the caul. I knows you hates that I looked, but I had to, along with Syllie, he was so broken, Addie, the prettiest little thing, I always felt you should've looked, seen how pretty your baby was, it was a awful thing to look at, the caul, but that baby—that pretty little baby—"

Adelaide stopped, her hand to her chest, gaping for breath. Suze stood before her. "Are you all right?" she cried. "Lord, Addie, it's this damn old wind—smother you, it would."

"It's not the wind," said Adelaide quietly. "Just leave me now, please. Just leave me. I'm fine. I'll think about what you said, if you'll just leave me."

"You hates me," cried Suze. "I shouldn't have said nothing, I promised Syllie—"

Adelaide shook her head, in silent praise of the tears tumbling down the Suze's cheek. Impulsively, as though willing those healing waters inside her own cramped self, she leaned toward Suze and pressed her lips against one of the tears. "Now, go on," she whispered to the surprised girl. "I wants to be by myself."

Speechless, Suze nodded. She stood for a second, not knowing if there was more to be said, then turned, casting worried looks back over her shoulder as the wind pummelled her along the shore.

Adelaide stood, the huge September sky barrelling clouds overhead and the overly bright sun bouncing sharply off the cemetery's white picket fence. The wind gusted harder, jiggling the loosely toggled gate, as though bidding her entry. She glanced about, noting a few fishermen tarring their boats way down the beach, another hammering at his stage, a couple of boys yelling and tussling as they gathered wood chips for kindling.

Almost furtively, she untoggled the gate, stepping inside. She could scarcely breathe now, yet the wind was heedless, nudging her along the footpath trailing around the knolls, some marked with crumbling clay tombstones, most not. Her step slowed and she crept nearer those three sleeping graves as though in fear of waking them. Foolish, she thought, yet she faltered, lowering her eyes, and knelt a foot away, the grass so cool it felt wet beneath her knees. For the second time that day she felt the timid stranger, an encroacher, as she lifted her eyes almost warily onto the three little crosses. Immediately she recoiled, her eyes moored onto the names—Eva, Elikum, Eliza—all painted black against the garish whiteness of the crosses.

He'd named them. Syllie had named them. She reached out her hands as though to touch them. Eva. Elikum. Eliza. Her babies. They were her babies, gone, banished to the underground, and with no grieving mother bargaining their return. The tightening in her chest gave way to deep remorse, and she lowered her eyes, wanting to shrink, to cover her face, to hide amidst the tuckamores and the trenches of Eva's garden, to withdraw into the tuck of her

own arid self. Eva. Which one was Eva? The son she knew
was the last born, but which one had been Eva? Eliza?

She grasped at the grass on one of the mounds, a wave
of hysteria growing within her as she struggled through
that dim corridor of memory whose walls were dank with
the sweat of her suffering and the wretched stench of
death. The labyrinth, she was reaching back into the
labyrinth again, not wandering this time, but searching for
some one thing, for Eva—that little hand hidden within
the white of her caul, for she'd be the one he'd name after
his mother, wouldn't she? The first born, wrapped into a
misshapen wing and buried without a mother's blessing?
All of them, banished, forsaken. The thaw was complete,
and her flesh, no longer anaesthetized by cold, was racked
with grief as she leaned upon that second grave, Eliza's
grave. That startling blue of an eye, that's what she
remembered of the second, and the old midwife saying,
"It's a girl, my dear, it's a girl," and she had shut it out, had
shut it out. Something came to her—"Like Janie." Isn't
that what Syllie had said, that one had looked like Janie?
Yes, yes, he'd said that, Eliza, that's who. That startling
blue of an eye—she'd seen that, she'd seen that, and for
sure it did look like Janie's, and her cheek had been cold,
he'd said. Her cheek had been cold. "Oh, my Lord," she
whispered, and not knowing if it was an exclamation of
prayer or pain, she lay down her head, feeling a prickling
of tears upon her cheek, and watched them drip onto
that shorn grass, gliding along its blade as it might a
child's lock, before soaking through to the underground,
baptizing the fretting brows of her babies, Eva, Eliza,
Elikum. Poor things. Poor, poor things, and she started
a slow rocking, her weeping growing deeper.

After a while, despite her sobs, a curious calm betook
her. She remembered back to something of Eva's, about
souls at rest and those still labouring. And that's how she
felt, sitting there beside those little engraved markers, her
sobs subsiding, like a mother's release when the babe is
finally brought forth from her labours. Eva. Eliza. Elikum.
And she sat there awhile longer, after all had stilled, quietly
rocking her babies. Forgiveness. She knew it now. From
herself it had to come, and onto that skinny-kneed girl
whose sustenance demanded she paste life around her as if
it were wallpaper, but then who had scrambled into hiding
after it started crimping and peeling and falling in strips
around her. She touched her hand upon the coolness of
a cross—the middle one, Eliza's—the bluest eye, and was
besieged by the teary blue of her sister Janie's, and her
softly whispered *bye* that had dispersed yesterday's
treacheries like ashes in the wind. Was hers not a cheek
deserving of warmth?

Holding back what sobs were left, Adelaide wiped her
face and rose. Stepping carefully around the graves, she let
herself out of the cemetery and toggled the gate. Cursing
the tears that still wanted to flow, she hurried toward
Eva's, sniffling into sleeves that were now wet, and cut
around to the back of the house so's not to encounter the
old woman who was surely watching her from some
window. Rooting through the tools in the old wooden
wheelbarrow, she pulled out the gardening shears,
exclaiming loudly as she jabbed a finger on their pointed
top. Sticking her finger into her mouth, she headed
toward what was left of the rhubarb patch. Shunning the
old and the young, she cut what was left of the medium-
sized stalks, snapped off the oversized leaves, and when

she had a good-sized pile beside her, she lifted it into her arms. Eva appeared in the doorway, but she took no notice, marching steadily onwards.

"Go help Am with the boxes," she said to Syllie, as he straightened up from cleaving wood at her approach, "and make your mother some hot brandy." Shutting the door upon his curious look, she set about scrubbing and chopping the rhubarb, and digging out the flour and shortening from the cupboards below, the salt and baking powder from the cupboards above, and the oblong syrup bottle with the long, skinny neck that she kept on the mantel-shelf for a rolling pin.

And whilst the rhubarb was stewing, she blended the flour, shortening, and butter, adding a bit of salt, water, and sugar, dumping all onto the table, rolling and stretching the dough as she herself was being plied and stretched from the coiled little self she'd become into that greater sphere of selflessness, where thought was more focused onto sisters despairing before bake sales, and brothers swaggering before sisters, and mothers rising or sinking to the needs put forth by their children, and fathers resurrecting the long-lost love for a child.

And as she fitted the rolled-out dough into the pie pans, trimming the edges and pouring into their centres the tart sweet jam of the rhubarb stalks, her heart quivered with the hope she was resurrecting within it, for that's what she had done by burying God along with her babies, she had buried hope—hope of any precious thing: the bliss of a meadow, the comfort of a kitchen, the love of her man. Like the fantasies of her youth, those things had been, and without hope, they had been dead, all dead, her soul more frozen than the winter soil and weighing like a mantle of rock upon her. And now once again, she felt that greater Hand moulding her, soothing her, for what is hope if not faith?

Slipping Janie's pies into the oven, she walked out to her little speckled rock by the brook and sat, watching the sun sink red over Big Arm Head.

THE FOLLOWING MORNING after Sylvanus had left for his fishing grounds, she wrapped her pies and sought out Ambrose, begging a ride back to Ragged Rock. Eva watched through her window at her comings and goings, like a lost soul, thought Adelaide, like her man must look on those nights he comes back and finds no place set for him at his supper table. Guiltily, she laid her pies beside the gatepost and ran up to the door.

"I got to go back to Ragged Rock," she said, breathlessly, ducking her head into the kitchen. "Are you resting?"

Eva pulled back from the window, dabbing at her reddened nose with a bit of balled-up tissue. "Bit late in the fall to be on the water so much," she said, her voice hoarse.

"Ooh, mind now, you're scared of a boat ride," scoffed Adelaide. "Get yourself in bed, crouped up like that. Sure, you can hardly talk. You want me to rub you with Vicks?"

Eva shook her head. "Go on, you're going," she said and looked back out the window.

Adelaide hesitated. "Is everything all right?"

Several hooted coughs were her reply, and a scrawny hand waving her on. "I never did like the bloody sea," Eva croaked, hobbling away from the window to her rocker. "Always darkens the second you leans over it." She sat back, dabbing at her nose and her rheumy eyes. "I'm fine, I'm fine," she added crossly, as Adelaide stood, ill at ease. "Bit of peace is what I'd like to have."

"My, you're the one, this morning. Worrying, that's what you're doing, and I already told you, you're worrying for nothing. We're not going nowhere, and who knows, it's probably just talk yet. Nobody's been around, telling us for sure."

Eva nodded, settling back—more to get rid of her than reassure her, thought Adelaide, and why wouldn't she worry with all this moving business, and Syllie not getting his fish, and she, Adelaide, running off to Ragged Rock two days in a row, and nothing solid, nowhere, to cast her mind upon? Lost, that's how Eva looked to her, sitting there in her chair all by herself, lost. Like her drowned man.

Eva sat forward, pointing a crooked finger at the window. "Is that pies them goats are eating?"

Adelaide beat it out the door. There was no goat in sight. "Blasted woman," she uttered, the corners of her mouth hooking on to a grin. Scooping up the pies, she waved goodbye to Eva, who was peering out the window again, her features drawn, tense. She thought to lay down the pies and run back in, assuring her again, but Ambrose was already in the boat, calling out to Suze, who was running down the path with her coat on.

Damn, she didn't want that woman's company today, she thought tiredly. A last worried look at Eva, and drawing a breath of resignation, she walked slowly to the boat.

Once they putted off from shore, Adelaide settled back, half listening as Suze launched into a running commentary for the next half hour about the coming shutdown of Cooney Arm, and Am's mother's bad stomach ever since she heard the news, and the old midwife declaring she'd be dead before they got her out of the arm, and Wessy and his brothers already planning where to build, and Elsie and Jake fighting over where to spend all the money they were going to get. "And you can be sure they're not the only ones fighting. People never had this much money before, and I dare say there'll be lots making a mistake—going for the money, and after they gets it spent, wanting to come home agin. Because it's not working out the way the government thinks, is it, Am? Those ones from Bear Cove, they're not too pleased, moving all the way to Hampden and finding out everybody already got the good fishing holes staked. Not surprising, seeing's how they've been living there all their lives. And all them jobs that huddling people together was suppose to make, sure that's not happening at all, not in Hampden, leastways. So I wouldn't expect it to happen much anywhere else, either. And besides, all them old people—sure they're all homesick two days after they leaves their houses, and the government got a real job, then, brother, keeping them from climbing in their boats and moving back to their old houses agin—especially since they got their money spent. Well, sir!" Suze broke off, her eyes widening in astonishment.

Adelaide turned to see what had caught Suze's attention, and rose, her eyes gaping at a sight that would be forever imprinted on her mind. It was the Trapps from Little Trite, all of them, old and young, crowded into their boats—two skiffs and two motorboats, and each with a punt in tow—all loaded down with tables and chairs and beds and highboys and brooms and dishes and all else it takes to furnish a house, along with rakes and shovels and wheelbarrows and hoes, and never mind the dogs howling over the sides, and two pigs grunting from one of the

punts, and two goats neighing in another, and two sheep
baaing from the last, and a cat wailing from somewhere in
their midst, and the flock of gulls circling, screaming overhead, as though trying to banish this oddity from the seas.

"Don't go too close, Am," Suze warned as one of the
Trapp men, upon seeing their boat, stood up and deliber-
ately turned his back toward them. "Cripes, no trusting a
Trapp. What're they doing? What's they packed up for?
Well, sir, they're not being resettled, are they? Is that what
they're doing, resettling somewhere?"

Adelaide shook her head, bereft of words. Ambrose
simply stared.

"Well, sir." Suze clucked her tongue. "Now isn't that
something? Just like the Trapps—resettle and not tell
nobody till the day comes. I tell you, they're sly as
conners. Where's they moving to? Where'd you think
they're moving, Am?"

Ambrose shook his head. "Don't ask me about a
Trapp."

"Well, sir, I knows you're not sly. And I always
thought that of the Trapp women—smile to your face,
then wear your guts for garters." Suze clucked her tongue
again, as Ambrose slowly overtook the last of the Trapps'
boats, pulling ahead, leaving them putting slowly behind.

It was all the talk in Ragged Rock. The Trapps had
secretly put in to the government for resettlement from
Little Trite the year before and had made a secret deal
with Hector Rideout to buy the old house he had abandoned few years back and another falling-down old thing
belonging to his father and the wood-house and stages
still standing alongside, with not a word, sir; not a word
about them getting resettled.

"Not sly, are they, sneaking in and buying up the houses like that," said Florry, looking through the window, along with everybody else in Ragged Rock, watching for the Trapps. "This is the third trip they made this morning. How much stuff, in the name of gawd, do they own? Sly, by cripes, they're sly. And now we got the whole brood living right alongside. I say they'd better keep their noses out on the point, then, because nobody wants mixing with their blood, sir. Robbed poor old Hector blind, they did."

"How could they rob him if they outright bought the houses?" asked Adelaide. She had laid the pies on her mother's table and was looking around for Janie and Ivy.

"They're out on the quay by the fish store, watching for the Trapps," said Florry. "And you knows they robbed him. He could've got a lot more money for them buildings if he knew the government was paying, and that all ye from Cooney Arm would be moving as well."

"Sounds like the Trapps got him before he got them. When's the girls getting back? When's the bake sale?"

"Not till two. Did you tell your father you wants the yard? There's people looking for land, and if you're not taking it, he might get a price for it."

"I don't allow we'll want it," said Adelaide. "Tell Janie—"

"Where you going to live, then, you don't want the garden? Is that what Syllie said? Did you tell him your father wants to go partners?"

Adelaide was shaking her head. "I—oh—I don't know—just tell him I'll talk to Syllie tomorrow. And tell Janie I made the pies from medium stalk. Just tell her," she insisted, as Florry exclaimed anew over the senselessness of such a thing. "Now, I got to go. Am's at the boat, waiting."

"Did you tell him your father wants to share his berth?"

"His what?"

"Sir, she don't know nothing. Fishing spot, maid. You got to have your fishing spot."

"I knows that. I just never heard it called anything before. Don't forget to tell Janie."

"I can't see Syllie passing up a chance to get a good berth. He knows the good ones are all took. You sure you told him?"

Adelaide nodded, trying to close the door. Her mother kept it open, following her out in the yard. "That's the problem with everybody moving here—there's no berths for them. Everybody that lives here already got the spots—unless they goes off in a skiff or liner somewhere. Be sure and tell Syllie. Like your father says, there's more and more people going fishing all the time. It don't make sense to he, herding people together when they should be spreading them out, finding different berths and different fish. Sure way to clean out a fishing ground, everybody anchoring over the same spot. Anyway, that's what your father's arguing about these days."

Adelaide let herself out the gate. "I'll tell him. See you now."

"But he's willing to share with Syllie. He don't like being by his self on the water. Makes him nervous, that far out in a small boat. His nerves is gone, your father's nerves is. That's why he'd take Syllie on with him. Mind you tells Syllie, that. My gawd, here comes the Trapps. Not the sight, are they?"

Sight, indeed, agreed Adelaide, joining Ambrose and Suze amongst a knot of people on the quay by the fish store, watching as the Trapps motored shoreward, looking like a bastardized version of Noah's ark with their boats in line, two by two, and two heads to a seat, and the couplings of pigs and goats and sheep taking up the punts in the rear.

But that wasn't the last sight that would keep her awake that night, and nor would it be the everlasting one. They were motoring near the bend beyond which Little Trite sat, when the first grey billows of smoke rose above the trees. Rounding the point, all three started in alarm as black smoke coiled out over the water beyond which flamed Little Trite, its houses, sheds, and wharves, all convulsing into an orange wall of fire.

"Oh, my gawd, get clear, Am," cried Suze as the acrid smoke curled toward them, shedding black ashes onto the water. Ambrose swerved shoreward, motoring along the outer edge of the smoke, taking them closer to the fire.

"What's you doing?" yelled Suze. "Don't take us no closer, Am!"

"Sit down. I'm trying to see who's that," said Ambrose. Adelaide, her eyes watering from the greyish haze enveloping them, saw, as Ambrose did, a boat pulled upon the beach and several men milling about.

"Figures," said Ambrose hotly. "Goddamn government men. Suze, sit down."

"I can't breathe in this," cried Suze. "Get us clear. Don't go no closer."

"Just a second," said Adelaide, patting Suze's shoulder to calm her. "What government people?" she asked Ambrose, her eyes torn between the men, the fire, and what used to be Little Trite.

"They goes in burning houses after the people leaves," said Ambrose, "so they won't go back. I heard tell of them doing it few years back out Trinity way. Never saw them around here before. Jake heard something, though," he said as an afterthought. "He was saying something to his mother about it this morning."

"To Eva?" Adelaide asked, startled. "About the houses being burned?"

"I never got it all …" He faltered as the roof of one of the houses collapsed, silencing them with a roar of flames shooting upward, burnishing the heavens and sending a heat wave rolling over their faces. Adelaide gripped Suze's shoulder, her awe of the fire overtaken by the image of Eva's face, and that of her man's, shooting out of every blazing window left in Little Trite.

No wonder she was all bothered this morning, thought Adelaide. Full of fear that her house was going to be burnt, and no place for either her or her man to come home to. Well, that's not going to happen, she thought calmly. Eva's house would remain standing. She had promised her that, and that promise now felt like the one good thing she had ever done. And like that good daughter, Ruth, she turned her attention back to Ragged Rock, pointing not to where her mother's yard might be, despite its being so generously offered, but to the fish store out on the quay.

"Go back," she said with a quiet determination to Ambrose. "To the fish store. I-I forgot something."

"It's getting on, Addie," said Suze, her voice tremulous from the fire, "and we're almost home."

"You must," implored Adelaide. She leaned against the side of the boat as though she'd jump overboard and start swimming if they didn't listen. "I knows it's a nuisance, but really I've got to go back. I've got to."

Ambrose nodded. Turning the tiller, he steered them around and started them back the way they'd just come. Clenching the thwart beneath her, Adelaide ignored their questioning eyes till they arrived back in Ragged Rock.

"A gill net," she said to Ambrose after they had motored past the plant, past her mother's house, and were now tied up at the quay in front of the fish store. "Would you go in and get me a gill net? Please."

"A gill net?" He stared at her blankly. "I don't think—"

"You won't get Syllie using a gill net, Addie," Suze cut in, "if that's what you're thinking. He's all out against them, hey, Am?"

"Just go get me one," said Adelaide, her eyes fixed onto Ambrose. "That's all you have to do—go get me one."

"He'll—uh, he'll think I said something."

"Syllie wouldn't think that of you."

Ambrose shifted uncomfortably, then raised his brow in acceptance. "If that's what you wants," he said. With a beseeching look at Suze, he climbed out on the quay, a disquieted look ruffling his smooth features as he went inside the fish store.

"I got nothing to say," said Adelaide firmly as the door closed behind Ambrose, and Suze, fair busting with curiosity, turned to her.

"Not much to say, is there?" said Suze. "You got in mind to stay in Cooney Arm. You're the case, Ad—I always said that about you." She grinned. "I always liked that about you, too. I allows Syllie got some answering to do when you gets back. My Lord, I wish I had your nerve. I might've stood up more to Am if I did, back when he was buying the longliner. I knew he was making a mistake, buying that big thing. Now we're so far in the hole we'll never see the light of day agin."

"Quit, then," said Adelaide, and looked as surprised as Suze as the words left her mouth.

"Quit what? Fishing?"

Adelaide shrugged. "I don't mean quit, quit! Just—I don't know, find other ways of making more money, is all. We don't have to go overseas to sell a bit of fish. Or be stuck doing what we don't want to."

"For sure it's not what Syllie wants, then, dropping drift nets into the water."

Adelaide fell quiet. For sure it isn't, she thought. A tinge of discomfort dampened the growing sense of purpose in her breast—along with a tinge of fear as Ambrose came out of the store shortly after, dragging what looked to be two gill nets.

"He'll need two," he said. "Ties them together to make them big enough."

Adelaide shifted aside her feet as Ambrose toppled the netting into the boat. She stared, the bulk of the netting bringing reality to the enormity of what she was doing— stepping over Sylvanus's word, and about something she was mostly ignorant of.

Well, it's done now, she thought as Ambrose unlooped the painter from the grump and started them off to sea. And her relief was as great as Eva's would be, for it was as she had once said: she had grown into the soil of Cooney Arm and was now rooted in its garden, in Syllie, in Eva. She smiled. For the first time, since swinging her legs on a church pew, she felt a fit with those things around her, and with it came a buoyancy that near lifted her off her seat. Freed. This settling of her fate freed her from that darkened corner where she had sought refuge those past years. And she hadn't even noticed at what point she'd started walking above ground again. We're like time, she thought, clenching her hands urgently in her lap, too busy coming and going to take notice of the present. And was not time a thing of the earth—seeding a thought one day, then returning it some days, weeks, months later, bearing no resemblance to what it once was?

Undoubtedly, a thing forever blooming is the soul, no matter how barren the soil. And only through that frightening abyss of the unknown self does the mind root out the light upon which it nourishes.

She clung to her thwart as they motored past Little Trite, no more than a smoking ruin, a blackening scar against the cornsilk yellow of the autumn grass. Worry you not, Eva, she thought. You'll always have your seat in the window, you and your man. And you, Syllie, put aside your false comforts, for that's all your offerings are, false comforts so's to please me and your mother. In the end they'll please nobody, most definitely not you. And I'm not allowing you to do that.

It was toward this end she strained as they cut through the neck and entered the arm, and she saw Syllie standing on the stage, watching them draw near.

If the flushed look on Ambrose's face didn't give it away to him, then certainly Suze's "My son, she's the case" left no doubt in his mind who the gill nets were for, she thought, seeing the repulsed look marring his face as he caught the painter Am was tossing him, staring down at the nets.

"Before you says anything, let me say this," she said clearly enough. "I'm staying in Cooney Arm whether you stays or not."

Sylvanus beckoned toward his mother's. "Go on in," he said deeply.

"I means what I say, Syllie, you never listens—"

"And you do, I suppose. Oh, don't argue with me, Addie, just bloody listen for once, and get the hell in. Mother wants a toddy."

She rose, feeling suitably chastened, and allowed him to help her onto the stage. Unexpectedly, he squeezed her hand, dropping a kiss to the side of her mouth. She stood for a second, watching the back of his head as he helped up Suze, a flush of warmth foolishly flooding her face. Cutting through the stage, she waved at Eva, who was standing by her gate.

Waiting for me, I suppose, she thought, and hurried onto the path. Something across the footbridge caught her eye, and she stumbled, her mouth falling open. It was ripped out. The back of her house was mostly ripped out. Perched beside it was a window, a big window, bigger than the southern one overlooking the neck.

"Well, sir," she whispered in some surprise. "Well, sir."

THE SUN HAD YET TO RISE the following morning, and the sea was white, without wrinkle, beneath a pearly sky. Just the nose of Sylvanus's boat was onshore. Tipping it onto its keel, he put his shoulder to the bow, easing it into the water. Loath to disturb the mother's quiet on this morning, he left his motor alone and drifted instead from shore, his boat slipping quietly with the current across the arm. Closer to the neck, the mother stirred beneath him, her swells rubbing lazily against the loins of that narrow opening. Outside the head, he kept drifting, his back to the open ocean. Old Saw Tooth passed his portside, and then the scarred remnants of Little Trite. He sat forward, jolted by her blackened grass, the trickles of smoke rising from her deeply smouldering coals.

He turned from the sight, toward the bend where Pollock's Brook flowed out of the estuary into the sea. He remembered standing there, jigging, that first morning he'd finished building his house, and how he had wished his Addie was standing beside him, seeing how he had created himself out of the sea, out of his father's stage, and how, if he were to constellate himself against the heavens, he'd be the swan in the Milky Way, his bowed legs its wings, and the sea of stars around him the milt from which his creation was spawned.

He grunted this morning at the unlikelihood of such a notion. He hove on his flywheel, opened throttle, and motored quickly past the brook, past Gregan's Hole and Widow's Inlet and Gull Rock and Peggy's Plate, and then, upon approaching Nolly's Shelf, he veered straight out to sea till he could look back and see a gorge cut deep by Petticoat Falls on top of the fourth rolling hill east of the head. Cutting his motor, he stood straddling his boat, seeing in the distance the dark shapes of five, maybe six trawlers hovering on the horizon. He couldn't turn his back today as he'd done the days before. He couldn't spit in disdain toward their presence, curse them, hate them. He turned instead to the bulk of netting filling his bow, and started lifting the lead line that would anchor it. It slipped from his hands and he cursed, snatching hold of it again, hauling it free from the hoard of netting resting beneath it. With a good ten, twenty feet of the netting bundled into his arms, he turned awkwardly portside. Taking a long look at the mother, he heaved it overboard and stood back, a lesser god than yesterday.

EPILOGUE

L IKE A CLOT OF BLOOD against the morning was the red cloth his mother stood waving furiously from the front of his house. Sylvanus, sitting motionless in his rowboat, drifting about the arm, sickened. Then, with a wildly beating heart, he snatched his paddles and rowed ashore. Leaping onto the beach, he bolted up over the landwash, across the footbridge, and stood breathing heavily outside his door. His mother opened it for him. He stepped inside, near buckling from the heat and the smell of raw blood. The infant lay swaddled on the oven door as still as death in the waves of heat brimming over it from the oven.

Is it all right? he wanted to ask, but a thick saliva filled his mouth, and he fell back dizzily, dragging in air that smelled like death; his child was born and it smelled like death. An upsurge of nausea gagged him, and he shrank back outside, laying his head against the hard, cold wood of his house.

"Syllie." It was Eva. She tugged on his arm, coaxing him back inside. He stumbled behind her and stood weakly as she laid the infant in his arms, all scrawny and wrinkled and red and encrusted with what appeared to be fish gurry. His vision blurred and he felt that he might be sick again. Immediately, the infant was whisked out of his hands. He watched as its mouth opened and a whimper sounded from it, then another.

Not for nothing is it said that the lungs are the wings of the heart, for he fair flew toward the door, heeding not his mother's cries that he stay put, and pushed through it. Ignoring the old midwife's orders to "Get out, get out, I'm not done, yet!" he lurched to his Addie's bedside, staring down at her face, white as marble, her hair damp upon her pillow.

She opened her eyes, more blue than the mother's, and closed them again, weakly reaching for his hand.

"Sylvia," she said. "Her name is Sylvia. Sylvia Now."

ACKNOWLEDGMENTS

THANK YOU to biologists Michael Chadwick and Jeffery Hutchings, and to the researched work of fishery historians Cynthia Boyd, Miriam Carol Wright, Raymond Blake, and Barbara Nies. Much appreciation to Ralph Getson at the Fisheries Museum of the Atlantic in Lunenburg, Nova Scotia; to Douglas Laporte for his many referrals and errands; to the Department of Fisheries and Oceans in Moncton, New Brunswick, for the use of their library; and to John Dalton for his invaluable sermonizing.

Thank you to the Canada Council for the Arts and the Nova Scotia Arts Council. Without their financial support, this book would not have been written.

Thank you to my story editor, Cynthia Good, line editor Jennifer Glossop, editor Sandra Tooze for bailing me out again, my agent, Beverley Slopen, and my heart friend, Jill Aslin.

And thank you to my uncle Bill Dyke, who stands witness to the historical drama of this novel, and to that woman, Connie Jodrey, who wept over her hoe.

And for their appreciation of my solitude, I wish to thank my children, David and Bridgette Morrissey; my siblings, Wanda, Glenn, Tommy, and Karen; and their partners, Charlene, Lindy, Dianna, Frony, and Andy.

And most especially, my dad, Mr. Enerchius Osmond from the Beaches, Hampden.

Sylvanus Now

A Penguin Readers Guide

ABOUT THE BOOK

Sylvanus Now is a simple man. Born without book smarts, he nevertheless learned early on what he wants in life, and he's succeeded in nearly everything he's set out to do—but there are some things he can't control.

Donna Morrissey's third novel, *Sylvanus Now*, is set in the 1950s in Cooney Arm, a small Newfoundland outport struggling to survive in the wake of national and international fishing trawlers and their overfishing of the ocean. Like all of Morrissey's settings, this one is dominated by the sea, rocky shores, and an outport full of neighbours who can't help themselves from sticking their noses in everybody's business. But although the issues of conservation, modernization, and government regulation of international waters touch the inhabitants of Cooney Arm, the novel is much more a romantic love story than a polemic.

At its heart are Sylvanus and Adelaide, a mismatched couple destined for misery. The youngest son of a fisherman and his wife, Eva, Sylvanus is "the unsanctioned egg, the one who shuddered from her old woman's body long after the others had been born and grown, and a month after her husband and eldest had been lost to sea." He's full of hope and faith that love will conquer loss, that the sea, the mother, will provide, and that Addie will eventually find happiness in Cooney Arm.

But happiness has never come easy to Adelaide. With her pale skin, brilliant mind, and revulsion of the sea, Addie's an outcast in her childhood home of Rocky Head, a fishing village not much different from Cooney Arm. Not that she cares. Addie has no use for the boys who smell of fish and the girls who long to marry and have babies and, perhaps, end up working the flakes. She resents the endless trail of brothers and sisters who follow her, making noise and mess and not caring that it's Addie who'll have to pick up after them and cook their meals. And she comes to despise her own parents, a hardworking couple who have child after child, and whose abandon in the bedroom spells the end of Addie's education.

Indeed, at fifteen, Addie has all but given up. Forced to leave school to work the flakes, she faces the two truths of outport life: a girl who leaves school never goes back, and without an education or money she never leaves the outport. Unless, of course, she marries.

And so Addie and Sylvanus settle into a house built on a meadow with the door facing the woods, the window facing the sea, and a solid wall facing the town and flakes of Cooney Arm. Sylvanus has everything he's always wanted. He's master of his own boat and he loves and worships his wife, but changes outside of his control are occurring, both in the fishery and in his beloved Adelaide.

As Addie begins to lose her battle with depression, Sylvanus realizes that he, too, is sunk. The haddock fishery is on the verge of collapse, and every fisherman—along with governments, corporations, and merchants—knows that "a fish once lost can never be found." So what now?

Caught between his desire to please his wife—his promise that she will never work the flakes—and his own desire for independence as well as his determination to treat his other great love, the sea, as she must be treated, Sylvanus must navigate his and Addie's rocky future. ■

AN INTERVIEW WITH DONNA MORRISSEY

Q: Your second novel, *Downhill Chance*, was as successful and acclaimed as *Kit's Law*. How did you feel when you set out to write *Sylvanus Now*? Was it easier to write your third book than it was to write the second? Do you feel you've honed the writing process in any way?

With *Sylvanus Now* I felt less anxiety than writing *Downhill Chance*. I knew that I wasn't a "one book" phenomenon. I also learned from writing the previous two books to trust the process of writing, that the difficult passages will be resolved, that the most I could do was give it time, not desert it, stay with it, and as before, it would come. ■

Q: Sylvanus is a captivating and very likable character. He has a huge capacity to love and an inner calm. He reminds me a bit of Luke in *Downhill Chance*. What or who was the inspiration for Sylvanus?

Sylvanus was inspired by my father. My father wasn't a fisherman (he fished in his early years, and the opening passage regarding the suit on hold at the merchant's was taken directly from my father's life), but he was mainly a logger. He loved the woods, and I transplanted that love to Sylvanus's love of the sea. ■

Q: Adelaide is clearly suffering from depression after several miscarriages, yet people expect her to get over it. And, after the birth of Sylvie, we're left with hope that she might. Is this how mental illness is handled in these outports?

In the past—as most anywhere—there certainly wasn't much known about postpartum depression. Depression was acknowledged, but the most a friend could offer was help with the housework during those trying first weeks, and no doubt the woman was expected to "get herself together" within a reasonable time period. Today there is much more help for such illnesses (thank God). ■

Q: The lives of Addie and Sylvanus are constrained by their place of birth. Although some of your characters long to leave their home province and venture forth into the wider world, very few actually do. What is it that ties them to their homes?

In most of the outports in Newfoundland, travel was exceedingly difficult during the fifties and early sixties. Newfoundland has ten thousand kilometres of coastline. There were few roads during those early years, and fewer dollars. It wasn't until those outports became integrated with a cash economy and the outports linked to larger communities did travel become prevalent. And too, Newfoundlanders are known for their deep familial ties. ■

Q: You write about fishing and the fishing industry, and life on the flakes or in the plants, with such clarity. How did you research this aspect of the novel? How do your own life experiences manifest themselves in your book?

I grew up in the outports, where fishing and curing and flakes were a part of everyday life. I also read quite a few books on the industry during the researching of this book. Two years preceding my university years I worked in a fish plant. This was invaluable to me in describing Adelaide's experiences. ■

Q: Themes from the Bible run through all your novels, including *Sylvanus Now*. Why? Which comes first when you're writing—stories and passages from the Bible, or the story itself?

I love the imagery and profundities found in the Bible. It gives such strong impressions and says so much more than mere words. Story always comes first. Imagery from the Bible helps strengthen the story. ■

Q: Since *Sylvanus Now* was first published, the public perception of our need to act on environmental issues has heightened dramatically. If you were writing this story today, would you change anything?

No. *Sylvanus Now* is about character and the impact of the devastation of the fishery on his life and that of his family. I don't write to give messages. I write to tell stories. ■

Q: One review of *Downhill Chance* commented that there's no mention of the greater political situation in Newfoundland. There's no talk of Joey Smallwood; people aren't "ferociously political." Why is this? Why aren't your books more political?

I write about characters who are near to my heart and to my experience. Given that I have not been politically inclined, there has been no need to delve more deeply into the political scene. ■

Q: Your characters seem particularly real, and much has been said about your expert use of the Newfoundland dialect in the novel. How did you go about crafting characters and dialogue that ring so true?

The Newfoundland dialect isn't a thing I need to craft, as it is still very much present in the outport where I was born and raised. I continue hearing it every day from my brothers, sisters, aunts, etc. We always speak in dialect when we're together. Times when I'm writing and I go too far afield, I simply close my eyes and listen for one of my aunts' or my uncles' voices and there it is … a whole sentence, a thought, totally rewritten in that beautiful, metaphoric manner the outport Newfoundlanders so casually call upon. ■

Q: *What They Wanted*, published in 2008, continues Addie and Sylvanus's story. It's the first time you've followed up on some of your characters. What was it about Sylvanus and Addie that made you want to return to them? Has their story ended with this last book?

What They Wanted was supposed to have been part two of *Sylvanus Now*. But a book has a way of dictating what it wants, not what the author wants. Thus, there wasn't room for *What They Wanted* in *Sylvanus Now*. It demanded its own covers. Stubborn, eh?? And I'm not sure if their story has ended. Well, actually, I know their story hasn't ended. But will it continue in the characters already put forth? I don't know yet. ■

DISCUSSION QUESTIONS

1. Why do you think Morrissey named her main character Sylvanus Now?

2. Sylvanus knows he isn't good at math, but that he has other smarts. He knows how many cords of wood it takes to fill a crawlspace and how long it takes to cure a fish in brine. Addie, on the other hand, laments that she can't go further in her education. But given their prospects, is a formal education a good thing? Would Addie have been better off without learning things that lie beyond her own reality?

3. Sylvanus feels proud when he releases a mother fish, her belly filled with roe. Where do you think Sylvanus

gained his respect for the natural world? How can pride be used to motivate others to respect the environment?

4. Morrissey once said in an interview, "People either had to compromise who they were or leave, which was also compromising who they were. It was either be exploited or become an exploiter." What do you think Sylvanus and Addie should have done when faced with this choice?

5. Sylvanus can't imagine leaving his home; it would mean leaving behind too large a piece of himself. Do you think this is the result of living in a small community? Does it hold true for you?

6. It seems commonplace for people to lose their loved ones to the sea in Newfoundland. Eva handled it by taking walks by herself. Do you think, though, that she's really accepted the death of her son and husband?

7. The Trapps are clearly the villains of the novel. Do you think they deserve the treatment they receive?

8. What do you think of Eva's "widow's walk" and the idea of marking the steps of "those still labouring"?

9. Addie and Sylvanus finally succeed in their struggle to have a baby. How do you think Addie will fare as a mother? Will their child face similar disappointments in life?

10. If you've read Donna Morrissey's other books, *Downhill Chance* and *Kit's Law*, how does *Sylvanus Now* compare? If you haven't, how did Morrissey's novel change your perception of Newfoundland?